Praise for the Novels of Lauren Willig

The Secret History of the Pink Carnation

"Lauren Willig balances her knowledge of English history with a veritable passion for English spies, turning out a deftly hilarious, sexy novel."
—Eloisa James, author of *A Kiss at Midnight*

"A fun read." —Mary Balogh, author of *A Secret Affair*

"A historical novel with a modern twist. I loved the way Willig dips back and forth from Eloise's love affair and her swish parties to the Purple Gentian and of course the lovely, feisty Amy. The unmasking of the Pink Carnation is a real surprise." —Mina Ford, author of *My Fake Wedding*

"In her swashbuckling debut . . . Willig reimagines France under Napoleon besieged by a whole bouquet of spying floral foes . . . bad news for the Bonapartes but barrels of good-natured fun for the rest of us." —*Library Journal*

"A juicy mystery." —*Complete Woman*

"Imaginative . . . a decidedly delightful romp." —*Booklist*

"[A] breezy historical romance. . . . The sparks fly."
—*Publishers Weekly*

"Funny, entertaining, and witty." —A Romance Review

"A delightful debut." —Roundtable Reviews

"An adventurous, witty blend of historical romance and chick lit . . . will delight readers who like their love stories with a bit of a twist." —*The Jamestown News* (NC)

"[A] playful romp . . . effervescent prose . . . a sexy [and] determined-to-charm historical romance debut."
—*Kirkus Reviews*

continued . . .

S0-AFN-332

The Temptation of the Night Jasmine

"The author's conflation of historical fact, quirky observations, and nicely rendered romances results in an elegant and grandly entertaining book." —*Publishers Weekly*

"Smart characters of both genders, fast-paced plotting, and a dash of self-conscious humor make this installment a winner." —*Kirkus Reviews*

"Another well-written chapter in the series that began with *The Secret History of the Pink Carnation*." —*Library Journal*

"Witty, smart, carefully detailed, and highly entertaining, Willig's latest novel is an inventive, addictive novel." —*Romantic Times*

The Seduction of the Crimson Rose

"This historical romance is filled with witty repartee. . . . The novel handily fulfills its promise of intrigue and romance." —*Publishers Weekly*

"Willig's series gets better with each addition, and her latest is filled with swashbuckling fun, romance, and intrigue." —*Booklist*

"There are few authors capable of matching Lauren Willig's ability to merge historical accuracy, heart-pounding romance, and biting wit." —*BookPage*

"Romantic adventure executed with wit." —*Kirkus Reviews*

"An exciting historical espionage romance that fans of the series will enjoy." —The Best Reviews

The Deception of the Emerald Ring

"History textbook meets Bridget Jones. . . . [T]he story alternates between two heroines . . . so you basically get two novels for the price of one." —*Marie Claire*

"A fun and zany time warp full of history, digestible violence, and plenty of romance." —*New York Daily News*

"Heaving bodices, embellished history, and witty dialogue: What more could you ask for?" —*Kirkus Reviews*

"Willig's latest is riveting, providing a great diversion and lots of fun." —*Booklist*

"[A] fast-paced narrative with mistaken identities, double agents, and high-stakes espionage. . . . The historic action is taut and twisting. Fans of the series will clamor for more." —*Publishers Weekly*

The Masque of the Black Tulip

"Clever [and] playful. . . . What's most delicious about Willig's novels is that the damsels of 1803 bravely put it all on the line for love and country." —*Detroit Free Press*

"Studded with clever literary and historical nuggets, this charming historical/contemporary romance moves back and forth in time." —*USA Today*

"This is a genre-bending soup of mystery, romance, and espionage, laced with wit." —*Taconic Press*

"Willig has great fun with the conventions of the genre, throwing obstacles between her lovers at every opportunity . . . a great escape." —*The Boston Globe*

"Delightful." —*Kirkus Reviews*

"Willig picks up where she left readers breathlessly hanging. . . . Many more will delight in this easy-to-read romp and line up for the next installment." —*Publishers Weekly*

"Terribly clever and funny . . . will keep readers guessing until the final un-Masquing." —*Library Journal*

The Betrayal of the Blood Lily

"Sure to please . . . this outing has all the charm of the previous books in the series." —*Publishers Weekly*

"Reading [this book] is like getting a plate of warm-from-the-oven chocolate chip cookies; it's hard not to eat them all at once, but you also want to savor each bite . . . a great choice for readers who like their mysteries with historical or romantic elements." —*Library Journal*

"Will delight readers with its vivid historical detail, deeply honorable characters fighting against truly wicked villains, and a plot filled with baffling mystery and heart-pounding danger." —*BookPage*

The
Secret History
of the
Pink Carnation

Lauren Willig

A SIGNET SELECT BOOK

SIGNET SELECT
Published by New American Library, a division of
Penguin Group (USA) Inc., 375 Hudson Street,
New York, New York 10014, USA
Penguin Group (Canada), 90 Eglinton Avenue East, Suite 700, Toronto,
Ontario M4P 2Y3, Canada (a division of Pearson Penguin Canada Inc.)
Penguin Books Ltd., 80 Strand, London WC2R 0RL, England
Penguin Ireland, 25 St. Stephen's Green, Dublin 2,
Ireland (a division of Penguin Books Ltd.)
Penguin Group (Australia), 250 Camberwell Road, Camberwell, Victoria 3124,
Australia (a division of Pearson Australia Group Pty. Ltd.)
Penguin Books India Pvt. Ltd., 11 Community Centre, Panchsheel Park,
New Delhi - 110 017, India
Penguin Group (NZ), 67 Apollo Drive, Rosedale, Auckland 0632,
New Zealand (a division of Pearson New Zealand Ltd.)
Penguin Books (South Africa) (Pty.) Ltd., 24 Sturdee Avenue,
Rosebank, Johannesburg 2196, South Africa

Penguin Books Ltd., Registered Offices:
80 Strand, London WC2R 0RL, England

Published by Signet Select, an imprint of New American Library, a division of
Penguin Group (USA) Inc. Previously published in Dutton and New American
Library editions.

First Signet Select Printing, October 2010
First Signet Select Printing (Read Pink Edition), September 2011
10 9 8 7 6 5 4 3 2 1

To my parents

Acknowledgments

Like first-time Oscar winners, who thank everyone from their first-grade teacher to that great chiropractor they saw last month, and have to be hauled offstage by the scruff of their tuxes, I have many, many people to whom I owe most humble thanks for the existence of this book. Unlike those Oscar winners, there's no orchestra waiting to strike up if I babble too long. Don't say I didn't warn you.

And the acknowledgments go to . . .

Brooke, little sister and favorite heroine-in-training, for providing plot ideas, giggling over the giggly bits, and nobly refraining from bludgeoning me every time I squealed, "Ooh! Come see this bit of dialogue I just wrote!" The next book is yours, Brookie-fly!

Nancy Flynn, most kindred spirit ever, for scads of publishing advice, even more scads of moral support, and for giving the Purple Gentian his name.

Abby Vietor, for playing fairy godmother to the Pink Carnation all the way, from reading early chapters to whisking the finished manuscript off to Joe (see under Agent, Super)—this book wouldn't be here without you.

Claudia Brittenham, for knowing my characters better than I do, care packages of candied violets, and retrieving my sense of humor when I misplace it.

Eric Friedman, for listening to three years of babble about the Purple Gentian—even if he did want to call it *The Rogue Less Traveled.*

The wonderful women of the Harvard history department, Jenny Davis, Liz Mellyn, Rebecca Goetz, and Sara Byala, for always being there with a coffee or a cosmo.

Joe Veltre, aka Super Agent, for taking a mix of sheep

jokes, French bashing, and the occasional heaving bosom and molding it into a book.

Laurie Chittenden, my fabulous editor, for shooing away the sheep, and keeping the manuscript from bloating to *War and Peace* proportions.

Finally, the brilliant ladies of the Beau Monde and Writing Regency, for knowing about everything from Napoleon's politics to the cut of Beau Brummel's waistcoat, and sharing it all with me despite my lapse into the modern.

Thank you all!

Prologue

The Tube had broken down. Again.

I clutched the overhead rail by dint of standing on the tippiest bit of my tippy toes. My nose banged into the arm of the man next to me. A Frenchman, judging from the black turtleneck and the fact that his armpit was a deodorant-free zone. Murmuring apologies in my best faux English accent, I tried to squirm out from under his arm, tripped over a protruding umbrella, and stumbled into the denim-covered lap of the man sitting in front of me.

"Cheers," he said with a wink as I wiggled my way off his leg.

Ah, "cheers," that wonderful multipurpose English term for anything from "hello" to "thank you" to "nice ass you have there." Bright red (a shade that doesn't do much for my auburn hair), I peered about for a place to hide. But the Tube was packed solid, full of tired, cranky Londoners on their way home from work. There wasn't enough room for a reasonably emaciated snake to slither its way through the crowd, much less a healthy American girl who had eaten one too many portions of fish and chips over the past two months.

Um, make that about fifty too many portions of fish and chips. Living in a basement flat with a kitchen the size of a peapod doesn't inspire culinary exertions.

Resuming my spot next to the smirking Frenchman, I wondered, for the five hundredth time, what had ever possessed me to come to London.

Sitting in my carrel in Harvard's Widener Library, peering out of my little scrap of window at the undergrads scuttling back and forth beneath the underpass, bowed double under their backpacks like so many worker ants, applying for a fellowship to spend the year researching at the British Library seemed like a brilliant idea. No more student papers to grade! No more hours of peering at microfilm! No more Grant.

Grant.

My mind lightly touched the name, then shied away again. Grant. The other reason I was playing sardines on the Tube in London, rather than happily spooling through microfilm in the basement of Widener.

I ended it with him. Well, mostly. Finding him in the cloakroom of the Faculty Club at the history department Christmas party in a passionate embrace with a giggly art historian fresh out of undergrad did have something to do with it, so I couldn't claim he was entirely without a part in the breakup. But I was the one who tugged the ring off my finger and flung it across the room at him in time-honored, pissed-off female fashion.

Just in case anyone was wondering, it wasn't an engagement ring.

The Tube lurched back to life, eliciting a ragged cheer from the other passengers. I was too busy trying not to fall back into the lap of the man sitting in front of me. To land in someone's lap once is carelessness; to do so twice might be considered an invitation.

Right now, the only men I was interested in were long-dead ones.

The Scarlet Pimpernel, the Purple Gentian, the Pink Carnation . . . The very music of their names invoked a forgotten era, an era of men in knee breeches and frock coats who dueled with witty barbs sharper than the points of their swords. An era when men could be heroes.

The Scarlet Pimpernel, rescuing countless men from the guillotine; the Purple Gentian, driving the French Ministry of Police mad with his escapades, and foiling at least two attempts to assassinate King George III; and the Pink Carnation . . . I don't think there was a single newspaper in London between 1803 and 1814 that didn't carry at least one mention of the Pink Carnation, the most elusive spy of them all.

The other two, the Scarlet Pimpernel and the Purple Gentian, had each, in their turn, been unmasked by the French as Sir Percy Blakeney and Lord Richard Selwick. They had retired to their estates in England to raise precocious children and tell long stories of their days in France over their postdinner port. But the Pink Carnation had never been caught.

At least not yet.

That was what I planned to do—to hunt the elusive Pink Carnation through the archives of England, to track down any sliver of long-dead gossip that might lead me to what the finest minds in the French government had failed to discover.

Of course, that wasn't how I phrased it when I suggested the idea to my dissertation advisor.

I made scholarly noises about filling a gap in the historiography, and the deep sociological significance of spying as a means of asserting manhood, and other silly ideas couched in intellectual unintelligibility. I called it "Aristocratic Espionage during the Wars with France: 1789–1815."

Rather a dry title, but somehow I doubt "Why I Love Men in Black Masks" would have made it past my dissertation committee.

It all seemed perfectly simple back in Cambridge. There must have been some sort of contact between the three aristocrats who had donned black masks in order to outwit the French; the world of the upper class in early nineteenth-century England was a small one, and I couldn't imagine that men who had all spied in France wouldn't share their expertise with one another. I knew the identities of Sir Percy Blakeney and Lord Richard Selwick—in fact, there was a sizable correspondence between those two men. Surely there would be something in their papers, some slip of the pen that would lead me to the Pink Carnation.

But there was *nothing* in the archives. Nothing. So far, I'd read twenty years' worth of Blakeney estate accounts and Selwick laundry lists. I'd even trekked out to the sprawling Public Record Office in Kew, hauling myself and my laptop through the locker rooms and bag searches to get to the early nineteenth-century records of the War Office. I should have remembered that they call it the *secret service* for a reason. Nothing, nothing, nothing. Not even a cryptic reference to "our flowery friend" in an official report.

Getting panicky, because I didn't really want to have to write about espionage as an allegory for manhood, I resorted to my plan of last resort. I sat on the floor of Waterstones, with a copy of *Debrett's Peerage* open in my lap, and wrote letters to all the surviving descendants of Sir Percy Blakeney and Lord Richard Selwick. I didn't even care if they had access to the family archives (that was how desperate I was getting), I'd settle for family stories, half-remembered tales Grandpapa used to tell about that crazy ancestor who was a spy in the 1800s, anything that might give me some sort of lead as to where to look next.

I sent out twenty letters. I received three responses.

The proprietors of the Blakeney estate sent me an impersonal form letter listing the days the estate was open to the public; they helpfully included the fall 2003 schedule for Scarlet Pimpernel reenactments. I could think of few things more depressing than watching overeager tourists prancing around in black capes, twirling quizzing glasses, and exclaiming, "Sink me!"

The current owner of Selwick Hall was even more discouraging. He sent a letter typed on crested stationery designed to intimidate, informing me that Selwick Hall was still a private home, it was not open to the public in any capacity, and any papers the family intended for the public to view were in the British Library. Although Mr. Colin Selwick did not specifically say "sod off," it was heavily implied.

But all it takes is one, right?

And that one, Mrs. Arabella Selwick-Alderly, was currently waiting for me at—I dug the dog-eared scrap of paper out of my pocket as I scurried up the stairs in the South Kensington Tube station—43 Onslow Square.

It was raining, of course. It generally is when one has forgotten one's umbrella.

Pausing on the doorstep of 43 Onslow Square, I ran my fingers through my rain-dampened hair and took stock of my appearance. The brown suede Jimmy Choo boots that had looked so chic in the shoe store in Harvard Square were beyond repair, matted with rain and mud. My knee-length herringbone skirt had somehow twisted itself all the way around, so that the zipper stuck out stiffly in front instead of lying flat in back. And there was a sizable brownish blotch on the hem of my thick beige sweater—the battle stain of an unfortunate collision with someone's cup of coffee at the British Library cafeteria that afternoon.

So much for impressing Mrs. Selwick-Alderly with my sophistication and charm.

Tugging my skirt right way round, I rang the buzzer. A crackly voice quavered, "Hello?"

I leaned on the reply button. "It's Eloise," I shouted into the metal grating. I hate talking into intercoms; I'm never sure if I'm pressing the right button, or speaking into the right receiver, or about to be beamed up by aliens. "Eloise Kelly. About the Purple Gentian?"

I managed to catch the door just before it stopped buzzing. "Up here," called a disembodied voice.

Tipping my head back, I gazed up the stairwell. I couldn't see anyone, but I knew just what Mrs. Selwick-Alderly would look like. She would have a wrinkled face under a frizz of snowy white hair, dress in ancient tweeds, and be bent over a cane as gnarled as her skin. Following the directive from on high, I began up the stairs, rehearsing the little speech I had prepared in my head the night before. I would say something gracious about how lovely it was of her to take the time to see me. I would smile modestly and express how much I hoped I could help in my own small way to rescue her esteemed ancestor from historical oblivion. And I would remember to speak loudly, in deference to elderly ears.

"Poor girl, you look utterly knackered."

An elegant woman in a navy blue suit made of nubby wool, with a vivid crimson-and-gold scarf tied at her neck, smiled sympathetically at me. Her snowy hair—that part of my image at least had been correct!—was coiled about her head in an elaborate confection of braids that should have been old-fashioned, but on her looked queenly. Perhaps her straight spine and air of authority made her appear taller than she was, but she made me (five feet nine inches if one counts the three-inch heels that are essential to daily life) feel short. This was not a woman with an osteoporosis problem.

My polished speech dripped away like the drops of water trickling from the hem of my raincoat.

"Um, hello," I stammered.

"Hideous weather today, isn't it?" Mrs. Selwick-Alderly ushered me through a cream-colored foyer, indicating that I should drop my sodden raincoat on a chair in the hall. "How good of you to come all the way from—the British Library, was it?—to see me on such an inhospitable day."

I followed her into a cheerful living room, my ruined boots making squelching noises that boded ill to the faded Persian rug. A chintz sofa and two chairs were drawn up around the fire that crackled comfortably away beneath a marble mantel-piece. On the coffee table, an eclectic assortment of books had been pushed aside to make room for a heavily laden tea tray.

Mrs. Selwick-Alderly glanced at the tea tray and made a

little noise of annoyance. "I've forgotten the biscuits. I won't be a minute. Do make yourself comfortable."

Comfortable. I didn't think there was much chance of that. Despite Mrs. Selwick-Alderly's charm, I felt like an awkward fifth grader waiting for the headmistress to return.

Hands clasped behind my back, I wandered over to the mantel. It boasted an assortment of family photos, jumbled together in no particular order. At the far right towered a large sepia portrait photo of a debutante with her hair in the short waves of the late 1930s, a single strand of pearls about her neck, gazing soulfully upwards. The other photos were more modern and less formal, a crowd of family photos, taken in black tie, in jeans, indoors and out, people making faces at the camera or each other; they were clearly a large clan, and a close-knit one.

One picture in particular drew my attention. It sat towards the middle of the mantel, half-hidden behind a picture of two little girls decked out as flower girls. Unlike the others, it only featured a single subject—unless you counted his horse. One arm casually rested on his horse's flank. His dark blond hair had been tousled by the wind and a hard ride. There was something about the quirk of the lips and the clean beauty of the cheekbones that reminded me of Mrs. Selwick-Alderly. But where her good looks were a thing of elegance, like a finely carved piece of ivory, this man was as vibrantly alive as the sun on his hair or the horse beneath his arm. He smiled out of the photo with such complicit good humor—as if he and the viewer shared some sort of delightful joke—that it was impossible not to smile back.

Which was exactly what I was doing when my hostess returned with a plate filled with chocolate-covered biscuits.

I started guiltily, as though I had been caught out in some embarrassing intimacy.

Mrs. Selwick-Alderly placed the biscuits next to the tea tray. "I see you've found the photos. There is something irresistible about other people's pictures, isn't there?"

I joined her on the couch, setting my damp herringbone derriere gingerly on the very edge of a flowered cushion. "It's so much easier to make up stories about people you don't know," I temporized. "Especially older pictures. You wonder what their lives were like, what happened to them. . . ."

"That's part of the fascination of history, isn't it?" she said, applying herself to the teapot. Over the rituals of the tea table, the choice of milk or sugar, the passing of biscuits and cutting of cake, we slipped into an easy discussion of English history, and the awkward moment passed.

At Mrs. Selwick-Alderly's gentle prompting, I found myself rambling on about how I'd become interested in history (too many historical novels at an impressionable age), the politics of the Harvard history department (too complicated to even begin to go into), and why I'd decided to come to England. When the conversation began to verge onto what had gone wrong with Grant (everything), I hastily changed the subject, asking Mrs. Selwick-Alderly if she had heard any stories about the nineteenth-century spies as a small child.

"Oh, dear, yes!" Mrs. Selwick-Alderly smiled nostalgically into her teacup. "I spent a large part of my youth playing spy with my cousins. We would take it in turns to be the Purple Gentian and the Pink Carnation. My cousin Charles always insisted on playing Delaroche, the evil French operative. The French accent that boy affected! It put Maurice Chevalier to shame. After all these years, it still makes me laugh just to think of it. He would paint on an extravagant mustache—in those days, all the best villains had mustaches—and put on a cloak made out of one of Mother's old wraps, and storm up and down the lawn, shaking his fist and swearing vengeance against the Pink Carnation."

"Who was your favorite character?" I asked, charmed by the image.

"Why, the Pink Carnation, of course."

We smiled over the rims of our teacups in complete complicity.

"But you have an added interest in the Pink Carnation," Mrs. Selwick-Alderly said meaningfully. "Your dissertation, wasn't it?"

"Oh! Yes! My dissertation!" I outlined the work I had done so far: the chapters on the Scarlet Pimpernel's missions, the Purple Gentian's disguises, the little I had been able to discover about the way they ran their leagues.

"But I haven't been able to find anything at all about the Pink Carnation," I finished. "I've read the old newspaper accounts, of course, so I know about the Pink Carnation's more spectacular missions, but that's it."

"What had you hoped to find?"

I stared sheepishly down into my tea. "Oh, every historian's dream. An overlooked manuscript entitled *How I Be-*

came the Pink Carnation and Why. Or I'd settle for a hint of his identity in a letter or a War Office report. Just something to give me some idea of where to look next."

"I think I may be able to help you." A slight smile lurked about Mrs. Selwick-Alderly's lips.

"Really?" I perked up—literally. I sat so bolt upright that my teacup nearly toppled off my lap. "Are there family stories?"

Mrs. Selwick-Alderly's faded blue eyes twinkled. She leaned forward conspiratorially. "Better."

Possibilities were flying through my mind. An old letter, perhaps, or a deathbed message passed along from Selwick to Selwick, with Mrs. Selwick-Alderly the current keeper of the trust. But, then, if there were a Selwick Family Secret, why would she tell me? I abandoned imagination for the hope of reality. "What is it?" I asked breathlessly.

Mrs. Selwick-Alderly rose from the sofa with effortless grace. Setting her teacup down on the coffee table, she beckoned me to follow. "Come see."

I divested myself of my teacup with a clatter, and eagerly followed her towards the twin windows that looked onto the square. Between the windows hung two small portrait miniatures, and for a disappointed moment, I thought she meant merely to lead me to the pictures—there didn't seem to be anything else that might warrant attention. A small octagonal table to the right of the windows bore a pink-shaded lamp and a china candy dish, but little else. To the left, a row of bookcases lined the back of the room, but Mrs. Selwick-Alderly didn't so much as glance in that direction.

Instead, she knelt before a large trunk that sat directly beneath the portrait miniatures. I've never been into domestic art, or material history, or whatever they're calling it, but I'd spent enough afternoons loafing around the British galleries of the Victoria and Albert to recognize it as early eighteenth century, or an extraordinarily good reproduction. Different-colored woods marked out fanciful patterns of flowers and birds across the lid of the trunk, while a large bird of paradise adorned the center.

Mrs. Selwick-Alderly withdrew an elaborate key from her pocket.

"In this trunk"—she held the key poised before the lock—"lies the true identity of the Pink Carnation."

Stooping, Mrs. Selwick-Alderly fitted the key—almost as ornately constructed as the chest itself, with the end twisted into elaborate curlicues—into the brass-bound lock. The lid sprang open with well-oiled ease. I joined Mrs. Selwick-Alderly on the floor, without even realizing how I'd gotten there.

My first glance was a disappointing one. Not a paper in sight, not even the scrap of a forgotten love letter. Instead, my sweeping gaze took in the faded ivory of an old fan, a yellowed scrap of embroidered cloth, the skeletal remains of a bouquet still bound with a tattered ribbon. There were other such trinkets, but I didn't take much notice as I sank down onto my haunches beside the trunk.

But Mrs. Selwick-Alderly wasn't finished. Deliberately, she eased one blue-veined hand along either side of the velvet lining and tugged. The top tray slid easily out of its supports. Within . . . I was back on my knees, hands gripping the edge of the trunk.

"This . . . it's amazing!" I stuttered. "Are these all . . . ?"

"All early nineteenth century," Mrs. Selwick-Alderly finished for me, regarding the contents of the trunk fondly. "They've all been sorted by chronological order, so you should find it easy going." She reached into the trunk, picked up a folio, and then put it aside with a muttered "That won't do." After a moment's peering into the trunk and making the occasional clucking noise, she seized on a rectangular packet, one of those special acid-free cardboard boxes they use to protect old library books.

"You'd best start here," she advised, "with Amy."

"Amy?" I asked, picking at the string binding the box together.

Mrs. Selwick-Alderly started to respond, and then checked herself, rising to her feet with the help of the edge of the box.

"These letters tell the tale far better than I could." She cut off my incoherent questions with a kindly, "If you need anything, I'll be in my study. It's just down the hall to the right."

"But, who is he?" I pleaded, pivoting after her as she walked towards the door. "The Pink Carnation?"

"Read and see. . . ." Mrs. Selwick-Alderly's voice drifted behind her through the open door.

Urgh. Gnawing on my lower lip, I stared down at the manuscript box in my hands. The gray cardboard was smooth and clean beneath my fingers; unlike the battered, dusty old boxes in the stacks of Widener Library, someone cared for these papers well. The identity of the Pink Carnation. Did she really mean it?

I should have been tearing at the twine that bound the box, but there was something about the waiting stillness of the room, broken only by the occasional crackle of burning bark upon the grate, that barred abrupt movement. I could almost feel the portrait miniatures on the wall straining to peer over my shoulder.

Besides, I counseled myself, mechanically unwinding the string, I shouldn't let myself get too excited. Mrs. Selwick-Alderly might be exaggerating. Or mad. True, she didn't look mad, but maybe her delusion took the form of thinking she held the key to the identity of the Pink Carnation. I would open the box to find it contained a stack of Beatles lyrics or amateur poetry.

The last loop of string came free. The cardboard flap fell open, revealing a pile of yellowed papers. The date on the first letter, in a scrawling, uneven hand, read 4 MARCH 1803.

Not amateur poetry.

Dizzy with excitement, I flipped through the thick packet of papers. Some were in better condition than others; in places, ink had run, or lines had been lost in folds. Hints of reddish sealing wax clung to the edges of some, while others had lost corners to the depredations of time and the clutching fingers of eager readers. Some were written in a bold black hand, others in a spiky copperplate, and many in a barely legible scribble. But they all had one thing in common: They were all dated 1803. Phrases rose out of the sea of squiggles as I thumbed through . . . "provoking man . . . brother would never. . . ."

I forced myself to return to the first page. Sinking down onto the carpet before the fire, I adjusted my skirt, refreshed my cold cup of tea, and began to read the first letter. It was written in ungrammatical French, and I translated as I read.

4 March 1803. Dear Sister—With the end of the late hostilities, I find myself at last in a position to urge you to return to your rightful place in the House of Balcourt. . . .

Chapter One

"   The city of your birth awaits your return. Please
 . . . send word of your travel arrangements by cou-
rier at first opportunity. I remain, your devoted brother,
Edouard."

"The city of your birth awaits your return." Amy whispered the words aloud.

At last! Fingers tightening around the paper in her hands,
she gazed rapturously at the sky. For an event of such magni-
tude, she expected bolts of lightning, or thunderclouds at the
very least. But the Shropshire sky gazed calmly back at her,
utterly unperturbed by the momentous events taking place
below.

Wasn't that just like Shropshire?

Sinking to the grass, Amy contemplated the place where
she had spent the majority of her life. Behind her, over the
rolling fields, the redbrick manor house sat placidly on its rise.
Uncle Bertrand was sure to be right there, three windows
from the left, sitting in his cracked leather chair, poring over
the latest findings of the Royal Agricultural Society, just as he
did every day. Aunt Prudence would be sitting in the yellow-
and-cream morning room, squinting over her embroidery
threads, just as she did every day. All peaceful, and bucolic,
and boring.

The prospect before her wasn't any more exciting, nothing
but long swaths of green, enlivened only by woolly balls of
sheep.

But now, at last, the long years of boredom were at an end.
In her hand she grasped the opportunity to leave Wooliston
Manor and its pampered flock behind her forever. She would
no longer be plain Amy Balcourt, niece to the most ambitious

sheep breeder in Shropshire, but Aimée, Mlle de Balcourt. Amy conveniently ignored the fact that revolutionary France had banished titles when they beheaded their nobility.

She had been six years old when revolution exiled her to rural England. In late May of 1789, she and Mama had sailed across the Channel for what was meant to be merely a two-month visit, time enough for Mama to see her sisters and show her daughter something of English ways. For all the years she had spent in France, Mama was still an English-woman at heart.

Uncle Bertrand, sporting a slightly askew periwig, had stridden out to meet them. Behind him stood Aunt Prudence, embroidery hoop clutched in her hand. Clustered in the doorway were three little girls in identical muslin dresses, Amy's cousins Sophia, Jane, and Agnes. "See, darling," whispered Mama. "You shall have other little girls to play with. Won't that be lovely?"

It wasn't lovely. Agnes, still in the lisping and stumbling stage, was too young to be a playmate. Sophia spent all of her time bent virtuously over her sampler. Jane, quiet and shy, Amy dismissed as a poor-spirited thing. Even the sheep soon lost their charm. Within a month, Amy was quite ready to re-turn to France. She packed her little trunk, heaved and pushed it down the hall to her mother's room, and announced that she was prepared to go.

Mama had half-smiled, but her smile twisted into a sob. She plucked her daughter off the trunk and squeezed her very, very tightly.

"Mais, maman, qu'est-ce que se passe?" demanded Amy, who still thought in French in those days.

"We can't go back, darling. Not now. I don't know if we'll ever . . . Oh, your poor father! Poor us! And Edouard, what must they be doing to him?"

Amy didn't know who *they* were, but remembering the way Edouard had yanked at her curls and pinched her arm while supposedly hugging her good-bye, she couldn't help but think her brother deserved anything he got. She said as much to Mama.

Mama looked down at her miserably. "Oh no, darling, not this. Nobody deserves this." Very slowly, in between deep breaths, she had explained to Amy that mobs had taken over

Paris, that the king and queen were prisoners, and that Papa and Edouard were very much in danger.

Over the next few months, Wooliston Manor became the unlikely center of an antirevolutionary movement. Everyone pored over the weekly papers, wincing at news of atrocities across the Channel. Mama ruined quill after quill penning desperate letters to connections in France, London, Austria. When the Scarlet Pimpernel appeared on the scene, snatching aristocrats from the sharp embrace of Madame Guillotine, Mama brimmed over with fresh hope. She peppered every news sheet within a hundred miles of London with advertisements begging the Scarlet Pimpernel to save her son and husband.

Amidst all this hubbub, Amy lay awake at night in the nursery, wishing she were old enough to go back to France herself and save Papa. She would go disguised, of course, since everyone knew a proper rescue had to be done in disguise. When no one was about, Amy would creep down to the servants' quarters to try on their clothes and practice speaking in the rough, peasant French of the countryside. If anyone happened upon her, Amy explained that she was preparing amateur theatricals. With so much to worry about, none of the grown-ups who absently said, "How nice, dear," and patted her on the head ever bothered to wonder why the promised performance never materialized.

Except Jane. When Jane came upon Amy clad in an assortment of old petticoats from the ragbag and a discarded periwig of Uncle Bertrand's, Amy huffily informed her that she was rehearsing for a one-woman production of *Two Gentlemen of Verona*.

Jane regarded her thoughtfully. Half apologetically, she said, "I don't think you're telling the truth."

Unable to think of a crushing response, Amy just glared. Jane clutched her rag doll tighter, but managed to ask, "Please, won't you tell me what you're really doing?"

"You won't tell Mama or any of the others?" Amy tried to look suitably fierce, but the effect was quite ruined by her periwig sliding askew and dangling from one ear.

Jane hastily nodded.

"I," declared Amy importantly, "am going to join the League of the Scarlet Pimpernel and rescue Papa."

Jane pondered this new information, doll dangling forgotten from one hand.

"May I help?" she asked.

Her cousin's unexpected aid proved a boon to Amy. It was Jane who figured out how to rub soot and gum on teeth to make them look like those of a desiccated old hag—and then how to rub it all off again before Nanny saw. It was Jane who plotted a route to France on the nursery globe and Jane who discovered a way to creep down the back stairs without making them creak.

They never had the chance to execute their plans. Little beknownst to the two small girls preparing themselves to enter his service, the Scarlet Pimpernel foolishly attempted the rescue of the Vicomte de Balcourt without them. From the papers, Amy learned that the Pimpernel had spirited Papa out of prison disguised as a cask of cheap red wine. The rescue might have gone without a hitch had a thirsty guard at the gates of the city not insisted on tapping the cask. When he encountered Papa instead of Beaujolais, the guard angrily sounded the alert. Papa, the papers claimed, had fought manfully, but he was no match for an entire troop of revolutionary soldiers. A week later, a small card had arrived for Mama. It said simply, "I'm sorry," and was signed with a scarlet flower.

The news sent Mama into a decline and Amy into a fury. With Jane as her witness, she vowed to avenge Papa and Mama as soon as she was old enough to return to France. She would need excellent French for that, and Amy could already feel her native tongue beginning to slip away under the onslaught of constant English conversation. At first, she tried conversing in French with their governesses, but those worthy ladies tended to have a vocabulary limited to shades of cloth and the newest types of millinery. So Amy took her Molière outside and read aloud to the sheep.

Latin and Greek would do her no good in her mission, but Amy read them anyway, in memory of Papa. Papa had told her nightly bedtime stories of capricious gods and vengeful goddesses; Amy tracked all his stories down among the books in the little-used library at Wooliston Manor. Uncle Bertrand's own taste ran more towards manuals on animal husbandry, but *someone* in the family must have read once, because the library possessed quite a creditable collection of classics. Amy read Ovid and Virgil and Aristophanes and Homer. She read dry histories and scandalous love poetry (her governesses, who had little Latin and less Greek, naïvely assumed that anything in a classical tongue must be respectable), but mostly she returned again and again to *The Odyssey*. Odysseus had fought to go home, and so would Amy.

When Amy was ten, the illustrated newsletters announced that the Scarlet Pimpernel had retired upon discovery of his identity—although the newsletters were rather unclear as to whether they or the French government had been the first to get the scoop. SCARLET PIMPERNEL UNMASKED! proclaimed the *Shropshire Intelligencer*. Meanwhile *The Cosmopolitan Lady's Book* carried a ten-page spread on "Fashions of the Scarlet Pimpernel: Costume Tips from the Man Who Brought You the French Aristocracy."

Amy was devastated. True, the Pimpernel had botched her father's rescue, but, on the whole, his tally of aristocrats saved was quite impressive, and who on earth was she to offer her French language skills to if the Pimpernel retired? Amy was all ready to start constructing her own band when a line in the article in the *Shropshire Intelligencer* caught her eye. "I have every faith that the Purple Gentian will take up where I was forced to leave off," they reported Sir Percy as saying.

Puzzled, Amy shoved the paper at Jane. "Who is the Purple Gentian?"

The same question was on everyone else's lips. Soon the Purple Gentian became a regular feature in the news sheets. One week, he spirited fifteen aristocrats out of Paris as a traveling circus. The Purple Gentian, it was whispered, had played the dancing bear. Why, some said Robespierre himself had patted the animal on the head, never knowing it was his greatest enemy! When France stopped killing its aristocrats and directed its attention to fighting England instead, the Purple Gentian became the War Office's most reliable spy.

"This victory would never have happened, but for the bravery of one man—one man represented by a small purple flower," Admiral Nelson announced after destroying the French fleet in Egypt.

English and French alike were united in their burning curiosity to learn the identity of the Purple Gentian. Speculation ran rife on both sides of the Channel. Some claimed the Purple Gentian was an English aristocrat, a darling of the London *ton* like Sir Percy Blakeney. Indeed, some said he *was* Sir

Percy Blakeney, fooling the foolish French by returning under a different name. London gossip named everyone from Beau Brummel (on the grounds that no one could genuinely be *that* interested in fashion) to the Prince of Wales's dissolute brother, the Duke of York. Others declared that the Purple Gentian must be an exiled French noble, fighting for his homeland. Some said he was a soldier; others said he was a renegade priest. The French just said he was a damned nuisance. Or they would have, had they the good fortune to speak English. Instead, being French, they were forced to say it in their own language.

Amy said he was her hero.

She only said it to Jane, of course. All of the old plans were revived, only this time it was the League of the Purple Gentian to whom Amy planned to offer her services.

But the years went by, Amy remained in Shropshire, and the only masked man she saw was her small cousin Ned playing at being a highwayman. At times Amy considered running away to Paris, but how would she even get there? With war raging between England and France, normal travel across the Channel had been disrupted. Amy began to despair of ever reaching France, much less finding the Purple Gentian. She envisioned a dreary future of pastoral peace.

Until Edouard's letter.

"I thought I'd find you here."

"What?" Amy was jolted out of her blissful contemplation of Edouard's letter as a blue flounce brushed against her arm.

A basket of wildflowers on Jane's arm testified to a walk along the grounds, but she bore no sign of outdoor exertion. No creases dared to settle in the folds of her muslin dress; her pale brown hair remained obediently coiled at the base of her neck; and even the loops of the bow holding her bonnet were remarkably even. Aside from a bit of windburn on her pale cheeks, she might have been sitting in the parlor all afternoon.

"Mama has been looking all over for you. She wants to know what you did with her skein of rose-pink embroidery silk."

"What makes her think I have it? Besides"—Amy cut off what looked to be a highly logical response from Jane with a wave of Edouard's letter—"who can think of embroidery silks when *this* just arrived?"

"A letter? Not another love poem from Derek?"

"Ugh!" Amy shuddered dramatically. "Really, Jane! What a vile thought! No"—she leaned forward, lowering her voice dramatically—"it's a letter from Edouard."

"Edward?" Jane, being Jane, automatically gave the name its English pronunciation. "So he has finally deigned to remember your existence after all these years?"

"Oh, Jane, don't be harsh! He wants me to go live with him!"

Jane dropped her basket of flowers.

"You can't be serious, Amy!"

"But I am! Isn't it glorious!" Amy joined her cousin in gathering up scattered blooms, piling them willy-nilly back in the basket with more enthusiasm than grace.

"What *exactly* does Edward's letter say?"

"It's splendid, Jane! Now that we're no longer at war, he says it's finally safe for me to come back. He says he wants me to act as hostess for him."

"But are you sure it's safe?" Jane's gray eyes darkened with concern.

Amy laughed. "It's not all screaming mobs, Jane. After all, Bonaparte has been consul for—how long has it been? Three years now? Actually, that's exactly why Edouard wants me there. Bonaparte is desperately trying to make his jumped-up, murderous, usurping government look legitimate . . ."

"Not that you're at all biased," murmured Jane.

". . . so he's been courting the old nobility," Amy went on, pointedly ignoring her cousin's comment. "But the courting has mostly been going on through his wife, Josephine—she has a *salon* for the ladies of the old regime—so Edouard needs me to be his *entrée*."

"To that jumped-up, murderous, usurping government?" Jane's voice was politely quizzical.

Amy tossed a daisy at her in annoyance. "Make fun all you like, Jane! Don't you see? This is exactly the opportunity I needed!"

"To become the belle of Bonaparte's court?"

Amy forbore to waste another flower. "No." She clasped her hands, eyes gleaming. "To join the League of the Purple Gentian!"

Chapter Two

The Purple Gentian was not having a good day. Lord Richard Selwick, second son of the Marquess of Uppington, prime object of matchmaking mamas, and chief foiler of Napoleonic ambitions, stood in the front hall of his parents' London home and scuffed his boots like a sulky schoolboy.

"That will be enough of that." His mother shook her head at him in fond exasperation, setting the egret feathers precariously perched on her coiffure wafting in the still air of the front hall. "It's an evening at Almack's, not a firing squad."

"But, Mother . . ." Richard caught the whine in his own voice and winced. Bloody hell. What was it about being home that instantly drove him back to the manners and maturity of a twelve-year-old?

Richard took a deep breath and made sure his voice came out in its proper register. "Look, Mother, I'm quite busy right now. I'm only in London for another two weeks, and there are a number of things . . ."

His mother made a noise that in anyone of lower rank than a countess would have been given the unmannerly name of snort. As a cowed member of the *ton* had once commented, "Nobody *harrumphs* quite like the Marchioness of Uppington."

"Tush!" His mother waved his words away with a sweep of her feathery fan. "Just because you're a secret agent doesn't mean that you can put off settling down forever. Really, Richard." She took a furtive look around the hall to make sure no servants were in evidence, as, after all, it wouldn't do to have her son's secret identity getting out, and servants did gossip so. Having ascertained that none were about, she warmed to her theme. "You're nearly thirty already! Just because you're the Purple Gentian—ridiculous name!—doesn't mean that you don't have *responsibilities*!"

"I'd say saving Europe from a tyrant is a jolly good responsibility," Richard muttered under his breath. Unfortunately, the marble foyer had excellent acoustics.

"I meant responsibilities to your family. What if the Uppington title were to die out entirely because you couldn't be bothered to spend one little evening at Almack's and meet a nice girl? Hmmm?" She cocked her head to one side, narrowing her green eyes at him, green eyes which were, Richard thought sourly, altogether too shrewd for either his good or hers. His mother, as he knew from unfortunate past experience, had the rhetorical slipperiness of Cicero, the vocal endurance of an opera singer, and the sheer bloody-minded tenacity of Napoleon Bonaparte. Sometimes Richard had the sinking suspicion that he had a far better chance of preventing Bonaparte from conquering Europe than he had of thwarting his mother's plans to see him married off within the next Season.

Nonetheless, Richard battled on valiantly. "Mother, Charles has produced a child for every year he's been married. I sincerely doubt that the title is in any danger."

His mother frowned. "Accidents do happen. But that's not even to be thought of." Reconsidering her tactics, Lady Uppington began to pace along the expanse of the foyer, bronze silk skirts swishing in time to her steps. "What I meant to point out was that sooner or later you're going to have to give up playing at espionage."

Richard's jaw dropped. *Playing* at espionage? He shot his mother a look of equal parts outrage and incredulity. Just who had provided Nelson the intelligence that destroyed Napoleon's fleet at Aboukir? And who had prevented four determined French assassins from murdering the king in his gardens at Kew? Lord Richard Selwick, alias the Purple Gentian, that was who! Had he not been constrained by the immense respect and filial affection he bore his mother, Richard would have produced a *harrumph* that would put the marchioness's to shame.

But as all this never made its way from Richard's mind to his mouth, his mother blithely carried on with her lecture. "All this gadding about on the Continent—you've been at it for almost a decade, Richard. Even Percy retired after he met his Marguerite."

"Percy retired because the French discovered he was the Scarlet Pimpernel," Richard grumbled unthinkingly. Hit by a sudden, horrible surmise, he jerked his head up. "Mother, you wouldn't . . ."

Lady Uppington paused in her perambulations. "No, I wouldn't," she said regretfully. For a moment, she gazed dreamily off at an arrangement of flowers in one of the alcoves in the wall. "Such a pity. It would be so effective."

Shaking her head as if to whisk away the temptation of the thought, she resumed her brisk progress around the room. "Darling, you know I could never sabotage you. And you know both your father and I are terribly proud of you. Don't think we don't appreciate that you trusted us enough to confide in us. Look at poor Lady Falconstone—she only found out her son was an agent for the War Office after he was captured by that French spy and they started sending her all of those nasty ransom notes in French. And he never even had a special name or made it into the illustrated papers." The marchioness indulged in a maternal smirk. "We just want to see you *happy*," she finished earnestly.

Sensing another maternal oration coming on, one of those I-bore-you-and-thus-know-what's-best-for-you lectures, Richard made a pointed move towards the door. "If that's all for the moment, Mother, I really must be off. The War Office . . ."

The marchioness gave another of her infamous *harrumphs*. "Have a good time at White's, darling," she said pointedly.

Richard paused halfway out the door and flashed her an incredulous look. "How do you always know?"

Lady Uppington looked smug. "Because I'm your mother. Now, shoo! Get along with you!"

As the door closed behind him, Richard heard his mother call out gleefully, "Almack's at nine! Don't forget to wear knee breeches!"

The banging of the door drowned out Richard's heartfelt groan. Knee breeches. Bloody hell. It had been so long since he had last been dragged by the ear through the dreaded doors of Almack's Assembly Rooms that he had completely forgotten about the knee breeches. Richard looked understandably glum as he headed down Upper Brook Street toward St. James Street. The prospect was enough to send anyone into a precipitate decline. How did his mother contrive to rope him into these things? If the Foreign Office had thought to let his mother loose on France . . . she'd probably have the entire country married off within a month.

"Afternoon, Selwick!"

Richard absently nodded to an acquaintance in a passing curricle. As it was just after five, the hour for flirting while on horseback, a steady stream of fashionable people in carriages or on horseback passed Richard as they made their way to Hyde Park. Richard smiled and nodded by rote, but his mind was already slipping away, across the Channel, to his work in France.

When he was very little, Richard had resolved to be a hero. It might have had something to do with his mother reading him the more stirring bits of *Henry V* at far too young an age. Richard charged about the nursery, dueling with invisible Frenchmen. Or maybe it came from afternoons playing King Arthur and his knights of the Round Table in the gardens with his father. For years Richard was convinced that the Holy Grail lay hidden under the floor of the ornamental Greek temple his mother used for tea parties. When Richard appeared with a shovel and a pickax while the Dowager Duchess of Dovedale was partaking of an *al fresco* tea, his mother was not amused. She declared an end to the grail-searching sessions at once.

Sent to Eton to learn the classics, Richard raced through the adventures of Odysseus and Aeneas, earning an utterly undeserved reputation as a scholar. Richard burned for the day when he could set out on his own adventures.

There was only one problem. There seemed to be very little call for heroes nowadays. He had, he realized, the ill fortune to be living in a time of singular peace and civility. Other employment would have to be found.

With that in mind, Richard looked first to estate management. He did have his own little estate, but the steward was a genial man of middle years, universally liked and unusually competent. There was little for Richard to do but ride about making polite conversation with his tenants and kissing the occasional baby. There was certainly something satisfying about it, but Richard knew that playing the role of gentleman farmer would leave him bored and restless.

So Richard did what any other young man in his position would do. He set out to become a rake. By the time he was sixteen, the second son of the Marquess of Uppington was a familiar figure in the fashionable gaming dens and bawdy houses of London. He played faro for high stakes, drove his horses too fast, and changed his mistresses as frequently as he did his linen. But he was still bored.

And then, just when Richard had resigned himself to a life of empty debauchery, good fortune smiled upon him in the form of the French Revolution. For hundreds of years, the Uppington estates had adjoined those of the Blakeneys. Richard had spent countless afternoons hunting with Sir Percy, raiding his kitchens for tarts, and kicking about the Blakeney library, reading Percy's extensive collection of classical works, all of which contained bookplates with the Blakeney coat of arms, which happened to contain a small scarlet flower. When the Scarlet Pimpernel began making headlines, it didn't take much for Richard to put two and two together and come up with the fact that his next-door neighbor was the greatest hero to appear in England since Henry V.

Richard had begged and pleaded until Percy agreed to take him along on a mission. That one mission went well, and became two, and then three missions, until Richard, with his gift for the heroic, became absolutely indispensable to the League of the Scarlet Pimpernel. So indispensable that Percy and the others had forgiven him when . . . No. Richard squashed the thought before it could grow into memory, stomping up the steps to his club with unnecessary vigor.

Richard felt himself relaxing as he entered the masculine stronghold of White's. The smells of tobacco and spirits hung heavy in the air, and from a chamber to his right, he could hear the heavy thud of darts being flung against a target—and missing, if the curses coming from that room were any indication. Meandering through the first floor, he spotted several hands of cards in progress, but none that he cared to join. One of his sister's many suitors made enthusiastic welcoming motions at Richard from the small table where he was ensconced with two friends over a bottle of port. Unfortunately, his welcome was a little too enthusiastic. He toppled himself right over the side of his chair, taking the table, port decanter, and three glasses with him. "Well, that's one person we won't be seeing at Almack's tonight," murmured Richard to himself as he nodded in passing at the flailing boy and his port-sodden companions.

Richard found his quarry in the library.

"Selwick!" The Honorable Miles Dorrington flung aside the news sheet he had been reading, leaped up from his chair, and pounded his friend on the back. He then hastily reseated himself, looking slightly abashed at his unseemly display of affection.

In a fit of temper, Richard's sister Henrietta had once referred irritably to Miles as "that overeager sheepdog," and there was something to be said for the description. With his sandy blond hair flopping into his face, and his brown eyes alight with good fellowship, Miles did bear a striking resemblance to the more amiable varieties of man's best friend. He was, in fact, Richard's best friend. They had been fast friends since their first days at Eton.

"When did you get back to London?" Miles asked.

Richard dropped into the seat next to him, sinking contentedly into the worn leather chair. He stretched his long legs comfortably out in front of him. "Late last night. I left Paris Thursday, stopped for a couple of nights at Uppington Hall, and got into town about midnight." He grinned at his friend. "I'm in hiding."

Miles instantly stiffened. Anxiously, he looked left, then right, before leaning forward and hissing, "From whom? Did they follow you here?"

Richard shouted with laughter. "Good God, nothing like that, man! No, I'm a fugitive from my mother."

Miles relaxed. "You might have said so," he commented crossly. "As you can imagine, we're all a bit on edge."

"Sorry, old chap." Richard smiled his thanks as a glass of his favorite brand of scotch materialized in his hands. Ah, it was good to be back at his club!

Miles accepted a whisky and leaned back in his chair. "What is it this time? Is she throwing another distant cousin at you?"

"Worse," Richard said. He took a long swig of scotch. "Almack's."

Miles grimaced in sympathy. "Not the knee breeches."

"Knee breeches and all."

There was a moment of companionable silence as the men, both fashionably turned out in tight tan trousers, contemplated the horror of knee breeches. Miles finished his whisky and set it down on a low table beside his chair. Taking a more thorough look around the room, he asked Richard quietly, "How is Paris?"

Not only Richard's oldest and closest friend, Miles also served as his contact at the War Office. When Richard had switched from rescuing aristocrats to gathering secrets, the Minister of War had wisely pointed out that the best possible way to communicate with Richard was through young Miles Dorrington. After all, the two men moved in the same set, shared the same friends, and could frequently be seen reminiscing over the tables at White's. Nobody would see anything suspicious about finding two old friends in hushed conversation. As an excuse for his frequent calls at Uppington House, Miles had put it about that he was thinking of courting Richard's sister. Henrietta had entered into the deception with, to Richard's big-brotherly mind, a little too much relish.

Richard took his own survey of the room, noting the back of a white head poking out over a chairback. He lifted an eyebrow quizzically at Miles.

Miles shrugged. "It's only old Falconstone. Deaf as a post and fast asleep to boot."

"And his son is one of ours. Right. Paris has been . . . busy."

Miles tugged at his cravat. "Busy how?"

"Stop that, or you'll have your valet baying for your blood."

Miles looked sheepish and tried to rearrange the folds of his cravat, which had gone from being a perfect waterfall to simply falling all over.

"Lots of comings and goings from the Tuilleries—more than usual," Richard continued. "I've sent a full report to the office. Along with some information helpfully compiled by our mutual friend Monsieur Delaroche at the Ministry of Police." His lips curved in a grin of sheer glee.

"Good man! I knew you could do it! A list of all their agents in London—and right out from under Delaroche's nose, no less! You do have the devil's own luck." Richard's back was too far away to reach, so Miles slapped the arm of his chair appreciatively instead. "And your connections to the First Consul?"

"Better than ever," Richard said. "He's moved the collection of Egyptian artifacts into the palace."

Egyptian artifacts might seem a topic beyond the scope of

the War Office. But not when their top agent played the role of Bonaparte's pet scholar.

When Richard created the Purple Gentian, the talent for ancient languages that had stunned his schoolmasters at Eton had come to his aid once again. While Sir Percy had pretended to be a fop, Richard bored the French into complacency with long lectures about antiquity. When Frenchmen demanded to know what he was doing in France, and Englishmen reproached him for fraternizing with the enemy, Richard opened his eyes wide and proclaimed, "But a scholar is a citizen of the world!" Then he quoted Greek at them. They usually didn't ask again. Even Gaston Delaroche, the Assistant Minister of Police, who had sworn in blood to be avenged on the Purple Gentian and had the tenacity of . . . well, of Richard's mother, had stopped snooping around Richard after being subjected to two particularly knotty passages from the *Odyssey*.

Bonaparte's decision to invade Egypt had been a disaster for France but a triumph for Richard. He already had a reputation as a scholar and an antiquarian; who better to join the group of academics Bonaparte was bringing with him to Egypt? Under cover of antiquarian fervor, Richard had gathered more information about French activities than Egyptian antiquities. With Richard's reports, the English had been able to destroy the French fleet and strand Bonaparte in Egypt for months.

Over those long months in Egypt, Richard became fast friends with Bonaparte's stepson, Eugene de Beauharnais, a sunny, goodnatured boy with a genius for friendship. When Eugene introduced Richard to Bonaparte, presenting him as a scholar of antiquities, Bonaparte had immediately engaged Richard in a long debate over Suetonius's *Lives of the Caesars*. Impressed by Richard's cool argument and immense store of quotations, he had extended an open invitation to drop by his tent and dispute the ancient past. Within a month, he had appointed Richard his director of Egyptian antiquities. Among the sands of the French camp in Egypt, it was a rather empty title. But on their return to Paris, Richard found himself with two rooms full of artifacts and an entrée into the palace. What spy could ask for more? And now his artifacts had been moved into the palace, Bonaparte's lair. . . .

Miles looked as though he had been handed a pile of Christmas presents in July. "And your office with it?"

"And my office with it."

"Damn it, Richard, this is brilliant! Brilliant!" Miles so forgot himself as to raise his voice above a whisper. Quite far above a whisper.

At the far end of the room, old Falconstone stirred. "Whaaat? Eh, what?"

"I quite agree," Richard said loudly. "Wordsworth's poetry is quite brilliant, but I shall always prefer Catullus."

Miles cast him a dubious glance. "Wordsworth and Catullus?" he whispered.

"Look, you were the one who shouted," cast back Richard. "I had to come up with something."

"If it gets around that I've been reading Wordsworth, I'll be booted out of my clubs. My mistress will disown me. My reputation will be ruined," Miles hissed in exaggerated distress.

Meanwhile, Falconstone had staggered to his feet and did a bizarre little dance as he tried to catch his balance with his cane. Spotting Richard across the room, his face darkened to match his burgundy waistcoat.

"Blasted cheek showing your face here! After you been consorting with them Frenchies, eh, what?" Falconstone roared with the complete lack of shame of the extremely deaf and the complete lack of grammar of the extremely inbred. "Blasted cheek, I say!" He tried to poke at Richard with his cane, but the effort proved too much for him, and he would have gone tumbling had Richard not steadied him.

Glowering, Falconstone yanked his arm away and stalked off, mumbling.

Miles had jumped to his feet when Falconstone had charged Richard. He looked at his friend with concern. "Do you get much of that?"

"Only from Falconstone. I really do have to get around to freeing his son from the Temple prison one of these days." Richard resumed his seat and drained the remainder of his scotch in a single swallow. "Don't be such an old woman, Miles. It doesn't bother me. Look, I prefer Falconstone's rantings to all those debutantes twittering about the Purple Gentian. Can you imagine what I'd have to put up with if the truth got out?"

Miles cocked his head thoughtfully, sending a lock of floppy blond hair tumbling in front of his eyes. "Hmm, adoring debutantes . . ."

"Think how jealous your mistress would be," Richard said dryly.

Miles flinched. His current mistress was an opera singer as well known for the range of her throwing arm as that of her voice. He had already courted concussion by flirting openly with a ballet dancer and had no desire to repeat the experience. "All right, all right, point taken," he said. "Oh, damnation! I promised her I would have supper with her before the opera. She'll probably break half the dishes in the house if I'm late."

"Most of them over your head," commented Richard helpfully. "Since I prefer you with your head all in one piece, you'd better relay my assignment quickly."

"How right you are!" Miles replied fervently. He struggled to collect himself and regain the gravity incumbent upon a representative of the War Office. "All right. Your assignment. We're pretty sure that Bonaparte is using the peace to plot an invasion of England."

Richard nodded grimly. "I thought as much."

"Your job is to uncover as much as you can about his preparations. We want dates, locations, and numbers, as quickly as you can get them. We'll have a string of couriers posted from Paris to Calais to relay the information as you find it. This is it, Richard!" Miles's eyes glowed with sporting fervor, like a hound on the trail of a fox. "*The* assignment. We're relying on *you* to keep old Boney out of England."

A familiar tingle of anticipation rushed through Richard. How had Percy been able to give this up? The rush, the excitement, the challenge! Heady stuff, to know the safety of England depended upon him. Of course, Richard didn't delude himself that he was the country's sole hope. He knew the War Office had a good dozen spies scattered around the French capital, all striving to uncover the same things. But he also knew, without false modesty, that he was their best.

"The usual code, I suppose?" They had developed the code their first year at Eton as part of an elaborate plan to outwit their bullying proctor.

Miles nodded. "You'll leave for Paris in two weeks?"

Richard rubbed his forehead. "Yes. I have some personal

business to take care of—and I've promised my mother to squire Hen around to scare the fortune hunters away. Bonaparte should be away at Malmaison for most of next week, anyway, and I've left Geoff to keep an eye on things while I'm gone."

"Good man, Geoff." Miles rose and stretched. "Now, if he were here, the three of us could have a bang-up night of carousing just like old times. I guess it'll have to wait till we've foiled old Boney once and for all. Cry God for England, Harry, and St. George, and all that." Miles was frantically trying to rearrange his cravat and smooth down his hair. "Damn. No time to stop off at home and get my valet to tidy me up. Oh well. Give Hen a kiss for me."

Richard shot him a sharp look.

"On the cheek, man, on the cheek. God knows I'd never try anything improper with your sister. Not that she isn't a beautiful girl and all that, it's just, well, she's your *sister*."

Richard clapped his friend on the shoulder in approval. "Well said! That's exactly the way I want you to think of her."

Miles muttered something about being grateful that his sisters were a good deal older. "You turn into a complete bore when you're chaperoning Hen, you know," he grumbled.

Richard raised one eyebrow at Miles, a skill that had taken several months of practice in front of his mirror when he was twelve, but had been well worth the investment. "At least I didn't let my sister dress me up in her petticoat when I was five."

Miles's jaw dropped. "Who told you about that?" he demanded indignantly.

Richard grinned. "I have my sources," he said airily.

Miles, not a top agent of the War Office for nothing, considered for a moment and his eyes narrowed. "You can tell your source that she's going to have to find someone else to fetch her lemonade at the Alsworthys' ball tomorrow night unless she apologizes. You can also tell her that I'll accept either a verbal or a written apology as long as it's suitably abject. And that means very, very abject," he added darkly. Miles snatched his hat and gloves up from a side table. "Oh, stop grinning already! It wasn't that amusing."

Richard rubbed his chin as though in deep thought. "Tell me, Miles, was it a lacy petticoat?"

With a wordless grunt of annoyance, Miles turned on his heel and stomped out of the room.

Picking up the news sheet Miles had left behind, Richard settled back down into the comfortable leather chair.

Two weeks, he thought. In two weeks he would be back in France, risking discovery and death.

Richard couldn't wait.

Chapter Three

"How do you possibly expect to find the Purple Gentian?" Jane hurried after Amy into the airy white-and-blue-papered room they had shared since they were old enough to abandon the nursery. "The French have been trying for years!"

Their bedroom was beginning to look like a modiste's shop struck by a hurricane. A garter dangled off the clock on the mantelpiece, Amy's bed was snowed under by a pile of frothy petticoats, and, somehow, with one wild fling, Amy had even managed to land a bonnet on the canopy of Jane's bed. Jane could just make out the tips of pink ribbons dangling over the edge of the canopy.

Amy had gotten it into her head that if she packed at once she might be able to leave the next day. It was, reflected Jane, a typically Amy reaction. If Amy had been around for the creation of the world, Jane had no doubt that she would have chivvied the Lord into creating the earth in two days rather than seven.

Several pairs of stockings came whizzing Jane's way. "Remember that inn the papers said the Scarlet Pimpernel always stopped at? The one in Dover?"

"The Fisherman's Rest," Jane supplied.

"Well the *Shropshire Intelligencer* said that they thought the Purple Gentian might be continuing the tradition. So . . . what if we were to stop at the Fisherman's Rest before we sail? With a little careful eavesdropping, who knows?"

"The *Shropshire Intelligencer*," Jane reminded her, "also carried a piece about the birth of a two-headed goat in Nottingham. And last month's edition claimed that His Majesty had gone mad again and appointed Queen Charlotte Regent."

"Oh, all right, I'll grant you that it's not the most reliable publication—"

"Not the *most* reliable?"

"Did you see today's headline, Jane? In the *Spectator,* mind you, not the *Intelligencer.*" Snatching up the much-thumbed sheet of paper, Amy read rapturously, "ENGLAND'S FAVORITE FLOWER FILCHES FRENCH FILES IN DARING RAID."

Amy was cut off by the scrape of the door inching open. It couldn't move more than an inch or two, because Amy's trunk, which she had dragged out from under the bed, was blocking it. "Begging your pardon, Miss Jane, Miss Amy"— Mary, the upstairs maid, poked her head in and bobbed a curtsy—"but the mistress said I was to see if you would be needing any help dressing for dinner."

Amy's face contorted with horror like Mrs. Siddons performing Lady Macbeth's mad scene. "Oh, no! It's Thursday!"

"Yes, miss, and tomorrow's Friday," Mary supplied helpfully.

"Oh, drat, drat, drat, drat," Amy was muttering to herself, so it was left to Jane to smile graciously and say, "We won't be requiring your assistance, Mary. You may tell Mama that Miss Amy and I will be down shortly."

"Yes, miss." The maid curtsied again, closing the door carefully behind her.

"Drat, drat, drat," said Amy.

"You might wear your peach muslin," suggested Jane.

"Tell them I have the headache—no, the plague! I need something nice and contagious."

"At least half a dozen people saw you running across the lawn in perfect health not half an hour ago."

"We'll tell them it was a sudden case?" Jane shook her head at Amy and handed her the peach gown. Amy docilely turned her back to Jane to be unbuttoned. "I haven't the patience for Derek tonight! Not tonight of all nights! I have to *plan*!" Her voice was slightly muffled as Jane pulled the clean frock over her head. "Why did it have to be a Thursday?"

Jane gave Amy a sympathetic pat on the back as she began buttoning her into the peach dress.

They would be twelve for dinner tonight, as they were every Thursday. Every Thursday night, with the same inevitable regularity as the shearing of the sheep, an outmoded carriage with a blurred crest on the side rattled down the drive. Every Thursday, out piled their nearest neighbors: Mr. Henry Meadows, his wife, his spinster sister, and his son, Derek.

Amy flung herself into the low chair before the dressing table and began to brush her short curls with a violence that made them crackle and frizz around her face. "I really don't think I can take it much longer, Jane. Derek is more than anyone should be expected to bear!"

"There are easier ways to escape Derek than to go chasing the Purple Gentian." Jane reached around Amy to pluck a locket on a blue ribbon off the dressing table.

"How can you even combine their names in the same sentence?" Amy protested with a grimace. Resting her chin on clasped hands, she grinned up at Jane in the mirror. "Admit it. You want to go chasing the Purple Gentian just as much as I do. Don't try to pretend you're not excited."

"I suppose someone needs to go with you and keep you out of scrapes." There was no mistaking the glint in Jane's gray eyes.

Amy leaped up from her stool and flung her arms around her cousin. "Finally!" she crowed. "After all these years!"

"And all our planning." Jane hugged Amy back exultantly. She added, "I do draw the line at soot on my teeth and Papa's old periwig."

"Agreed. I'm sure I can think of something much, much cleverer than that. . . ."

Jane pulled back with a sudden frown. "What do we do if Papa says no?"

"Oh, Jane! How could he possibly refuse?"

"Absolutely out of the question," said Uncle Bertrand.

Amy bristled in indignation. "But . . ."

Uncle Bertrand forestalled her with a wave of his fork, sending a trail of gravy snaking across the dining room. "I'll not see a niece of mine among those murderous French. Black sheep, the lot of them! Eh, vicar?" Uncle Bertrand drove an elbow into the vicar's black frock coat, causing the vicar to reel into the footman and the footman to spill half the carafe of claret onto the Aubusson rug.

Amy put down her heavily engraved silver fork. "May I remind you, Uncle Bertrand, that I myself am half French?"

Uncle Bertrand had little sense of tone or nuance. "Never

mind that, lass," he replied jovially. "Your pa was a good chap for all that he was a Frenchman. We don't hold it against you. Eh, Derek?"

Derek smirked across the table at Amy. In his Nile green frock coat, he looked like a particularly foppish frog, thought Amy disgustedly.

"If you feel the need to move about more, Amy, dear, you're always welcome to call on us!" chirped Derek's mother from Uncle Bertrand's right. Her double chins bounced with enthusiasm. "I'm sure Derek can find the time to take you for a lovely turn in the rose gardens—properly chaperoned, of course!"

She waved a plump hand at the obvious proper chaperone, Mr. Meadows's maiden sister, commonly known as Miss Gwen. Miss Gwen responded in her usual fashion: she glowered. Amy supposed that if she had to live with Mrs. Meadows and Derek, she would glower, too.

"Oh, my love is like a red, red rose . . . ," Derek began, making sheep's eyes at Amy.

He was drowned out by his father. "None of your rose gardens! They'll go riding," barked Mr. Meadows, from the opposite end of the table, next to Aunt Prudence. "Survey the land. Kill two birds with one stone. Derek, you'll call for the girl tomorrow. Need you to take a look at the fences near Scraggle Corner."

"I'm sure she'd much rather see my roses, wouldn't you, dear?" Mrs. Meadows sent what was meant to be a meaningful glance at her husband. "They're so much more . . . romantic."

Turning to her left, Amy caught Jane's eye and grimaced.

She sent a look of appeal to Aunt Prudence at the foot of the table, but there was no help forthcoming from that corner. Aunt Prudence's one passion in life was covering all surfaces in Wooliston Manor with miles of needlepoint, and she was blind to all else.

Amy launched into plan B. She squared her shoulders and looked directly at her uncle. "Uncle Bertrand, I am going to France. If I cannot leave with your assent, I shall leave without it." She braced herself for argument.

"Feisty one, ain't she!" Mr. Meadows declared approvingly. "Would've thought the French line would weaken the blood," he continued, eyeing Amy as though she were a ewe at market.

"The dam's line bred true! You can see it in my girls, too,

eh, Marcus? Good Hereford stock." It was highly unclear whether Uncle Bertrand was referring to his niece, his sheep, his daughters, or all three.

"Bought a ram from Hereford once . . ."

"Ha! That's nothing to the ewe I purchased from old Ticklepenny. Annabelle, he called her. There was a look in her eye . . ." Uncle Bertrand waxed lyrical in the candlelight.

The conversation seemed on the verge of degenerating into a nostalgic catalog of sheep they had known and loved. Amy was mentally packing for a midnight flight to the mail coach to Dover (plan C), when Jane's gentle voice cut through the listing of ovine pedigrees.

"Such a pity about the tapestries," was all she said. Her voice was pitched low, but somehow it carried over both the shouting men.

Amy glanced sharply at Jane, and was rewarded by a swift kick to the ankle. Had that been a "say something now!" kick, or a "be quiet and sit still" kick? Amy kicked back in inquiry. Jane put her foot down hard over Amy's. Amy decided that could be interpreted as either "be quiet and sit still" or "please stop kicking me now!"

Aunt Prudence had snapped out of her reverie with what was nearly an audible click. "Tapestries?" she inquired eagerly.

"Why, yes, Mama," Jane replied demurely. "I had hoped that while Amy and I were in France we might be granted access to the tapestries at the Tuilleries."

Jane's quiet words sent the table into a state of electric expectancy. Forks hovered over plates in midair; wineglasses tilted halfway to open mouths; little Ned paused in the act of slipping a pea down the back of Agnes's dress. Even Miss Gwen stopped glaring long enough to eye Jane with what looked more like speculation than rancor.

"Not the Gobelins series of Daphne and Apollo!" cried Aunt Prudence.

"But, of course, Aunt Prudence," Amy plunged in. Amy just barely restrained herself from turning and flinging her arms around her cousin. Aunt Prudence had spent long hours lamenting that she had never taken the time before the war to copy the pattern of the tapestries that hung in the Tuilleries Palace. "Jane and I had hoped to sketch them for you, hadn't we, Jane?"

"We had," Jane affirmed, her graceful neck dipping in assent. "Yet if Papa feels that France remains unsafe, we shall bow to his greater wisdom."

At the other end of the table, Aunt Prudence was wavering. Literally. Torn between her trust in her husband and her burning desire for needlepoint patterns, she swayed a bit in her chair, the feather in her small silk turban quivering with her agitation. "It surely can't be as unsafe as that, can it, Bertrand?" She leaned across the table to peer at her husband through eyes gone nearsighted from long hours over her embroidery frame. "After all, if dear Edouard is willing to take responsibility for the girls . . ."

"Edouard will take very good care of us, I'm sure, Aunt Prudence! If you'll just read his letter, you'll see—ouch!" Jane had kicked her again.

"You know I don't hold with gadding about with foreigners," Uncle Bertrand was saying with a forbidding shake of his wineglass. "Why your sister ever . . ."

"Yes, yes, dear, I know, but that's all past, and Edouard *is* our nephew."

Amy clenched her hands in her lap. It took all of her willpower not to speak; she could feel her chest heave with the effort of containing the angry words. Noticing, Jane gave her a small, warning shake of the head. Noticing something else entirely, Derek leered at Amy's décolletage. Amy glared at Derek. Derek failed to notice. His eyes, after all, were not on Amy's face.

". . . just for a few weeks." As Aunt Prudence's words drifted past her, Amy realized she had missed a couple of rounds of the conversation. "It's not that terribly far, and we can fetch them back if there's any trouble."

Uncle Bertrand, Amy noticed, with the dawning of delight, was visibly weakening. He was regarding Aunt Prudence across the table in a rather bemused way. In a younger man, Amy would have called the look besotted. As for Aunt Prudence, if she had been a younger woman, Amy would have termed her expression positively coquettish! Her head was tilted at its most becoming angle, and she was smiling fondly at Uncle Bertrand. Amy's twelve-year-old cousin Ned looked horrified.

So did Derek. His head swiveled anxiously back and forth from one to the other. "You can't mean to let them go!" he yelped, adding belatedly, "sir," as Uncle Bertrand dragged his eyes away from Aunt Prudence.

Mrs. Meadows's lips narrowed into a tight line. To Aunt Prudence, she said, "You won't be able to send the girls off for months, anyway, I suppose. You'll have to hire a proper chaperone, and that can take quite some time. Good duennas are so hard to find these days."

"I'm sure Edouard has a chaperone waiting for us in Paris," Amy said hastily. "If we left immediately—"

"But who is to travel with you?" Mrs. Meadows drew herself up and cast a censorious eye across the table at Amy. "You and Jane cannot think of traveling alone! Two delicate young ladies at the mercy of ruffians and highwaymen!"

"You could send a manservant with us, couldn't you, Uncle Bertrand?" Amy asked her uncle. "To fight off all the highwaymen?"

Derek slumped down in his chair, an unattractive pout blowing out his thick lips.

Mrs. Meadows redoubled her efforts. "Think of your reputations!" she howled.

"I suppose I shall have to advertise," sighed Aunt Prudence.

"You shall have to," Mrs. Meadows declared officiously. "There's really no other alternative."

Amy wondered if she would be able to make the midnight mail coach if she crept out of her room by eleven.

"*I* shall chaperone them."

Ten heads (Ned was still involved in coaxing the remains of his vegetables down Agnes's back) turned to stare at Miss Gwen in astonishment. Ten mouths opened at once.

"When can we leave? I can be finished packing by tomorrow morning!" Amy shouted gleefully above the din.

In the hullabaloo, nobody even noticed when Agnes clapped a hand to the back of her neck, shrieked, shook Ned by the collar until he turned a rich shade of purple, and fled from the room scattering small green blobs.

Still calmly cutting her meat, Miss Gwen stared down the various speakers one by one. "You may be assured, Prudence, I shall keep a close eye on Jane and Amy. As for you, Miss Amy, *you* may be packed, but *I* am not."

Miss Gwen speared a pea with military precision.

"We leave in two weeks."

Chapter Four

At the sound of the door cracking against the wall, Richard automatically whirled toward the entrance, his whole body tensing for trouble. Blast it all, nobody was supposed to be on the packet from Dover to Calais but him. Ten crowns he had pressed into the hands of the rather oily-looking captain, ten crowns of good British sterling, with another five promised upon arrival. The captain had assured him that the boat would be his alone and would set sail at the next promising gust of wind, instead of lolling about for a week, waiting for passengers.

So who was banging doors? The sound of oak bashing oak, in his experience, generally preceded flying chairs, toppling candlesticks, snarled oaths in three languages, and, if one were really unlucky, the acrid smoke of powder from a pistol. The cabin of a Channel boat was a damnable place to be ambushed. The ceiling was too low for a man to stand and fight properly. And if the bloody boat began swaying . . . Richard winced at the prospect. It could lend a whole new aspect to fencing. Richard whirled towards the door in a grim frame of mind.

The figure in the doorway nearly made Richard tip his chair over backwards in surprise. In the place of the burly oafs he had expected, he saw one rather agitated young lady, planted indignantly in the middle of the entrance. "But why not?" she was arguing with someone in front of her.

"Harrumph," said Richard. The girl's back, clad in a narrowly cut yellow frock, was quite as pleasing a back as one could hope for, but this was *his* boat, blast it, and no one else had any business being on it, not even young ladies with fetching backs.

The young lady paid no attention.

"Really, Miss Gwen! The captain said the wind won't be right for *hours* yet! We could just stop in at the Fisherman's Rest for a lemonade. I'm sure there can't possibly be anything improper about stopping for a lemonade."

Richard *harrumphed* again. Very loudly. The girl in yellow half-turned, affording Richard a momentary view of a pert nose, a determined chin, and one large blue eye. The eye settled briefly on Richard and as rapidly dismissed him. With a toss of her mahogany curls, she continued pleading with her invisible chaperone.

"And Jane agrees with me, don't you, Jane?" the girl went on. "Just *one* lemonade, Miss Gwen!"

Could anyone really be that thirsty? Richard failed to see the earth-shattering importance of a lemonade. Unless, of course, the girl had some unfortunate medical condition which could only be soothed by constant application of lemonade. From the energy with which the girl was arguing her case, and the enthusiastic way she bounced on her feet, like a prizefighter waiting to be let into the ring, Richard rather doubted she was suffering from any weakening, wasting malady.

Richard listened to the ridiculous one-sided argument for a few more minutes before reminding himself that, much as he enjoyed speculating on the girl's reasons and pleasing as it was to watch her skirts sway with every vehement word, the time had come to intervene. He had dispatches to read, and if he tarried too long, he risked the boat setting sail with these noisy interlopers still aboard.

"I say," Richard drawled, loudly enough that they might have heard him say it back in London.

That finally got her attention. The girl turned. In full, her face fulfilled the promise of her profile. It wasn't what one would call a classically beautiful face; her features lacked the sort of sculpted dignity one expected from a statue in marble. Instead, her face was a talented engraver's etching, small and decisive, her cupid's bow of a mouth in constant movement, exclaiming, talking, laughing. No, Richard changed his mind, not an etching after all. Her coloring was too vivid for the stark black and white of a print. The deep brown of her hair glimmered with hidden alloys of red gold, like fire shining through a screen of mahogany. Between dark lashes and fair cheeks, her eyes gleamed startlingly blue.

Her face bore a perplexed look, as if she had only just noticed Richard and wasn't quite sure what to do about him. To help her along, Richard raised a sardonic brow. It was an expression that had been known to make cardsharps fling in their aces and the secretest of secret agents babble like babes. For a moment, confusion continued to hover in the girl's narrowed blue eyes. Then she beamed at Richard and bounded into the room towards him.

"You look like you've traveled a great deal! Don't you agree that there's plenty of time to stop off at the inn for a lemonade?"

Before Richard could suggest that she do just that—preferably lingering over her lemonade until after his boat had sailed—another figure appeared behind her. Ah, the chaperone, Richard decided. There were, he had come to the conclusion after many tedious evenings at Almack's, two types of chaperone. Given the number of events he had been forced to squire Hen to, Richard considered he had conducted something of an exhaustive study of chaperones.

Both types were aging spinsters (Richard discounted young widows looking after their younger sisters' debuts; those tended to need a chaperone even more than the young ladies they were ostensibly supervising), but that was all they had in common. The first was the frumpy henwit. Although of indeterminate age, she dressed in the ruffles of a seventeen-year-old. Her hair, no matter how sparse or gray, was curled and frizzed until it looked like a nest built by a particularly talentless blue jay. She twittered and simpered when spoken to, read the sappiest sort of novels in her spare time, and generally contrived to accidentally lose her charge at least twice a day. Rogues and seducers loved the first sort of chaperone; she made their endeavors that much easier.

And then there was the other type of chaperone. The grim dragon of a chaperone. The sort who looked like her spine had been reinforced with a few Doric columns. Chaperone number two would sneer at a flounce or a frizz. She never simpered when she could snarl, read forbidding sermons by seventeenth-century puritans, and all but chained her charge to her wrist.

As the woman bore down on him, Richard, using his brilliant powers of deduction, was quickly able to conclude that this chaperone fell into the second type. Gray hair rigidly pulled back. Mouth pressed into a grim line. The only incongruous note was the cluster of alarmingly purple flowers on the top of her otherwise severe gray bonnet. Maybe the milliner confused her order and she didn't have time to change it, Richard concluded charitably.

At any rate, he decided, here was someone he could deal with sensibly. One of the benefits of type number two was that they were nearly always extremely sensible. Richard darted a quick glance down at her feet. Underneath the gray hem of her skirt, he could just make out two sturdy, thick-soled black boots. Yes, definitely sensible.

Richard opened his mouth to speak, and the tip of a parasol jammed in between his ribs.

"Who are you, young man, and what are you doing on our boat?"

"I beg your pardon, madam." The words came out somewhat more raggedly than Richard would have liked, but it was hard sounding sophisticated when all the air had just been forced out of your lungs in a most unpleasant fashion. "*Your* boat?"

"Why don't Jane and I just pop by the inn while you straighten matters out with this gentleman . . . ," began the girl in yellow brightly, but she was cut off by the forbidding voice of her duenna.

"You, miss, are staying right here." The dragon managed to reach out and snag the girl's arm without taking her beady eyes from Richard. "Yes, sirrah, *our* boat. That greasy-looking fellow who calls himself the captain assured us that we should be the only passengers. If you are one of the crew—which, judging from your dress and speech, I assume you are not—go about your duties. If not, kindly depart at once."

She looked as though she were ready to enforce her words with the point of her parasol. Richard judged it wise to move out of range. Who had ever heard of a parasol with a steel tip that sharp and pointy? They were supposed to be dainty, feminine things, not lethal weapons.

Rising from his chair, Richard sidestepped the gleaming parasol point and executed a small but elegant bow. "Forgive me, madam, I have been remiss in my social obligations. I am Lord Richard Selwick."

The chaperone still looked like she would rather poke him than chat with him, but she obviously knew what was proper.

With a bend of the knees that only just resembled a curtsy, she inclined her head and said, "I, my lord, am Miss Gwendolyn Meadows. Allow me to make known to you my two charges, Miss Jane Wooliston"—a girl Richard had failed to notice moved out from the shadows behind Miss Meadows and made her curtsy—"and Miss Amy Balcourt."

The quiet girl in blue subtly took Amy's arm and tried to lead her away. Squeezing the other girl's hand affectionately, Amy shook her head and stayed where she was. Richard was so caught up in this byplay that he completely lost track of what the chaperone was saying until the point of her parasol made another sortie at his waistcoat.

"Sir! Have you been attending?"

As Richard had learned from his youthful encounters with the Dowager Duchess of Dovedale, the best way to deal with irate ladies of a certain age was to be disarmingly honest.

"No, madam, I fear I was not."

"Hmph. I said that now that the amenities have been served we would be pleased if you would take yourself off our boat."

"I was afraid that was what you might have said." Richard smiled winningly, while taking care to move himself out of the path of the parasol. "You see, I also paid the captain for the sole use of this ship."

Miss Gwen's face darkened alarmingly. Richard watched in some fascination as the flowers on her hat began to quiver with rage. Had she been a man, she would undoubtedly be indulging in strong language. As it was, given the ominous way she was swinging her parasol, it appeared that she was planning severe bodily harm to the captain, Richard, or both.

The quiet girl, Jane, moved forward to put a reassuring hand on the chaperone's arm. "There must have been some mistake," she said soothingly. "I'm sure we can all reach an amiable conclusion."

Miss Gwen looked about as amiable as Attila the Hun.

"The only possible conclusion is for this gentleman to remove his person from our conveyance."

Richard felt himself beginning to grow annoyed. Watching the chaperone bicker with her charge had been a mildly amusing diversion, but, blast it all, he had real work to do. Important work. War Office work. And, anyway, he had been here first.

That fact seemed like a particularly conclusive one to Richard, so he decided to point it out.

"Who was here first, madam?"

That argument had failed the Saxons in 1066; it was equally ineffectual with Miss Gwen, who regarded Richard with all the imperiousness of William the Conquerer. "You, my lord, may have been here first, but we are *ladies*," Miss Gwen responded with a most unladylike scowl. "And there are more of us. Therefore, you should cede your place."

"Why don't we all go to the inn for a nice glass of lemonade and talk it over?" suggested Amy hopefully.

Neither of the combatants paid the least bit of attention to her.

Standing back with her arms folded across her chest—highly unladylike, but then, Miss Gwen wasn't looking—Amy watched the debacle with the avid interest she would have accorded to a duel. As the two sparred, their barbed sentences ended with incongruous civilities, like protective tips on epées.

Lord Richard took a step closer to Miss Gwen, close enough that the chaperone had to tip her head back to see him. Miss Gwen was fairly tall for a woman, but Lord Richard Selwick topped her by nearly half a foot. His blond head loomed over the waving purple flowers on her bonnet, gleaming with its own light in the dim cabin. Unlike the men Amy had known back in Shropshire, who still wore their hair clubbed back with a ribbon, Lord Richard's was cut short in the new French style. Lord Richard carried himself with an air of easy assurance infinitely more convincing than Derek's swaggering. From his highly polished boots to his waistcoat embroidered in a subtle pattern in silver, he was dressed with a casual elegance that made Derek and his ilk look foppish and overdone. He had evidently anticipated being alone on the boat, because his black frock coat was tossed over a chair, his waistcoat unbuttoned and his cravat loosened. Where his collar gaped open, Amy could see the strong lines of his throat. He looked, Amy thought, like an illustration she had once seen of Horatius at the bridge, defending Rome against all comers.

Her cheeks flushed a deep, uncomfortable red as she realized that the cords of his throat had gone still, the room was silent, and Lord Richard was staring at her staring at him.

Amy covered her confusion by saying hastily, "This is absolutely ridiculous! There's no reason at all why anybody should be forced to wait for the next boat. After all, there's plenty of room for all of us." With a sweeping gesture, she indicated the four walls of the room.

"Out of the question," snapped Miss Gwen.

Amy shook her dark curls in an unconscious gesture of defiance. "Why?"

"Because," Miss Gwen pronounced witheringly, "you cannot stay the night in the same room as a gentleman."

"Oh." Amy took a quick look at the watch pinned to Miss Gwen's bony chest. From what she could make out, it looked to be just a little past four. Edouard's carriage wasn't due to pick them up until the following morning, anyway, so they would put up for the night at an inn in Calais. Surely it couldn't take all that long to cross such a narrow body of water as the Channel. As long as they reached France before midnight, remaining in the cabin with Lord Richard couldn't really be counted as spending the night in the same room as a man. After all, Amy resolved with splendid illogic, if nobody went to bed, it wasn't spending the night.

"How long does it take to reach Calais, my lord?"

"That depends on the weather. Anywhere from two hours to three days."

"Three days?"

"Only in very bad weather," Richard drawled.

"Oh. But look! It's absolutely lovely outside. Really, what's the harm of sharing the space for an insignificant two hours?"

Amy looked around the small group expectantly. Jane suddenly turned toward the window, and held up her hand for silence. "Listen," she said.

Amy listened. She heard the steady slap of waves at the keel of the boat, the keening cry of a seagull, and the scrape of their bags on the wood floor as the motion of the boat made them shift back and forth. Nothing more.

"What am I supposed to hear?" she asked curiously. "I don't hear anything. Just—oh."

From the disgruntled expression on Lord Richard's face, she knew he had reached a similar conclusion.

Miss Gwen rapped her parasol impatiently on the ground. "Just what? Speak up, girl."

Amy glanced from Jane to Lord Richard for confirmation. "I don't hear the sounds of the people on the dock anymore."

"That's right." Lord Richard nodded grimly. "We've set sail."

Amy's face fell for a moment. "So much for plan A," she muttered. Stopping at the inn had ceased to be an option. At least she had the consolation of knowing that the odds of running into the Purple Gentian there had been slim in the extreme. For all she knew, he was in France at this very moment, giving instructions to his band of devoted men or filching documents from under the noses of French officials or . . . Upon reflection, it really was best that they get to France as quickly as possible.

"Well, that's that, then!" Amy proclaimed cheerfully, making for the porthole to peer out. "There's no point in arguing about it anymore, is there? Two hours and we'll be in France! Do come look, Jane—don't they look like dolls on the wharf?"

Miss Gwen stayed where she was, standing ramrod straight smack in the center of the room. Richard sank back down into the chair he had been occupying when the ladies had barreled into the room. "I don't like this any better than you do," he said softly. "But I shall endeavor to stay out of your path if you will keep your charges out of mine."

Miss Gwen afforded him a grudging nod. "We must hope it doesn't rain," she said tartly, and stalked off to join her young ladies at the window.

Precisely three-quarters of an hour later, the first drops hit the porthole. Richard was alerted to it by Amy's loud cry of distress.

"It can't be raining, it can't be raining, it just can't be raining," she muttered, like an incantation.

"Yes, it can," said Richard.

Amy's expression indicated that she was not amused. She cast him a look of great disdain that was somewhat diminished by the fact that the boat swayed suddenly and she had to stagger to catch her balance. "I can see that, can't I?" She returned to her mournful vigil by the window, but couldn't resist turning around to ask anxiously, "How much longer do you think the trip will take?"

"My dear girl, I already told you, anywhere from—"

"I know, I know, anywhere from two hours to three days." She looked as frustrated as his mother's cat when someone dangled a cloth mouse in front of her and then drew it away.

"It depends on how bad the storm is."

"How bad do you—?" A low growl of thunder cut off her words. "Never mind," she finished, just as Richard answered her unfinished question, "That bad."

Despite herself, Amy laughed. The sound rang an unexpected note of gaiety in the rain-dimmed chamber. The portholes were too small to let in much light under any circumstances, and with the sun overcast with clouds, only the eerie gray glow of a stormy sky crept into the room. The gloom created a Sleeping Beauty effect. Jane had succumbed to sleep on a berth across the room, her embroidery still in her hand, her feet discreetly tucked up under the hem of her gown. Defying the usual laws of nature, Miss Gwen had managed to fall asleep upright in a rickety wooden chair. Even the combined forces of sleep and the rocking motion of the boat failed to relax Miss Gwen's iron spine; she sat as bolt upright asleep as she had awake.

The only other person awake was Lord Richard Selwick.

Amy stifled the ignoble impulse to shake Jane awake. She needed to speak to someone about something, anything, just to dull the anticipatory jitters that were making her palms tingle. If she didn't do something to distract herself soon, she would probably start running madly about the room or jumping up and down or twirling wildly in circles, just to spin off some of her excess energy. Even one of Uncle Bertrand's lectures on cross-breeding sheep would be welcome.

Across the room, Lord Richard was sitting in a stiff wooden chair too small for his large frame, an ankle propped against the opposite knee, utterly engrossed in what looked to be some sort of journal. Amy stared shamelessly across the room, but she couldn't make out the title. Whatever it was, it couldn't possibly be worse than Uncle Bertrand's husbandry manuals. Unless . . . she had heard of one journal devoted entirely to the planting of small root vegetables. But Lord Richard really didn't look the sort to have a turnip obsession and Amy could feel the pins and needles of nervous energy darting from her hands all the way down to her feet, pushing her forward.

Her yellow skirts made a bright splotch of color in the rapidly darkening cabin as she crossed the room.

"What are you reading?"

Richard flipped the fat pamphlet over to the other side of the table for her. Antiquarian literature usually worked as well for discouraging inquisitive young ladies as it did French spies.

Amy strained to see in the dim light. "*Proceedings of the Royal Egyptological Society*? I didn't know we had one."

"We do," said Richard dryly.

Amy cast him an exasperated look. "Well, that much is clear." She flipped through the pages, tilting the periodical to try to catch the light. "Has there been any progress on the Rosetta Stone?"

"You've heard of the Rosetta Stone?" Richard knew he sounded rude; he just couldn't help himself. The last young lady to whom he had delivered his Rosetta Stone soliloquy had asked him if the Rosetta Stone was a new kind of gemstone, and if so, what color was it, and did he think it would look better with her blue silk than sapphires.

Amy made a face at him. "We do get the papers, even in the wilds of Shropshire, you know."

"Are you interested in antiquities?"

For the life of him, he couldn't figure out why he was going to the bother of carrying on a conversation with the chit. First off, he had better things to do, such as plot the Purple Gentian's next escapade. Daring plans didn't just invent themselves; they took time, and thought, and imagination. Secondly, voluntarily entering into conversation with young ladies of good family was inevitably a perilous venture. It gave them ideas. It gave them terrifying ideas that involved heirloom veils, ten-foot-long trains, and bouquets of orange flowers.

Yet here he was encouraging the girl to talk. Absurd.

"I don't really know much about antiquities," said Amy frankly. "But I love the old stories! Penelope fooling all of her suitors, Aeneas fighting his way down to the underworld . . ."

It was too dark to read, reasoned Richard. And the girl didn't seem to be flirting with him, so carrying on a conversation with her was a harmless and sensible means of passing the time. Nothing at all absurd about that.

"I haven't read any Ancient Egyptian literature, though. Is there any? All I know about Ancient Egypt is what I've read in Herodotus," Amy went on. "And, really, I get the sense that about half of what he wrote about the Egyptians is pure sensationalism. All of that nonsense about sucking peoples' brains out through their noses and putting them in jars. He's worse than the *Shropshire Intelligencer*!"

Richard managed to stop himself from asking whether she had really read Herodotus in the original Greek. Coming on the heels of his Rosetta Stone comment, it might seem a bit insulting. "Actually, we think Herodotus may have been telling the truth on that one. In the burial chambers of tombs, we found canopic jars with the remains of human organs." If the girl wasn't genuinely interested, she was putting on a far better act than any Richard had ever seen.

"We? Were you actually there, my lord?"

"Yes, several years ago."

Questions tumbled out of Amy's mouth so quickly that Richard scarcely had time to answer one before another rolled his way. She leaned forward across the table in a way that would have had Miss Gwen barking, "Posture!" had she been awake to see it. She listened avidly as Richard described the ancient Egyptian pantheon, interrupting him occasionally to compare them to the gods of the ancient Greeks.

"After all," she argued, "there must have been some sort of communication between the Greeks and the Egyptians. Oh, not just Herodotus! Look at *Antigone*—that's set in Thebes. And so are the myths of Jason, aren't they? Unless, do you think the Greek authors used Egypt the way Shakespeare used Italy? As a sort of miraculous once upon a time where anything could happen?"

Outside, the storm still splattered across the windows and rocked the little boat away from its destination, but neither Amy nor Richard noticed. "I cannot tell you," Amy confessed frankly, "how good it is to finally have a genuinely *interesting* conversation with someone! Nobody at home talks about anything but sheep or embroidery. No, really, I'm not exaggerating. And whenever I come across someone who has actually done something interesting, they change the subject and talk about the weather!"

Amy's face was so disgruntled that Richard had to laugh. "Surely you must allow the weather some consequence?" he teased. "Look at the impact it has had upon us."

"Yes, but if you start talking about it, I shall have to remember something I've forgotten on the other side of the room or develop a passionate desire to take a nap."

"Do you think it will be fair tomorrow?"

"Oh, so that's your ploy, sir! You really want to read your journal in peace, so you've decided to bore me away! That's terribly devious of you. But, if I'm not wanted . . ." Amy swished her yellow skirts off her chair.

The plan she described did rather resemble his intentions of an hour before, but, without even taking the time to think about it, Richard found himself grinning and saying, "Stay. I'll give you my word not to talk about the weather if you swear you won't mention gowns, jewels, or the latest gossip columns."

"Is that all the young ladies of your acquaintance talk about?"

"With a few notable exceptions, yes."

Amy wondered who those notable exceptions might be. A betrothed, perhaps? "You should count yourself lucky, my lord. At least it's not sheep."

"No, they just behave like them."

Their shared laughter rolled softly through the dim room.

Richard leaned back and regarded Amy intently. Amy's laughter caught in her throat. Somehow, his gaze cut through the gloom, as if all the light in the dim cabin were concentrated in his eyes. Suddenly dizzy, Amy lowered her hands to the sides of her chair and held on tightly. It must be that the boat is swaying more now because of the storm, she thought vaguely. That really must be it.

Richard contemplated Amy with puzzled pleasure. He did know other intelligent women—Henrietta, for one, and a few others of his sister's circle, bright, intelligent women who were too pretty to be dismissed as bluestockings. He had even, of his own free will, dropped by the drawing room to join them in their conversations on one or two occasions. But he couldn't imagine bantering so easily with any of Hen's entourage.

Perhaps it was the intimacy of darkness, or of the small quarters, but absurdly, he felt quite as comfortable chatting with Amy Balcourt as he ever had with Miles or Geoff. Only Miles didn't have immense blue eyes fringed with dark lashes. And Geoff certainly didn't possess a slender white neck with kissable indentations over the collarbones. . . .

At any rate, Richard concluded, the Fates had known what they were doing when they set Amy Balcourt upon his boat.

"I am truly delighted to have met you, Miss Balcourt. And I promise not to talk about the weather *or* sheep unless it is absolutely imperative."

"In that case . . ." Amy clasped her hands under her chin and launched back into her eager inquisition.

Only once she had satisfied her curiosity on such important subjects as tombs, mummies, and curses did Amy ask, "But wasn't Egypt swarming with French soldiers? How did you manage to slip in?"

"I was with the French."

For a moment, the words just hung there. Amy frowned, trying to make sense of what he had just said. "Did you—were you a prisoner of war?" she asked hesitantly.

"No. I went at Bonaparte's invitation, as one of his scholars."

Amy's spine snapped upright. Head up, shoulders back, as she stared at Richard her posture locked into a steely rigidity to please even Miss Gwen. "You were in Bonaparte's pay?"

"Actually"—Richard lounged back in his chair—"he didn't pay me. I went at my own expense."

"You weren't coerced? You went of your own free will?"

"You sound horrified, Miss Balcourt. You must admit, it is the chance of a lifetime for a scholar."

Amy's mouth opened but no sound came out.

Richard was right; she *was* horrified.

For an Englishman to accompany his country's enemy . . . to disregard all duty and honor in the pursuit of scholarship . . . Couldn't he have waited for the English to take control of Egypt before pursuing his pyramids? And how could any man, any thinking man, any intelligent man with a modicum of feeling, have anything to do with a nation which had so cruelly and senselessly slaughtered so many of its own people on the guillotine! And to disregard all that for the sake of a few tombs! It was a slight to his country and a slight to mankind.

But, if she was being quite, quite honest, what stung most wasn't the slight to mankind, but the sense of betrayal his words caused. It was utterly ridiculous. She had known the man all of two hours. One couldn't really claim betrayal after two hours' acquaintance. Even so, in those two hours, it wasn't as though he had lied and claimed to have fought for the English and then let slip by accident that he had been with the French.

He had been witty and interesting and charming. He had argued antiquities with Amy as though she were an equal, and not just a young girl who had never been out of the country and knew only what she had stumbled across in her uncle's library. Good heavens, he had even told her, in the most sincere of tones, that he was honored to know her. In short, he had committed the crime of acting as though he liked her and the even greater crime of charming her into liking him. And then to reveal that he had defected to the French . . .

Suddenly, the man seated across from her took on all sorts of sinister attributes. The smile that a half an hour ago had seemed genial was now mocking. The gleam in his green eyes that had been good-natured became sinister. Even the dark hues of his clothing went from elegant to dangerous, the sleek pelt of a panther on the prowl. He was probably quite practiced at gulling the unwary into liking and trusting him. Good heavens, for all she knew he might be a French spy! Why else would he have been back in England? The logical part of her brain, the bit that always sounded like Jane, reminded her that he might very well have family back in England he wished to visit. Amy silenced it.

Across the table, Richard raised an eyebrow at her in silent inquiry. The gesture made Amy want to whack him over the head with *The Proceedings of the Royal Egyptological Society*.

Amy struggled for words to voice her revulsion. "Scholarship is all very well and good, but after what the French did—while your own country was at war with them! To join the French army!"

"I wasn't in the French army," Richard corrected. "I merely traveled with them."

Amy rediscovered her voice and her vocabulary. "Egypt was a military action first and a scholarly expedition second! You can't claim not to have known—I'm sure even the savages in the wilds of America knew!"

"Priorities, my dear, priorities." Richard realized that he was being provoking, but something about the way Amy was looking at him, as though she had just discovered nine dismembered wives in a cupboard in his bedchamber, brought out the worst in him. The fact that he agreed with everything she was saying annoyed him even more. He brushed an imaginary speck of lint off his sleeve. "I chose to concentrate on the second."

"You chose to ignore the thousands of innocent people slaughtered on the guillotine. You chose to range yourself with a murderous rabble against your own country!" Amy retorted.

How many people had he saved from the guillotine since he had first joined Percy and the League of the Scarlet Pimpernel? Fifty? A hundred? One lost count after the first few dozen. Richard was trying to remain calm and urbane, but irritation rose through him like heat radiating from the Egyptian sands.

"What," he asked languidly, "has the guillotine to do with my researches?"

It was quite a credible imitation of a vapid London fop, and Amy reacted just as expected. She sputtered.

Rationally, Richard knew that in her position he, too, would have sputtered, appalled by such selfish callousness. Rationally, he knew that he was behaving in an absolutely appalling fashion. Rationally. Of course, Richard was feeling quite irrationally irate just now and thus enjoying her distress accordingly. The five-year-old in him was of the firm opinion that it served her right. Just what it served her right for, he wasn't quite sure, but why fret about details?

"That army was led by the same people who cold-bloodedly slaughtered thousands of their compatriots! The ground of the Place da la Guillotine was still red with the blood of the murdered when you went to Egypt. By your very presence, you condoned their villainy!" Amy's voice rose and cracked with the intensity of her emotions.

"I quite agree, dear girl. What the French did was reprehensible. *Did.* Past tense. You're a bit behind the times. They stopped killing off their aristocrats several years ago now."

"You might as well say that just because a cannibal eats vegetables for a few years, he's no longer a cannibal," choked Amy. "The fact still remains that he once feasted on human flesh and he can't be allowed to get away with it!"

The sheer oddity of the analogy left Richard speechless for a moment. He devoted his energy to fighting off a horrible image of Bonaparte, in the gilded dining room of the Tuilleries, polishing off a human leg, while his elegant wife, Josephine, munched on an arm. Richard winced. "Let's keep cannibals out of this, shall we? I assure you, the French may eat horse but they haven't descended to human."

"I don't want to discuss the eating habits of the French!"

"You brought them up."

"I did no such—oh, for heaven's sake, it was a metaphor!"

"So, metaphorically speaking, by going to Egypt I metaphorically feasted with the metaphorical cannibals."

"Yes!"

"You are on a packet bound for Calais."

Amy blinked. "If you so desperately want to change the subject, you could find a more subtle way of doing it, you know."

"I'm not trying to change the subject. I'm simply pointing out that you, O scourge of metaphorical cannibals, are on a boat bound for France."

Amy squirmed slightly in her chair, silent with frustrated anger. She had an uncomfortable inkling of where he was going with that statement.

"I say now, what was that comment you made about guilt by association?" Richard continued loftily. "Something about condoning their evil with my presence, wasn't it? That's all very well and good, but isn't there an old saw about people in glass houses not lobbing stones at their neighbors?

"And that dress you're wearing." Amy's hands flew automatically to her bodice. "Isn't that in the French style? The revolutionary style? If associating with the revolutionaries is a hanging crime, what about aping their fashions? Speak to me again of condoning."

Amy stood so suddenly her chair toppled over behind her. "It's not at all equivalent! It's been five years—"

"But a cannibal is still a cannibal, isn't he, Miss Balcourt?"

"—and England is no longer at war with France . . . and . . ."

Amy couldn't think of any more logical arguments, but she knew, just knew that she was right and he was absolutely, positively *wrong*. Blast him and blast his nasty, underhanded, sophistic debating techniques! This had gone on far too long. She should have gotten up and left the minute he'd told her he had accompanied the French, not stayed to argue like an idealistic fool.

"And?" Richard looked up from toying idly with the lace on his cuffs.

Amy fought back tears of pure rage. Oh, to be a man, to be able to just punch someone when she didn't know what to say! "And how dare you judge me when you know nothing of my reasons! *Nothing*!"

Sweeping her skirts away as though from something infected, she resumed her post by the porthole, her back to Lord Richard.

Left alone in splendid solitude at the little table, Richard realized he finally had the quiet he had craved. After all, hadn't he just wanted to be left in peace to work? Lighting one of the covered lamps, Richard moved to a berth at the far end of the room and took out the latest dispatches from the War Office. He went so far as to prop a page against his knee and stare at the words on the paper. But all he saw was a pair of angry blue eyes.

Chapter Five

"What right does she have"—*whap*—"to judge me? She has no idea what she's talking about." *Whap!* Richard pounded the nearly flat pillow under his head into a more hospitable shape. "And why should it bloody well bother me?" *Whap!* "It shouldn't bother me. I'm *not* bothered." Richard punched the pillow again. He had no illusions that his pounding would render the pillow comfortable, but punching something made him feel better, and he couldn't very well punch Amy.

After his altercation with Amy, Richard had kept punctiliously to his side of the cabin. There might as well have been a line drawn across the scarred wooden floor. When true dark fell, replacing the rainy gray gloom, Miss Gwen had insisted on raising a literal barrier down the center of the room. "I will not have you share a bedchamber with a person of the opposite sex," she had declared to the two girls, and gone off to badger the captain for spare sailcloth. The captain had refused to be badgered. Not to be thwarted, Miss Gwen had commandeered Richard's cloak. Strung up along the center of the room with Miss Gwen's, Amy's, and Jane's cloaks, it made a rather uneven but passable partition.

Unfortunately, it did nothing to keep out the image of Amy's furious face.

Richard pummeled his pillow again. So the girl had condemned him for hobnobbing with the French. He had thought he was used to that by now. Old Falconstone wasn't the only one to have taken umbrage at Richard's activities. Over the past few years, Richard had run the gamut of disapproval, from snide remarks hissed behind his back to outright lectures delivered to his face. Considering the tongue-lashing he had received from the Dowager Duchess of Dovedale in the middle of the Alsworthys' ballroom, Amy's protest was mild indeed.

But he hadn't spent the night awake, abusing his pillow, after being reproved by the Dowager Duchess.

"You are a prize idiot," he mumbled to himself. He should be delighted to have rid himself of the tedious company of a simpering young female. Usually, he had to employ every ounce of his ingenuity to be rid of them. But to be fair, Amy's company hadn't been tedious and she hadn't simpered. She had bounced, giggled, and occasionally squealed, but she hadn't simpered. And she had read Herodotus in the original. He wondered if she had stumbled across the plays of Sophocles and what she thought of . . . Richard nipped that line of inquiry in the bud. No matter how many classics the girl had perused, young ladies were a liability that an intrepid spy could not afford. Richard had learned that lesson well five years ago.

He pushed the recollection away. Some things did not bear remembering.

At any rate, the last thing he needed in Paris was an English debutante clinging to him while he tried to ferret out Napoleon's plan for invasion. Richard had been waiting for this assignment for years. They had all known that Bonaparte would try to invade England sooner or later—it was one of the few countries he hadn't gotten around to yet. Italy, the Netherlands, Austria, all had fallen. England had the advantage of a watery moat, but how long could it hold out against Bonaparte's tactical brilliance?

It bothered him that she disliked him.

Richard tried to push aside the uneasy suspicion that it might be guilt keeping him awake. He had, after all, behaved very badly indeed. And it was compounded by the fact that the girl had had the right of it. Maybe a little naïve, a little too self-righteous, but essentially right. Hell, had their positions been reversed, he would have said the same himself. In a more logical, less emotional fashion, of course. In return, he had been not only ungentlemanly, but downright unkind.

Damn it, he didn't have time for this! England still needed to be saved, and he couldn't save England unless he got some *sleep*. Richard dragged his blanket up around his ears and prepared to settle down for a much-needed rest.

Unfortunately, the blanket was as thin and flat as the pil-low. Even with the emaciated cloth pulled halfway over his head, Richard's trained ear heard the soft thud of someone swinging her legs out of bed. And then, close on the heels of the previous noise, a series of slow, soft footfalls. It had to be Amy, thought Richard resignedly. Neither the chaperone nor the other girl looked the sort who would wander about after hours. Poking his head out of the nest of blanket (which smelled regretfully like its last occupant, someone who obvi-ously took a very dim view of bathing), Richard heard a thud, and a muffled cry. Ah, he wisely concluded, someone stubbed her toe. The footfalls resumed with a slight limp. Richard's lips twitched into a grin in the darkness.

The grin disappeared as the midnight prowler slipped out the door of the cabin and closed it behind herself with a cau-tious click. Richard sat bolt upright in bed, no longer the least bit amused. Of all the damn fool things to do! Didn't the little ninny realize that the deck could be teeming with rough men? If she happened across a drunken sailor at this time of night . . . Richard cursed and threw his own legs over the side of the bed.

Wait! What was he doing going after her? Richard paused in a half-crouch. She was certainly none of his responsibility. Hadn't she made it more than clear that she wanted nothing to do with him? And that was all very well and good since he wanted nothing to do with her either, and she could bloody well take care of herself.

Richard flung himself back upon his bed with enough force to bang his head against the wall. Hard. Maybe it was the bump on his head affecting his judgment—at least, Richard was pretty sure it was the bump on his head—but as he rubbed his aching cranium, Richard began to have disturbing images of Amy alone on deck. Leaning over the railing to stare at a star, slipping, and tumbling into the hungry waters. Or being backed into a corner by a drunken sailor with no-body to hear her scream.

With one leap, Richard was off the bed and three-quarters of the way to the door.

Amy couldn't sleep. With all the portholes closed, the air in the cabin was heavy and dusty and scarred by the rasping of Miss Gwen's snores. The gentle rocking of the ship should have put Amy to sleep. It had put Jane to sleep. When Amy pulled herself up and peeked over the edge—which she had at least twice in the past fifteen minutes—she could see Jane in the berth above her, the blankets over her lightly rising and falling with her regular breaths. But Amy remained hideously, uncomfortably awake.

Amy rolled over irritably. "I will fall asleep, I will fall asleep," she muttered. The noise evoked a new crescendo of snores from Miss Gwen. Amy flopped back onto her back. She tried counting sheep, but all that did was bring back memories of Shropshire. Shropshire, which had seemed so detestable for the last decade or so, took on a far more attractive aspect in retrospect. There was the blue and white room she shared with Jane; the back staircase she had sneaked down so many times; her favorite climbing tree in the orchard . . . and what on earth did she think she was doing?

It had all seemed quite, quite simple back in Shropshire. They would stop off at the Fisherman's Rest inn for a glass of lemonade, and Jane would distract Miss Gwen, while Amy pretended to have to use the facilities. Amy would have a great deal of trouble finding the necessary room, and would have to linger about the common room of the inn, glancing about as if searching for the correct door, and looking vague. In the process, she would be able to drift in the direction of two men having an intent conversation (there were sure to be two men having an intent conversation), and would overhear one whisper to the other in anxious tones something that would clearly mark him as the Purple Gentian (Amy couldn't think of any such phrase off the top of her head, but she was sure to recognize it once she heard it).

But that hadn't happened. And plan A had been such an easy plan! True, Amy had plans B through G in reserve, but they were all much more complicated, and involved a freedom of movement that Amy wasn't sure she could acquire under Miss Gwen's watchful eye. For example, plan B, dressing as a stable boy and eavesdropping in the stables of any suspects, involved finding boy's clothes, finding enough time away from Miss Gwen, and, well, finding suspects. And plan C grew even more intricate. . . .

What if Jane was right? What if she was dragging them all across the Channel on a fool's errand?

The dark pressed in on Amy like a physical force. Suddenly,

she couldn't stand it anymore, not the sweltering blackness of the cabin, not Miss Gwen's muffled snores, not Jane's quiet breathing. She needed to be *alone*. Stumbling off the bed, Amy fumbled in the dark for her shawl. Amy left her slippers untouched on the floor; bare feet would make less noise. Feeling her way carefully in the dark, she made her way along the partition with the silent grace of an experienced spy.

"Argh!" Amy doubled over and clutched her toe. Good heavens, what had Miss Gwen been thinking to leave her portmanteau right there, where anyone could trip over it! Amy scowled and nursed her wounded toe. And why had she felt the need to pack the blasted thing with bricks?

Aggrieved, Amy limped to the door. It really was quite a challenge to limp stealthily. Amy paused by the doorframe and listened again. All was still. The storm had spent itself several hours ago and the calm water lapped gently at the boat. Lifting her skirts, Amy tiptoed up the stairs to the deck.

About halfway up the narrow stairway, she paused, arrested by a sudden thought. All of these doubts, these fears, these worries . . . none of them had appeared until after her run-in with Lord Richard. It was Lord Richard, questioning her motives, calling her a hypocrite, who was clearly to blame for her sleeplessness.

"I can't believe I let that man make me doubt myself," Amy mumbled as she continued up the stairs. She breathed in the cool night air on a deep breath of relief and satisfaction. "Everything will go splendidly. I just know it will."

It was such a pity she hadn't thought of a better retort this afternoon.

Her eyes accustomed to the darkness, Amy made her way carefully to the edge of the deck and rested her arms on the railing. After the musty air of the cabin, even the bouquet of tar and damp wood that rose from the deck smelled of freedom to Amy. A gentle mist had succeeded the rain. The moon, hidden behind the clouds, threaded the sky with delicate silver strands. Their supernatural glow reminded Amy of the three Fates of Greek myth, spinning peoples' destinies on their spindles. For a moment, alone on the moonlit deck, she had a fancy that if she looked long and hard enough, she would be able to distinguish her own thread, disentangle it from the rest, and follow its glistening length to her destiny.

"Silly." Amy shook her head at herself. After all, she already knew her destiny. She didn't need to search in the clouds to discern it. She would track down the Purple Gentian, make herself an indispensable member of his league, and, of course, restore the monarchy. It would take more than one treacherous scholar with mocking green eyes to discourage her!

Amy leaned against the railing. Had it been on a boat such as this that she had come to England fifteen years ago? Amy had only the vaguest recollections of that journey. Most of them had to do with Mama bribing her with sugarplums so she wouldn't cry over forgetting her favorite doll at home. Amy wondered if Mama had held her up over a rail like this one to wave good-bye to France. In her imagination, she could see Papa, tall and elegant, flapping his handkerchief at them from the wharf, and Mama putting Amy down to blow kisses at her husband, while Amy jumped up and down and cried, *"Au revoir, Papa! Au revoir!"* until Mama caught Amy up in her arms again before she could tumble off the side of the boat. Amy had imagined the scene so often that she could no longer distinguish invention from memory. It might have happened that way. Amy liked to think it had.

Peering into the mist, she could almost see Papa smiling on the wharf and smell Mama's lavender scent beside her.

I'll avenge you soon, she promised them silently.

Amy was concentrating so hard that she never heard the soft footfalls on the deck behind her. She didn't see the shadows lengthen around her. She didn't feel the gentle breath at the nape of her neck.

But she couldn't fail to hear the voice that boomed, practically in her ear.

"You shouldn't be out here."

Chapter Six

The unexpected sound of a voice behind her, too close behind her, nearly sent Amy catapulting over the railing. Her parents' shades vanished abruptly into the silvery night. The spell was broken.

Clutching the wood for support, she snapped, not looking around, "And you shouldn't sneak up on people like that!"

"And you shouldn't lean on the railing like that," the infuriatingly unflustered voice behind her went on. "These ships are seldom in good repair."

"I'm perfectly—agh!" Amy staggered back as the rail obligingly wobbled.

"Safe?" he finished for her. "I think not."

Amy shook off the hand he had put out to steady her. "I thank you for your warning, but I am quite all right."

Richard followed her as she turned her back on him and walked across the deck in search of silence and a more stable piece of railing. Despite his earlier pique, he had to repress a chuckle as he watched her plant her elbows on the wooden plank, as if defying it to wobble.

"You'll get splinters," he warned.

Amy ignored him. Poised on the prow of the ship, shoulders back, chin set, she looked like a particularly fierce figurehead. She was obviously trying quite, quite hard to ignore him. Well, let her try. Richard stared at her unabashedly, watching the way the moonlight made her skin glow white against her dark hair. When he had first ascended to the deck, with her face tilted to the night sky, she had looked like Joan of Arc having visions.

Shaking his head, Richard recalled his original objective. "Come inside," he advised Amy's back.

"I am quite comfortable where I am." As if in illustration, Amy sat herself down on the damp deck and circled her knees with her arms.

Richard sat down beside her.

Amy looked at him in surprise. Derek would never have risked getting brown streaks on his tan trousers. Or grass stains or rust stains or any other kind of blemish. Amy had frequently been able to avoid his clumsy advances by climbing over a fence or traipsing off into places where dandies feared to tread.

"You'll stain your breeches."

"You'll stain your skirt," Richard returned equably.

"This is an utterly inane conversation!"

"Would you rather discuss the weather?"

"I'd rather not discuss anything at all."

"Good." Richard stood, leaning over to offer her a hand up. "Then we can go back inside."

Amy batted at his outstretched hand like a cat rejecting a substandard ball of yarn. "No, *you* can go back inside."

"Miss Balcourt, you cannot remain out here alone."

His tone set her teeth on edge, but Amy remained silent.

"Someone might come upon you in the darkness."

"Someone already *has*."

"That's not what I meant. *I* came out here to see that you were safe."

"Well, I am. You've seen that. Now go *away*."

"You don't take awfully well to being rescued, do you? All right, then." Richard executed a bow so formal it could only be meant as an insult. "Good night, Miss Balcourt. Enjoy your lonely sojourn on the deck. If any sailors come after you, don't scream for me."

Amy sniffed.

Richard turned sharply on his heel and stalked off towards the stairs. Two yards away, he stopped and stalked right back again. Shaking his head at Amy, who was watching him with an expression compounded of contempt and confusion (although confusion seemed to be winning out), he said, "No. Sorry. Can't."

"Can't what, my lord? Walk? It's really quite simple. You just put one foot in front of the other and keep on going until you're all the way down the stairs and in your own berth."

"No." Richard lowered himself back down next to her. "I

can't just leave you here. Unfortunately for both of us, I was raised with a sense of honor that precludes leaving a young lady alone in the middle of the night with a crew of ruffians sleeping just below. My obligation is clear; if you persist in remaining outside, I shall have to remain, too. Besides," he added, before Amy could make a sharp comment about his sense of honor not extending to avoiding his country's enemies, "it's easier for me to stay here with you now than to come running when you start screaming."

"I wouldn't."

"Let's not put it to the test, shall we? Carry on with whatever you were thinking about. You'll scarcely know I'm here." As if to prove his point, Richard swiveled his head and gazed ostentatiously off at the ocean.

Amy tried to rekindle the memory of her parents, but the image had taken on the flat quality of a set of cardboard dolls against a clumsily illustrated backdrop. The very reality of the man sitting next to her rendered the daydream weak and insubstantial. His presence crowded her thoughts. He was sitting a good foot away from her, far enough to be proper, far enough to satisfy the most particular of chaperones (in other words, Miss Gwen), but far too close for Amy's liking. She could smell the citrus of his cologne, hear the even exhalations of his breathing, feel the heat rising from his body in the chilliness of the night. Every time he shifted on the hard deck she tensed. Every time she heard his hair whisper against his high collar as he turned his head, she wondered if he was looking at her.

You'll scarcely know I'm here? Amy thought. Ha!

Resting her chin on her knees, she squeezed her eyes shut. She tried to conjure up the Purple Gentian (her very favorite daydream, the one where he pressed her hand in his and told her he could do nothing without her), but the image was as flat as an amateur painting, and the Purple Gentian's voice kept taking on the inflections of Lord Richard Selwick.

Sneaking a little sideways glance, Amy wondered if she had, perhaps, been too hard on him that afternoon. It was absolutely appalling of him to have worked for the French, but that had been a full five years ago. He must have been quite young five years ago, and Mrs. Meadows was always going on about how young people did foolish and thoughtless things. Perhaps he truly hadn't considered the situation in

France when he charged off to Egypt. Perhaps he had since repented of his actions.

Perhaps she really should go back inside, before his presence beside her spurred her on to even more ridiculous flights of fancy.

It might have eased Amy somewhat to know that the object of her thoughts was having equal difficulty concentrating. Richard had tried to consider strategies for ferreting out Bonaparte's plans for the invasion of England, but Amy conquered his concentration more effectively than any number of units of artillery.

Under cover of the darkness, he shifted his weight to face Amy and asked softly, "What brings you to France?"

Amy snapped her head up, instantly on the defensive. Richard put out a hand as though in his own defense. "Retract your claws! I'm scarred enough from this afternoon. Can we cry a truce, at least for the night?"

Amy eyed him askance.

"Consider it our own personal Peace of Amiens. I'll be France and you can be England."

Some of the wariness crept out of Amy's stance. "You can be England and I'll be France before the Revolution," she offered.

"Sorry. I'm afraid you're stuck with the present."

"Only if you stay on your own side of the Channel, then." Amy indicated the sliver of deck that separated them.

"What would you do if I tried to invade?" Richard wiggled his eyebrows in mock flirtation.

"I'd call out the heavy artillery." She motioned to the hatch leading down to the cabin.

"I'm sorry. You can't pass off a dragon as a brace of guns. Not allowed. And I assure you, dragons are not an acceptable weapon in modern warfare."

"Why not? They both breathe fire."

"Yes, but . . ." Richard cast about for a rejoinder, but all he could come up with was, "but dragons are *frightening*!" which didn't sound terribly brave and manly.

"I win!" Amy crowed.

"But dragons are *obsolete*," Richard finished smugly. "As the victor of that round, I claim a boon."

"I don't believe you deserve one, Sir Knight. After all, you didn't slay any dragons."

"Nevertheless"—he held up a magisterial hand—"I still claim a boon. Outwitting you ought to rank with slaying dragons."

"I don't know if I'd call that outwitting," protested Amy.

"It was a compliment."

"You don't compliment people often, do you? That was really an awfully poor attempt. If you'd like, I'll help you practice. We could start out with something simple, like, 'Why, Amy, how clever you are!' and proceed from there."

"Nonetheless." Richard leaned forward, his dark blond hair shimmering in the moonlight. "Do I get my boon?"

Amy's pulse picked up speed at a reckless rate. "What sort of boon did you have in mind?"

"I would like you"—his voice was low and intimate—"to tell me what brings you to France."

"Oh."

"Is it that much of a secret?" Richard teased.

Amy fought against an unreasonable sense of disappointment. "No, no, of course not. It's quite dull really. I'm going to live with my brother in Paris."

"I'm disappointed in you, Miss Balcourt. How can someone who so disapproves of the French have a brother there?"

Amy stumbled to her feet, catching her skirt on her bare toes and clutching the railing to steady herself. She towered over Richard. "My brother is half French; I am half French; good heavens, you really are the most provoking man! Is there anything else you wanted to know, or may I go back to the cabin?"

Richard took Amy's hand and tugged her back down. "If your brother's in France and you were in England, where are your parents?"

Amy allowed herself to be tugged, but settled on her heels, as if ready to spring up again at any moment. "They suffered the embrace of Madame Guillotine," she said tersely.

Still holding her hand, Richard squeezed it lightly, for comfort.

"Actually, only Papa was really murdered, but Mama might as well have been. She loved Papa so much—they must have said good-bye three dozen times before we left. When they killed Papa, they killed her, too. Theirs was a love match, you see."

Oddly enough—for one who had thus far assiduously avoided matrimony—Richard did see. His own parents had married for love, and had stayed in love, rather distressingly so. At least it had been distressing for the poor adolescent boy forced to witness his parents holding hands under the table. Not to mention all the times Richard had accidentally stumbled upon his parents kissing in corridors. But for all he made faces and the occasional inarticulate noise indicating extreme disgust (because everyone knew that *parents* weren't supposed to engage in intimate behavior), Richard secretly thought it was rather sweet. He thought it was rather sweet the way his indomitable mother would blush and flutter at a whispered comment from his father, and he thought it was rather sweet the way his dignified father would bolt abruptly out of debates in the House of Lords just to take tea with his mother. Of course, you wouldn't catch him confiding that to just anybody.

It wasn't until he had hit the London social scene as a rakehell, fresh from the innocence of Eton, that Richard had realized how unusual it was, that sort of connection his parents enjoyed. Until then, he had naïvely assumed that all married couples were like that, holding hands under the breakfast table and kissing in corridors. But then he saw married men in brothels, received scented solicitations from married women, and watched marriages contracted with no more feeling on either side than . . . well, no feeling at all. In all of his meanderings from ballroom to ballroom, Richard had seen perhaps one couple in ten who shared some sort of affection, one couple in a hundred truly in love. And he had realized, for the first time, that what his parents had was something wonderful and rare, and that he himself could never stoop to settle for anything less.

And Amy had seen that, too, and had been forced to see it wrenched away.

"I'm sorry," he said softly.

"Why should you be? You didn't wield the ax."

"If I had known, I wouldn't have baited you so. I didn't realize you had a personal interest."

Amy looked up at him in confusion, wondering at the sudden change in his demeanor. The moon had gone behind a cloud, leaving his face in shadow, no glimmer of light to reveal whether he spoke sincerely. If only the clouds would part and she could see—she wasn't sure what she hoped to see. Something that would tell her whether he was honest or a thorough blackguard.

"I am truly sorry," he said again, and with his deep voice vibrating through her ears, Amy knew, just knew, he was sincere, the same way she knew that Jane was good, and that sheep were vile, and that she was going to find the Purple Gentian.

And somehow it seemed the most natural thing in the world that he would take her free hand in his own, and even more natural that he was leaning towards her and she towards him. Their joined hands formed a bridge across the sliver of deck she had laughingly called their Channel. Amy couldn't tell if he was pulling or she was; there no longer seemed to be a place where her arms ended and his began. And what did it matter if there was? Amy closed her eyes, and felt his warm breath on her lips.

Chapter Seven

Crack!

The piece of railing Amy had been leaning upon earlier detached itself from the deck and tumbled into the water. Suddenly, Amy's hands were her own again. Blinking dazedly as she opened her eyes, she saw that their own personal Channel was back in place between them and that Richard had his own hands planted firmly on the deck on either side of him. It was enough to make her think she had imagined those past few moments, if she still hadn't been able to feel the tingliness left by Richard's breath on her lips.

"The captain should see to getting that repaired," Richard commented, his voice the slightest touch unsteady. "I'll say something to him in the morning."

Amy nodded. For once in her life—and such occasions were rare indeed—she couldn't think of anything to say. "Excuse me, were you about to kiss me?" didn't seem at all a proper thing for a young lady to ask, even a young lady who had been so unladylike as to sit unchaperoned with a man on the deck of a boat at midnight. Besides, what if he said no? Drat that railing!

Amy bit down on her lower lip, utterly at sea. Plans, plans . . . when was she ever without a plan? True, it was terribly hard to plan when one wasn't at all sure what one wanted. Did she want him to kiss her? Or just to admit that he had intended to kiss her? And why did it matter if he had? Oh, heavens! Amy squirmed on the hard deck. Planning the restoration of the monarchy was so much easier than dealing with the aftermath of an almost-kiss!

And really, Amy reminded herself, she should be concentrating entirely on her plans to find the Purple Gentian and restore the monarchy, not agonizing over a man of dubious morals. Even if that man did have cheekbones to make a sculptor weep, and the most intriguing play of muscles along his back . . . Amy went back to gnawing her lower lip.

Richard leaned back on his hands, letting the rough wood against his palms drag him back to his senses. Kissing Amy. Bad idea. What the devil had he been thinking? He hadn't been thinking at all; that was the problem. At least, he hadn't been thinking with any part of him that worked in a logical manner. Logic. Richard scraped his hands against the splintery deck and tried to approach the situation logically. Logically, kissing Amy was a terrible idea. He repeated that to himself a couple of times. After all, if he'd kissed Amy, he would have some sort of obligation to her, and that would mean spending time with her once they both got to France.

Of course, he really wouldn't mind spending time with her. . . . Richard squashed that thought posthaste. No matter how much he might enjoy spending time with Amy, he couldn't. He just didn't have the time to spend. Not if he wanted to discover Bonaparte's invasion plans before French troops set foot on English soil. Nobody knew better than Richard how quickly Bonaparte could move (except, perhaps, the Italians, and the Austrians, and the Dutch), and as for Amy . . . Richard sensed that she could be a rather massive distraction.

But if he didn't kiss her, he wouldn't be obligated to her, and therefore she wouldn't distract him. It all made perfect sense. Logically.

Richard glanced at Amy, sitting uncharacteristically silent beside him. She had drawn her knees back up to her chest, and she was staring straight out over the dark waters, biting her lip. It was too dark to discern the color of her lips, but Richard remembered them well, a surprisingly deep pink against her pale skin, soft, inviting. He remembered watching the way her lips moved as she talked, as she smiled. Biting them was probably making them red and swollen, just as his kisses would. Logic, logic, logic, Richard reminded himself, tilting his head back and staring at the sky. When he looked back, Amy was still biting her lip.

Richard hastily looked away again.

"What is your brother's name?" Richard asked, just to ask something. She couldn't bite her lip and talk at the same time, could she?

"Edouard," Amy replied absently. "He's several years older than me."

"Edouard." Richard sat upright so hastily that his head swam. "Not Edouard de Balcourt?"

"Yes! Do you know—"

"Edouard de Balcourt is your *brother*?"

"You *do* know him, then?" Amy asked eagerly.

"We know each other slightly," Richard replied cautiously. That was true as far as it went; Richard had done his very best to keep the acquaintance slight.

"Would you tell me about him? Please? Whatever you know. I haven't seen him since I was five. He doesn't write much," she confessed. Knowing Balcourt, Richard could well believe it. "I suppose he's afraid any letters to England would be searched. What can you tell me about him?"

"Um . . ." Richard drummed his fingers against the deck. From the glowing expression on Amy's face, it was clear that she cherished high hopes of her brother. Blast it all, why should he have to be the one to tell her that her brother was one of the laughingstocks of Bonaparte's court? Edouard de Balcourt was a fop, a toady, a man without taste, morals, or scruple. And that was putting it in the most generous way possible.

How could Balcourt be Amy's *brother*? Perhaps he was a changeling? One of them had to be.

Amy tapped her foot impatiently. "So?" she prompted.

"He doesn't look like you." It was the only harmless thing Richard could think of to say.

"We did a bit when we were younger," reflected Amy. She smiled wistfully. "Mama always used to say it wasn't fair that we both took after Papa's side of the family. Mama's family was all tall and fair and stately, like Jane, but Edouard and I were both small and dark. Papa was tall, though. When he lifted me onto his shoulders, I thought I could touch the stars."

For a moment, Amy lost herself in the memory of bouncing on Papa's shoulders, grabbing for stars. He had even given her a tiny little diamond bracelet—a string of stars, he had sworn, gathered while she was asleep in the nursery.

"He promised, when I was older, that he would lift me into the night sky so that I could string myself a necklace. A necklace of stars." Amy blinked back tears and stared longingly into the sky.

There were no stars tonight.

But there was one very silent man beside her, watching her closely, and Amy plummeted abruptly into the present, like Icarus falling from the sky, shaken and a little abashed.

What had possessed her to reveal so much? Her memories of Mama and Papa were her own, her treasured cache, more precious than any number of necklaces of stars. She spoke of them to no one, not even to Jane, who was the sister of her heart, her one confidante, and the person who knew her better than anyone in the world. Yet it had been so easy to speak of them to Lord Richard. Obviously, her wits had been addled by the almost kiss and the moonlight. People did silly things by moonlight. It didn't matter that the moon had gone behind the clouds quite some time ago; it was still there, affecting her actions, even if she couldn't see it.

Though there was also something about Lord Richard. Something that made it quite easy and natural to confide in him. Something she couldn't blame on the moon. Something that made Amy feel quite, quite vulnerable, and she wasn't at all sure she liked it.

Amy broke the fragile silence by saying with forced bravado, "Now that you know all about me, it's your turn. Why are *you* going to France?"

Busy admiring Amy's courage, Richard spoke without thinking. "I'm the First Consul's director of Egyptian antiquities." It was a response he had made so often, to so many people, that it came out by rote.

Amy blinked. "The First Consul's director of antiquities?"

"Yes, after we returned from Egypt, the First Consul invited me to . . ." Richard's voice trailed off as Amy stumbled clumsily to her feet. "Is something wrong?"

"You weren't sorry at all, were you?" she whispered.

"I beg your pardon?"

"You weren't baiting me, you were saying what you felt, and *you weren't sorry*."

"Amy, I—" Richard reached up to take Amy's hands, but she backed away, wiping her hands furiously on her skirt as though to exorcise his touch.

"I don't understand it." Her voice had an edge of tears that lashed him far more harshly than her shouting that afternoon. "You've been with the French all along. You never left. You've been with *them* the whole time. If you stayed with them, you can't have thought that what they did was so terrible. Why pretend to be sympathetic when you weren't? I've been such a fool!"

"You're not a fool. Amy—"

"Don't you dare tell me I'm not a fool! Don't you dare presume to tell me anything, ever again!"

Stunned by her outburst, Richard sat staring as Amy whirled like a small dervish in angry circles around the deck.

"I liked you. I trusted you. Oh, goodness, I told you about my *parents*!"

More than a little irritated by that string of past tenses, Richard snapped, "What has that got to do with anything?"

He grabbed the railing and yanked himself to his feet.

"Nothing. Nothing!" Amy waved her arms wildly. "It has nothing to do with the fact that you are a rogue and a cad and a bounder and a traitor to your country and—"

Rogue and cad and bounder had been bad enough, but traitor to his country? Richard had harbored some vague idea of suffering her insults in patient silence, but that was really the utter end.

"Oh, am I?" Richard advanced with the stealthy prowl of a panther, his voice a low purr more threatening than any growl. "Define treachery, Miss Balcourt."

Amy noticed the dangerous light in Lord Richard's green eyes, but somehow the jade glare only fueled her own rising anger. Rather than backing away, she stomped forward to meet him. "Treachery," she declared furiously, tipping her head back till her upturned nose practically brushed his chin, "is when a man willfully allies with the enemies of his country!"

Amy took a half step back, not from intimidation—never that!—but because her neck hurt. Blast the advantage of height! It was thoroughly unfair that he should be able to look down his nose at her in that ridiculously supercilious way, just because some good fairy had waved her wand over his cradle and given him an utterly undeserved collection of inches. If his physique were to mirror his character, why, he should be a nasty, shriveled, twisted gnome of a man. Not a towering golden Adonis designed to lead innocent females into indiscretions. The injustice of it all rendered Amy even angrier.

"Treachery," repeated Amy shrilly, "is when an unscrupulous man deceives innocent young ladies into believing he is a—a person of sense and sensibility! When all the while—"

"Innocent?" roared Richard. "Innocent? You're the one who's always picking fights with me! You call yourself innocent? *I* was innocently discussing Egyptology this afternoon, when you hauled off and started abusing my character!"

"That might be because *you're* the one in the employ of Bonaparte!"

"At least I don't go about throwing stones at other people's glass houses!"

"Oh no, you'd just guillotine them, wouldn't you?"

Richard grabbed Amy by the shoulders. "You"—*shake*—"are absolutely"—*shake—shake*—"ABSURD!"

Amy stamped her foot. Hard. On Richard's.

"That's for calling me absurd!"

"Owwwww!" Richard released Amy somewhat more abruptly than he would have liked. How could one small foot pack such a punch? He'd been attacked by grown men who hadn't managed to cause him quite so much pain.

Amy backed away from him, visibly seething. "Don't touch me; don't talk to me; don't follow me," she spat, stalking towards the stairs. "I'm going to bed!"

"That's the first sensible thing you've said all evening!" Richard snapped, hobbling after her.

Amy whirled on one—as Richard now knew—very dangerous little heel. Richard flinched, an involuntary movement that brought a flicker of malicious pleasure to Amy's blue eyes. It might have just been a stray glimmer of moonlight, but Richard and his aching instep were pretty sure it was malice.

"I thought I told you not to follow me!"

"Do you expect me to sleep on the deck?" Richard inquired acidly.

Amy muttered something unintelligible, and started down the short flight of stairs.

Richard poked her in the shoulder blades, just below her tangled dark curls, which jerked satisfyingly in response. "What was that you said?" he asked.

Amy's hands clenched into fists at her sides as she kept walking. "I said I'm not speaking to you!"

"Oh, that's logical," drawled Richard.

Amy emitted an inarticulate noise of great emotion.

"I say, that doesn't count as speaking, does it?"

One hand on the door of the cabin, Amy gave an agitated hop that looked like it wanted to be a temper tantrum when it grew up. "Just leave me alone!" she whispered fiercely, yanking open the door. "Stay on your side of the room, and leave me alone!"

"Your wish is my command." Richard bowed mockingly and disappeared without a sound behind the wall of cloaks.

Amy flounced over to her side of the partition, promptly tripped over the same portmanteau of Miss Gwen's that she had whacked into earlier, and experienced no difficulty in convincing herself that it was all Lord Richard's fault. Amy hopped into her berth, nursing her wounded toes. She had no doubt that, in some roundabout way, the storm that had stranded them on this dratted boat was Lord Richard's fault, too. Most likely some minor deity he had offended getting back at him.

"I hate him, I hate him, I hate him," Amy muttered as she drifted into sleep.

Within moments, Amy found herself on a balcony outside a ballroom. Through the open French doors came the sound of laughter and music. The candlelight traced intriguing patterns at Amy's feet, but they failed to hold Amy's attention.

She was looking over a garden—a large, elaborate, formal garden, with bowers of roses, a false classical temple on a distant hill, and a large, surprisingly unruly hedge-maze smack in the middle of the patterned paths and beds of flowers. And that's when she saw him. Practically a shadow himself in a dark, hooded cloak, he slipped out of the maze and swung over the edge of her balcony. Amy reached out an eager hand to help haul him over.

"I knew you'd come!" Through the kid of his glove, she could feel the signet ring on his hand, a signet ring that bore a small, purple flower.

"How could I stay away?" he murmured.

Amy clung to his hand. "I so badly want to help you! It's all I've ever wanted! Won't you tell me who you are?"

The Purple Gentian ran one gloved finger down her cheek in a way that made Amy shiver with delight. "Why don't I show you?"

Usually, at this point in the dream—because Amy had dreamed this same dream, not once, but several dozen times, down to the very colors of the flowers in the garden—Amy woke up, anxious, bereft, and more eager than ever to track the real Gentian down to his lair.

But tonight she watched with quivering anticipation as the Gentian painstakingly undid the knot holding his cloak at his throat, as he slowly pushed back the enveloping hood to reveal a head that glinted gold in the candlelight and a pair of shrewd and mocking green eyes.

"I'll wager you didn't expect to see me," drawled Lord Richard Selwick.

Amy woke with a gasp of horror.

"Drat him!" You would think the nasty cad could at least leave her to dream in peace! Amy punched the pillow, rolled over, and went back to sleep. Lord Richard invaded her slumbers once more, but this time Amy didn't mind. She dreamed with great satisfaction of pushing Lord Richard off the side of the boat, and then sticking out her tongue at him as he thrashed in the cold waters of the Channel.

On the other side of the cabin, Richard's slumbers were equally uneasy—even though he had no idea that Amy was mentally chucking him into the Channel. He had lain awake for some time, alternately fuming over his own behavior and that of Amy. He had dismissed a ridiculous voice in his head (which sounded unsettlingly like Henrietta's) that rather caustically informed him that if he wanted Amy's attention behaving like a seven-year-old was not the best way to go about it. "She started it," Richard grumbled, and then felt even worse, because, devil take it, he had sunk to the level of arguing with people who weren't even there. If he continued like this, he'd be more fit for Bedlam than espionage.

Richard fell asleep while mentally drafting an instructional pamphlet for the War Office entitled *Some Thoughts on the Necessity of the Avoidance of the Opposite Sex While Engaged in Espionage: A Practical Guide.* The title itself took him some effort to get just right. By the time he finished composing Item One ("Under no circumstances allow yourself to be drawn into conversation, no matter how well read the young lady in question, or how fine her eyes"), Richard slid seamlessly into a familiar nightmare.

He was just outside Paris, making his way through the Bois de Vincennes to the rendezvous with Andrew, Tony, and the Marquis de Sommelier. Percy was to meet them at Calais with his yacht and the Comte and Comtesse de St. Antoine. Another successful week's work for the League of the Scarlet Pimpernel.

Richard wasn't feeling particularly buoyed with success; he

was still brooding over that last call on Deirdre. She had been arranging flowers from Baron Jerard when he had arrived. Baron Jerard! What sort of rival was that! Forty if he was a day! Richard would be willing to wager the man couldn't sit the back of a horse for the duration of a hunt, much less pull off dashing rescues with half the military might of revolutionary France in pursuit. It had been the way Deirdre said his name when Richard asked about the flowers that had set Richard off. "Baron Jerard called," she'd said, and there was just a hint of something secret, something almost smug, only his Deirdre, his perfect, beautiful Deirdre would never possibly be smug. That's when Richard rashly spilled *his* secret.

But when he'd told her . . . well, what he wasn't supposed to tell her, she'd just kept on arranging Jerard's pestilential flowers, and trilled, "La, you are droll, my lord!"

"What will it take to convince you, the head of a Frenchman on a platter?" Richard had cried in anguish, and stormed from the parlor.

Geoff poked Richard in the ribs. "Richard, something's not right."

Blinking, Richard realized they were already at the small shack they used for their rendezvous. And Geoff was right—something was quite, quite wrong. There should have been a scrap of scarlet cloth in one of the rough rectangles that passed for windows. The door of the shack hung ominously ajar.

The two old friends exchanged a long look, and crept silently along the side of the shack. "Ready?" Richard breathed. Geoff nodded, and they exploded into the hovel. Only to find one man lying twisted on the floor, his clothes dark and wet with his own blood.

Tony.

And then Geoff uttered the words that Richard couldn't erase from his brain, not with a hundred bottles of port. "Someone must have tipped them off."

"Damn her!" Richard cursed, as he thrashed in his sleep. "Damn her!"

Chapter Eight

Voices in the foyer jolted me out of Amy's world.

Expecting to hear only waves lapping against the keel of a boat, the sound of laughter in the next room knocked me unwillingly back into the twenty-first century. I blinked to rid myself of the last phantom images of tarry decks and canvas sails. It took me a moment to remember where I was; my head felt as muzzy as though I'd just taken a double dose of cold medicine. A quick glance around informed me that I was still sprawled out on the Persian rug in Mrs. Selwick-Alderly's drawing room and the fire next to me had burned down to mere embers from lack of tending. I had no idea what time it was, or how long I'd been reading, but one leg seemed to have gone numb, and there was a vague ache in my shoulders.

I was experimentally stretching out one stiff leg—just to make sure it still worked—when he appeared in the doorway.

It was the Golden Man. He of the photograph on Mrs. Selwick-Alderly's mantel. For a moment, in my befuddled state, caught between past and present, I half fancied that he'd just strolled out of the photograph. All right, I know it sounds silly, but I actually took a quick look to make sure the man in the picture was still where he ought to be, frozen in perpetual laughter next to his horse. He was. And on a second glance at the man in the doorway, I picked up the differences I had missed the first time around. The man in the photograph hadn't been wearing gray slacks and a blazer, and his blond hair had been bright with sun, not dark with wet.

He also hadn't been wearing an unspeakably chic woman on his arm.

She was about my height, but there the resemblance

ended. Her long, glossy dark brown hair floated around her face as though it was auditioning for a Pantene commercial. Her brown suede boots were as immaculate as if she had just walked out of the Harrods shoe department, and her smart little brown wool dress screamed Notting Hill boutique. They made an attractive pair, like something out of *Town and Country*: Mr. and Mrs. Fabulously Fabulous Show Off their Gracious Home.

It was enough to make one feel like a miserable mugwump.

I was so deep in mugwump land that it took me a moment to realize that not only was the smiling, golden man of the photograph not smiling, his expression was positively explosive. And it was aimed at me. .

"Hi!" I struggled to my feet, a few yellowed pages tumbling from my lap as I levered myself up with one hand, the other hand clutching the bundle of letters. "I'm Elo—"

Golden Man stalked across the drawing room, snatched up the papers I'd left on the floor, flung them into the open chest, and slammed the lid shut.

"Who gave you leave to take those papers?"

I was so shocked by the transformation of the friendly man of the photograph that my brain and my mouth stopped working in partnership.

"Who gave me . . . ?" I glanced down dumbly at the papers in my hand. "Oh, these! Mrs. Selwick-Alderly said—"

Golden Man bellowed, "Aunt Arabella!"

"Mrs. Selwick-Alderly said I could—"

"Serena, would you go fetch Aunt Arabella?"

Chic Girl bit her lip. "I'll just go see if she's ready to leave, shall I?" she murmured, and hurried off down the hallway.

Golden Man plunked himself down on the chest, as though defying me to snatch it out from under him, and glowered at me.

I stared at him in dismayed confusion, automatically clutching Amy's letters closer to my coffee-blotched sweater. Could he be under some sort of misapprehension about my intentions towards his family papers? Maybe he thought I was an appraiser from Britain's equivalent of the IRS, come to charge his aunt great gobs of money for possessing a national treasure, or a rogue librarian, come to steal the papers for my library. After all, if there was art theft, maybe there was document theft, too, and he thought I was a dastardly document thief. I didn't think I looked particularly dastardly, just disheveled—it's hard to look dastardly when one has wide blue eyes, and one of those easy-to-blush complexions—but maybe document thieves came in all shapes and sizes.

"Mrs. Selwick-Alderly said I could look at these papers for my dissertation research," I tried to reassure him.

He continued to eye me as though I were a Victorian scullery maid caught parading around in the mistress's best diamond tiara.

"I'm getting a PhD," I added. "From Harvard."

Why had I felt the need to say that? I sounded like one of those intolerable academic types who wore leather patches on their tweed jackets, affected horn-rimmed spectacles, and pronounced "Hahvahd" without any Rs.

Golden Man clearly thought so, too. "I don't care if you're David bloody Starkey," he snapped. "Those papers aren't open to the public."

Forget golden. He was being rapidly demoted to bronze. Tarnished bronze, at that.

"I'm not the public," I pointed out as Chic Girl slipped unobtrusively back through the open doorway. "Your aunt invited me here, and offered me the use of these papers."

"Damn!" he cursed explosively.

"Really, Colin," she of the enviable boots broke in, "I don't think—"

"*Colin*?" I took a step forward, eyes narrowing as a nasty suspicion began to form. "Not Mr. Colin Selwick of Selwick Hall?"

Suddenly, it all made sense.

I dropped the disputed bundle of papers on an overstuffed chair. "Not Mr. Colin Selwick who likes to send nasty letters to American scholars?"

"I wouldn't say—" he began, looking harried, but I didn't let him get any further. After all, if I was going to be flung out of the house like a disobedient Victorian scullery maid, I might as well go out with style.

" 'Badgering private persons with impertinent requests for personal papers may be appropriate on your side of the Atlantic'?" I quoted triumphantly.

Chic Girl looked horrified. "Colin, you didn't!"

I began to think I could forgive her the boots. "Oh, yes, he did."

"I was having a bad day," Colin Selwick muttered, shifting uncomfortably on the wooden chest. I hoped he was sitting on a splinter. Make that several splinters. "Look, you've got hold of the wrong end of the—"

"Oh, I don't think so," I said sweetly. "You were quite, *quite* clear, Mr. Selwick. Oh, wait, wasn't there also something about academics who have nothing better to do than waste taxpayer money on dilatory pursuits that are about as much good to the public as a moldy ham sandwich?"

"I never—"

"I just added the moldy ham sandwich bit," I clarified for Chic Girl's benefit, "since I'm afraid I don't remember just which thrilling analogy Mr. Selwick employed to describe my utter uselessness to human existence."

"Do you always memorize your correspondence?" he demanded in exasperation, pushing off from the trunk.

"Only when it's as memorable as this one was. You have quite a knack with the poison pen."

"And *you* have quite an overwrought imagination." With two long strides, he bridged the swath of carpet separating us.

"Are you saying I'm making this up?" I yelped.

Colin Selwick shrugged. "I'm saying you're exaggerating wildly."

"Right. I'm sure your behaving like a boorish lout just now was all a product of my hyperactive imagination, too." I had to tilt my head back to glower at him.

From my vantage point just beneath his chin, I could see the muscles of his throat constrict. Swallowing some choice Anglo-Saxon words, no doubt.

"Look," he said in strangled tones, "how would you feel if you saw a perfect stranger pawing through your private possessions?"

"This isn't exactly your underwear drawer. And as far as I can tell, these papers aren't even yours."

Mr. Colin Selwick didn't like that. Underneath his sportsman's tan, his face was turning a mottled red. "They belong to my family."

A slow smile spread across my face. "You don't have any authority over these documents, do you?"

"Those. Papers. Are. Private."

I'd never actually seen anyone speak through gritted teeth before. No wonder English dentistry was in such a dreadful state.

"Why?" I demanded recklessly. "What is it that you don't want me seeing? What are you so afraid of?"

"Colin . . ." Chic Girl tugged anxiously at his arm. We both ignored her.

"Did the Purple Gentian sell out to the French? Have a thing for women's underwear? Or maybe it's the Pink Carnation you don't want me finding out about? Ha!" An involuntary twitch—perhaps a repressed attempt to strangle me?—gave me the clue I was looking for.

I shoved my hair back behind my ears and leaned forward for the kill, never taking my eyes from his. "I've got it! The Pink Carnation was . . . *French*!"

At that inconvenient moment, Mrs. Selwick-Alderly hurried in, dressed for going out in black and pearls. We all froze like naughty schoolchildren caught brawling in the playground.

"Sorry to keep you waiting, dears! Colin, I see you've met Eloise?"

That was one way of putting it.

Colin mumbled something in the general direction of the carpet.

Draping a cashmere stole around her shoulders, Mrs. Selwick-Alderly added, "Eloise is working on a fascinating project about the Pink Carnation. You must tell Colin about it sometime, Eloise. The Pink Carnation has always been something of a passion of his."

"So I gathered." My tone was as dry as well-aged sherry.

Colin sent me a sharp look.

I permitted myself a slight, sardonic smirk.

Colin returned the smirk with interest. "Too bad she has to be going."

Going. My smirk disintegrated faster than the embers of the fading fire. He who smirks last . . . There was no denying that Colin Selwick had won that round. Of course, I should have realized that if Mrs. Selwick-Alderly was going out, I would have to go home, home to my lonely basement flat, and my frozen Sainsbury's dinner, and the All-England televised darts championship. And if Colin Selwick had his way, I would never be invited back.

What time was it? *Late,* said the midnight-dark sky beyond the cream-colored drapes. At a guess, it was dinnertime at least, probably later. I cast an agonized glance at the half-read papers on the chair—not only was I no closer to the identity of the Pink Carnation, but I was dying to know if Lord Richard ever did kiss Miss Amy Balcourt. Did he tiptoe over to her side of the boat in the dead of night, stand on his tiptoes . . . and smooch Miss Gwen by accident? It was like being torn away midway through an episode of *The Bachelor*.

But Mrs. Selwick-Alderly, stole around her shoulders, was clearly ready to leave.

"I'm so sorry." I turned penitently to Mrs. Selwick-Alderly. "I probably should have left ages ago, but I was so wrapped up in Amy's letters that I lost all track of time. I can't thank you enough for your kindness and hospitality."

"We wouldn't want you to be late for an engagement," Colin Selwick broke in impatiently.

"That would only be a problem if I were going somewhere."

"In that case . . . ," Mrs. Selwick-Alderly began.

"Well, we are," Colin said rudely. "Good-bye."

"In that case," Mrs. Selwick-Alderly repeated, with a look of gentle reproach for her erring nephew. "There's no reason you can't stay."

It was like Santa Claus and the Tooth Fairy and the Easter Bunny all rolled into one. "Do you really mean it? Are you sure it wouldn't be too much of an inconvenience?"

"No reason?"

"It's not an inconvenience at all. Serena, would you show Eloise to the spare room before we go? There should be some old nightgowns in the wardrobe."

Colin made a low, grumbling noise. "Aunt Arabella, are you sure this is wise?"

She met his agitated gaze serenely. "You know the contents of that chest."

"But the Pink—"

Her head swayed infinitesimally in negation. "The one doesn't necessarily lead to the other, you know," and in her voice was both reassurance and warning.

She slipped quickly back into the prosaic. "Now, Eloise, the bathroom is the third door to the right, and you'll find the kitchen straight back and to the left. Please don't hesitate to help yourself to anything in the cupboards. And don't worry about the washing up; Consuela will be here in the morning to take care of that. Is there anything I've forgotten?"

Colin mumbled something. It sounded like, "Common sense."

Mrs. Selwick-Alderly ignored him. So did I.

"I'll take very good care of the papers," I promised, eyes shifting to the treasure chest in the corner. All those lovely letters to read . . .

"Be sure that you do," Colin Selwick said shortly. "Aunt Arabella?"

He did a very good job of stalking from the room, back straight, head high. But he spoiled it with a backwards glance over his shoulder. His face was rigid with frustrated anger, and I could tell that he wanted nothing more than to sling me over his shoulder and fling me out the nearest doorway. Or window. He didn't look like he was in the mood to be picky about the means of egress.

I wish I could say that I met his gaze with level dignity. I didn't.

I grinned—an honest-to-goodness, gum-baring, playground grin.

Turning on his heel, Mr. Colin Selwick slammed out of the room. A moment later I heard the front door close—not quite emphatically enough to be a slam, but with enough wrist behind it to imply that somebody was more than a little bit miffed.

Still grinning, I sank back down onto the Persian rug. Round two to Eloise. It might not be dignified, but, oh, it did feel good to see Mr. Colin Selwick seething and helpless. Leaving aside his unpardonable rudeness to a guest, I'd been longing for revenge ever since I'd opened that insufferable letter of his. Did I mention that the envelope gave me a paper cut? Just to add injury to insult.

What on earth was his obsession with family privacy, anyway? I wondered as I stretched out an arm to snag the papers I'd dropped on the armchair. You'd think he'd caught me reading his diary.

It was curious that he had felt the need to curb his temper in front of his aunt. Maybe he stood to inherit from her and was afraid of incurring her ire? It was a classic television drama plot: elderly, eccentric relative, bad-tempered young heir. That could put a whole new complexion on Mr. Colin Selwick's explosive reaction to me. Maybe it wasn't really about the Pink Carnation papers at all. Perhaps his real fear was that I'd worm my way into his aunt's good graces through my interest in the family history and oust him from his inheritance.

It was an amusing image. I pictured myself in a smartly cut black dress and a 1920s hat with spotted veil, perched on a little gilt chair while a gray-faced solicitor droned, "And the bulk of my estate I leave to Miss Eloise Kelly." Colin Selwick, in spats and slouch hat, would curse loudly and storm from the room, his hopes forever thwarted. That would teach him to write rude letters. An amusing image, but Colin Selwick would have to be more than a little bit mad to see a potential rival in every little American grad student who wandered into his aunt's flat. And the inheritance theory failed to explain the intolerable rudeness of his letter to me well before he had seen me cozily ensconced in his aunt's parlor.

Not that it mattered. Mr. Colin Selwick's psychoses—and I was sure a good psychiatrist could diagnose him with quite a few—were his own concern. In the meantime, I had the trunk of papers all to myself, and a whole night to read them in. Why waste time speculating about insufferable modern men when one could read about swashbucklers in capes and knee breeches?

Even if, from Amy's letters, it appeared that Lord Richard Selwick was quite as infuriating as his obnoxious descendant.

At least Lord Richard had a good excuse, I decided charitably. Hiding a secret identity must put a considerable strain on a man.

Setting the precious bundle of papers down next to me, I tugged off my gangrenous boots, tucked my feet up under me, and leaned my back against the side of the armchair. Ruffling through the documents in my hands, I selected one from Lord Richard Selwick to his friend Miles Dorrington and resumed reading.

I would give Lord Richard a chance to prove himself more congenial than his aggravating descendant. . . .

Chapter Nine

E douard's carriage wasn't there.

Amy looked out over the street for the fifth time in as many minutes. There was still no sign of a carriage bearing the Balcourt crest. The dock at Calais lacked the bustle and flurry Miss Gwen had frowned over at Dover. In the weak, early morning light, the wharf was almost eerily deserted. Only one carriage had braved the dawn chill, a battered black carriage with a broken sidelamp, and starbursts of mud along its sides. When they had wobbled off the ship an hour before in predawn dark, Amy had seen the bulk of a carriage, and assumed it must be Edouard's. The coachman's striding past them and making straight for the cargo in the hold had dispelled that happy notion. With little else to do, Amy tugged her shawl tighter and watched idly as three men in rough work clothes trotted up and down the gangplank, heaving assorted boxes and bundles into the carriage. Surely Edouard would arrive soon?

Amy started at the sound of hooves racketing against cobblestones. Four black horses trotted into view, followed by a sleek black carriage. The coachman rose on his box and gave an unservile halloo in a decidedly English voice. He was answered by the all too familiar tones of Lord Richard Selwick. It was utterly unfair, thought Amy, that a man as devoid of honor as Lord Richard should have his coach arrive on time while theirs was nowhere in sight. Where was the justice in that? Shouldn't he be at the top of the list for divine retribution for his perfidy? Oh well, there was yet time for justice to be served. Maybe his carriage wheel fall off and leave him stranded in a ditch.

"Hullo, Robbins!" Richard left his perch atop a pile of trunks and strode over to his carriage. "Have a nice drive?"

"As nice as can be had on them damned French roads, milord—begging your pardon, ladies," the coachman hastily added as Miss Gwen's loud sniff of reproach alerted him to the presence of three rather disheveled female persons on the wharf. "All pits and potholes, they are," he earnestly explained to Miss Gwen.

Miss Gwen sniffed again.

Feeling that he'd done the best he could to atone for his profanity, Robbins shrugged and turned his back on the old harpy with the strange hat. "When do I get to drive on good English roads again, milord?"

"When Bonaparte donates his collection of antiquities to the British Museum," Richard said dryly. The words came out by rote; he and Robbins had been through the same routine several times before. Richard's attention had shifted to the tousled collection of females huddling on the windy wharf.

The second he looked at Amy, she scowled violently.

It would have been quite an effective scowl if the wind hadn't blown her curls into her face. Richard couldn't help grinning as he watched Amy paw clumps of hair out of her mouth. She looked like a bedraggled kitten dealing with fur balls.

He, of course, didn't feel one way or the other about the girl. Well, all right, he did feel quite an uncomfortable tightening in certain parts of his breeches when the wind flattened her skirts against her legs, just as it was doing now, outlining her—Richard let out his breath in a rush. It was best not to think about what the wind was outlining. At any rate, aside from lust—which, he quickly reminded himself, was a physical reaction, which could have been brought on by any other female with kissable Cupid's-bow lips and intriguing curves outlined by fine yellow muslin—he felt nothing for her. She was just a chance acquaintance, and if she happened to dislike him, that was her own affair. He scarcely knew her.

He did, however, know Edouard de Balcourt. Balcourt would think nothing of leaving his female relations stranded in Calais for a week, if sending the carriage to pick them up didn't suit his own schedule. Richard could easily imagine Balcourt being distracted by a fitting for the latest style of breeches and completely forgetting to send the carriage at all. He didn't like to think of three gently bred young ladies being stranded by the wharf. Certainly, there were inns in

Calais, but they catered to a very different sort of clientele. No doubt there was at least one respectable establishment, but docks, as Richard knew far too well from his peregrinations back and forth across the Channel, tended to attract the most unsavory sort of riffraff. With that deadly parasol of hers, Miss Gwen made a formidable guard—whoever picked her to look after Amy and Jane had known what they were about—but, even so . . . Richard imagined Henrietta stranded for a week in Calais and his lips tightened grimly. There was nothing for it but to take the women back to Paris with him.

Amy caught Richard's eye, flushed, and quickly looked away again. "Insufferable man!" she muttered.

"Amy, I really wish you would tell me what happened between you and Lord Richard."

"Shhhh! He's coming this way!"

Casually swinging his hat in one hand, Lord Richard strolled towards them . . . and past them, bowing to Miss Gwen.

"Madam, your carriage seems to have been . . . delayed. May I be so bold as to offer the use of mine?"

Oh no, thought Amy. Oh no, no, no.

Amy drew herself to her full five feet and three inches and set her chin. "That really won't be necessary! I'm sure Edouard's coach will arrive any minute now, don't you think? There are dozens of reasons why it might have been delayed. Broken wheels or bandits or . . ." Amy's voice petered out. Miss Gwen and Lord Richard, on either side, were looking down at her with frighteningly similar expressions of polite incredulity. "Well, I'm sure there *must* be bandits, and a broken wheel could happen to anyone!"

"Indeed." Lord Richard positively exuded skepticism in a highly unpleasant way.

Richard *felt* highly unpleasant. Here he was, trying to do something nice for the girl, dash it all, despite all of the extremely rude things she had said to him the night before, and she was treating him as though he had offered to convey her to a leper colony! She could at least attempt to be civil in return. For heaven's sake, it wasn't as though *he* had murdered her parents.

Amy took a deep breath and resisted the urge to stamp her foot. Preferably on Lord Richard's. Again. "At any rate, when Edouard's carriage does arrive—which it *will*—it would be dreadfully rude of us not to have waited for it, after he's put his coachman to so much trouble. And what if the coachman thinks we haven't arrived yet and stays to wait for us? Why, the poor man could be stranded here for days!"

"Your concern for your brother's coachman does you credit, Miss Balcourt," Lord Richard commented dryly, with a wry twist of the lips that suggested that he knew it was not Edouard's coachman who troubled her, "but, at present, *you* seem to be the one stranded, not he."

Amy squared her shoulders for further argument, but Miss Gwen prevented her with a commanding thump of her parasol. "I will have no more argument from you, Miss Amy! Your brother's coach was to have been here this morning. It was not. Therefore we are accepting Lord Richard's kind offer, and I trust that your brother's coachman, should he appear, shall have the basic sense to return to Paris. Is that understood? My lord, you may instruct your man to load our baggage."

"Miss Meadows, I am yours to command. Miss Balcourt, the opportunity to extend our acquaintance, as I am sure you will agree, is an unexpected delight."

"Indeed." Amy tossed his own word back at him with twice the skepticism.

And he laughed. The bounder actually laughed.

Amy stomped off to the side of the dock as Richard's coachman joined two sailors in loading all of their trunks onto the top of the carriage. At least, she tried to stomp. Her kid boots made disappointingly little noise on the wooden planks. Amy longed for loud noises—stomping boots, slamming doors, breaking china—to vent her displeasure. Oh for a parasol to thump like Miss Gwen! "Maybe that's why she carries it," Amy murmured to the waves. The waves crashed obligingly in affirmative response.

"It *is* very good of him." Jane slipped an arm through Amy's.

"It gives the appearance of goodness," Amy corrected crossly. She stole a glance at Richard, who was speaking gravely to Miss Gwen. "All the better to hide a thoroughly black heart."

Jane's pale brows drew together in concern. "What did he do to make you feel so about him? Amy, he didn't behave improperly to you?"

"No," Amy said grumpily, feeling, if possible, even crosser than before. The memory of the almost-kiss—had it even been an almost-kiss?—danced mockingly at the edge of memory, taunting her with her own foolishness. Good heavens, how could she even have considered kissing such a base rogue? Amy wasn't sure whether she was more irate with Richard for charming her into liking him or with herself for allowing herself to be charmed when she ought to have known better. Either way, she was irate.

Jane was still watching her expectantly. Jane, Amy decided, could not be told of the almost-kiss. "No," Amy repeated. "It was his principles, not his actions, that offended me. Can you believe that the man is employed by Bonaparte! An Englishman, a member of the peerage, working for that—"

"It might be well not to judge him too hastily," Jane interjected as Amy's voice rose dangerously above the slapping of the waves.

"Trust me, Jane, it's a *very* well-considered judgment!"

"Amy, you've known him all of a day."

"That was more than long enough," Amy stated stubbornly. "Oh blast, the trunks are loaded. I was so hoping Edouard's coach would appear before we had to leave with *him*."

Lord Richard greeted each girl with a deep bow as they fell in beside Miss Gwen. Such an excess of civility, thought Amy grimly, could only be meant as insult. Her darkest suspicions were confirmed when Richard followed up his bows with, "Good morning, Miss Wooliston, Miss Balcourt. I trust you slept well." He spoke lightly, his gaze resting impersonally on Jane and Amy in turn.

"Quite well, thank you," said Jane.

Amy glowered. "I was kept awake by the sound of someone stamping about on deck."

Richard smiled blandly. "It's well you didn't go up to investigate. You never know what rough sorts you might encounter on a Dover packet."

"I believe I have a fair idea, my lord."

Jane's bonneted head swiveled from one to the other. She gave Amy a hard look from under the straw brim. "There's something you're not telling me," she whispered.

"Later," Amy whispered back.

Richard regarded them with that infuriatingly benign look

of condescension men assume when women whisper in front of them.

Miss Gwen was less benign; she rapped her parasol against the ground like an exasperated orchestra conductor. "Are we to stand here taking the air or shall we depart? Sir?" Grabbing Richard's outstretched arm, she climbed regally into the carriage. Murmuring her thanks to Richard, Jane followed, taking the seat beside Miss Gwen.

Pointedly avoiding resting her fingers on the arm Richard proffered, Amy peered into the interior of the carriage. Oh, drat! She would have to sit next to Lord Richard.

Amy wedged herself into the very farthest corner of the bench. Richard gave her a somewhat sardonic look as he settled down on his side. He called an order to the coachman, and the carriage jostled into movement. Under pretense of picking up a fallen glove from the floor, Richard leaned towards Amy.

"It's not catching, you know."

Amy opened her mouth to retort, but Miss Gwen's eye was upon her like a falcon sighting its prey. With as much dignity as she could muster, Amy turned her back on Richard and stared out the window.

Amy stared out the window for quite some time. She stared out the window until there was no sign of the coast in sight. She stared out the window until her neck ached. After an hour, she began to wonder if she would ever be able to move her head again. Beside her, Lord Richard was conversing with Jane in low, pleasant tones. "Compared with the works of Mozart, Herr Beethoven . . ." Jane was saying earnestly. Next to Amy, Richard's voice rumbled in reply, but it was fading . . . fading . . . fading . . . Amy only had time to think, confusedly, how odd that his voice should be so pleasant when he was so very unpleasant himself, before she fell into sleep.

Amy slept through a debate on the merits of the new romantic music and Jane leaning precariously across the coach to tuck a shawl around her sleeping form.

"I'll do it," Richard volunteered as Jane tottered on the edge of her seat. He reached for the shawl, and Jane handed it to him gratefully before sliding back against the velvet squabs. Robbins tended to display his feelings for the French by lurching violently into every pothole he could find, which meant that the coach was swaying from side to side with greater force than the boat in last night's storm.

Richard toppled back into his own seat more hastily than intended and turned toward Amy. She had fallen asleep curled up against the window, one hand under her cheek, and her back rather pointedly towards Richard. With her booted feet dangling an inch or two off the floor, she looked quite tiny and fragile. Funny, she hadn't seemed all that little before. Probably, thought Richard ruefully, because she never stayed still long enough for one to notice. Awake, she exuded enough energy for a whole troupe of Amazons. And packed as furious a punch. Or did he mean a kick? Richard half smiled. He knew the memory of Amy's assault on his foot—and his honor—should anger rather than amuse him, but, for the life of him, he couldn't seem to muster up a decent spurt of indignation. Instead, he found himself squelching down an entirely inappropriate feeling of fondness.

It really was just as well that he would be rid of her in a few hours. Of course, since she was Balcourt's sister, they would be bound to run into each other at the Tuilleries, but with any luck—and it was luck, Richard firmly reminded himself— she'd likely avoid him like the plague. And he could get back to his real job. This whole boat interlude . . . well, necessity made odd bedfellows.

Brusquely, Richard flung the shawl over the sleeping girl.

Amy mumbled something and flopped over. Right into Richard's shoulder.

She must have been very soundly asleep, indeed, because rather than springing away in horror, she nuzzled against the fine wool of Richard's coat. Instinctively, Richard's arm rose to wrap around her shoulders. It was, of course, just a reflex reaction. With a quick, guilty look at Miss Gwen, who, thank goodness, was deep in a book and didn't seem to notice that her charge was snuggled up against a member of the opposite sex, Richard clamped his arm to his side. He had no desire to find himself on the pointy end of Miss Gwen's parasol for improper advances. And how much more infuriating it would be to earn a punctured kidney for half-unconscious improper advances to a girl who wouldn't give him a civil how-do-you-do if she were awake. If he were to get poked by anyone's parasol, it might at least be for something enjoyable. Not that it wasn't rather pleasant having Amy curled up against him.

She was soft, and warm, and smelled nice, too, notwithstanding their bathless night on the boat. Like—Richard gave an experimental sniff—lavender water. Nice. Richard sniffed again.

Thump! Miss Gwen's book slammed shut.

Richard's head jerked up with enough force to make him dizzy.

"Could you kindly contrive to breathe in a more decorous fashion?" Miss Gwen admonished. "I have known sheepdogs with more genteel respiratory habits. Amy! Yes, you!" Amy had begun to stir next to Richard and seemed to be trying very hard to lodge her nose permanently in a fold of his coat.

"What sheep?" murmured Amy into Richard's collarbone. "I detest sheep."

A sound suspiciously like a chuckle emerged from Jane. Miss Gwen reached for her parasol. Richard prepared to dodge, but this time Miss Gwen's instrument of torture had another victim at its tip. One well-placed poke in the ribs, and Amy's eyes fluttered open.

"Whaaa?"

"You are to remove yourself from Lord Richard *at once*."

Her words had far more effect on Amy than the point of the parasol; Amy looked down at Richard's coat, up at his face, and recoiled with such force that she nearly rebounded off the wall of the coach. "I . . . did I . . . oh goodness, I never intended . . ."

Richard plucked a curling brown hair from the wool of his jacket. Holding it out towards Amy, he said gravely, "I believe this belongs to you."

"What? Oh. Um, you may keep it." Amy was busy wedging herself back into the far corner of the seat.

"Most obliged."

Amy looked at him skeptically through bleary eyes and leaned her head against the side of the coach. In front of her, Miss Gwen had resumed reading intently. Amy squinted at the letters on the spine.

"You're reading *The Mysteries of Udolpho*."

"How very clever of you, Amy." Miss Gwen turned a page.

"I didn't think you cared for—that is, I didn't know you read novels."

"I don't." Miss Gwen looked up over the top of the volume that gave the lie to her statement. "There was nothing else to read in the carriage and not all of us care to sleep in public." Looking much more cheerful once she had made her jab at Amy, Miss Gwen continued. "The style of the book is quite arresting, but I find the heroine entirely unsympathetic. Swooning solves nothing."

"You should write your own," suggested Richard. "For the purpose of edifying young females, of course."

Amy's and Richard's eyes met in a moment of pure amusement. Amy started to return Richard's grin when it suddenly hit her that she had just exchanged a significant glance with Lord Richard Selwick. Amy hunched down in her seat, feeling beleaguered.

Good heavens, why couldn't the man leave her be!

Abruptly, she turned her head and stared out the window. Paris couldn't be that much farther, could it?

It could. It was well past teatime, or what would have been teatime had they been back in Shropshire, by the time the coach lurched its way through the gates of the city.

Robbins had slowed down to a pace little faster than a walk, not out of concern for Miss Gwen's sensibilities (despite Miss Gwen's threat after one hairpin turn that unless he slowed down she would take her parasol to him), but because the narrow streets would not permit anything more. Most were missing cobblestones; water and refuse ran in streams down the center of the street, and Amy had to duck back as a rivulet of filth poured from one window to join the muck below. People scurried back and forth through the refuse, occasionally stopping to curse at the carriage. Amy added more colloquialisms to her rapidly growing collection.

"How very French." Miss Gwen conspicuously held a handkerchief to her nose.

"It's not all like this, is it, my lord?" Jane asked Richard in tones of such polite distress that Richard laughed.

"Your cousin's house is in a far nicer neighborhood, I assure you, but, yes, much of Paris is in a sorry state. Bonaparte has grand plans to rebuild, but he hasn't had the time to put his schemes into practice."

"Too busy conquering the world?"

"I'm sure he would be flattered by your summation, Miss Balcourt."

Amy flushed irritably and returned to her window.

Making a sharp turn that nearly sent Miss Gwen's parasol into Richard's ribs, the carriage clattered into the stone courtyard of the Hotel de Balcourt—and stopped abruptly. The drive was blocked by a shabby black carriage; mud splattered its sides, and a shattered lamp hung drunkenly on the side nearer Amy. Several men were occupied in unloading large, brown paper packages tied up with string.

"Why have we stopped?" demanded Miss Gwen.

"A coach is blocking the door," Amy explained. She poked her head back out. "Mr. Robbins, could you please ask them to let us pass? Tell them the vicomte's sister has arrived."

Robbins puffed out his chest. With great enthusiasm, he shouted out in his ungrammatical French that they were all to clear out as the lady of the house had arrived.

One of the workers paused to shout back that there was no lady of the house.

"There is now!" declared Robbins. "Just who do you think that there lady is if she ain't the lady of the 'ouse?"

The worker made an extremely rude suggestion in French. Amy, abruptly remembering that she wasn't supposed to understand the language, opened her eyes wide at Richard and inquired, "What did he say?"

"He voiced his disbelief as to your identity," Richard translated blandly.

Robbins, red-faced with fury, retorted with an inventive blend of French and English invective.

"Really!" exclaimed Miss Gwen, who had caught the English half.

"Really, indeed," echoed Richard, looking quite impressed. That one comment about the reproductive habits of camels had been quite original.

"This is ridiculous!" Amy exclaimed.

"I quite agree." *Thump!* "To refer to an innocent camel in that salacious way—"

"No! Not that! This!" Amy's arm gesture encompassed the stalled carriage, the courtyard, and almost decked Richard on the chin. Richard eyed Amy speculatively but concluded that bodily harm to him had been a by-product, not a goal. "Don't you see? It's ridiculous to remain mewed up in the carriage when we're here already. Why on earth can't we just walk to the door? That's why we have legs, for heaven's sake! I'm going to find Edouard." And with that, Amy unlatched her carriage door and prepared to hop out.

Only to be unceremoniously hauled back into the carriage by the scruff of her skirt.

"Oh no, you don't," said Richard, making up in firmness what he lacked in originality. "You are not going out there."

It was hard to glare at someone when he still had his fist wound in the back of her skirt. Amy yanked irritably away and twisted to face Richard. Much better. Able to glare at him full on, she demanded, "Why not?"

Richard raised a sardonic eyebrow and indicated the courtyard where two other men in varying states of dirt and undress had joined the first in exchanging less than witty repartee with Robbins. Amy hated to admit it, but he had a point.

"But we can't just sit here!"

"I agree. I'll go."

"You'll go?" Amy echoed idiotically. Wait—had Lord Richard just agreed with her?

"I'm the only one who knows what your brother looks like."

"I suppose I can recognize my own brother," Amy muttered, but since she wasn't awfully sure on that point, she muttered it very softly.

It was at that point that the door to the house opened and a portly man with too much lace on his cuffs emerged and began chastising the workers in the courtyard in rapid French, demanding to know the cause of the delay.

Richard swung out of the carriage.

"Ho! Balcourt!"

The man raised his head. Like Richard, his hair had been cut short in the classical style made popular by the Revolution, but this man had a pair of fuzzy sideburns crawling down his face towards his chin. They stretched so far down his face that they touched the absurdly high points of his shirt collar. It was a wonder that he was able to turn his head to look at Richard at all; his shirt points stretched up to his cheeks, and his chin was entirely buried by an exuberant cravat.

A voice emerged from the folds of the cravat. "Selwick? What are you doing here?"

Oh dear, that couldn't be Edouard, could it?

Amy's suspicions were confirmed by Richard's next words.

"I'm delivering your sister, Balcourt. You seem to have misplaced her."

The last time she had seen Edouard, he had been a gawky youth of thirteen, preening in front of the mirror in the gold salon and tripping over his court sword. He had worn his hair in a queue tied with a blue ribbon and dusted over his adolescent spots with powder filched from Mama's boudoir. To her five-year-old eyes, he had seemed impossibly tall. Of course, that might also have owed something to the heels then in fashion. Edouard had been so infuriated when she had sneaked into his room and paraded about in his heels. . . . This man, his puce waistcoat straining across his stomach, his puffy cheeks pinched behind his starched collar—he was a stranger.

But then he looked towards the carriage.

"My sister, you say?"

And all of a sudden, his face took on that exact same look it had worn all those years ago when he had caught Amy with his favorite heels.

"*Edouard*! It *is* you!"

Amy flung herself from the carriage. She stumbled a bit on the uneven cobblestones as she landed, but by dint of waving her arms about managed to keep herself upright. She heard a quickly muffled chuckle from Richard. Amy ignored it, the same way she ignored the bold stares of the French servants and the nasty smell rising from the cobblestones. Grabbing her skirts in both hands, she dashed at her brother. "Edouard! It's me! Amy! I've finally come home!"

Edouard's face—or what one could see of it—wavered between bewilderment and horror.

"Amy? You weren't supposed to arrive until tomorrow!"

Chapter Ten

"Oh, that explains why your coach wasn't there! I knew there had to be a good reason! I was so sure we'd told you we would arrive today—"

"We did," inserted Miss Gwen coldly.

"—but we're here and that's all that matters! Oh, Edouard, I am so glad to see you again!" Amy threw her arms impulsively around her brother.

Edouard patted her rather awkwardly on the back. "Likewise, I'm sure."

"And this is our cousin Jane, who is one of the cleverest, most wonderful people you will ever meet." Amy tugged Edouard across the courtyard towards the carriage. A great deal of tugging was required; Edouard eyed the filth on the cobbles with extreme distaste, mincing in Amy's wake with all the care of a young lady in new white slippers on a rainy day. Richard grinned at the sight. Everyone knew that Edouard de Balcourt had servants run ahead of him to lay wooden planks across the streets so he wouldn't get his fine shoes and stockings dirty. But Amy was a force not to be gainsaid.

"Jane! Jane, this is Edouard!"

Edouard murmured his greetings through the lace-edged handkerchief he had pressed to his nose.

"Are we to sit here all day?" demanded an imperious voice from the carriage.

"Oh, and that's Miss Gwendolyn Meadows, our chaperone and our neighbor in Shropshire. Miss Gwen, do come down and meet my brother, Edouard!"

"I am waiting," pronounced Miss Gwen, "for the carriage to deliver us to the house." Her disembodied voice emerged from the carriage with all the solemnity and terror of the Delphic Oracle.

"Of course, of course!" Recovering from his shock, Edouard scurried across the courtyard and muttered something to the waiting servants. The last brown packages made their way hurriedly into the house and the carriage clattered off through the gates.

Edouard intercepted Richard's curious stare and hastily explained, "I've been redecorating the west wing—finally time to get rid of all that musty stuff my parents left, don't you think? Anyway, it requires a lot of draperies. That's what those were, you know. Draperies." Edouard rubbed his lace handkerchief across his perspiring forehead.

"You haven't changed everything, have you?" Amy asked anxiously as Richard's carriage pulled up to the door.

"No, no. Redecorating takes some time, you know. Mama's room hasn't changed a bit. You can use it as your own if you like."

"May I? Really?"

"Well, yes, if you like." Edouard's tone made quite clear that he couldn't understand why she would, but as older brother would humor younger sister. He tried to exchange one of those male looks of complicity with Richard, but Richard was busy watching Amy.

Amy's eyes were shining as though she had been promised an extra Christmas in July.

Richard's stomach turned over on itself in a sickening lurch. He hadn't experienced anything like this since that time Miles had gotten carried away and whapped him full force in the gut at Gentleman Jackson's. For one brief, insane moment, he wondered what it would be like to have her look at him like that.

Abruptly, Richard turned away and went to hand Jane and Miss Gwen down from the carriage. It seemed safer. Suddenly, he wanted nothing more than to put a safe distance between himself and the Balcourts and all of their connections. They were far, far too distracting. Who the devil did he think he was fooling? There was no *they* about it. It certainly wasn't Edouard de Balcourt who had kept him awake, pounding his pillow, or imperious Miss Gwen, or even levelheaded Jane. *Amy* was far, far too distracting.

Having spent the whole day avoiding him—or as much as one could avoid someone sitting next to one in the confines of a coach—Amy was utterly unprepared for the wave of disappointment that swept over her as she watched Lord Richard flee into his carriage and rapidly clatter out of the courtyard.

Gradually, Amy realized that Edouard was trying to steer her inside, jabbering away all the while. "So nice of Selwick to bring you—watch that step there—I trust you had a good journey?"

Amy pushed all thoughts of Lord Richard to a cupboard in the back of her head emphatically marked DO NOT OPEN. "What does the journey matter now that we're here?" she exclaimed a little too cheerfully. She gave her brother's arm a quick, affectionate squeeze. "Thank you so much for inviting us, Edouard! I've been wanting to come home for the longest time and . . . oh my goodness."

"Isn't it splendid?"

In contemplation of his front hall, Edouard's agitation momentarily ebbed. His waistcoat threatened to explode as he puffed out his chest with pride.

"Incredible might be the better word," Miss Gwen commented sharply.

"It's . . . it's . . ." Amy groped for words. "It's quite the thing, I'm sure," she finished weakly.

Gone was the elegantly appointed foyer of her youth. Only the sweeping marble staircase remained the same. The tapestries and gilded mirrors had been stripped from the walls, the Louis XV tables from their posts on either side of the stairs, and the classical statues from their niches. In their place . . . Amy's eyes bugged out. Was that really a sarcophagus in the corner of the room? Imitation obelisks flanked the entry to the east wing and mock sphinxes guarded the staircase. Unobtrusively, Jane placed a comforting hand on Amy's shoulder.

Edouard beamed, at ease for the first time since Amy had arrived. "*Retour d'Egypte* is all the rage," he said complacently.

Amy stared incredulously about her. "Do we have to answer the sphinx's riddle before we can go upstairs to bed?"

Edouard looked blank. "Are you tired?"

"Don't you remember the story Papa used to tell about—oh, never mind," said Amy. "Are the new draperies also Egyptian in theme?"

"New draperies? Oh. Right. Um, no." Edouard stiffened again. He waddled over to one of his faux sphinxes and began absently stroking its stone head. "Um, Amy, about Mama's room . . ."

"It was so thoughtful of you to offer it to me."

Edouard tugged uncomfortably at his immense cravat. "About that . . . It might be best to wait a week or two before you move to Mama's room. The west wing's rather a mess. Lots of dust and, uh, rats. Yes, definitely rats. So, um, you might not want to go into the west wing at all. Dangerous. And dirty. Very dirty," Edouard stammered.

"If you think it's unsafe . . ."

"Oh, it is! Maid will show you to your rooms—bring you dinner on a tray—theater engagement—must go—good evening!" Edouard shouted for servants, aimed two kisses in the general direction of Amy's cheeks, nearly toppled himself over bowing hastily towards Jane and Miss Gwen, and fled in the direction of the west wing.

"Most odd," commented Miss Gwen.

Amy couldn't help but concur. She would have to inspect the west wing at the first opportunity.

The first opportunity presented itself quite quickly. Miss Gwen, *Mysteries of Udolpho* firmly tucked under one arm, pronounced that she was having an early night and closed the door behind her with an emphatic clack that rattled the vase perched on a table outside her room and caused the footman following them to drop three hatboxes.

From her bedroom door, Amy paused and considered her route. The Hotel de Balcourt had been built, like so many houses of the seventeenth century, in a square around a central courtyard, with the wings sticking out in front just enough to create the small cobblestone courtyard they had driven in through. Once she had figured that out, it was surprisingly easy to make her way towards the west wing. As long as she could see the greenery of the courtyard through the windows to her left, there was no way she could possibly get lost. Amy's own bedroom was on the bit that jutted out to form the stone courtyard. Turning, she retraced her steps along the corridor towards the back of the house, past Jane's and Miss Gwen's rooms, past the closed doors of guest bedrooms, past a narrow servants' stair.

After an age, the hallway finally turned, leading her into

what, she thought, must be the north wing. A half-open door revealed a large suite that could only be Edouard's. A heavy reek of cologne wafted through the doorway. Inside, Edouard's valet hummed a bawdy ballad as he brushed his master's frock coats. Amy tiptoed past very, very quickly.

More closed doors. Amy hadn't realized quite how large the house was; by now, she had counted at least fifteen bedrooms, and she still hadn't reached the west wing. But at bedroom seventeen, the hallway just stopped. Amy put her hands on her hips and advanced on the wall. The simpering shepherdesses in a large tapestry to her left shook their crooks at her and laughed at her perturbation. Amy disregarded them and stared at the plain red wall ahead of her. There had to be another wing there! Bearing in mind Edouard's valet down the hall, she tapped lightly at the red wallpaper. Ouch. Amy nursed her bruised knuckles. The wall was decidedly solid. In fact, she was quite sure that had been stone under the red wallpaper.

Amy wandered back to the window overlooking the central courtyard. Ha! To her right, there was most definitely another set of windows. One was so close that she could probably climb from her current post onto the sill of the other. . . . No. Amy discarded the idea. The courtyard below was elegant and flowering, but the shrubbery did not look like it had been designed to break a fall. There had to be an easier way in.

Of course! On the other side of the hall, the turn had occurred right after the window. Amy gave the immense tapestry another look. The rococo splendor of gazebos and gardens and lovers was really quite out of step with the cool classicism of the rest of the hallway. The red paper with its frieze on the top was designed to suggest Pompeii and ancient pottery. The few paintings scattered along the wall were classical scenes in the style of David, all bold colors, strong lines, and not a garden, gazebo, or lover among the lot.

Yet here the shepherdesses and their swains remained locked in eternal flirtation next to . . . a unicorn? That couldn't be right! What were eighteenth-century lovers doing next to a medieval unicorn hunt? And on the other side of the unicorn hunt, the scene switched again, to a classical tragedy, where a lady in a charred white robe cried out in grief against a relief of burning temples. *Troy,* Amy's mind automatically provided. *Hecuba.* My goodness, it wasn't one tapestry, but three! All hung side by side—and rather clumsily at that, now that she knew what to look for—as if to hide something.

Amy burrowed in the dusty fabric at the point where Patroclus seemed to be pointing his spear at a mangy unicorn. Groping for a door, she practically fell into the room behind the tapestry.

"Papa . . . ," Amy murmured. "Oh, Mama . . ."

Amy stumbled into her parents' suite, dizzy with memory. There were no dust sheets. Under a gray film of disuse, everything had been left exactly as it was fifteen years before when she and Mama departed for England, leaving Edouard and Papa behind. Her mother's writing case lay open on her escritoire, the ink dry and caked at the bottom of the well. In her father's dressing room, Papa's wigs still perched in a row on their stands. Amy clenched her eyes shut, fighting off waves of recollection. Any moment now, Mama would scoop her up, and . . .

Amy could understand why Edouard had closed off their parents' rooms.

Steeling herself, she followed the small spiral staircase down from her father's study to the floor below. The boards creaked slightly under her slippers, but they held her weight. She was in what had once been the library, before the Revolution had intervened. The dusty books called to her—through the grime, Amy could see the works of Homer in Greek, and a whole shelf of Latin works in elegantly tooled bindings. They could only have been Papa's—Papa, who used to snuggle her in his lap in Mama's sitting room and tell her fabulous tales of centaurs and heroes and maidens turned into trees.

Amy scrubbed furiously at her damp cheeks and hurried into the next room. Papa's books would have to wait for another time; now her mission was to explore the west wing before Edouard returned.

Why, this was the ballroom! All of the furniture, a series of elegant couches and chairs, was pushed to the sides of the room, clearing the center of the floor for dancing. The immense room stretched most of the length of the wing, and had a series of French doors opening onto the flowering courtyard on one side. At least Amy assumed they opened onto the courtyard. The glass was opaque with fifteen years' filth. Squinting in the darkness, Amy wished she had thought to bring a candle. Along the walls, cobwebs draped candle sconces like lace, and spiders swayed inside their creations to the tunes of music only they could hear. At the very end of the room was a little raised area, which the musicians must once have occupied. It still contained a harpsichord, a harp—and a pile of brown-paper packages.

Amy crossed the room at a run, slipping and skidding on the parquet floor.

Those were the mysterious packages! And there were others, too: big wooden crates of all sizes stacked against the wall, next to more and more of the floppy paper parcels. Amy's imagination thundered away like post-horses pounding down the Calais road. Draperies, ha! More likely disguises for the League of the Purple Gentian!

She ached to rip into the paper, but she forced herself to painstakingly unpick the knot of one of the packages. Finally, the last strand gave way and the parcel fell open in Amy's lap.

It was white muslin.

Amy stared stupidly at the cloth flowing over the dusty lap of her dress. It was nothing but yards and yards of white India muslin.

Of course! Amy's face brightened. There must be pistols . . . or epées . . . or masks . . . hidden among the folds of the cloth! How very clever to wrap them in cloth in case they were intercepted!

Amy scrabbled through the material. There was nothing hidden within the India muslin except more India muslin.

Disappointed and perplexed, Amy settled back on her heels.

Ah, but there were still the crates to be examined! Amy fell eagerly upon one of the wooden boxes, tugging at the lid. Three splinters and one lost fingernail later, the crate remained obdurate. Whoever had hammered the lid shut had not stinted on nails.

"Drat!" Amy kicked the crate with one booted foot. The contents made an interesting swishing noise.

Intrigued, Amy knelt on the ground, grabbed the crate, and tried to shake. It was too heavy for her to do more than rock it slightly, but she could hear whatever was inside shifting. Something fine, like a leaf or a powder.

Gunpowder.

Amy staggered to her feet, clutching the lid of the crate.

There had to be something she could use to pry that lid off, a stick or a poker. Or, maybe, if she knocked the crate over, she could jar the lid off. That struck Amy as infinitely preferable to leaving the crate to search for a poker. Kneeling, Amy wedged her fingers under the edge of the crate, ignoring the abrasion of wood against her palms. She heaved. The box tottered right back into place. Gritting her teeth, Amy wiggled her fingers back under the box, and heaved again.

The box toppled over onto the parquet floor with a tremendous crash. Lid intact.

Hands on her hips, Amy glowered at the crate. She would have to find a poker.

That was when Amy heard the sound. It was half a breath, half a groan. Like the sigh of a spirit in torment. A frisson of terror quivered through Amy. Oh, for heaven's sake! She didn't believe in ghosts. Muttering to herself in annoyance, Amy tottered towards the edge of the ballroom. It was more likely wind she had heard. A house of this age nearly always had drafts. Or rats. Ugh. Amy didn't like to think of herself as squeamish, but she could definitely do without rats. Pulling her skirts close to her ankles, she peered along the floorboards on either side of the room.

Someone had left a boot dangling off the edge of a sofa. With a leg still inside it.

On a sofa by the wall, under a portrait of Mme de la Vallière, lay a sleeping man with a bloody bandage wrapped around his brow.

Chapter Eleven

"Jane! You'll never believe what I found!"

Racing into Jane's room without knocking, Amy slammed the door behind her and collapsed panting against the doorframe.

"Two skeletons, three ghosts, and a lunatic in the attic?" Jane suggested absently.

"A wounded man!"

"What?" Jane dropped the heavy tome she had been reading into her lap. "Oh dear, now I've lost my page. Amy, a servant with a scratched finger does not count as a wounded man."

"Very funny. He had a bandage wrapped around his head, and—do you have smelling salts?"

"I do have smelling salts, but why do you need . . . ?" Jane put her book down on the coverlet next to her and fixed confused eyes on her cousin.

"Well, I wanted to wake him up to question him, but I didn't want to shake him, because heaven only knows what that would do to a man with a head injury—oh, we don't have time for this, Jane! We have to go back to the west wing!"

"It doesn't sound as if he'll be going anywhere," said Jane mildly, searching in her reticule. She held up a small, green glass vial. "What were you planning to ask him?"

Practically dancing with impatience, Amy yanked her cousin out the door. "Where the Purple Gentian is, of course!"

"What makes you think . . . ?" Jane began, but Amy was muttering to herself about shorter ways to the west wing.

"If we go down the front stairs and to our right . . ." Amy suited action to words, running towards the stairs. Jane caught her hand.

"We'll be less conspicuous if we walk."

Amy cast her cousin an agonized glance, but admitted the wisdom of her words. She had been fortunate enough not to see any servants on her hectic flight back from the west wing, but the odds of escaping the staff twice were slim. Wait—she had seen Edouard's valet, who had been emerging from her brother's room with a pile of crumpled linen in his arms. Oh well, if he told Edouard, she could always explain that she had been looking at the tapestries when a rat jumped out at her, or something like that.

They descended the stairs at a sedate pace that made Amy dig her fingernails into her palms with impatience. At the base of the stairs, they checked quickly for servants. Although the candles were still lit in the foyer, nobody seemed to be about. To their left lay the rooms of the east wing, to their right, a seeming dead end.

Now that Amy knew what she was looking for, the entrance to the west wing was as clearly marked as though someone had slapped a sign on it. Edouard had hung yet another tapestry, this time one depicting the rape of Lucrece. As the entrance downstairs was more prominent than the one upstairs, Edouard had taken an extra precaution. In front of the tapestry, he had placed a bust of Julius Caesar on a marble pedestal.

Tense with excitement, Amy pointed towards Julius. "There. That's the entrance."

Jane picked up a small candelabrum from a marble chest designed to look like a sarcophagus. "Shall we?"

Together, they lifted the heavy tapestry high enough to clear the candles and slipped underneath. They found themselves in an anteroom, a pretty little chamber with gilded walls and dainty chairs that looked as though they would collapse if anyone so much as looked at them. The antechamber led into a music room, complete with a large pianoforte, painted with scenes of pastoral merriment. Jane looked longingly at the yellowed keys, but Amy hurried her onwards into the ballroom. At first, Jane couldn't see anything at all. Her vision was entirely blocked by piles and piles of brown paper packages.

"There wasn't anything interesting in them," Amy whispered as they skirted around the piles. "Just muslin."

"What an odd place to keep muslin."

"Maybe they ran out of space in the airing cupboard. My wounded man is just down there, on the sofa underneath Mme de la Vallière." Amy took the candelabrum from Jane and hurried forward. "I couldn't get the lids off the crates, but I think—" Amy broke off as she brandished the flames above the sofa to illuminate . . . absolutely nothing.

"Where is he?" In her agitation, Amy forgot to whisper. She waved the candles about, peering under the sofa, running to the next sofa and the next. "I know he was right there! Right under Mme de la Vallière . . . He was fast asleep!"

"Amy . . ."

Amy whirled around to face Jane, flames swirling with her in a diabolical sort of halo. "Please, please don't tell me I must have imagined him, Jane. I *know* I saw him!"

"I wasn't going to," Jane said gravely. "Bring the candle over here."

Complying, Amy followed Jane's gaze. Against the faded white silk of the couch burned a streak of fresh blood.

Jane experimentally reached out a finger. "He can't have been moved more than a few minutes ago. It's still wet."

"But who moved him? And where?" Amy swiveled with the candle as though the malefactors might be hiding in the corners of the room.

"They likely took him out through the French doors into the courtyard," Jane said thoughtfully.

Amy raced to the nearest door and pulled it open. For something so begrimed with age, it opened without a squeak.

"It's been newly oiled," commented Jane under her breath.

Thrusting the candles at Jane, Amy dashed down a shallow flight of three steps and out into the garden while Jane examined the doors. It hadn't rained recently, so the earth wasn't damp enough to hold footprints, nor was there mud to track along the stone paths. And there were doors, doors, doors on three sides. Doors into the east wing, the north wing, the west wing. Far too many doors. The man could have been carried through any one of them. Amy prowled the perimeter of the garden, peering through door after door. Unlike the windows and French doors to the west wing, the ones to the east and north were well scrubbed. Amy peered in turn into two drawing rooms, another music room, a breakfast room, and an immense state dining room that took up a large portion of the north wing.

"Amy." Jane was whispering at her shoulder, the candles in her hand casting odd shadows on the stone of the balustrade. "Come back, I want to show you something."

"They must have taken him out through one of these rooms."

Jane considered. "And then downstairs through the servants' quarters? I think you may have lost your wounded man, Amy." They were making their way around the garden back to the ballroom doors. Jane paused next to an armless statue of Aphrodite. "None of this explains why he was lying in the ballroom with . . . what kind of wound was it?"

"On his head." Amy gestured to her own head to demonstrate where. "I couldn't tell exactly what it was since it was bandaged, but there seemed to be some sort of gash on the left side of his head, or at least that's where the blood was on the bandage."

"He could," Jane commented slowly, "have simply hit his head on something while unloading those packages from the carriage. There might be as simple an explanation as that."

"Then why all the subterfuge? Why hide him in the ballroom and then whisk him away again?" A breeze whipped Amy's dark curls into her face and she hastily pushed them out of her way.

"He could have felt better and left."

"*Really,* Jane!" The warmth had departed with the sun, and Amy shuddered in the twilight chill, feeling the evening breeze pierce the thin fabric of her frock. "Can you really believe that?"

Jane leaned briefly against Aphrodite, looking perturbed. She finally straightened up and made a face at Amy. "No, I can't. Come with me and I'll show you why."

Amy hurried with her cousin back to the ballroom, where Jane paused just within the entrance.

"Yes?" Amy prompted Jane, who had a regrettable habit of thinking things through before acting on them.

"Look at this." Jane indicated the door.

"It's dirty?"

"That's just it. It's too dirty. It looks like someone deliberately took garden dirt and smeared it along the glass. See? Here and here? It's too thick and too uniform to be merely dust and age. It's as if . . ."

". . . someone didn't want anyone seeing in!" Amy finished

for her excitedly. Jane quickly moved the candles aside as
Amy leaned in to peer at the dirt on the doors, her short curls
swinging recklessly close to the flames.

Jane nodded. "That's just it. But why? What does Edouard
have to hide?"

Amy shut the door with a decisive click, and beamed at her
cousin. "But, Jane, that's obvious. Don't you see? It's proof
that he's in league with the Purple Gentian!"

The Purple Gentian swung down from his carriage in the
courtyard of his own modest bachelor residence—only five
bedrooms and a small staff of ten servants, not counting his
valet, cook, and coachman—with a heartfelt sigh of relief.

"Zounds, Geoff, it's good to be back," he announced to the
slender man in waistcoat and shirtsleeves who waited by the
door.

"After your dangerous mission into the heart of London
society?" his second-oldest friend responded with the quiet
humor that had drawn Geoff into Richard and Miles's circle
at Eton.

"Don't mock," Richard chided, pulling off his hat and
scrubbing one hand through his hair. "I only just made it out
of there alive."

Having displayed their decades of affection by a brisk
handshake, Richard surged into the foyer and began dropping
his hat, cloak, and gloves on any surfaces that presented themselves. His butler, Stiles, cast his eyes up to the ceiling as he
followed in Richard's wake, gathering up gloves from the
floor, cloak from a chair, and hat from the doorknob.

"Will that be all, my lord?" Stiles inquired in the afflicted
tones of King Lear.

"Could you see what Cook can rummage up for me? I'm
famished."

"As you wish, my lord," Stiles intoned, looking, if possible,
even more pained than before, and hobbled his way out in the
direction of the kitchen.

"He does make a convincing octogenarian," Richard commented to Geoff as they headed for the dining room in the
optimistic anticipation that food would rapidly be forthcoming. "Hell, if I didn't know better, *I* would be fooled."

Geoff darted into the study and emerged shuffling a stack
of papers. "You're not the only one he's fooled. I gave him last

Saturday off, thinking he would wash the gray out of his hair, do the rounds of the taverns, what have you. Instead, he pulled up a chair before the kitchen fire, threw an afghan around his shoulders, and complained about his lumbago."

The two friends exchanged looks of mingled amusement and distress.

"Well, good butlers are hard to find . . . ," commented Richard.

"And Stiles will be with you for a great many decades to come," concluded Geoff.

"That's the last time we accept an out-of-work actor into the League," groaned Richard. "I suppose it could have been worse—he could have had delusions of being Julius Caesar and gone about in a toga."

"He would have fit right in with the members of the Council of Five Hundred," Geoff commented wryly, referring to the legislative body set up by the revolutionaries in 1795 in an attempt to imitate classical models of government. "About half of them were convinced they were Brutus."

Richard shook his head sadly. "They read too many classics; such men are dangerous. At any rate, I prefer Stiles's current delusion. I take it, as matters stand, that he hasn't lost all track of why he's really here?"

"If anything, he's entered into it with even more gusto ever since he decided that he really *is* an eighty-year-old butler. He plays cards with Fouché's butler every Wednesday—apparently they exchange remedies for their rheumatism and complain about the poor quality of employers nowadays," Geoff added with a twinkle in his eye. "And he's been carrying on a rather bizarre—if informative—flirtation with one of the upstairs maids at the Tuilleries."

"Bizarre?" Richard sniffed hopefully as he entered the dining room, but comestibles had not preceded them.

Geoff pulled out a chair towards the head of the table and sent the pile of papers he had been holding scooting across the polished wood towards Richard. "He attained her good graces by complimenting her special formula for silver polish. They then proceeded to the intimacies of cleaning crystal."

"Good God." Richard began riffling through the stack of correspondence that had accumulated in his absence. "To each his own, I suppose."

The pile Geoff had brought him contained the usual

accumulations—reports from his estate manager, invitations to balls, and perfumed letters from Bonaparte's promiscuous sister Pauline. Pauline had been trying to entice Richard into her bed since he had returned from Egypt, and the amount of perfume she poured on her letters increased with each failed attempt. Richard could smell the latest all the way from the bottom of the pile.

"How was London?" Geoff asked, signaling to a footman to fetch the claret decanter. "You look like you're in need of a restorative."

"You don't know the half of it." Richard abandoned his letters and flung himself into a chair across the table from Geoff. "Mother must have dragged me to every major gathering in London. If there was an affair of over three hundred people, I was there. I attended enough musicals to render me tone deaf, if not deaf in actuality. I—"

"No more, please," Geoff shook his head. "I refuse to believe that it could have all been that bad."

"Oh, really?" Richard raised one brow. He shot his friend a swift, sideways glance. "Mary Alsworthy asked after you."

"And?" Geoff's voice was studiedly unconcerned.

"I told her you had taken up with a Frenchwoman of ill repute and were currently expecting your third illegitimate child. By the way, you're hoping for a girl this time."

Geoff choked on his claret. "You didn't. I'm sure I would have heard from my mother by now if you had."

Richard tipped his chair back with a sigh of pure regret. "No, I didn't. But I wanted to. It would have been informative to see if she could count high enough to realize three children in less than two years was an impossibility."

Geoff looked away, displaying a deep interest in the arrangement of silver on the sideboard behind Richard. "There were a number of interesting developments while you were away."

Richard let the subject drop. With any luck, by the time Geoff returned to England some other poor blighter would have fallen prey to Mary Alsworthy's overused lures.

Richard leaned across the table, green eyes glittering. "What sort of developments?"

Geoff regaled him with tales of changes in security at the Ministry of Police ("Rather a case of closing the stable door once the horses have fled, don't you think?" remarked Richard smugly), the frustrated ambitions of Napoleon's brother-in-law Murat ("A weak-willed man, if ever I saw one," commented Geoff. "He may be of use to us yet."), and strange goings-on along the coast.

Richard's ears pricked up. "Do you think he could be shipping munitions in for the invasion of England?" There was no need to ask whom Richard meant by "he."

"That's still unclear. We haven't been able to get anyone close enough to see what's being transported. Our connection in Calais—"

"The innkeeper at the Sign of the Scratching Cat?"

"The very one. He's noticed an unusual amount of activity over the past few months. The serving wench at the Drowned Rat in Le Havre has similar reports. She says she saw a group of men transferring a series of large packages from a Channel packet to an unmarked carriage, and taking off down the road towards Paris."

"Could it be just the usual smuggling activity?" Richard nodded his thanks as the footman set a bowl of potato-and-leek soup down before him, trying to quell the anticipation thrilling through him at Geoff's news. He felt like a hound eager to bounce off after a fox. Of course, he had better make jolly sure first that it was a fox, and not just a rabbit, or a bunch of waving leaves. Or something like that. Richard rapidly abandoned the metaphor. Ever since war had broken out between England and France, the smugglers of both countries had done a brisk trade, hauling French brandies and silks to England, and returning laden with English goods. There had been one or two occasions in the past where Richard had gone haring off into the night, convinced he was on the trail of French agents carrying valuable intelligence to England, only to wind up with a boat full of disgruntled French smugglers and ten-year-old brandy. Not that Richard minded the brandy, but still. . . .

"There is that," Geoff conceded. "But Stiles heard from Fouché's butler that the Ministry of Police has been very quietly detailing men to guard shipments of something coming in from Switzerland. He wasn't sure what, and he didn't know when—at least not yet—but he did say that it was top priority, whatever it was."

"That does sound promising, if somewhat vague. I take it you've had someone watching the major roads and waterways?"

"I will ignore the implicit insult," Geoff said calmly. "Yes, I have. In addition to another three cases of brandy in the cellar, we also have a few leads. Whatever these shipments are, Georges Marston is up to his neck in it."

Richard's lip curled in distaste. "Why does that come as no surprise?" he inquired of the portrait on the wall behind Geoff's head.

The portrait, presumably an ancestor of the former owner of the house, which Richard had purchased furnished, sneered silently. One might assume that the gentleman in the portrait would have turned up his nose at the likes of Marston, even had he been able to speak. While Marston claimed a relation with a distinguished English family through his father, it was an open secret that he had been raised by his French mother in circumstances that could hardly be called respectable. Having wrangled his father's family into buying him a commission in the English army, he had promptly deserted in the midst of battle and decamped to the French.

"Marston has been frequenting the docks," Geoff continued. "I've had our boys watching him. We've noticed a pattern—every few days, someone will come to his lodgings with a note, and then he hares off in a carriage to the waterfront."

"Then what? Oh, devil take it!" Richard mopped at his lap, where a little puddle of soup was collecting from the spoon that he had suspended halfway to his lips.

"Not the devil, Marston," Geoff corrected with a twitch of his lips. "I hope those weren't new trousers?"

Richard scowled.

"At any rate," Geoff went on, "he always takes an unmarked black coach and four—"

"I thought he only had that flashy curricle of his." Richard made sure to put his soup spoon down before speaking. "That hideous bright red thing."

"It wouldn't be at all bad if it weren't for the color," commented Geoff wistfully.

"Marston?" Richard prompted.

"Right." Geoff shook himself out of his reverie of curricles and phaetons. "The use of the carriage heightened our suspicions. We traced it to a livery stable not far from Marston's lodgings."

"The curricle would be too noticeable," mused Richard.

Seeing the gleam of the carriage lover rekindle in Geoff's eye, Richard hastily asked, "What does he do once at the docks?"

"Cleverly disguised as a sailor, I followed Marston to a rather disreputable tavern called the Staves and Cutlass. They named it that for good reason, I might add," Geoff commented thoughtfully. "It was quite a good thing that I was wearing a hook."

"And there I was with the debutantes while you were having all the fun," mourned Richard.

"Calling it *fun* might be stretching matters a bit. When I wasn't otherwise occupied in retaining my skin in one piece, I did notice Marston first engage in conversation with a bunch of ruffians, and then slip into a back room. When he didn't return, I left the establishment just in time to see Marston and his cronies finish loading the carriage with a number of brown paper packages."

"What were they?"

Geoff cast Richard a mildly exasperated look. "If we knew that, why would we still be following him? However, I can tell you that at least some of the shipments have made their way to the Hotel de Balcourt."

"Balcourt?"

"You know, little toady of a man, always hanging about the Tuilleries," Geoff clarified.

"I know who you mean," Richard said through a mouthful of soup. Swallowing, he explained, "It's just a devilish odd coincidence. I shared a boat—and a carriage—with Balcourt's sister and cousin."

"I didn't realize he had a sister."

"Well, he does." Richard abruptly pushed away his empty bowl.

"What a great stroke of luck! Could you use the acquaintance with the sister to discover more about Balcourt's activities?"

"That," Richard said grimly, "is not an option."

Geoff eyed him quizzically. "I realize that any sister of Balcourt's is most likely repugnant at best, but you don't need to propose to the girl. Just flirt with her a bit. Take her for a drive, call on her at home, use her as an entrée into the house. You've done it before."

"Miss Balcourt is not repugnant." Richard twisted in his chair, and stared at the door. "What the devil is keeping supper?"

Geoff leaned across the table. "Well, if she's not repugnant, then what's the—ah."

"Ah? Ah? What the deuce do you mean by 'ah'? Of all the nonsensical . . ."

"You"—Geoff pointed at him with fiendish glee—"are unsettled not because you find her repugnant, but because you find her *not* repugnant."

Richard was about to deliver a baleful look in lieu of a response, when he was saved by the arrival of the footman bearing a large platter of something covered with sauce. Richard leaned forward and speared what looked like it might once have been part of a chicken, as the footman whisked off with his soup dish.

"Have some," Richard suggested to Geoff, ever so subtly diverting the conversation to culinary appreciation.

"Thank you." Undiverted, Geoff continued, "Tell me about your Miss Balcourt."

"Leaving aside the fact that she is by no means *my* Miss Balcourt"—Richard ignored the sardonic stare coming from across the table—"the girl is as complete an opposite to her brother as you can imagine. She was raised in England, somewhere out in the countryside. She's read Homer in the original Greek—"

"This *is* serious," murmured Geoff. "Is she comely?"

"Comely?"

"You know, nice hair, nice eyes, nice . . ." Geoff made a gesture that Richard would have expected more readily from Miles.

"She doesn't look like her brother, if that's what you're asking," Richard bit out.

Geoff slapped the table. "But if you're taken with her, that's wonderful!" His lips twitched. "You can court her *and* investigate her brother at the same time."

Richard gave the napkin he had just lifted to his lips an irritable twitch. "No, I cannot. First of all, you know that I will never again allow my personal life to interfere with a mission. And secondly . . . secondly," he repeated more loudly, as Geoff opened his mouth to protest, "did I forget to mention that she hates me?"

"That's quick work. How did you get her to hate you in all of one day?"

"It was a day and a half."

Something between a snort and a snicker escaped Geoff's lips.

"Easy for you to laugh," retorted Richard.

"No arguing with that," chuckled Geoff. "No, really, what did you do?"

Richard planted his elbows on the polished wood of the table. "I told her I worked for Bonaparte."

"And that was all?"

Richard's lips quirked. "She's rather passionate on the subject of the Revolution."

"Then why is she—"

"I know, I know. I asked her the same thing."

"And you won't tell her—"

"No!" Richard pushed back from the table so hard that the legs of his chair nearly splintered.

"You could let me finish a sentence once in a while, you know," Geoff said mildly.

"Sorry," Richard muttered.

Geoff took advantage of Richard's momentary silence to say, "I'm not suggesting you go shouting your identity to every comely young lady who wanders your way. But if this one is special, wouldn't it be better to take the chance of confiding in her—in a limited way," he added hastily, "than risk losing her? If she's so fanatical about the Revolution, it seems rather unlikely that she would betray you."

Richard was mustering his objections when Geoff silenced him again with the softly spoken words, "Not every woman is as shallow as Deirdre."

Richard pressed his lips together. "You sound like my mother."

"Since I like your mother, I'll take that as a compliment, and not as the insult for which it was intended." Geoff leaned both elbows on the table. "In some ways, it was a fortunate escape for you."

"But not for Tony."

"You can't go on blaming yourself for Tony's death. Good gad, the odds of something like that happening were nonexistent! It was an accident, Richard, a foolish, unfortunate accident."

"It would never have happened if infatuation hadn't impeded my judgment."

Richard remembered the nervous anticipation he had felt

each time he galloped over to call on Deirdre, the way the heady scent of her perfume made his pulse race and his head spin. Funny, he couldn't remember exactly what she looked like. He had once written a sonnet to her blue, blue eyes, but he could recall the sonnet, with its limping meter and forced rhymes, far better than he could the eyes themselves. And yet this fuzzy image of a woman, so utterly unmemorable now, had exercised a strong enough effect on him to make him completely forget his obligations. Let this be a lesson to you, he advised himself. Passion was fleeting; dishonor lingered. *Sic transit* . . . well, everything.

Richard tried to think of a more fitting Latin tag, but couldn't. Amy would probably . . . Richard quelled that counterproductive thought before it could go any further.

Geoff poured himself a second cup of claret. "Besides, as hideously as the business with Deirdre ended, she wasn't malicious, just henwitted. It was pure ill luck that her maid happened to be a French operative."

Richard closed his eyes and pressed the heel of his hand hard against his forehead. "So it wasn't Deirdre, it was her bloody French maid who was the spy. That didn't make any difference to Tony."

"It exonerated her of ill intent."

"But not me of idiocy." Richard's green eyes darkened with remembered pain. "Don't you see? That makes it that much worse. A chance word to her maid while she was fixing her hair—her damned hair!—and Tony's life was forfeit. Say I tell Amy . . ."

"So that's her name."

"And Amy makes some comment—in strictest secrecy, because, of course, these things are always passed along in strictest secrecy," Richard spat out, "to her cousin Jane. Jane's a discreet sort of girl; she might not repeat it. But the house is teeming with servants. Even if they don't have a bloody lady's maid in the room with them, there's bound to be a footman lurking somewhere about. And then there's Balcourt himself, who may or may not be on Bonaparte's payroll, but who would do anything to ingratiate himself to him. How long would the League of the Purple Gentian last if my identity were to become known to him? I give it the time it would take for him to call his carriage and waddle his way to the consul's study." Richard raised his wineglass in an ironic salute. "Farewell, Purple Gentian."

"That's only the very worst case."

Richard's lips twisted in a humorless smile. "Isn't that what we ought to plan for then? I can't risk it, Geoff. Even if there weren't other impediments, I couldn't risk it. Too many people depend on me."

Geoff looked at him steadily, a friend of too long standing to be daunted by either irony or idealism. "You know what Miles would tell you if he were here. He'd say, 'You're being too bloody noble.' And, in this instance, he'd be right."

Breaking Geoff's gaze, Richard lounged back in his chair and changed the subject. "Did anything else thrilling transpire while I was away? Like Delaroche choking on a chicken bone?"

Geoff pushed aside the remains of his own cold chicken. "Delaroche, I regret to inform you, is still alive and kicking. I must say, the man does have an instinct for theater. He strode into the Tuilleries the other day and informed Bonaparte that, as the Purple Gentian hadn't struck for over a fortnight, it was clear that he, Delaroche, had scared him away."

"That will never do," Richard drawled. He rocked back and forth in his chair, a devilish gleam creeping into his emerald eyes. "After all, it would be deuced unkind of us to let the man continue to entertain these delusions, wouldn't you say?"

Geoff hunched forward, his own eyes taking on an answering sheen. "What do you think one might do to disabuse him of these unhealthy fantasies?"

"Well . . ." Richard toyed with the stem of his wineglass, admiring the way the candlelight struck crimson glints off the dark liquid. "One might raid his secret files . . . but one has done that already, so what's the fun in that?"

"Or," Geoff mused, getting into the spirit of the game, "one might leave mocking notes on his pillow, but . . ."

"One has done that already, too," Richard concluded sadly. "Does Delaroche have any files we haven't looked at yet?"

Geoff shook his head. "No. I'd say you made a rather thorough job of that. How about rescuing someone from the Temple prison? We haven't done that in a while, and it's sure to infuriate Delaroche."

"The very thing!" Richard rocked upright so fast that he banged into the table, setting dishes and cutlery jumping. "I knew I kept you around for a reason!"

Geoff grimaced. "You flatter me."

"Think nothing of it," Richard advised him graciously. "Young Falconstone *has* been imposing on the hospitality of the Bastille for far too long. We wouldn't want to overstrain their supplies."

"The moldy bread and moldier water?"

"Don't forget the occasional rat as a treat on holidays. I'm sure the French consider it a great delicacy. Like frogs, or cow's brains."

Geoff groaned. "No wonder they had a revolution! They were probably all suffering from chronic indigestion."

"There may be something in that theory." Richard pushed back from the table and stood. "But let's save writing your *History of the Causes of the French Revolution* for another night. We have far more diverting activities ahead of us. . . ."

Chapter Twelve

In a little room in the Ministry of Police, a man stood looking out the window. His hands were clasped loosely behind his back, fingers and arms relaxed. The hair combed forward on his forehead in the classical style gave him the serene air of a bust of a Roman senator, a man of calm and *gravitas*. But when he spoke, his voice shook with controlled rage.

"This has gone on too long, Delaroche. Bonaparte is displeased. *I* am displeased. This man cannot be allowed to make us the laughingstock of Europe." The Minister of Police slowly turned and fixed icy eyes on his subordinate. "What do you intend to do about it?"

"Kill him."

A whir of movement, and a silver-handled letter opener quivered as if in fear, its point embedded in the blotter of Delaroche's desk. The sentry at the door cringed back, but Fouché regarded the palpitating knife with a jaundiced eye. "That's all very well, but you have to find him first, do you not? How many years has it been, Delaroche? Four? Five?"

"He won't live to see another." Delaroche's sallow countenance burned with the fanatic fervor of a sixteenth-century inquisitor. "I'll draw up a short list of suspects. My best men will shadow them day and night. They won't so much as piss but we'll know of it! He will *not* slip through my fingers again. I'll have him strung up before you within the month." Delaroche's lips curled into a feral snarl.

"See that you do," Fouché said coolly. "The invasion of England relies on the strictest secrecy. We cannot afford any more breaches of security."

Reaching over, he retrieved his hat from the corner of Delaroche's desk. "We can only hope that the papers have not yet gotten wind of this latest embarrassment. I suggest you hold to your promise, or the Purple Gentian may not be the only man to swing. Good day, Delaroche."

The door clicked smartly shut behind the Minister of Police.

Delaroche stalked over to his desk, flipped back the tails of his coat, and sat down heavily. On the blotter, where Fouché had tossed it upon his entrance, lay a small, cream-colored card.

Fingers steepled in front of him, Delaroche stared at the note. The card itself was useless. Delaroche had an entire drawer full of nothing but cream-colored cards bearing the Gentian's distinctive purple stamp. He had long ago traced the cards to a very exclusive stationer in London which boasted a wide clientele among the *ton*. If Delaroche were to go on the make of the paper alone, he could easily accuse anyone from the Prince of Wales to Lady Mary Wortley Montague. Inside—Delaroche did not need to release the card from the letter opener to look; he recalled the contents in painful detail—inside, that rogue had inscribed a bill for the accommodations. One shilling for stale bread, one shilling for rank water, two shillings for rats, three shillings for amusing insults from the guards, and so on, before signing it with the customary small purple flower. On top of the note had been a small pile of English coins, as per the reckoning.

Damn him! The list was in Falconstone's hand—Delaroche knew the handwriting of every man whose correspondence he had ever intercepted. Delaroche could picture the Gentian standing there, dictating, in the middle of the most carefully guarded prison in Paris. The man's cheek was unbelievable.

Which would make killing him all the sweeter.

Reaching into a desk drawer, Delaroche retrieved a plain sheet of writing paper. He dabbed a quill savagely into the inkpot, wishing it were a knife plunging into the Gentian's heart. He would have that pleasure soon enough. The man had played him for a fool one too many times. Delaroche had enjoyed the game; he would be the last to deny that. He had enjoyed the excitement of an adversary worthy of his attention—most of these would-be spies were pitifully easy to discover, and even more pitifully easy to coerce into full disclosure. A few fingernails pulled and they babbled like babes. Pathetic.

Attacking the paper with an explosion of inkblots, Delaroche scrawled the first name on his list: Sir Percy Blakeney, Baronet.

The Gentian had to be an Englishman, of that Delaroche was sure. Only an Englishman would have such an utterly inappropriate sense of humor. Who else but an Englishman would disguise himself as a dancing bear or leave itemized payment for a jailer? Those English! Didn't they realize that espionage was no laughing matter?

During his time as the Scarlet Pimpernel, Sir Percy had played similar jokes on the French government. He still spent large parts of each year in Paris with his French wife. He was even now in residence in his town house in the Faubourg St. Germain. He was, of course, kept under close surveillance, but hadn't the Scarlet Pimpernel eluded the closest of surveillance before? Bonaparte insisted that Sir Percy was harmless, a serpent whose fangs had been drawn. Bonaparte found him amusing. Delaroche found him highly suspect. Like the London news sheets, he had always retained a nagging suspicion that Sir Percy had changed only his *nom de guerre,* not his spots.

Delaroche returned to his list. Unlike the London news sheets, he did not proceed to name Beau Brummel (after an unpleasant encounter with the man in London, Delaroche had concluded that Brummel was, indeed, quite that interested in fashion). Instead, Delaroche penned the name Georges Marston.

Marston's comings and goings from the docks had not escaped the notice of the Assistant to the Minister of Police. Marston claimed the call of his French blood drew him back to the service of his homeland. Others claimed it had been the stronger siren call of higher pay. Delaroche considered a third explanation. How easy it would be for a man to claim a change of allegiance, infiltrate the highest reaches of government . . . all the while reporting to his former masters.

Marston had used his acquaintance with that idiot brother-in-law of the consul's, Joachim Murat, to propel himself into the inner circles at the Tuilleries. The friendship, Delaroche gathered, had been founded on a basis of imbibing, gaming, and wenching. Delaroche himself had no use for such pastimes. He had heard, however, that they provided an excellent pretense under which to gather intelligence.

Delaroche's nostrils flared scornfully. Amateurs!

For a moment, Delaroche toyed with the delicious notion of subverting the Purple Gentian to Bonaparte's cause. Georges Marston was a soldier of fortune. If he were the

Purple Gentian, one need only find out what the British were paying him and double it. Throw in a commission in the French army—colonel, perhaps?—marry him off to one of Mme Bonaparte's ladies-in-waiting, and Marston would be theirs for life. What a coup that would be! PURPLE GENTIAN DESERTS TO BONAPARTE the headlines on those despicable English news sheets would read.

Such an outcome might almost be more pleasurable than killing him. Delaroche caressed the blade of the letter opener with one scarred finger. Almost.

Ah, well, one could always subvert the man, enjoy the embarrassment of the English for a few weeks, and then arrange for a little accident to befall the newest colonel in Bonaparte's forces.

Regretfully putting aside the knife with one last, loving caress, Delaroche penned a third name, jotting the characters tersely onto the page: Edouard de Balcourt.

Underneath his thoroughly French name, Balcourt was half English. It had not escaped the attention of the Ministry of Police that Balcourt had been sending couriers into England over the years under the pretense of letters to his sister. Sister, ha! True, the girl existed, but what man went to such trouble over a mere sister? Delaroche hadn't given his own sister a thought since she married that butcher in Rouen fifteen years ago.

Balcourt had seen his father's head roll into the straw below the guillotine (a particularly fine day for an execution, Delaroche recalled fondly); his estates had been looted, his vineyards torched. All in the interests of the Republic, of course, but someone without civic spirit might take such acts as a personal affront.

Balcourt's gaudy waistcoats, his overlarge cravats . . . No French tailor would produce clothing that execrable unless it was deliberate. Those cravats bespoke a man who had something to hide.

But no cravat in France was large enough to shield Balcourt from the all-seeing eyes of the Ministry of Police.

Without hesitation, Delaroche continued on to his fourth and final suspect, Augustus Whittlesby. Whittlesby proclaimed himself a romantic poet seeking inspiration among the splendors of *la belle France*. He could usually be found languishing among the inns of the Latin quarter, flowing white shirt askew, one pale hand pressed to his brow, the other wrapped around a carafe of burgundy. When Delaroche had asked him sharply if he suffered a medical condition (Whittlesby having inconveniently swooned onto his boots just as Delaroche was preparing to follow a suspect), Whittlesby had declared in dramatic tones that he was overcome, not with any weakness of the body, but with the soul-searing joys of poetic inspiration. He had then, with Delaroche held captive by his boot-tops, insisted on reciting an impromptu ode to the cobblestones of Paris that began, "Hail to thee, thou sylvan stones!/ Upon whose adamantine brilliance tread many feet!/ Tread there more feet! More happy, happy feet!/ In boots with merry tassels and polish bright/ That never know the scum of a dirt road." The happy, happy feet had trotted along the merry, merry cobbles for twenty-five further stanzas, while Delaroche's feet had remained very unhappily immobile on cobbles more muddy than merry.

Delaroche eyed his letter opener speculatively. Perhaps Whittlesby might be dispatched even if not identified as the Purple Gentian.

Delaroche was about to shout to the sentry to summon him four agents, when a sudden recollection barreled out of the miscellany of information he acquired every day, giving him pause. Yesterday, another Englishman had returned to Paris. That same Englishman had left Paris directly following the Purple Gentian's theft of Delaroche's dossiers.

This man had come to Delaroche's attention before. That alone was little distinction, as most of Paris had come to Delaroche's attention at some point. But Delaroche's attention had been so arrested that he had cornered the gentleman in question at no fewer than seven of Mme Bonaparte's receptions, and personally shadowed him for over a fortnight. Delaroche's efforts had proven fruitless (unless one counted a new understanding of several passages in Homer). In the end, Delaroche had reluctantly dismissed him because, to all appearances, he was exactly what he claimed to be: a gentleman scholar with an utter disregard for current affairs and a knowledge of the classics to make a schoolmaster weep with joy. Yet . . . the coincidence of the dates tugged at Delaroche with almost physical force.

Before calling for his spies, Delaroche penned one last name.

Lord Richard Selwick.

Chapter Thirteen

~~~~~~~~~~~~~~~~

L ord Richard Selwick regarded the assemblage in the Yellow Salon of the Tuilleries Palace with a yawn. Not terribly much, it seemed, had changed in his two weeks' absence. Richard resisted the urge to tug at his carefully arranged neckcloth; the room was uncomfortably warm with the heat of too many bodies and too many candles. Scantily clad women drifted from cluster to cluster like moths flitting from lamp to lamp—only, Richard noted with some amusement, unlike the insects, the ladies stayed as far away as possible from the telling light of the flames. Josephine, herself older than she liked to admit, had draped the candle sconces and mirrors in gauze, but even the gentle light betrayed cheeks layered with rouge.

A burst of raucous laughter sounded from across the room. Over the curled and turbaned heads of the crowd, Richard trained his quizzing glass on the source of the sound. Ah, Marston. Between his long, curly sideburns, Marston's face was flushed with heat and drink. He had one arm propped against the mantelpiece; the other was gesticulating with a snifter of brandy to an appreciative audience composed of Murat and a couple of other chaps in military attire hung with far more medals than their age made likely. Richard considered wandering over to investigate, but decided he needn't push his way through the crush of perfumed bodies just yet. From the sound of the guffaws wafting from the fireplace, Marston was telling jokes, not deep secrets.

Richard let his quizzing glass trail about the room. The usual gossip, the usual flirtations, the usual crowd of underdressed women and overdressed men. It was enough to make one understand why the French were always moaning on and on about *ennui*.

"Who are those provincials with Balcourt?" Vivant Denon elbowed Richard in his ribs. "The two young ones are not ill-favored, but those clothes!"

Denon, who had headed the scholars in Egypt, and was at present in charge of setting up Bonaparte's new museum in the Louvre Palace, had very decided ideas about aesthetics. Especially regarding women. Denon's own elegantly attired mistress, Mme de Kremy, was just two yards away, occasionally sending steamy looks in Denon's direction. At least Richard hoped they had been intended for Denon; Mme de Kremy was not at all the sort of woman he preferred.

As for the sort of woman Richard preferred . . . Following Denon's gaze, Richard sighted Amy Balcourt, one gloved hand lightly resting on her brother's arm. Richard's *ennui* evaporated in an instant. With some amusement, Richard noted that Amy fidgeted like a horse at the start of the Derby, straining to see around her brother into the crowded salon. Balcourt had paused in the doorway to exchange pleasantries with Laure Junot, and Amy was not weathering the delay well. As Richard watched, Jane, standing behind Amy with Miss Gwen, leaned forward and whispered something in Amy's ear, to which Amy responded with a quick, rueful smile. Richard started to smile back at her, even though the look had not been intended for him.

"They should hand all young women from the provinces a fashion plate and march them to the dressmaker before they let them into the Tuilleries!" Denon was saying.

"These have the handicap of being from England," Richard commented dryly.

"Ah, that explains it!" Denon stared unabashedly at Amy and Jane. "Those heavy fabrics, those boxy styles, they are so sadly English. As charity to them, we ought to send a boatload of dressmakers across the Channel."

Richard wouldn't have called Amy's form boxy. True, Amy's dress didn't hug her body like those of the French-women, who wore their filmy dresses with only a single slip, dampened to make the fabric cling to their legs (more than one woman had caught her death of cold by doing so in winter, but Frenchwomen seemed to agree that style was worth the risk of death). Instead, Amy's dress fell gracefully from its high waist, lightly skimming her hips, merely hinting at the feminine form beneath. Next to the plain white lawn worn by the other women, the satin of Amy's dress glimmered in the candlelight like snow seen by moonlight.

"Put them in French clothes and they will still be English-women," Richard commented admiringly.

Misunderstanding, Denon shook his head. "So sad."

Balcourt had finished introducing his sister to Mme Junot and was beginning to make his way through the crowd towards Josephine Bonaparte, who sat like a queen in state towards the back of the room. As Denon went on about the sad state of fashion on the other side of the Channel, using the purple ostrich feathers stuck in the tight gray knot of Miss Gwen's hair as a prime example, Richard entertained himself by observing Amy. It couldn't hurt just to watch her.

All of her reactions passed across her face with the colorful variety of a sky at sunset. Amy's face flared with interest as her brother introduced her to Mme Campan, one of Marie Antoinette's former ladies-in-waiting. As Georges Marston folded into an elaborate bow, she blinked incredulously at his gold-embroidered, peacock-blue coat, and giggled something to Jane under cover of her fan that made serene Jane's eyes water with suppressed laughter. Amy's lip gave a perceptible curl of distaste as she made her curtsy to Joseph Fouché and Gaston Delaroche, who brooded in the lighthearted assembly like two ravens amidst a gathering of doves. And then Amy's eyes lighted on Richard.

She tripped over the hem of her dress.

It was just a small stumble, not enough for anyone else to mark, but enough for Richard to be oddly pleased. Well, one did like to have one's presence noted. Amy quickly regained her balance and continued walking with her head tilted to prevent Richard from entering her line of vision. So she didn't intend to acknowledge the acquaintance, did she?

Denon elbowed Richard. "You know these English-women, no?"

"No. I mean, yes, I do know them. We shared the boat over from Dover two days ago. One is Balcourt's sister, the other his cousin, and the dragon with the purple plumage is their chaperone."

"Une femme formidable!" breathed Denon, eyeing Miss Gwen's plumage with considerable alarm. "I feel for you, my friend. These English—their women are lacking of all the so-

cial graces. They do not realize that the flirtation, it is an art! The boredom you must have endured upon that ship!"

"Not at all. You do these ladies an injustice." Just because Amy bore him a grudge didn't mean *he* had to be uncivil. "Miss Balcourt—the small, dark-haired one—is surprisingly well read. She has some very original observations about the relations between the Greeks and the Egyptians."

Denon squinted at Amy's back through his quizzing glass. "Ah, a—how do you call them?—a bluestocking?"

"She's certainly not a bluestocking." Richard contemplated Amy's dark curls before adding, very, very softly, "I'm not sure what to call her."

"An Original, perhaps?" Denon was peering through his quizzing glass at Amy with an intensity that had his mistress's fan fluttering indignantly.

"An Original." Richard couldn't repress a smile as he remembered Amy's comments on metaphorical cannibalism and the French Revolution. "Assuredly."

On the other side of the room, waiting among the crush of people paying their respects to Mme Bonaparte, Jane whispered to her assuredly Original cousin, "How long do you intend to keep your head at that angle?"

"Is he still looking at me?"

"No." If it was possible to whisper with asperity, Jane did so. "You're being ridiculous, Amy!"

"I don't want to have to talk to him. He annoys me."

"And if you pretend not to see him, you don't have to talk to him?"

"Exactly!"

"Girls! It is not polite to whisper!" whispered Miss Gwen.

Amy rolled her eyes at Jane behind her fan.

Resisting the urge to lift one gloved hand to massage her sore neck, Amy lurked behind her fan and contemplated the progress of the search for the Purple Gentian. Or, rather, the lack of progress. Since their arrival, she had eavesdropped on ten conversations with great stealth and skill. As a result, she now knew exactly how deeply M. Murat was in debt to his tailor, where to find the best kid gloves in Paris, and that a Mme Rochefort, whomever that might be, was supposedly engaging in illicit amorous relations with her footman, or maybe her groom (the woman in the large, green-silk turban telling the story hadn't been entirely clear on that point). Unless the energetic Mme Rochefort somehow knew the identity of the Purple Gentian and could be blackmailed, Amy really didn't see how any of this information could be the slightest bit useful.

As for the Gentian himself . . . Amy had dismissed most of the guests as far too French. Unless the Gentian were merely aping the Scarlet Pimpernel, the Gentian's very name was an indication of his nationality. So far she had met only two men of English extraction. One, a Mr. Whittlesby, with hair and sleeves both flowing in romantic disorder, had taken one look at Jane, flung himself prostrate at her blue slippers, and composed an on-the-spot ode to "the pulchritudinous princess of the azure toes." It didn't scan. Mercifully, Miss Gwen stepped hard on the poet's hand, cutting him off with a squeak in the middle of his second stanza. True, it could all be a disguise, but . . . Amy frowned behind her fan.

Her second candidate, Mr. Georges Marston, was, like his name, only half English, and his bright regimentals were as off-putting in their own way as Mr. Whittlesby's rumpled white linen. But there was a certain bold gleam to Mr. Marston's blue eyes that might bespeak a man of action hidden under all that gold braid.

A hand with plump white fingers reached out and tugged Amy's fan down to below nose level. "Mme Bonaparte, it would please me very much to present to you my sister, Mlle Aimée de Balcourt," Edouard was saying in French.

Amy sank into a deep court curtsy. Mme Bonaparte half rose from her chair and nodded in acknowledgment. She smiled very sweetly at Amy and said in French, "I knew your dear mother before the Revolution. She was such a dear, lovely woman! Why, when she discovered that I loved roses, she sent me some cuttings I'd been longing to add to my garden. You shall have to come someday to see my little garden at Malmaison, which wouldn't be nearly so nice as it is but for your darling mama."

Mme Bonaparte spoke French with a lilting Creole accent that settled on its hearers with the benevolent warmth of island sunshine. Under her diamond diadem, her large hazel eyes gleamed with kindness. Amy had seen drawings of Bonaparte's wife, and puzzled over her reputation as a beauty. Face-to-face, Amy realized that her beauty resided not so much in regularity of feature, but in the serene goodwill that she seemed to exude as easily as breathing. Amy longed to curl up at her feet like a small child and beg for tales of her parents. But she couldn't sacrifice all of her plans for a moment of nostalgia. If Mme Bonaparte—and thus all of the court—knew that she spoke French, half of her utility to the Purple Gentian would be lost.

So Amy forced a puzzled look onto her face and said in very bad, broken, schoolgirl French, "Remembering the French I am not. The esteemed lady is speaking the English maybe?"

An expression of mild distress crossed Mme Bonaparte's pleasant face. From the corner of her eye, Amy could see Edouard turning bright red with horror and frustration. "I beg your pardon for my sister, your excellence," he began hurriedly, but a pretty blond girl leaned over the back of Mme Bonaparte's chair and said, "There's no need for apologies, M. de Balcourt!" Switching to English as poor as Amy's French, she said carefully, "Mama desire to tell to you zat she was 'aving zee acquaintance of your mama."

Edouard, looking for all the world as though he wished the polished parquet floor to part and swallow him up, performed hasty introductions, presenting the blond girl as Hortense de Beauharnais Bonaparte, Mme Bonaparte's daughter by her first marriage, now married herself to Napoleon's younger brother Louis. When Miss Gwen stamped heavily on Edouard's foot, he finally introduced Miss Gwen and Jane as well.

"I must to you beg pardon for my English *abominable*!" Hortense said with a self-deprecating wave of her fan. "My stepfather, 'ee was not liking of my tutor, so I 'ave lacked for lessons."

"Your English isn't bad at all," Jane reassured her. "It's much better than my French, I assure you."

"Yes, you do yourself far too little credit!" While Edouard waxed lyrical in showering the First Consul's stepdaughter with compliments on her linguistic abilities, Amy found herself seized by the most brilliant of plans. A plan that would secure her access to the palace on a regular basis. . . .

"I would be happy to teach you English!" she blurted out.

Hortense looked so delighted and grateful that Amy almost felt guilty for her subterfuge. Almost.

"Would you *vraiment*?"

"Of course, she will!" Edouard's face bore the expression of a man who has sighted the promised land after an uncomfortable session with brimstone and pitchforks down below. His sudden squeeze of Amy's hand informed her that she was back in her brother's good graces. "The Balcourts are always happy to be of service to the First Consul and his family! When would you like her to begin?"

Had Edouard always been such a deplorable toady?

With some mutual expressions of gratitude, much bad English from Hortense, and some even worse French from Amy, they settled upon the following afternoon for the first lesson. Edouard bowed himself out of the presence of the Bonaparte ladies to chat with some acquaintances, and Amy was about to do likewise, minus the bowing and the acquaintances, when someone cleared his throat behind her. Amy instantly knew just whose throat the sound had issued from. A strong, sun-browned throat she had once seen tantalizingly displayed by an opened collar and loosened cravat. The skin on her arms prickled and her neck ached with the pressure of not turning to look. Oh, blast the man, couldn't he have even left her a moment to gloat over her good fortune?

"Richard!" On Hortense's lips, the name was soft and exotic, *Reeshard*. She demanded of him in French, "When did you return?"

Richard bowed over Mme Bonaparte's hand before kissing her daughter's. "I returned Monday night."

"And you have not called until now! Cad! Is he not a beast, Mama, to have deprived us of his company for so long? Eugene will be disappointed to have missed you—he is off at the theater tonight."

Amy was about to back quietly away, when Hortense laid one gloved hand gently on Amy's arm. "There is a lovely countrywoman of yours to whom I would like to introduce you!" Beaming, Hortense tilted her head in Amy's direction, and drew Amy forward. Amy tried not to balk visibly under Lord Richard's knowing eye. "Mlle Balcourt, I would like to you make zee acquaintance of Lord Reeshard Selweeck."

"We've already met," said Amy hastily.

"You 'ave?" Obviously intrigued, Hortense looked up inquiringly at Richard from under her eyelashes.

"Don't matchmake, Hortense; it's a beastly habit," Richard advised in French. In English, he said to Amy, "If Hortense will spare you, I would like to introduce you to Vivant Denon, the director of the Egyptian expedition. Er—of the *secondary* part of the Egyptian expedition, that is. The scholarly bit."

"I caught your meaning, my lord. You don't have to belabor it." Amy narrowed her eyes at Richard over the lace fringe of her fan. Fans were truly wonderfully useful items. Amy wished she could carry one all the time. "Why?"

"Amy!" Miss Gwen's feathers shook reprovingly.

Richard ignored Amy's rudeness. "Because I thought you would enjoy discussing the classics with him."

"I would think my *absurd* efforts would have little to recommend them to scholars so widely traveled," riposted Amy, snapping her fan closed.

Lord Richard's green eyes glinted with amusement. "Oh, I wouldn't say *all* of your ideas are absurd," he said lightly. "Just some of them."

"Josephine!" A stentorian bellow shook the candles in their sconces.

Unconsciously, Amy grabbed Richard's arm, looking about anxiously for the source of the roar. About the room, people went on chatting as before.

"Steady there." Richard patted the delicate hand clutching the material of his coat. "It's just the First Consul."

Snatching her hand away as though his coat were made of live coals, Amy snapped, "You would know."

"Josephine!" The dreadful noise repeated itself, cutting off any further remarks. Out of an adjoining room charged a blur of red velvet, closely followed by the scurrying form of a young man. Amy sidestepped just in time, swaying on her slippers to avoid toppling into Lord Richard.

The red velvet came to an abrupt stop beside Mme Bonaparte's chair. "Oh. Visitors."

Once still, the red velvet resolved into a man of slightly less than medium height, clad in a long red velvet coat with breeches that must once have been white, but which now bore assorted stains that proclaimed as clearly as a menu what the wearer had eaten for supper.

"I do wish you wouldn't shout so, Bonaparte." Mme Bonaparte lifted one white hand and touched him gently on the cheek.

Bonaparte grabbed her hand and planted a resounding kiss on the palm. "How else am I to make myself heard?" Affectionately tweaking one of her curls, he demanded, "Well? Who is it tonight?"

"We have some visitors from England, sir," his stepdaughter responded. "I should like to present . . ." Hortense began listing their names. Bonaparte stood, legs slightly apart, eyes hooded with apparent boredom, and one arm thrust into the opposite side of his jacket, as though in a sling.

Bonaparte inclined his head, looked down at his wife, and demanded, "Are we done yet?"

Thwap!

Everyone within earshot jumped at the sound of Miss Gwen's reticule connecting with Bonaparte's arm. "Sir! Take that hand out of your jacket! It is rude *and* it ruins your posture. A man of your diminutive stature needs to stand up straight."

Something suspiciously like a chuckle emerged from Lord Richard's lips, but when Amy glanced sharply up at him, his expression was studiedly bland.

A dangerous hush fell over the room. Flirtations in the far corners of the room were abandoned. Business deals were dropped. The non-English speakers among the assemblage tugged at the sleeves of those who had the language, and instant translations began to be whispered about the room— suitably embellished, of course.

"It's an assassination attempt!" a woman next to Amy cried dramatically, swooning back into the arms of an officer who looked as though he didn't quite know what to do with her, but would really be happiest just dropping her.

"No, it's not, it's just Miss Gwen," Amy tried to explain.

Meanwhile, Miss Gwen was advancing on Bonaparte, backing him up so that he was nearly sitting on Josephine's lap. "While we are speaking, sir, this habit you have of barging into other people's countries without invitation—it is most rude. I will not have it! You should apologize to the Italians and the Dutch at the first opportunity!"

"*Mais* zee Italians, zey invited me!" Bonaparte exclaimed indignantly.

Miss Gwen cast Bonaparte the severe look of a governess listening to substandard excuses from a wayward child. "That may well be," she pronounced in a tone that implied she thought it highly unlikely. "But your behavior upon entering their country was inexcusable! If you were to be invited to someone's home for a weekend, sirrah, would you reorganize their domestic arrangements and seize the artwork from their walls? Would *you* countenance any guest who behaved so? I thought not."

Amy wondered if Bonaparte could declare war on Miss Gwen alone without breaking his peace with England. "So much for the Peace of Amiens!" she started to whisper to Jane, but Jane was no longer beside her.

Amy wondered if Jane had wandered away while she was sparring with Lord Richard. She thought, vaguely, that Jane had still been about when Lord Richard had intruded onto the scene, but after that her attention had been so filled by the presence of Lord Richard that she couldn't swear with any certainty to anything else at all. Amy slanted her eyes to the right, seeking a furtive glimpse of a strong arm in a superfine coat. Instead, Amy found herself eyeing a puffed sleeve. No longer furtive, Amy twisted to look at the spot that Lord Richard had been occupying beside her before the hullabaloo with Miss Gwen erupted.

Lord Richard Selwick had evaporated.

Amy tried to peer around the room, but the fascinated circle of bodies around Bonaparte and Miss Gwen was several people deep, and it seemed that Bonaparte had a penchant for employing very tall officers; Amy found herself staring straight into several gold-bedecked uniform coats. She would need a stepladder to see over them! Worming her way out of the crowd, Amy stepped on seven different toes, smelled fifteen different perfumes at close range, got tangled up with one ornamental sword, and almost tumbled over as she finally broke free.

Beyond the human wall, the rest of the room appeared deserted. To Amy's right, a woman had a man backed into the corner and was running a finger suggestively down his cheek. Some people have no shame, thought Amy. On the other side of the room . . . Wait a minute! Amy's eyes scooted back to the first corner.

That wasn't . . . ? Was it? It was!

Being caressed in plain view of anyone who cared to look, in Mme Bonaparte's salon, was none other than that infamous turncoat, Lord Richard Selwick.

Chapter Fourteen

❧❦❧

Good heavens, was that woman actually licking Lord Richard's ear?

Transfixed, Amy backed up a couple of steps on her soft slippers. A candle sconce was placed just above their heads, so Amy could view the scene and its actors with hideous clarity. The woman wore a white lawn gown so diaphanous that the light went right through it, revealing the decided absence of any slip at all, wetted or otherwise. Her dark hair fell in smooth curls from a circlet of pearls high on top of her head, one particularly long curl calling attention to the fact that the woman's dress had practically no bodice, unless one were willing to count a brief scrap of lace bristling two inches above the high waist. She was incredibly, undeniably beautiful.

Amy hated her on sight.

Edouard had pointed the woman out to her earlier. Amy racked her memory as the woman slid one hand into the shining golden waves of Richard's hair. Pauline! That was it. Bonaparte's younger sister, Pauline Leclerc. Her affairs were as legendary as her beauty, and she was said to have bedded half the men in Paris. Amy, of course, wasn't supposed to know such things, but she had read the gossip sheets assiduously for years. When it came to the French, the English papers had few qualms about reporting scandal at its most scandalous, without even the protective veil of a euphemism.

Watching Pauline twine herself sensuously around Lord Richard like Laocoön and the snakes, Amy smoothed down the opaque material of her skirt, aware for the first time that her own frock had been designed by a rural modiste in Shropshire, working off fashion papers several months old. Amy's hand went up to her own very modest scooped neckline, toying with the charm that hung in the hollow of her throat. Next to Pauline's diamonds, the little gold locket on a silk ribbon around her neck must look a trumpery affair, a child's trinket. Amy suddenly felt very young and very gauche, a little girl spying on an adult party.

Well, I wouldn't want to be like *that* anyway, Amy told herself firmly. And it was just typical that Lord Richard would be dallying with such a crass strumpet! Two people with no morals. They served each other right.

But how could he?

"Amy." Someone was plucking at her sleeve. *"Amy."*

"Oh, Jane! I was looking for you. Did you see *that*?" Amy packed as much outrage as possible into a whisper as she pointed at the couple caught in the candlelight. Her very finger shook with indignation.

Jane looked from Richard and Pauline to Amy. Her cousin was biting her lower lip so hard it was a wonder she hadn't drawn blood, and her arms were crossed firmly across her chest as though she were hugging herself for comfort.

"He doesn't look like he's enjoying her attentions," observed Jane. "Amy, Edouard—"

"Then why doesn't he just *move*?" hissed Amy.

"Perhaps because she has him backed against the wall? Amy, you must—"

"That's no excuse!"

"Amy, Edouard is engaged in an extremely suspect conversation and I think you ought to go listen *at once*!" Jane whispered in one long breath, before her cousin could interrupt yet again.

"If he really didn't—what?" Amy's glower disappeared as she swirled to face Jane. "Wait, what?"

"Edouard and Marston," Jane whispered urgently. "They slipped out while everyone was distracted by Miss Gwen."

Amy's entire body snapped to attention. "Well, what are you waiting for? Why are we wasting time talking about—ugh! Take me to them, Jane. We can't waste a moment!" Amy dashed for the door.

Jane permitted herself only the very slightest rolling of the eyes before following her cousin.

Had Amy waited a moment longer, she would have seen Richard reach up to pluck the woman's twining hand from his hair.

"You're wasting your wiles on me, Pauline. I'm not interested."

The First Consul's sister pouted and reached her arms around Richard's waist. "That is what you always say. Can't I . . . *persuade* you to say something else?" One hand slipped into the waistband of his breeches.

"No," said Richard bluntly.

Taking Pauline by the waist, he moved her aside and edged out of the corner she had backed him into. "Go and find someone more receptive to play with," he advised amiably. Pauline wasn't really a bad sort, and it was always mildly flattering to see someone so determined to have him in her bed. But Richard just wasn't interested. Pauline had made the rounds of the court far too many times for his taste. Richard strode purposefully towards the doorway—he had seen Balcourt and Marston exit that way. The two of them were certainly up to something, and Richard wanted to know what.

"But you are such a *challenge*!" Pauline called after him.

"And you are too bloody persistent," muttered Richard as he smiled and waggled his fingers. Pauline, already off in search of more accommodating company, failed to hear. Which was probably for the best, since the last thing Richard wanted to do was irritate Bonaparte's favorite sister badly enough to cause a rift with her brother. Hell, even if Pauline did appeal to him, the force of her charms would undoubtedly be outweighed by the risk of Bonaparte's displeasure.

How long ago had Balcourt left the salon? Five minutes? Ten? It was hard to tell time when one was pressed up against the wall and being forcibly caressed. Unfortunately, it was more than enough time for Balcourt and Marston to have effectively disappeared. The problem with the Tuilleries was that the deuced rooms were still all *en filade,* one room opening out onto another. Hallways, decided Richard, were architecture's gift to espionage. You could actually wander down a hallway, listening at door after door, instead of having to walk through rooms hoping you had taken the right direction, and hoping you didn't accidentally walk in on the very conversation you had hoped to spy on.

Pacing irritably through a deserted salon, Richard slowed as he came to the next door. He eased it open a crack, peeking through the narrow gap. No sound of voices, but that didn't necessarily mean no one was there. No scent of that obnoxiously strong cologne Balcourt favored. Richard took that as a more reliable guide and flung the door the rest of the way open.

Ah, the door at the far end of the room was ajar! Of course, it could have been left ajar by a servant, or a guest seeking the water closet, or any other number of innocent persons unrelated to Balcourt or Marston, but it was the closest thing to a lead Richard had. He tiptoed his way silently through the long gallery, past rows of armless deities, and peered through the crack in the door....

Only to encounter a nicely rounded female backside draped in white satin.

Once Richard's eyes fixed upon that object, it would have been hard for a disinterested observer—had there been one—to determine whether he was so much peering as leering through the crack in the door. There was no doubt to whom the nether regions in question belonged. The thin fabric molded itself obligingly to Amy's body as she leaned over, her ear against the keyhole of the door on the other side of the narrow room.

Her ear against the keyhole?

What was Amy doing with her ear against the keyhole? Never mind that the activity showed off certain parts of her anatomy to good effect.... Richard plucked his mind out of the gutter and coerced it back into reasonable patterns of thought.

Not only was her derriere distracting, but, by Jove, she had stolen his spot! *He* should have been the one in that antechamber. *He* should have been the one with his ear pressed against the door. Blast it all, what business did a mere chit of a girl from the country have usurping his keyhole?

Richard's lips thinned into a grim line.

Utterly unaware that she was causing such consternation, Amy pressed her ear against the convenient gap afforded by a keyhole. Thank goodness these locks had been designed for large keys! Amy could hear every word said, unmuffled by the wood of the door. Unfortunately, not terribly much had been said so far. Edouard had babbled—there was really no other word for it—on and on about the high favor in which he was held by the consular family. Amy rolled her eyes and made faces indicating boredom and disgust at Jane.

Had Edouard dragged Marston off in private just so he

could gloat at him? Yet Jane had been so sure their conversation was suspect, and Jane wasn't one to succumb to fancy. . . . Amy's neck was beginning to ache from tilting her head at an unnatural angle and the ornate brass ornamentation of the keyhole pricked against her ear. Had it not been for that wounded man in the ballroom, Amy would have been convinced that her brother was merely one of the more boring men in creation and left it at that. But there was that wounded man. . . . Maybe Edouard was speaking in code? No. The sound of booted feet pacing impatiently up and down the parquet floor in the next room seemed to indicate that Marston found Edouard's monologue equally irritating. That, Amy decided, indicated a certain amount of good sense on Marston's part.

Of all the men she had met that evening, Marston *was* the most likely candidate to be the Purple Gentian.

The steady rhythm of Marston's steps came to an abrupt stop. So did Edouard's monologue.

"Enough pleasantries. Have you squealed, Balcourt?"

Edouard's voice was oddly muffled as he gasped, "No! How could you think—no, never!"

"Good." The word was nearly obscured by a thud, as though someone had dropped something heavy.

The Purple Gentian. He *must* be the Purple Gentian. Amy was too excited for complete sentences; her thoughts exploded in ragged fragments.

"Tonight then?" Edouard asked breathlessly.

Tonight! Tonight! Amy mouthed excitedly to Jane. But where? She pressed her ear harder to the crack in the door.

"Might as well," drawled Marston. "No sense waiting."

"You could drive back with us and we could say we were retiring to my study for some port and cards and—"

"I know where to find you, Balcourt."

"Um, right." Edouard subsided.

"Though I must say"—Amy heard the boots begin to click again—"I wouldn't mind sharing a carriage with that sister of yours."

What?

Oh, blast, the footsteps were rapidly nearing the door. There was no time to dwell on that last, highly interesting comment, or await its sequel. Amy abandoned her keyhole and made anxious waving motions at Jane. The two of them scurried for cover behind a pair of rickety gilded chairs. Amy felt a bit like a child trying to hide behind its own hands. If the men brought a candle with them, the chairs would do little to hide them. Amy squeezed back more firmly into her corner. If caught, they would just have to brazen it out. They could say that they'd gone looking for Edouard because Miss Gwen was making a scene—that would distract Edouard in a hurry!— and if he asked what they were doing crawling about on the floor, well, Amy could always pretend she'd lost a hairpin. It would never occur to Edouard that she'd been wearing her hair down. And if that didn't work, for plan B . . .

The door swung open, nearly careening into Amy's chair. Amy just managed to keep herself from flinching.

"Sir!" Edouard was proclaiming in his most pompous tones. Even in the dark, he looked like a halibut. "That is my sister you are discussing!"

Marston crossed the antechamber in three long strides, Edouard puffing behind. "Your point?" And the door slammed behind the two men. Clip-clap, shuffle, shuffle . . . Marston's decisive tread and Edouard's shuffling gait receded along the marble gallery.

Jane's head poked out, turtlelike, from behind the back of her chair. "Amy," she whispered, "I don't like that man."

"Shhhhh!" Amy hissed. "Wait till we know they're gone!"

"Unless they tiptoed back, I think we're safe."

Amy bounced up, and gave an extra little hop of glee, just for good measure. "Isn't this exciting, Jane! What absolute luck! And if you hadn't followed Edouard, we'd never have—"

Jane was clearly not listening, because she broke in with a worried, "That Mr. Marston is no gentleman."

Amy glanced up from brushing dark smudges of dust off the satin of her dress. White was no color for a spy. "But, Jane, he *must* be the Purple Gentian! Who else could it be?"

"That doesn't make him a gentleman. Besides, we don't know he's the Purple Gentian, Amy." Amy didn't need to see her cousin's face to know what sort of look she was being given.

"Oh, *Jane.*" Before she gave way to pique, Amy recalled that her cousin hadn't had the benefit of the keyhole. In tones that rapidly escalated from a whisper, she hastily repeated the conversation she had overheard. As Edouard had slammed the door to the marble gallery behind him, neither Amy nor Jane noticed an ear being pressed to the keyhole. Neither saw a pair of green eyes glitter like a panther on the prowl at the words "study," and "tonight."

Neither heard the sound of muffled footsteps easing down the marble gallery as Richard slipped away to plan a midnight raid on Balcourt's study.

"So you see, Jane," Amy finished, curls bouncing as she pirouetted around the small room, "I'll just hide in Edouard's study and eavesdrop on their conversation. Obviously, they couldn't talk here with all of these revolutionaries about, but tonight . . ."

She had to make sure she got to Edouard's study before he did.

"We're so close, Jane!" she crowed. "I can't believe we've already found the Purple Gentian!"

"Nor can I," commented Jane uneasily.

Chapter Fifteen

⚮

Richard paused outside the window of Edouard de Balcourt's study, tugging the hood of his black cloak further down around his face. He always felt deuced silly in this getup. Black breeches, black shirt, black cloak, black mask . . . It was the sort of outfit worn by pretentious highwaymen with names like the Shadow or the Midnight Avenger, who hoped to be written up in the illustrated papers with lines like, "His heart is of the same unrelieved black as his clothes. . . ." Ugh. If the black weren't so bloody useful for blending into the night, Richard would have been much happier carrying out his missions in buff breeches. Besides, the mask tickled the bridge of his nose. Who ever heard of a sneezing spy?

Giving his nose one last good wriggle, Richard set his mask straight, and eased open the library window. The drapes had been left open, and unless Balcourt was lying on the floor in the dark—an image which boggled Richard's excellent imagination—the study was clearly deserted. Good. He would have time to do a little scouting and hide himself properly before Balcourt and Marston met for their rendezvous. If Richard had timed it right, it should be roughly a quarter to twelve. From what he knew of Balcourt, he was just the sort of hackneyed individual who was bound to hold any clandestine meeting just at the stroke of midnight. Hell, if Balcourt was a spy, he would probably *enjoy* wearing all black.

That was one thing Balcourt had in common with his sister—an instinct for drama.

Grasping the windowsill in both hands, Richard hoisted himself up and into the room, just managing not to get his legs tangled in his cloak. He wobbled a bit as he landed on the squishy cushions of the window seat, hopping down onto the floor rather more rapidly than he had intended.

Richard scanned the room. The recessed windows with their thick velvet drapes would be his line of retreat if he heard footsteps in the hall. A desk, a small table bearing a brandy decanter, a standing globe . . . the furnishings of the room, while expensive, were few. How could a man have a study without bookshelves? The bibliophile in Richard was appalled. The only reading matter of any kind apparent in Edouard Balcourt's study was a pile of well-thumbed fashion papers featuring the latest in waistcoats.

The obvious place to look would be the desk. But this desk was a spindly affair, little more than a glorified table, with room for only one narrow drawer. Besides, Balcourt might not be the brightest frog in the pond, but even he couldn't possibly be dim enough to store evidence of illicit activities in his desk.

Of course, Delaroche stored his most sensitive files in his desk—or, rather, *had* stored his most sensitive files in his desk, Richard amended with a smug smile—but to be fair to Delaroche, he had done so on the assumption that the Ministry of Police was impenetrable, not out of rank stupidity.

If not the desk, then where?

Balcourt had hung paintings above his desk and above the table on the far side of the room. Both gleamed with newness. There had been no time for dust to colonize the curlicues in the gilded frames, nor were the surfaces of the paintings themselves dulled by sunlight or grime. In most of his investigations, Richard followed the rule that anything conspicuously new was automatically suspect. Trust Balcourt to be difficult. Everything in the study was conspicuously new. The desk, with brass sphinxes' heads inlaid into the wood of the legs, couldn't be more than a year old, if that, and the small table bearing the decanter, aside from being too thin to boast a false bottom, was clearly from the same workshop. Even the mantelpiece on the fireplace was a recent addition.

In fact, in the entire room, the only object not new, fashionable, and, to Richard's mind, unpardonably ugly was the globe standing in the corner of the room, between the table and the window. There had been just such a globe in the library at Uppington Hall when Richard was young. Due to Richard's habit as a beastly eight-year-old of spinning the globe as fast as he could make it go for the joy of seeing the countries blur into multicolored blobs, the Uppington Hall library globe was no more. It had spun off its moorings, smashed out the window, and ended its existence by bouncing into an ornamental fountain under the shocked gaze of a marble water maiden. Richard had been confined to paper maps for years.

It was with a certain amount of eight-year-old glee that Richard approached Balcourt's globe.

Wrapping his fingers around the contours of the globe, Richard lifted it up off its stand and shook it. And shook it again, thrilling to the unmistakable swish of paper. Rather a lot of paper, unless he missed his guess. Huzzah!

His fingers probed for the catch, and he had just found a suspicious bump somewhere along the equator when Richard heard a bump of an entirely difference kind. And a noise that sounded curiously like the word "ouch."

Dash it all, Balcourt wasn't actually lying on the floor in the dark, was he?

Richard immediately dismissed the ridiculous thought. Balcourt's voice might be squeaky, but he wasn't a eunuch. Richard stood very still, weighing his options. That might not have been an ouch at all. It might have been a squeaky floorboard, or a mouse. Yet, if there was even the slightest chance of it being a human voice, the sensible thing to do was to dive out the window and make his escape before he was seen.

Being a sensible man, Richard intended to do just that.

He was quite surprised to hear his own voice whisper, in French, "Who's there?"

And he was even more surprised when a voice answered, in the same language, "Don't worry! It's just me. Ouch!"

"Just me," Richard repeated stupidly. A small and all-too-familiar figure was wriggling its way out from under the desk. "Dratted furniture!" he heard it mutter in English, as first a dark head and then a pair of shoulders slithered partway out. "Oh, blast, my hem's caught." The head disappeared again under the desk.

Too incredulous even to be angry, Richard stalked over to the desk, grabbed a pair of slim forearms, and pulled. There was a slight tearing sound, and out popped a rather disheveled Miss Amy Balcourt.

Amy didn't yelp as the Purple Gentian dragged her out from under her brother's desk. She didn't even wince when her knee scraped against the carpet. She was too busy staring unabashedly at the Purple Gentian.

The Purple Gentian was here, in the flesh, in her brother's study. True, not much flesh was revealed by the long black gloves, black mask, black pants, black cloak, and black hood, but two very lively eyes blazed through the holes of his mask, and his black-garbed chest rose and fell with his somewhat uneven breathing.

Despite her confident words to Jane earlier—one had to be confident with Jane, or else she logicked one to the point of despair—Amy had feared that her sojourn under the library desk would go unrewarded, unless one counted the gleaning of a fine crop of dust. The Purple Gentian, savior of royalists, scourge of the French, had haunted her daydreams for so long that it seemed scarcely possible that he could appear in any form more material than that of a phantom.

But here he was, real, alive, from his scuffed boots to the expression of shocked outrage on his shadowed face. Amy didn't even have to pinch herself to make sure she wasn't dreaming because the Gentian, unintentionally, had undertaken that task for her. The grip of his gloved fingers on her upper arms was painfully tight. Amy wiggled a bit in the Gentian's grasp as she began to lose feeling in her fingers.

"Um, do you think you could put me down?" Amy asked in French.

"What? Oh." He seemed to have pulled just a bit too far; although he was still holding Amy by the arms, she was now dangling six inches off the floor. Richard hastily set her down. "Sorry."

"That's quite all right." Amy shook out her skirts and flashed him a smile that dazzled even through the moonlit darkness of the study.

"May I inquire as to what you were doing under that desk?"

"Waiting for you," Amy said brightly, as if that were all the explanation that was needed. "You *are* the Purple Gentian, aren't you?"

"Don't you think it would be rather foolish of me to answer that question?" Richard asked dryly.

"Only if you fear that I might have the secret police stashed away behind the curtains." Impulsively, Amy grabbed one of his gloved hands and led him to the closed curtains of the other window and flung them open. She twirled to face him. "See? No Fouché, no Delaroche. You're perfectly safe."

Standing far closer to Amy than propriety would have ever allowed, in her brother's darkened, deserted study, Richard had his doubts about that statement. It would be so easy to lean just the slightest bit forward, to brush that unruly curl out of her eye, to cup her face with his hands. . . . Richard pulled back, away from Amy; if he couldn't make her leave, he would feign departure and lurk under the windowsill.

"You're not planning to leave! I've been under that desk for ages waiting to speak to you."

Amy fervently hoped that he wasn't considering a rapid leap out of the window. While she could grab on to the end of his cloak and refuse to let go, somehow, that wasn't the way she had envisaged her first meeting with the Gentian progressing. Bad enough to have him haul her out from under the desk—blasted hem!—when she so desperately needed to impress him with her intrepid espionage abilities.

"I want to help you," she said eagerly.

"*Help* me?"

Amy chose to ignore the skepticism in the Gentian's tone. "Yes! I could be a great help to you! I have an entrée into the palace—I'll be giving Bonaparte's daughter English lessons. No one except you knows I can speak French, so they'll talk freely in front of me and I can overhear all sorts of useful things. I'm not squeamish and I'm excellent at disguises and—"

"No." The Gentian stalked rapidly towards the window. "It's out of the question."

"Why?" Amy darted after him. "Do you not trust me? At least give me a trial! Let me do something to prove myself! If I fail, I'll go away, I promise, and you'll never hear from me again."

Richard paused, arrested by echoes of his own voice nearly a decade ago. He had stood there in Percy's study, pleading with him, begging him, promising anything at all for the chance to go on just one mission.

Richard's face hardened. It really wasn't the same thing at all, he decided. True, he had only been a little older than Amy at the time, but he rode, he boxed, he fenced, and, damn it, he wasn't a tiny female who could be flung over the shoulder of the first lout who happened along.

How could he let Amy wander off on missions on her own?

She had said she was excellent at disguises. Imagining Amy roaming the streets of Paris dressed as a highly unconvincing boy made Richard's blood run cold. Amy might be fine-boned, but Richard had conducted a thorough inspection of her form—in the interest of her safety, of course—and it was eminently clear that the curves so helpfully revealed by her scooped neckline could not easily be compressed into male proportions.

"Wouldn't you be happier practicing your embroidery?" Richard suggested irritably.

"Embroidery?"

"Or you could always take up an instrument." Richard tried to herd Amy towards the door. "Why don't you go see if there's a harp in the music room?"

"Are you trying to fob me off?"

There didn't seem to be any point in denying it. "Yes."

Amy planted her hands on her hips and looked the Gentian firmly in the eye—or, rather, in the mask. "You don't seem to understand. I came to France for the express purpose of joining your League. This isn't some silly whim. Unlike *some* people, who flit about the continent and consort with the enemy . . ."

Like Lord Richard Selwick, Amy added mentally.

Like me, Richard specified, with an inward smile. So she was still brooding about that, was she?

". . . I take the plight of France very seriously, and I intend to do something about it."

"An unusual interest for an English debutante."

"Most English debutantes," Amy explained with a wry twist of the lips, "don't have a father who died on the guillotine. I do. And I intend to make sure his death does not go unavenged."

Something about her demeanor killed the flippant reply that had rested on Richard's lips. "Your father," he said instead, "might consider it a greater tribute for his daughter to live long and happily. A spy cannot hope for either."

"My parents were robbed of long and happy life by the Revolution."

"All the more reason for you to aspire to both."

"How could I live long and happily knowing that their murderers prosper?" Amy's hands clenched into passionate fists. "I have spent my entire life in training for this moment!

You can't just turn me away with platitudes about playing the harp and living a happy life."

Damn, thought Richard, who had fervently hoped to do just that.

Amy took a deep breath, and tried to school her voice into a calmer tone.

"All I ask is one chance. Is that so unreasonable?"

"Yes. It is." The Purple Gentian seized Amy by the shoulders and marched her over to the mirror over the fireplace. "You"—he pointed at her image in the glass—"are a girl."

"That's not exactly an original observation." Amy squirmed out of his grasp. "And besides, I really don't see what that has to do with the matter at hand. I—"

"It has everything to do with the matter at hand," the Gentian cut her off. "Don't you realize the sort of risk you'd be putting yourself into?"

"No more than you do every time you undertake a mission. I understand the danger. And I'm not worried. Really."

The Gentian's gloved hands flexed impatiently. "Well, you ought to be. You shouldn't even be here now! It can only be termed criminally idiotic of you to be alone, in the dark, with a man whose identity is entirely unknown to you. With any man, for that matter," he ground out.

"But your identity *is* known to me. You're the Purple Gentian! And if it's propriety that you're worried about, who is there to see us? As long as no one knows you're here, my reputation is perfectly safe. And *I'm* certainly not telling."

Richard resisted the urge to drive a fist into the wall. "God, Amy, your naïveté is terrifying!"

Neither of them noticed that he had used her first name.

"I am not naïve," she said stiffly. "Unless it's naïve to weigh all the evidence and come to a reasonable conclusion. I've read about everything you've done. Everything! You've always been the very soul of honor. Why would you do so much good for so many people only to behave ill towards me? Is that naïve?"

"Yes," said the Gentian sharply. "And what proof do you have that I am the Purple Gentian? I could be a bloody highwayman for all you know."

"I felt your ring."

"You what?"

"I felt your ring. When I took your hand, when you first

came in. I could feel the shape of the flower engraved on your signet ring through your glove. After all," she added smugly, "there was no other way I could be sure it was you. I am not quite so naïve as you think."

"Minx!" the Gentian exclaimed with grudging admiration. "Subtle, too. I had no idea what you were about."

"That's because I didn't intend you to." Amy basked in his approbation. "Does this mean . . . Have I passed?"

Richard closed his eyes. Damn, damn, damn. If he were intelligent, he would leave now, before this ridiculous conversation went any further. Only, given the determined set of Amy's jaw, she would probably try to follow him. Just what he needed: Amy blundering after him down the midnight alleyways of Paris.

He could solve the problem by making her despise him. He could mock her ambitions, belittle her abilities, dwell crudely upon her physical attributes. Within ten minutes, rather than begging him to stay, Amy would be pushing the Purple Gentian headfirst out the window with a boot in his back for good measure. All he had to do was make her hate him.

He couldn't do it.

"I am losing my mind," muttered Richard.

"What was that you said?" Amy asked hopefully.

Ping! Ping! Ping! The china clock on the mantelpiece rocked alarmingly on its base as its high-pitched chimes rang out the hour.

Amy froze.

"Midnight," Richard said grimly. Blast! If his suspicions were right, Balcourt could be here at any moment.

The last chime of the clock was still reverberating through the room when it was replaced by a very different sort of sound. An uneven series of clumps and thuds filtered softly through the closed French doors. Just on time, Richard thought dourly, listening to the footfalls on the flagstones of the courtyard. Not only Edouard Balcourt, by the sound of it, but a whole series of booted feet.

Damn. He couldn't allow himself to be found here. Even if Balcourt wasn't an agent for Bonaparte, Richard's presence in his study, at midnight, in the company of his young and nubile sister, would be bloody hard to explain.

Swift action was required. So Richard acted. Swiftly.

Grabbing Amy's arm, Richard pulled her with him behind the curtains of the window seat.

Chapter Sixteen

Whump! Amy fell back with a thud against the Purple Gentian's chest.

Swallowing an automatic exclamation of surprise, she struggled to catch her breath and her balance. She had lost her footing entirely when the Purple Gentian hauled her behind the curtain, and was sprawled across his lap in a very unsettling way. Under her cheek, she could hear his heart beating in rapid staccato through the thin linen of his shirt. That made two of them—her own pulse was racing, whether from sudden movement, fear of discovery, or in imitation of the pulse beating in the masculine chest beneath her, Amy wasn't sure.

The linen of his shirt pressed warmly against her cheek, lightly scented with the clean, spicy tang of orange peel. Amy pushed against an uncomfortably hard cushion to lever herself up off the Purple Gentian. The cushion shifted beneath her hand in a most uncushionlike fashion, displaying an impressive array of muscles. Oh good heavens, had she just grabbed the Purple Gentian's thigh? Amy snatched her hand away with a speed that would have done Miss Gwen proud.

Losing her balance, Amy tumbled back against the Gentian. "Oof," grunted the Purple Gentian.

"Sorry, sorry, sorry," Amy mouthed, which was pointless, since she was facing away from the Gentian, but made her feel better anyway.

One would think he might lend her a hand, instead of lying there, impersonating a cushion. Oh, wait—his hand was pinned under her elbow.

Amy twisted her body to free the Gentian's hand, winding up with her nose wedged into a citrus-scented sleeve.

From the courtyard, the sound of the men's voices had

become louder, despite the extra barrier of the heavy fabric of the curtain. Not just one voice, but several. Grabbing the end of the window seat for balance, Amy wiggled off the Gentian's lap. The Gentian emitted a sort of muffled groan. Amy winced, mouthing another unseen apology. She really did have to stop injuring the man if she hoped to convince him to accept her into the League. Squirming around to face the draperies, she tucked her knees up underneath her so that her legs wouldn't dangle off the edge of the window seat and possibly disturb the fall of the fabric.

Outside, someone dropped something—was that wood splintering?—and a rough voice cursed loudly. It sounded, Amy thought, straining to hear, like that man who had been quarreling with Lord Richard's coachman in the courtyard several days ago. Good heavens, was he robbing the house?

Or could this be something to do with the plans of the Purple Gentian? Amy cast a quick, sideways glance at the man on the window seat beside her. His face revealed nothing. Which, Amy thought with a certain amount of aggravation, might have been due to the fact that, between the mask and the hood of his cloak, there was very little of his face revealed to begin with. Amy chafed at the futility of trying to read emotion from the set of someone's nose.

If the Purple Gentian was to meet Edouard, why was he hiding behind the curtains with her? Why hadn't the Gentian just shoved *her* behind the curtains, and gone on to his rendezvous with Edouard on his own? Maybe, mused Amy, because he had the good sense to realize that she wasn't likely to stay where he'd left her.

Amy turned her attention once more to the activity in the courtyard. How frustrating not to be able to see anything! Closing her eyes—not that it made much of a difference, since all she had been able to see with them open was the dusky fall of the curtain in front of her—Amy tried to concentrate her senses on the noises coming from the garden. Fragmented voices shifted and blended into each other. Against the blur of voices, another thud resounded through the night.

A new voice broke in. "Careful with that, you fools!"

Amy's eyes flew open. "It's Edouard," she whispered to the Purple Gentian.

"Shhh . . ." The Purple Gentian pressed a gloved finger to her lips.

He meant only to silence her. But once his finger touched Amy's lips, Richard found he couldn't move away. Her lower lip was full and soft under his finger, and even through the leather of his glove, he could feel the gentle exhalations of her breath through her slightly parted lips. Those pink, soft, perfect lips.

Amy's eyes flew to the Purple Gentian's face. Her breath stilled as she realized that through the slits of his mask, his gaze was riveted on her mouth. For a moment, time seemed to trail off into inconsequentiality. Amy's world narrowed to encompass only the Gentian's intent eyes, and the pressure of his finger against her lips.

Unheeding, unthinking, Richard brushed his finger back and forth along the ripe contours of her lower lip, tactilely memorizing each crease, each fold, lingering over the adorable indentation at the center. When Amy made no move to protest, he traced his way along the lush curves of her mouth to her upper lip.

Amy curled the fingers of her left hand around the edge of the window seat, trying to still the trembling the Gentian's caress evoked. Little shivers of feeling made their way from her lips down her arms; a quick memory of the tremors Lord Richard had caused on the boat flashed through her mind, but the Gentian's hand moving from her lips to her hair blotted out any thought of anyone else, or anything else. His fingers slid up through her curls, gently curving her face towards his as they knelt, facing each other, on the wide velvet window seat.

Shutting her eyes, Amy reveled in pure feeling. The feeling of his fingers twining through the strands of her hair, the feeling of his other hand stroking warm and firm down her back, the feeling of his breath caressing her lips as he moved closer and closer, until his lips were on hers and Amy couldn't concentrate at all; she couldn't even think about feeling, because the feelings were too acute for thought.

The Purple Gentian's arms tightened around her, pulling her intimately against him, her chest pressing against his. With her dress trapped by her knees, Amy's bodice lurched perilously as the Gentian drew her forward. The linen of his shirt brushed against the exposed flesh of her breasts as his lips brushed gently back and forth along hers. Wanting, needing more, Amy leaned into the kiss, moving her hands from their tentative perch by her sides up along the Gentian's forearms.

How wonderful to feel him shiver as she trailed her fingers from his wrist to his elbow, to feel the muscles tense beneath her hands as she slid from elbow to shoulder to—

Amy's hands clutched at the Gentian's shoulders as he teasingly touched his tongue to hers.

Neither of them noticed as the sounds in the courtyard faded voice by voice, footstep by footstep to nothingness. Neither of them noticed as a door on the other side of the courtyard clicked shut.

Neither of them noticed as a dark-clad figure on the other side of the windowpane rolled his eyes and melted back into the shrubbery.

Fearing for his sanity or Amy's virtue—since one or the other of them was going to have to go if matters continued as they were—Richard broke the kiss, wrenching his lips from Amy's. Their lips parted with an audible pop that made him wince and made her giggle at the absurdity of the sound and the sheer joy of the moment.

Richard, rather doubting that he could survive a repetition of the kiss without the instant application of large blocks of ice, evaded harm's way by firmly tucking Amy's head under his chin.

"You were wrong," he murmured ruefully, resting his cheek on top of Amy's head. "You weren't safe with me."

"I feel like Psyche kissing Cupid in the dark," Amy said dreamily.

Richard drew Amy's arms around his back under his cloak. "Feel. No wings."

Amy could hear the smile in the Gentian's voice. "Does that mean if I unmask you, you won't fly away?"

Richard tightened his grip on Amy's arms. "Don't even consider it."

"You could give me three trials, like Psyche."

"With what as the prize at the end? Me, or membership in the League?"

Amy managed the difficult feat of looking at him askance with her nose only inches from his. "It would be much easier for me to answer that question if I knew who you were."

"What's in a name? A Gentian by any other name would—"

"Be an entirely different flower," interjected Amy, swatting him on the arm. "I refuse to be fobbed off with poor imitations of Shakespeare."

"If you don't like *Romeo and Juliet,* how about a sonnet?" Richard suggested. " 'Shall I compare thee to a summer's day? Thou art—' "

"Not that easily deterred."

Amy extricated herself from Richard's arms—and his cloak, which had tangled around her knees—and hopped off the window seat.

"Damnation," muttered Richard.

"I'll ignore that," offered Amy generously. "And we can go straight to the crucial question of how I'm going to help you restore the monarchy."

"When did that topic go from *never* to *how*?" Richard inquired indignantly, pushing back the velvet drapes. "I never even said *if*!"

"But you thought it, didn't you?" argued Amy, with incontrovertible logic. "I'm just making things easier by verbalizing it for you."

"Easier for whom?" Richard grumbled.

"Now when I search the—"

"How do you know I'm even planning to restore the monarchy?" Richard interrupted desperately. He had to say something before Amy assigned herself some sort of ridiculous and dangerous task, on the argument that he would get around to appointing her eventually, so she might as well save everyone trouble by doing it for him. "That's not on my agenda for this month at all! In fact, the only thing on my mind right now is preventing the invasion of England. Not restoring the monarchy. So there's no point in your wasting your time. Amy—"

Amy's large blue eyes snapped open in a way that boded trouble for Richard.

"You know who I am. You called me Amy."

The Purple Gentian cast a panicked look over his shoulder at the unlatched window. "Let's ignore that, shall we?"

"Wait!" Amy grabbed his cloak in both hands. "Do I know you from the Tuilleries reception? From England?"

"I don't have time to argue with you." The Purple Gentian pulled her to him and pressed a quick, hard kiss on her lips, letting her go so abruptly that she almost overbalanced and tumbled backwards off the window seat into the study. In one polished movement, he swung himself over the windowsill onto the ground below. "Till we meet again, Amy."

"But when? Where?" Amy regained her balance and

leaned out the window after him. "You can't just—oh, drat." The Purple Gentian could. He disappeared around the corner of the house with a dramatic swish of his cape.

How could he just run off like that after—ooh! Amy gathered her already ripped skirts together and bunched them up above her knees. Miss Gwen would disapprove, but everything she had done this evening was well beyond the bounds of propriety, so why stop now?

Amy would have liked to have tried to swing off the windowsill like the Gentian, but one quick look down revealed it to be at least a ten-foot drop, all very well when you were the Gentian's height, but too far a fall to the flagstones for Amy's comfort. Maybe if she wiggled out one leg at a time, then lowered herself down by her arms?

Oh, for heaven's sake! By the time she finished figuring out how to climb out of the blasted window, the Purple Gentian could be halfway to England! Amy bravely positioned herself on the edge of the windowsill, allowed herself one last clutch at the sides of the window, closed her eyes, and jumped.

She landed with a jarring thud, stumbled, and sprinted towards the edge of the house. What she would do when she caught up with the Purple Gentian, Amy wasn't quite sure, but there would be ample time to figure that out after she had grabbed him by the tail of his cloak and dragged him to a stop. As she rounded the corner of the east wing, she thought she caught the faintest sight of a flutter of fabric swishing around the front of the house. Or was it just her blurry vision giving the illusion of movement? If only she had a lantern!

Ignoring the stitch in her side, Amy put on a new burst of speed. She slipped in something foul smelling, and performed an unintentional arabesque before righting herself and staggering onwards. Oh goodness, was this the gutter she was running in? On second thought, Amy decided she'd rather not know. The enveloping darkness that prevented her from seeing more than the dim outline of the stones of the wall and the rough shapes of shrubs and trees might not be an entirely negative thing. Fortunately, Amy's breath was coming in such short, sharp pants through her parted lips that it was impossible to smell much anyway.

Finally reaching the end of the house—and mentally upbraiding whichever ancestor had decided he really *must* have a town residence half the length of Versailles—Amy grabbed the wall as she wove around the corner and skidded to a ragged stop just before she would have gone headlong into one of the great iron gates that stood open before the entrance to the cobblestone courtyard.

The gates had been closed after their return from the Tuilleries, Amy was quite sure of it. What were they doing gaping open well past midnight? The gates had to be twelve feet tall, and were, as Amy knew from watching the grooms struggling with them earlier that day, heavy enough to require the efforts of two men to move. Not exactly the sort of door one might accidentally leave ajar. Had Edouard opened them to permit the egress of the Purple Gentian? Then why the dramatic entrance and exit through the study window?

Amy tiptoed cautiously towards the courtyard.

It was quite a different thing approaching the gates on foot, rather than sailing through them ensconced on the raised seat of a carriage. The gate in front of Amy reared forbiddingly into the air. The ornamental *fleurs de lys* that adorned the upper curve of the gate so charmingly in daylight bristled like the spears of a veritable regiment of sentries.

Flattening herself against the wall, Amy turned to peer through the bars. The elaborate ironwork of the gates, leaves and flowers and curlicues twining so closely together that they almost formed a solid barrier, hid her form from the view of anyone within—or at least she hoped it did. Amy twisted her head at an uncomfortable angle so she could look through the two-inch gap between a flower and a leaf.

A plain dark coach, horses moving restlessly, was preparing to leave the courtyard. Amy couldn't discern the features of the coachman perched on the box in the front; he wore a shapeless hat, and a long muffler had been wound round his face. On the lip of the coach, speaking softly to her brother, stood none other than Georges Marston. He wore a long black cloak.

Gesturing to Edouard with one black-gloved hand, he swung into the coach. Black gloves, black cloak . . . Amy's head swirled as she squeezed herself into the gap between the gate and wall. Could there be any doubt?

Her Purple Gentian must be Georges Marston.

Chapter Seventeen

~~~ෛ⌘ଇ~~~

My contact lenses were glued to my eyeballs.

Letting the paper I was holding drop into my lap, I rubbed my eyes. I hadn't pulled an all-nighter since college, and my eyes had clearly decided I was too old for this sort of thing. Hauling myself higher against the pillows, I glanced at the face of the china clock upon the night table. Two thirty in the morning. No wonder my contacts were killing me.

The bedside lamp cast intriguing shadows along the flocked wallpaper of Mrs. Selwick-Alderly's guest bedroom. Like all guest bedrooms, it had the musty, unused air a room gets when nobody has lived in it for quite some time. Silver-framed photographs of people I didn't know—but none of Colin—shared dresser space with an old-fashioned dresser set engraved with my hostess's initials, and a squat statue that looked to my untutored eyes like it might be African. Other exotic knickknacks occupied odd corners of the room, a tufted spear propped up against an armoire, a multilegged goddess sitting companionably next to a Dresden shepherdess on the writing table.

Once again, I tried to focus my bleary eyes on the paper in my lap, but the faded loops of inks slithered away from me. Amy's handwriting wasn't nearly as tidy as Jane's; her diary teemed with crossed-out phrases, blots of inks, and, in moments of agitation, extra loops on her letters. That last entry had been very, very agitated. One "m" alone had obtained three extra humps.

Of course, I'd have been agitated, too, if my favorite masked hero had caught me in a passionate embrace and then hopped blithely out the window. True, I might not have known the last name of a couple of the guys I'd kissed back in college, but at least I'd been able to see their faces. Talk about adding a whole new dimension to the "but does he really like me?" dilemma. Poor Amy.

I was one up on Amy in terms of knowing who the Purple Gentian was, but there had been nary a whiff of a Pink Carnation so far. I mulled over the possibilities. I had to agree with Amy that there was something rather suspect about Georges Marston. Could anyone really be that boorish unless he was trying to hide something? And the whole half-English, half-French thing . . . I paused, liking the notion. I had flung "The Pink Carnation might be French!" at Colin Selwick in a fit of temper, but wouldn't it be funny if it were true?

I smiled beatifically off into space. I'd just love to see the look on Mr. Colin Selwick's face as I disclosed to the Institute of Historical Research that not only had the Pink Carnation been half French, but he had held a commission in Napoleon's army.

Given my own long-lasting attachment to the Pink Carnation, I wasn't all that sure I wanted him to turn out to be Georges Marston just to spite Colin Selwick. There was something about Marston that put me in mind of those swaggering guys who latch onto you in a club, refusing to believe you're really there just to dance with your friends. The ones who won't take no for an answer, and call you nasty names when you wiggle away.

My money was on Augustus Whittlesby. I'd read the effusions he'd sent to Jane, fifteen poems under the collective title, *Odes to the Pulchritudinous Princess of the Azure Toes*. They might limp along from one rhyme to the next, but one couldn't really call them poetry. Not without offering up apologies to Keats and Milton. No man could write verse that bad unless it was on purpose. He had to have a secret identity. And both Pulchritudinous and Princess began with P, like Pink. . . .

I dropped my aching head into my hands with a heartfelt groan. Oh, goodness, I hadn't just really thought that, had I? "Pink Carnation, Pink Carnation starts with P . . ." sang my unregenerate mind in the tones of Cookie Monster.

I really had been awake too long.

What I needed was a cup of tea. I'd even settle for a plain old glass of water. Something to sip to wake me up so I could go on reading before Colin Selwick managed to convince his aunt never to let me darken their doorstep again.

Placing the unbound pages of Amy's diary carefully on the

bedside table, I shoved aside the covers, and clambered out of the high bed, tugging the long skirts of my borrowed nightgown out of my way.

Easing my way through the crack in the door, I paused, letting my eyes adjust to the darkness of the hallway and trying to get my bearings. As my friend Pammy likes to point out, I have an internal anticompass. Tell me to find my way to a destination, and I will invariably go in the exact opposite direction.

The steady tick-tock of a grandfather clock formed a backbeat to the other nighttime noises: the hum of the pipes, the creak of floorboards, the rustle of the wind through the bare branches of the trees in the square. I shimmied along the wall, hoping I was heading in the right direction for the kitchen. Ouch. I had discovered a doorframe with my elbow. Rubbing my injured extremity, I peered around the door. Silver gleamed in the faint light from the streetlamp outside. It was the dining room, a long table of polished wood in the center of the room, a silver-laden sideboard under the half-draped windows.

Where there was a dining room, shouldn't there be a kitchen? I'd try the next door down, I decided, turning back around, and if that didn't work. . . .

Ooof!

I whammed into something warm and unyielding. A large pair of hands clamped down on my elbows. Automatically, I tried to wiggle free.

"What in the hell—?" it rasped.

Colin Selwick. Who else would be profane to a guest in the wee hours of the morning? I pushed against him with both hands, coming into contact with pure muscle beneath a thin layer of fabric. The big lummox didn't so much as budge.

"Let go!" I whispered indignantly. "It's me. Eloise."

His viselike grip on my elbows loosened, but he didn't let go. I could feel the warmth of his hands seeping through the thin linen of Mrs. Selwick-Alderly's nightgown.

"What in the hell are you doing creeping around the house at this hour of the night?"

"Stealing the silver, what else?" I snapped.

"Oh, for heaven's sake." He released me and took a step back; I could barely make out the location of his face in the darkness of the hallway, much less see his expression. "Let's try this again, shall we?"

"I was looking for the kitchen," I amended hastily. "I wanted a glass of water."

"You're going the wrong way."

"Typical," I muttered.

"Come along before you wake Aunt Arabella," he ordered, and took off in the opposite direction. He didn't wait to see if I would follow.

He moved through the pitch-black hallway with the sureness of a man in his own home, weaving dexterously around such impediments as a small table (which I identified the hard way), a chair (ditto), and someone's discarded umbrella. For all I knew, it *was* his home. After all, what did I know of the Selwicks? Limping along behind the broad shadow of Colin Selwick's back, I had to remind myself that I'd only known them for one day; Mrs. Selwick-Alderly, kind as she had been to me, was still a stranger. Even if I was wearing her nightgown. Stumbling on the hem, I gathered up my linen skirts and followed Colin Selwick around a bend in the hallway, through a swinging door, and into the kitchen.

I covered my eyes with my hand as Colin flicked the switch, flooding the square room with light from the overhead fixture. He stood there, one hand still on the switch, just looking at me.

I countered his inspection with one of my own. With the light on, he was considerably less intimidating than he had been as a shadow in the dark hallway. There's something inherently unthreatening about plaid pajama bottoms and a ratty old T-shirt.

Even so, I missed the protective armor of my three-inch heels. With my bare feet poking out from under the flounce of my nightgown, I felt little, off-balance. I had to tilt my head back to meet Colin Selwick's speculative gaze. I didn't like it.

"Do you have something to say?" I prompted. "Or do you just enjoy propping up the wall?"

Colin considered me for a moment longer. "Aunt Arabella likes you."

He sounded unflatteringly perplexed.

"There is a small but vocal minority of people who do."

Colin had the good grace to look abashed. "Look, I didn't mean to—"

"Treat me like I have a loathsome social disease?"

His lips quirked with something that might have been amusement. "Do you?"

"None that I'd admit to in mixed company." After all, an unhealthy obsession with Cadbury Fruit & Nut bars isn't the sort of weakness a girl confides in just anybody.

He smiled—a real smile. Damn. It was easier to deal with him when he was being thoroughly vile. "Look, I'm sorry for being so rude earlier today. Your presence came as something of a shock and I reacted badly."

"Oh." Geared for battle, his apology took me utterly by surprise. I gaped.

"Aunt Arabella spoke very highly of you," he added, heaping coals of fire on my head. "She was impressed by your work on the Purple Gentian."

"Why all this sudden amiability?" I asked suspiciously, crossing my arms across my chest.

"Are you always this blunt?"

"I'm too tired to be tactful," I said honestly.

"Fair enough." Stretching, Colin detached himself from the wall. "Can I make you some hot chocolate as a token of peace? I was just about to have some myself," he added.

Suiting action to words, he loped over to the counter beside the sink and checked the level of water in a battered brown plastic electric kettle. Satisfied, he plugged it into the wall, flipping the red switch on the side.

I followed him over to the counter, the linen folds of the nightgown trailing after me across the linoleum. "As long as you promise not to slip any arsenic in it."

Colin rooted around in a cupboard above the sink for the cocoa tin and held it out to me to sniff. "See? Arsenic free."

I leaned back against the counter, my elbows behind me on the marble work surface. "I don't think arsenic is supposed to have a smell, is it?"

"Damn, foiled again." Colin spooned Cadbury's instant hot chocolate into two mugs, one decorated with large purple flowers, and the other with a quotation that I thought might be Jane Austen, but the author's name was hidden around the other side of the mug. "Look, if it makes you feel better, I promise to do a very bad job hiding your body."

"In that case, carry on." I yawned.

The red switch on the side of the electric kettle flipped to off as the water bubbled to a boil. Marveling at the unreality of it all, I watched as Colin efficiently unplugged the cord and poured steaming water into the two mugs. Here I was, in someone else's midnight kitchen, while the man who had told me to keep my grubby little hands off his family papers made me hot chocolate. I had to be hallucinating. Or asleep. Any moment now, Colin was going to morph into a dancing aardvark, and I'd find myself naked in the middle of a chemistry exam.

Colin held out one steaming mug. "Flowers suit you?"

In the interest of our truce, I refrained from making snide remarks about carnations.

"Do you live here?" I asked, carefully positioning my fingers at the very bottom of the handle so that they wouldn't touch his.

He shook his head, carrying his own mug over to the kitchen table. "I stay with Aunt Arabella when I'm in town."

"Is your girlfriend also staying over?" I asked.

I caught a flash of something in his eyes—probably distaste at my prying into his personal life—but he said neutrally, "Serena has her own flat."

It was on the tip of my tongue to ask why he was staying with an aged aunt instead of his beauteous lady love, but I bit it back. It really wasn't any of my business. For all I knew, they'd had a huge spat over dinner and he'd been banned from his girlfriend's bed. Maybe he was a cover hog, and she'd exiled him. Maybe she snored. I rather liked that theory. The glamorous Serena snuffling and snorting, while Colin, driven half mad with the noise, fled in his plaid pajamas to Onslow Square.

My amusement faded as another, more realistic option occurred to me. His return to his aunt's house might have more to do with concern that a certain unwanted houseguest didn't try to make off with the family silver in the middle of the night.

"Sorry?" I'd been so wrapped up in my speculations that I'd missed whatever the object of them was saying.

"Why don't you sit down," he repeated patiently. He nudged a chair towards me with one large, bare foot. "I won't bite."

"One would never have known it from that letter of yours." I maneuvered myself and my flounces into the straight-backed chair, setting my still-steaming cocoa on the table in front of me. "I half expected to be set upon by mastiffs if I dared to set foot upon the hallowed grounds of Selwick Hall."

Amusement danced in Colin Selwick's hazel eyes. "I only promised *I* wouldn't bite. That's what we keep the dogs for," he added with mock solemnity.

"Why *were* you so nasty?"

Colin shrugged, some of the amusement fading. For a second, I was almost sorry I'd forced the topic. "We've had some difficulty with academics in the past, wanting to see the family papers. Some of them were less than polite."

Personally, I thought that if he had behaved to them as he had to me, they had every reason to rave like demented harpies.

"We had one woman sniffing around two years ago, trying to prove that the Pink Carnation was a transvestite. She said that's why he picked such a poofy name."

"He was not!" I said indignantly. Not that I have anything against that splendid segment of the species with their highly developed fashion sense, but my—um, I mean, *the* Pink Carnation was all man. He was Zorro, Lancelot, and Robin Hood all rolled into one. And, yes, I know Robin Hood wore tights, but they were manly tights.

"At least we agree on that much," Colin said dryly.

"And why should it matter?" I took a gulp of my cocoa, scalding half the skin off my tongue in the process, but I was off on one of my favorite rants and not to be deterred. "How does that make any difference to the thousands of British soldiers he saved and the hundreds of French spies he uncovered? What does it matter who the Pink Carnation was, when what he *did*— oops!" I had gestured a little too grandly with my flowery mug, generating a waterfall of hot cocoa down my hand.

"And you're so keen to see these papers because?" Colin Selwick inquired delicately.

I made a face at him and said something rude.

He raised a smug eyebrow.

I plunked my mug down on the pine table and leaned forward. "Why did your family hide the identity of the Pink Carnation?"

Colin retracted his eyebrow. He developed a deep interest in poking at the gooey cocoa residue that had collected at the bottom of his mug. "Maybe nobody was interested."

"Bullshit."

"Language, language, Miss Kelly."

"Sorry to singe your tender ears. But, really, why didn't anyone ever tell?"

Colin leaned back in his chair, lips twisting wryly. "God, you are tenacious."

"Flattery won't make me any less so."

"Flattery?" he queried.

"Pink Carnation?" I prompted.

"Well." He lowered his voice conspiratorily. "If you really must know . . ."

"Yes!"

"Maybe the Pink Carnation had a loathsome social disease." He grinned.

"Awful!" I whacked the table in disgust. Cradling my wounded hand, I moaned, "Owwww . . ."

"Serves you right, attacking the poor, innocent table." Colin picked up his mug and carried it over to the sink.

"You drove me to it," I flung back at him. "Ouch!"

Colin sighed. "Oh, give me that. No, not that." I'd extended my half-full mug of cocoa. He took the cocoa out of my hand, placed it on the table, and took hold of my hand instead.

Moving closer, so close that his pajama leg whispered against the skirt of my nightgown, he leaned intently over my hand.

"Where does it hurt?" he asked.

Next to his, my hand looked fragile and transparently pale. A nervous joke about palmistry and fortune-tellers died on my lips as Colin turned my hand palm up, massaging the abused digits. He ran his thumb, large, tanned, calloused, along the fleshy mound at the base of my palm, probing for injury. A shiver that had nothing to do with the draft from the window ran down my spine.

"It's fine. Really," I croaked, jerking my hand away.

"Good." Chair legs scraped against linoleum. "We wouldn't want you suing us," Colin added briskly, dumping my mug into the sink with a clatter.

My mouth dropped open. "I wouldn't—"

Colin started towards the kitchen door. "Of course, you wouldn't," he said, as if he didn't care one way or the other. "Look, all of this we've discussed—and everything you've read—it stays between us."

I wrenched my chair around to face him. "What do you mean?" I demanded, still reeling from that lawsuit comment.

"The Pink Carnation. Anything you read, or discover, goes no further than this flat. I spoke with Aunt Arabella tonight, and we came to the agreement that you may read anything she sees fit to show you—but only on that condition."

I popped out of my chair. "But my dissertation!"

"Will no doubt contain all sorts of brilliant insights about the Purple Gentian and the Scarlet Pimpernel," he said smoothly. "You can use anything you read here for those purposes. Not the Pink Carnation."

"You're absurd!"

His eyes swept leisurely up and down my linen-clad form. And he grinned. The bastard had the nerve to grin.

"At least I'm not impersonating Jane Eyre. Good night, Eloise."

"Well, you're no Mr. Rochester!" I snapped.

A door clicked shut somewhere along the hallway, informing me that even my feeble sally had been too late.

Urgh!

I sank back down into my chair, fuming. That nasty, vile . . . I must really have been reading too many nineteenth-century letters if my first impulse was to call him a cad. Rogue and bounder might also apply. Whatever term one used—and I could also think of several modern ones that would do nicely—the result was the same. That walking ball of slime had lulled me into a false sense of security by plying me with apologies and hot chocolate, intending all the while to spring his little nondisclosure provision on me.

Did he think I was going to go all gooey and giggly over him just because he fed me some instant hot chocolate and spoke to me like a human being for half an hour?

Well, I wasn't falling for it. And I wasn't giving in that easily. So his aunt Arabella liked me, did she? We'd see what she had to say about the whole nothing-you-read-can-go-beyond-this-flat ultimatum.

In the meantime, I had reading to do. Lots and lots of reading, and only a few hours left before morning necessitated my departure.

Stomping purposefully down the hall to my temporary room, I flung myself onto the bed, and resolutely took up Amy's diary where I had left off. I didn't care if my contacts started dancing a tango; nothing was going to deter me from finding out as much as I possibly could, and to hell with Colin Selwick!

Chapter Eighteen

❧

Georges. Amy rolled the name through her mind and frowned. She tried Anglicizing it. George. George! George . . . No matter how she pronounced it or punctuated it, George just didn't sound like the sort of name the Purple Gentian ought to have. Spelled Georges it was far too French and slippery. Spelled George, the name called up images of corpulent old King George puttering about in the gardens of Kew. Not exactly an enticing prospect.

But after last night, how could she have any doubt as to the Gentian's identity? The evidence was overwhelming. If Marston's conversation with her brother hadn't been enough to prove his identity, seeing him climbing into his carriage, wearing a long black cloak of the same sort that Amy had been in such intimate contact with—her stomach did flip-flops at the recollection—had to be conclusive. *Two* men in black cloaks roaming about her brother's house in the dead of night strained the imagination. And that Marston would be leaving from the front of the house just after the Purple Gentian sped off in that direction was enough of a coincidence to beggar belief.

Amy squirmed fretfully against the gray velvet squabs as her brother's coach pulled out of the courtyard, the same courtyard into which she had spied so anxiously last night. In the midday sun, with light glancing off the windows of the house and glinting along the shiny black finish of the gates, it hardly seemed like the same place. In fact, had Amy not woken on her chaise longue to find a pair of hideously besmeared slippers kicked half into the fireplace grate (she vaguely remembered attempting to burn them, and being thwarted by the fact that the coals had already been banked), she would have been inclined to assume that she had dreamed the whole thing.

Finding her way back into the house last night had been an experience that Amy would as soon forget. Attempting to climb over the gates had not been one of her more inspired plans. Discovering that Edouard had returned to his study and latched the window—after Amy spent an uncomfortable fifteen minutes grappling with the wall before successfully hoisting herself up onto the sill—had been the sort of setback that would have reduced a woman of lesser spirit to tears. Finally, when she had sunk to the prospect of waking the household and was trying to concoct a convincing tale to explain why she was outside at well past midnight in a torn gown and filthy slippers, she had come upon an unlatched window in the dining room, and swarmed up over the sill with a strength born of desperation.

At least the treacherous journey into the house had kept Amy's mind occupied. Back in her room, she lit a candle by the bed, and changed out of her soiled clothes in the quivering point of light. She stuck her shoes in the grate, pulled on a clean white linen night rail, brushed her hair fifty times, turned down the covers, blew out the candle, and couldn't sleep.

She couldn't sleep on her side, and she couldn't sleep on her back, and she couldn't sleep rolled into a ball with her arms around her knees.

"Oh my goodness, I kissed the Purple Gentian," Amy whispered to the darkened room. She slid down along the pillow with a silly smile on her face. It really had been an incredibly nice kiss.

But she still had no proof of who he actually *was*. Or how to find him.

Who was he? Why had he kissed her? Did he want to see her again? Argh!

Two o'clock saw Amy flat on her stomach with her head at the footboard and her feet kicking the pillow, replaying her conversation with the Purple Gentian in a slightly improved version.

At three o'clock Amy had rolled the covers into a little ball at the foot of the bed, and was wondering whether the Purple Gentian had just kissed her to get her to stop pestering him.

By four o'clock Amy had been reduced to pulling little

tufts of fuzz off of the coverlet and chanting, "He loves me, he loves me not."

It had taken the combined efforts of Jane and Miss Gwen to drag Amy out of bed in time for her first English lesson with Hortense Bonaparte. Really, that jug of water had been completely unnecessary, Amy decided crossly.

Amy yawned broadly as the carriage drew up before the Tuilleries, decanting her and Edouard into the courtyard. A bored-looking sentry waved them into the palace. Amy made faces at Edouard's anxious reminders to be on her best behavior, promised to meet him back at the entryway in two hours, and breathed a sigh of relief as he scuttled off down a corridor on his own errands. Amy wasn't supposed to meet Hortense—she consulted the little enamel watch hanging from a gold chain around her neck—for another twenty minutes, which, now that she had divested herself of her brother, left her time to explore.

The Tuilleries by day was quite a different prospect from the Tuilleries by night. Last night, the rooms through which they had passed had been decked with orange blossoms and cunning arrangements of roses whose scent had clashed with the heavy perfumes worn by the guests. Not even the odd, crumpled petal remained; all had been swept away by efficient servants, leaving in their wake the less pleasant reek of ammonia and lye.

Last night grenadiers standing stiffly at attention (at least Bonaparte made no attempt to hide the source of his power!) had lined the staircase like human signposts. At the top of the landing they had followed the sound of martial music through a series of antechambers lit with candle sconces draped in gauze. By the time they were three rooms away, the hubbub of the Yellow Salon had been an unmistakable guide.

It wasn't as though the palace was deserted. As Amy wandered down the corridors looking for suspicious activities, she passed servants lugging pails of water, soldiers leaving their shifts, and a pale young man in an ill-fitting frock coat with ink-stained fingers, who Amy surmised was most likely someone's secretary.

Amy was contemplating following the secretary (after all, he might be on his way to a highly secret meeting), when her attention was arrested by a familiar puce frock coat in the next room. It was undeniably her brother—no one else would wear gold lace in that quantity at collar and cuffs—but his voice held a very uncharacteristic air of authority as he held forth in a rapid whisper.

Amy strained for a glimpse of his companion. Her pulse raced at the prospect of encountering the Purple Gentian again, and she leaned further forward around the doorframe. Why did Edouard have to wear coats with such ridiculously padded shoulders? All she could make out was a hand and a bit of black sleeve; Amy doubted even the most dedicated spy would be able to identify someone from a hand glimpsed from several yards away. Even that unhelpful appendage was soon blocked by a waterfall of gold lace as Edouard pressed something into the stranger's hand. Edouard's garish cuffs hindered Amy's view, but it looked like paper. A note of some kind?

Amy edged forward, right into the doorknob.

She bit down on her inadvertent gasp of pain and annoyance, but the soft exhalation of air was enough to alert Edouard's companion, who grabbed at Edouard's arm, said something in a rapid whisper, and propelled him through the door on the opposite side of the room. Edouard scurried out without so much as glancing back.

But his companion did.

As Edouard's companion swerved to yank the door shut behind him, his face came briefly into view before the oaken barrier slammed into place. Amy only saw his face for a moment, but that moment was enough. It was a face she recognized, but not the face of Georges Marston. It was a narrow, dark face, undistinguished in every way—except for the long, newly healed scab that slashed across his left temple.

"Drat!"

Amy raced across the room and peered through the door, but it was no use; her brother and his companion had already disappeared from sight.

How ever was she going to explain to Jane that she had lost her wounded man for a second time?

Chapter Nineteen

~~~~~~~~~~~~~~~

It was in considerably reduced spirits that Amy returned to her exploration of the Tuilleries. At first, she peered beneath tables and behind chairs in search of a familiar flash of puce and gold, but Edouard and his companion had disappeared with a speed of which Amy would never have believed her brother capable. He had whisked his padded shoulders and lacy ruffles out of her path faster than the Purple Gentian leaping through a study window.

Ought she, Amy wondered, to broach the topic with Edouard on the way home? Should she simply tell him she knew him to be in league with the Purple Gentian and demand to be allowed to participate? It would certainly save her much time spent skulking about, and give Edouard an opportunity to drop his foppish front in his own home. On the other hand, Edouard might tell her, as he frequently had when they were small children, to mind her own business. In fact, it seemed more than likely that was just what Edouard would do. He had never been amenable to sharing.

All things considered, Amy concluded, she was probably best off maintaining an air of ignorance—and spying on her brother whenever the opportunity arose. She would have to consult with Jane....

"DISGRACE!" someone bellowed.

Amy stopped abruptly, shocked out of her reverie. Good heavens, that wasn't directed at her, was it? She took a quick look around. No. She was alone in yet another of the little antechambers that separated the grander areas of the palace. The noise had emerged from the door towards which she had been thoughtlessly wandering, a door that stood slightly ajar, as though someone had just entered.

"YOU ARE A DISGRACE!" the bellower repeated, with, if possible, an increase in volume.

Amy was considering edging her way back out of the anteroom, when another much softer voice interposed, "But, Napoleon, I—"

Amy's breath caught in her throat. While not exactly a meeting with Fouché, the conversation held promise for the eavesdropper. Perhaps a scandal that she could convey back to the English news sheets? Lifting her muslin skirts in both hands, she tiptoed her way into the space between the door and the wall.

"Leclerc only dead for a year!"

Leclerc . . . The name might mean little in terms of international espionage, but Amy pressed her ear against the hinges of the door hard enough to leave a permanent dent. The last time she had spotted Pauline Bonaparte Leclerc, the shameless woman had had her tongue in Lord Richard Selwick's ear. Her interest, Amy assured herself, was purely professional, not personal. Lord Richard's amours meant nothing to her, nothing at all. It was just that . . . that . . . any scandal that might be damaging to the Bonaparte clan could be helpful to her cause, she rationalized triumphantly.

Through the gap in the door, Amy could hear the clomping of boots on the parquet floor as Bonaparte raged about the room. "You're out of mourning already!"

"But, Napoleon, I did cut off all my hair and place it in his coffin."

"Hair, ha!" The smack of a palm hitting wood. "Hair grows back! It already has! And you! Chasing anything in trousers!"

Amy waited eagerly for a reference to Lord Richard and that scandalous scene in the salon.

"My Assistant Minister of Police complained that you pinched him in an inappropriate place! Again!"

"Oh, but, Napoleon, it wasn't an inappropriate place," Pauline reassured him eagerly. "It was in my sitting room."

Amy eyed the wood of the door with incredulous disgust. Either Pauline Leclerc was one of the most truly addlepated people she had ever encountered (and there was stiff competition for that title, with Derek on that list, not to mention her cousin Agnes), or she was wickedly clever. Amy preferred the first option.

Bonaparte spoke in the simple monosyllables of someone who had also chosen the first option. "What was he doing there?"

"I had to have someone check for spies," Pauline answered innocently.

Crash! Bonaparte had hurled something against the wall. Amy squinted against the hinges. Ah, an inkwell, judging from the large black splotch adorning the wallpaper.

"Don't be angry with me, Napoleon," Pauline wheedled. "It's just that I am so bored...."

"Bored? Bored? Find a hobby! Go shopping!"

"You can't begrudge me my innocent little amusements...."

"Your innocent amusements are an international scandal! What do I have to do? Send you to a nunnery?"

An excellent solution! Amy would have seconded the idea had she been a legitimate part of the conversation, rather than an eavesdropper.

"How can you"—*sniff*—"be so unkind? All I want"—*sniff*—"is a little happiness."

"All *I* want is my family not to embarrass me!"

"This is Josephine's doing, isn't it? She's poisoned your mind against me!"

Amy had been decidedly right in liking the First Consul's wife. Josephine was clearly a woman of good taste and sound judgment—except in marrying Bonaparte.

To his credit, the First Consul rose to his wife's defense, or rather, roared in his wife's defense, "Hold your tongue!"

"If that's what you want, I'll just leave. You'll never have to see me again." The sound of chair legs scraping against wood was followed by Pauline sobbing her way out of the room. Amy cringed back against the wall, fearing both disclosure and the impact of the door, but Pauline slipped easily through the gap—nobody in the throes of distress should be that graceful, thought Amy critically—bawling into her handkerchief all the while.

"Pauline! Don't cry, damn you! Pauline!" Bonaparte charged out of the room after his sister.

The door slammed open. Fortunately, Bonaparte's shouts drowned out Amy's involuntary *oomph* as the heavy wood whacked all of the air out of her lungs.

When the little black spots in front of Amy's eyes had

faded away—except for the legitimate little spots of dust motes dancing in a beam of sunshine—she slipped cautiously out from behind the door. "I feel like a dress that was put in a clothespress," she muttered to herself.

Once Amy had flexed her shoulders and shaken out her arms, and felt more like herself and rather less like a piece of recently ironed fabric, she tiptoed around to peek into the room that Bonaparte and his sister had so recently vacated. After all, there was only so much one could see through the inch-wide gap between the door and the wall.

Amy's eye took in, one by one, a wall with a large ink splotch, an iron staircase that looked a bit like an ink splotch itself against the pale wall, and a carpet marred by yet more ink splotches. By far the most interesting feature of the room was a desk, piled with stacks of papers, and surrounded by enough broken quills to refeather a plump goose.

Bonaparte had left his study empty.

Amy allowed herself only a moment to gloat over her good fortune. With a quick glance either way to make sure no one else was about, she plunged into Bonaparte's study.

Amy picked her way across the broken quills and balled-up bits of paper on the floor. She really mustn't disturb anything; she must do nothing to arouse suspicion. And if he returned, she could legitimately claim to be lost and looking for Hortense. Who would ever suspect a bit of a girl in a yellow muslin dress? Amy practiced looking innocent and mildly daft as she made for the desk. Widen the eyes, drop the lower lip . . . and, if worse came to worst, cry. From that last interview, Amy had gleaned a crucial piece of intelligence; Bonaparte was a soft touch for crying women.

Ah, the desk! Amy briefly clasped her hands together to still their shaking, and then stooped over in earnest. In the center of the desk lay a piece of paper closely covered with writing, as well as an unintended design of ink dots splattered by the abandoned quill that lay next to it. Clearly, Bonaparte must have been working on this when his sister disturbed him.

Eagerly, Amy snatched it up and began to read. "Article 818. The husband may, without the concurrence of his wife, claim a distribution of objects movable or immovable fallen to her and which come into community . . ."

Oh, for goodness' sake, what was this drivel? Not only did

Amy disagree heartily with the sentiment—she defied any future husband to try to claim a distribution of her objects movable or otherwise without her concurrence—but it was utterly useless to her investigation. Unless Bonaparte's secret plan for conquering England was to contract a marriage between the two countries and then claim that as husband, France was entitled to all of England's objects, movable and immovable.

Not being an immovable object, Amy moved on, replacing the offending document in the center of the blotter, with the quill placed across it as though just dropped by Napoleon's hand.

A sheaf of papers bristled under a fragment of classical pottery serving as a paperweight. At any other time, Amy would have been intrigued by the artifact; keen on her mission, she went straight for the documents, which were folded and roughly bound together with a piece of string. Carefully, Amy eased the letter on the top out of the pile. Ten thousand francs. Amy squinted at the spidery writing. Had she misread it? No. It was a bill from Josephine's mantua-maker for a white lawn gown embroidered with gold thread. Amy yanked out the next paper from the pile, which turned out, unsurprisingly, to be an invoice for the matching slippers. Recklessly, Amy shook out all of the papers, and began to thumb through them. She flipped past bills for cashmere shawls, for diamond bracelets, for shipments of rose cuttings, for more pairs of slippers and gloves and fans than Amy could imagine using in a decade of continuous partygoing. There wasn't a clandestine note or a suspicious purchase among the lot.

Wait! Unless . . . Could the documents be a code? Perhaps what was meant by slippers was really rifles—different colors could refer to different types! And rose cuttings could refer to cannon balls, or something of that ilk. Buoyed by her own cleverness, Amy snatched back up the documents she had dropped in disgust seconds before. Perhaps by looking at them more closely, she would find a key to the code.

On second glance, it became quite clear that the bills were indeed bills. The only thing revealed by looking at them more closely was that Amy's imagination was more effective than her spying. And that Josephine, for all her charm, was a prodigious spendthrift, but that wasn't anything everybody didn't already know. The English papers delighted in carrying tales of Josephine's extravagances and Bonaparte's infuriated reaction. It was rumored—in the *Spectator,* not the *Shropshire Intelligencer*—that Josephine had already bankrupted the French treasury with her uncontrollable acquisitiveness.

Scowling, Amy bundled the folded papers back into their string. Marvelous. She had stumbled into Bonaparte's abandoned study in the spying opportunity of a lifetime, and what did she discover? A packet of bills.

Amy rested her hands on her hips and glared at the desk. Really, there had to be something more informative among the clutter. A bird landed on the windowsill, puffed out its chest, and unleashed an operatic series of trills. Absently, Amy flapped a hand at it, hissing, "Shh!" Offended, the bird gave a few indignant hops, relieved itself on the windowsill, and flew squawking back into the garden to complain to his fellows.

Amy returned to rifling halfheartedly through Bonaparte's desk. Perhaps the Purple Gentian had been right to call her naïve last night. It had certainly been naïve of her to believe that a man clever enough to take over the rule of a turbulent country, cutting out numerous competitors at home, and conquering a slew of countries abroad along the way, would be dim enough to leave his plans for the invasion of England in plain sight upon his desk.

All right then, if Bonaparte's secret papers *weren't* in plain sight upon his desk, she would just have to figure out where they were. By the time she emerged from this room, she would have something to report to the Gentian, something that would make his eyes widen with admiration and his jaw drop. "Amy, you astound me," he would say, and she would simply raise an eyebrow—well, both eyebrows, since she couldn't manage just the one—and murmur, "You doubted me?"

Amy's gaze drifted up around the walls, searching for secret caches. That painting on the far wall could conceal a safe of some kind. And over there, by the window, that long, dark line might be a relic of another inkpot that had perished for its country, or it might indicate a break of some kind in the wallpaper. Amy planted both her hands on the desk and leaned forward for a better look.

"Ouch!" Lesson one of spying: Never plant your hands anywhere without first checking to make sure you won't be maimed. Amy absently sucked on a cut on her index finger, and searched for the weapon of destruction. She wouldn't put it past the tyrant to have strewn poisoned tacks on his desk, or . . . Oh, it was a paper cut.

The sharp edge that had sliced her finger poked out from underneath the blotter. Grabbing the edge with her uninjured left hand, Amy yanked it free. Probably another bill, she thought irately. The series of numbers marching across the page gave credence to that theory, but the signature at the bottom said Joseph Fouché. Fouché had sent Bonaparte calculations for the cost of the Army for the Invasion of England.

Amy's first impulse was to stuff the paper into her bodice and flee. She went so far as to poise the paper over her neckline, but common sense prevailed. Not only would it create quite a lump under the thin fabric of her dress, but Bonaparte was sure to notice its absence. She would just have to memorize it. Two thousand four hundred ships, Amy repeated to herself, and one hundred and seventy-five thousand men. Amy felt a swell of indignation that had nothing to do with proving herself to the Purple Gentian or the ills done the monarchy. Her overactive imagination had presented her with an image of one hundred and seventy-five thousand Frenchmen marching grimly through Uncle Bertrand's peaceful meadows, trampling his fields and kicking his sheep.

"Not while I'm around to stop it," Amy muttered, and read on.

The treasury, Fouché wrote, could not support such an expense. No wonder, thought Amy, glancing at the pile of bills she had plunked back down on the desk in irritation moments before. The next time Amy saw Mme Bonaparte, she would be sure to bring her attention to the necessity of owning at least three diamond tiaras.

Unfortunately, Fouché had secured funds from the Swiss. Amy scowled at the letter. Secured, indeed! Extorted would doubtless be the better word. The money, in gold, was to be transported by coach from Switzerland to Paris on the evening of April thirtieth, and thence to what Fouché referred to as "a safe place."

"That's what he thinks." Amy regarded the scrap of paper with the smug sort of smile usually reserved by felines for canaries.

The last day of April. That gave her a week and a half to figure out how to intercept the money. Plenty of time, thought Amy blithely. First, she would notify the Purple Gentian, who, of course, would be so impressed that he would henceforth include her in all his counsels. Together, they could create a daring plan to make off with the money. Without money, Bonaparte's invasion of England would be thwarted. The discontented masses would rise against him. And the monarchy would be restored. Amy grinned as she stuck the letter carefully back under the blotter. Not bad work for a girl fresh from Shropshire.

Amy strode hurriedly out of the study. Before she continued on to Hortense, she would have to send a note to the Gentian, telling him to meet her . . . where? Perhaps in the Luxembourg gardens. She could find a page to—

Ooof! Amy collided at high speed with someone entering the anteroom from the other direction. Her head was still spinning as a pair of capable hands righted her, and a warm chuckle sounded somewhere above her ear. "What an original way to make your presence felt!"

Chapter Twenty

"**M**y lord!" Amy hastily stepped back, this time banging into a bust of Brutus that wobbled ominously on its marble pedestal. Amy grabbed at Brutus before he could take a suicidal leap off his stand. "I didn't . . . that is . . ."

"Had you known it was me you would have taken care to run into poor Brutus instead?" Lord Richard supplied with a smile of such conspiratorial goodwill that Amy nearly reeled back into poor Brutus once more.

"Something like that," admitted Amy weakly. Clearly, she was still slightly dazed from her two collisions.

Amy felt behind her to make sure she wasn't going to back into anything else. With Lord Richard in it, the anteroom shrank to nothingness. The tall figure in tight buff breeches and pale blue jacket filled Amy's line of vision. A dusty ray of sunshine from the one window in the room caressed his head, encircling him with a sort of halo. Halo? Amy caught herself up short before she could descend any further into folly. A man who abandoned his country? Who caressed scantily clad women in the middle of a party? Lord Richard was the last man in the world to deserve a halo.

"You just missed Mme Leclerc," blurted Amy.

"Pauline?" Lord Richard frowned in a way that could indicate either confusion or displeasure. "Was she looking for me?"

"Um . . ." Why on earth had she said that? Drat. Now if Lord Richard went and found Mme Leclerc she'd be sure to tell him that she had never even spoken to Amy, and Lord Richard would know Amy had made it up, and might even leap to the conclusion, the *incorrect* conclusion, that Amy cared the slightest little bit about his relationship with Mme Leclerc.

Amy evaded the danger of being caught out in a direct lie by pointing at the door and informing him, "She went that way."

"Oh," was Lord Richard's lengthy response.

Amy waited for him to charge off past the statue of Brutus, through the gilded doors, in pursuit of She of the Diaphanous Dress and Nonexistent Bodice. And waited.

Lord Richard leaned lazily against the paneled wall as though he had no other purpose in the world but to stand in a little anteroom with Amy.

"Don't you want to go that way?" Amy asked uncertainly.

Lord Richard considered for a moment. He shook his head. "Not really."

Amy's eyes searched Lord Richard's handsome face. She would have thought that he would be in more of a hurry to run off after his paramour. On second thought, maybe that wasn't all that surprising. Look how rapidly he had gone from flirting with Amy to dallying with Mme Leclerc. Just the way he had flitted off to join the French in Egypt when his very own country was at war with them. Faithless cad!

Amy's feelings towards Pauline Leclerc rapidly spiraled from animosity to pity. That poor, gullible woman had clearly been as thoroughly taken in by the glib charm of the perfidious Lord Richard as had Amy herself. The woman might wear dresses with as much substance as cobwebs, and her intellectual capacities might be even flimsier, but, still, she deserved better than to be treated like that.

"Well, you really *ought* to," said Amy hotly.

"Ought to what?"

"Go after Mme Leclerc." Amy glowered at Richard.

Richard regarded Amy quizzically. "Is this an attempt to free yourself of my presence? You could just say so."

"No!"

"No, you don't want to be rid of my presence?"

"Urgh!" Amy emitted an inarticulate noise somewhat akin to a snort. Heaving a deep breath, she clarified, "Ridding myself of your presence was not my intention—"

"Delighted to hear it."

"Rather," Amy bit out, "I was hoping to induce you to behave with some consideration—"

"By leaving you alone as quickly as possible?"

"No!" Amy bounced up and down in a way that would

have been the prelude to a temper tantrum had she been a decade younger.

As she was twenty, rather than ten, the effect was rather different. Richard's lips twisted into a bemused smile as he watched her breasts jiggle below the scooped neck of her bodice.

"Would you like to repeat that?" he asked hopefully.

Amy scowled at him. "What about the word *no* do you find difficult to comprehend?"

"What in the blazes you mean by it," Richard admitted honestly. "Let's back up a step, shall we? You want me to go away. . . ."

"No." Unfortunately, this time Amy didn't jiggle. Instead, she held up both hands. "No. That's not the point. You're twisting my words again. Don't interrupt me! What I've been trying to say is that the only decent thing to do is go after Mme Leclerc and make things right with her."

Richard blinked at Amy. "I didn't realize things were wrong with her."

Since it didn't look like Amy was going to bounce anymore, Richard took a moment to actually try to figure out what in the devil she was talking about. This sudden fascination with Pauline made very little sense. Unless Pauline had come upon Amy and bent her ears with tales of unanswered letters of love? That wasn't a terribly Pauline sort of thing to do. Pauline's attitude towards love affairs, Richard thought approvingly, could only be called *sporting*. She gave the chase her all, accepted her defeats with good grace, and seldom whined.

"How can you be so callous?"

Richard looked down into Amy's irate, flushed face, and enlightenment dawned.

"You don't mean to say that you thought that Pauline and I—good gad, no!"

"What do you mean, 'good gad, no!' I saw the two of you together last night, in Mme Bonaparte's salon. Do you deny it?"

For a moment, Richard struggled to recall what Amy could possibly be talking about. His encounter with Amy in her brother's study later that evening had done much to drive any other recollections out of his head, and he had been to so many receptions at the Tuilleries over the years that one tended to blend into another. What could he have been doing with Pauline?

Oh. Pauline had had him backed into a corner. She had also, if memory served, ventured into regions generally reserved for behind closed doors. Richard hoped Amy hadn't witnessed that. From the strength of Amy's glare, Richard rather feared that she had. Of course, this all begged the question of how Amy had come to witness that unfortunate moment in the first place. It wasn't as though he had been entwined with Pauline right in the middle of the room; they had been off in a far corner, well away from the throng of spectators clustering around Bonaparte and Miss Gwen. A group of which, Richard was quite sure, Amy had been a part. In which case, Amy must have followed him.

Richard beamed straight at Amy's scowling face.

"See? You can't deny it," Amy said in a suffocated voice.

"Deny it?" Richard shrugged. "What man wouldn't want to be seen with Pauline? She is, after all, an exceptionally beautiful woman, don't you agree?"

Amy nodded woodenly.

"With exceptionally fine eyes," he added devilishly. "The sort of eyes a man can lose himself in."

Amy's head jerked up and down by a fraction of an inch.

Richard lowered his voice and leaned forward conspiratorially. "And exceptionally little conversation."

Amy gaped.

Moving back a step, Richard waved a nonchalant hand. "She has very little to say about the Rosetta Stone, and absolutely no interest in Homer."

Amy leaned back against the wall, feeling completely thrown off balance. For the life of her, she couldn't remember why she had brought up Mme Leclerc in the first place, and fervently wished she hadn't.

"Amy," said Richard softly, "there is not, nor was there ever, anything between me and Pauline."

"Other than her dress," muttered Amy.

She hadn't meant the comment to be heard but Lord Richard's hearing was unfairly sharp. He gasped with laughter. As he laughed, his green eyes crinkled at the corners, glinting with flecks of gold like leaves touched by the sun.

"While I must confess that the only person I was looking for was Bonaparte—"

"He also went that way," interjected Amy.

"I am delighted to have stumbled across you," Richard continued with a grin.

"I can't imagine why."

"Can't you?" murmured Richard.

"You needed to discuss Homer with someone?" Amy suggested tartly, flinging out the first unromantic image that came to mind.

Only, unfortunately, once she had spoken, she couldn't help but imagine sitting curled up next to Lord Richard in a large leather chair, in front of a flaming fire on a cold winter's day, reading aloud the sonorous Greek phrases of the *Odyssey* to one another.

Amy mentally pushed the book aside and doused the fire, just as Lord Richard said, "Close enough. I was planning to send you a note, inviting you to come see my antiquities tomorrow."

Something about the way Richard said "my antiquities," as proud as a schoolboy with a particularly smashing toad to show off, made Amy want to smile despite herself. Only they weren't really his antiquities, were they? They belonged to Bonaparte, who had collected them in the course of leading the armies of the Revolution. No right-minded Englishman would admit to having anything to do with those antiquities. And no right-minded Englishwoman would have anything to do with Lord Richard Selwick, Amy reminded herself sternly. Teasing green eyes or no.

"That will not be possible," she said coldly.

Lord Richard's eyes lingered knowingly on her face. "No blood guilt can pass to you from a few harmless objects."

Amy lifted her nose in the air as though she hadn't the slightest notion of what he was talking about.

"Think of it," he continued softly. "These statues and jewels and fragile bits of humanity were buried deep in the earth centuries before the world ever heard of Bonaparte. Think of it. The relics of a civilization that was old while France was still covered in forest and London a mere gathering of mud huts."

His words cast a spell in the midafternoon quiet of the room, evoking images of shimmering sands and scurrying men in white robes and black-haired women keening their grief in elaborate burial chambers.

"Tomorrow afternoon, then. Your cousin and chaperone are, of course, included in the invitation." He grinned. "Miss Gwen might like a mummy case for use in her horrid novel."

"I haven't accepted!"

"But you want to."

Drat. The insufferable man was absolutely right; no matter her feelings for him, she longed to see hieroglyphs carved into stone and ornaments that might once have dazzled the eyes of Mark Antony. Miss Gwen wasn't the only one with an interest in mummy cases.

"Why hesitate?" Lord Richard pressed his advantage. "You're not afraid, are you?"

"Of what?"

"Of ancient curses? Of enjoying my company?"

Since that was precisely what terrified Amy, she bristled indignantly. "Of course not! Tomorrow afternoon, you said?"

"Two o'clock, perhaps? The artifacts are lodged in a wing of the Tuilleries, until we move them into the Louvre. Ask any sentry to show you the way," Lord Richard directed, with a smile that struck Amy as uncomfortably close to a smirk.

Too late, Amy realized how neatly she had been seduced and goaded into accepting.

"You don't have any apples to offer while you're at it, do you?" she asked sourly.

"Satan tempting Eve in the garden? Not a terribly flattering role for me, is it? And you're overdressed for the part."

Amy's blush rivaled the hue of the dangerous fruit they had been discussing. Somehow, Lord Richard's frankly admiring gaze made the yellow muslin of her gown feel as insubstantial as a string of fig leaves. Amy covered her confusion by saying quickly, "Might I ask a favor, my lord?"

"A phoenix feather from the farthest deserts of Arabia? The head of a dragon on a bejeweled platter?"

"Nothing quite that complicated," replied Amy, marveling once again at the chameleon quality of the man beside her. How could anyone be so utterly infuriating at one moment and equally charming the next? Untrustworthy, she reminded herself. Mercurial. Changeable. "A dragon's head wouldn't be much use to me just now, unless it could offer me directions."

Richard crooked an arm. "Tell me where you need to be, and I'll escort you."

Amy tentatively rested her hand on the soft blue fabric of

his coat. "That's quite a generous offer when you don't know where I'm going."

"Ten leagues beyond the wide world's end?" suggested Richard with a lazy grin.

"Methinks it is no journey?" Amy matched the quotation triumphantly, and was rewarded by the admiring light that flamed in Lord Richard's eyes. "No, not nearly that far—at least, I hope not. This palace does seem large enough to house a couple of continents. I was looking for Hortense Bonaparte's chambers."

The statement was close enough to the truth, and Lord Richard accepted it without a murmur of disbelief. "You're in the right place," he informed her, steering her back into Bonaparte's study, "just a flight below where you ought to be. That little staircase will take you right up to Josephine's chambers, and Hortense's are next door."

"Thank you." Amy lifted one foot to the first step.

"Think nothing of it." Lord Richard leaned an arm on the newel of the stair. Even with Amy a step up, he still smiled down at her. "It wasn't much of a journey. I owe you nine leagues at least."

"Bring me a phoenix feather, and we'll cancel the debt. Good day, my lord, and thank you for the directions." Amy lifted her skirt and ascended another step.

"You'll have to accept a mummy case or two instead." Lord Richard's voice arrested Amy midstep. Letting fall her skirt, she turned, only to discover that his smile was even more devastating when faced eye to eye. Or lip to lip, as the case might be. Amy swallowed hard.

"Why were you so eager for me to visit?" she asked suspiciously.

"Because," Richard said quite simply, "I like you."

And then he smiled and bowed as if his last statement hadn't made Amy's jaw drop till it practically hit the bottom stair, and, with a bland, "Good day, Miss Balcourt," took his leave before Amy could retrieve her jaw and her faculties of speech.

"And good day to you too," she muttered as she flounced up the stairs. " 'Because I like you.' What on earth is that supposed to mean? And why do I care? I don't care. Of course I don't care. What difference does it make if Richard Selwick likes me or not? None. None at all. Of course it makes no difference."

Amy stopped short on the upper landing and lifted her chin. "I have more important things to worry about."

Amy collared one of the young pages who seemed to do nothing but loiter about the corridors waiting to carry messages, clandestine or otherwise.

Which was why, when Amy hissed, "Can you take a message for me?" the page gave her a look that questioned her mental capacities.

"Yes, miss."

"Can you keep it secret?"

Another look, this time compounded with wounded dignity. Amy was sinking in the page's estimation by the moment. "Of course, miss."

"Oh, good!" Leaning forward, Amy whispered, "Tell him I must see him urgently. Don't forget! *Urgently*. Because I have something terribly important I have to tell him, and he'll know what it is, after our conversation last night. I'll meet him at the Luxembourg Gardens at midnight. And don't forget—*urgently*!"

The page looked understandably confused. "Tell who, miss?"

Amy refrained from banging her hand against her head in extreme self-disgust. Just because she had let Lord Richard rattle her . . .

"Georges Marston," she said, pressing a coin from her reticule into the boy's hand. "Make sure to deliver my message solely to the ears of Georges Marston. And don't forget—"

"I know," said the boy, with the world-weary air of one who had heard it all before. "Urgently."

Richard allowed himself a moment to watch the delightful sway of Amy's hips as she ascended the stairs towards Hortense's apartments. It was, he assured himself, a permissible luxury. Bounding up the stairs after her, flinging her over his shoulder, and bearing her off to the nearest empty chamber was not. Pity, that.

Shaking his head, Richard wandered back out of Bonaparte's study and through the anteroom, which suddenly seemed much darker without the cheerful yellow of Amy's dress. He wondered if she was as beset by memories of their kiss last night as he was.

It was ludicrous! He had kissed hundreds of women in his time. Actually . . . Richard did a quick calculation, casting his mind back over his teenage career as a rakehell. Well, maybe only dozens. At any rate, not one of them had plagued him nearly as much as Amy. None of them had kept him awake for the rest of the night in a state of uncomfortable desire, wondering whether such an opportunity would arise again.

Usually Richard made his own opportunities.

Back in his rakehell days, all it had taken had been a smile across a ballroom, a nod of the head towards a garden, a note passed surreptitiously from gloved hand to gloved hand. So easy. But then had come Deirdre and her betrayal, and Richard had become adept at sending opportunity scurrying away. And now . . . Richard frowned at a bird chirping with excessive force in the open window of an empty salon.

He could easily arrange another assignation with Amy. Ah, but only if he were willing to do so as the Purple Gentian. Therein lay the rub. The Purple Gentian and Lord Richard Selwick unanimously concurred that Amy was to have nothing more to do with the former. Just look at last night. She had curtailed his inspection of Balcourt's study, just as he had gotten to the good part, the mysterious cache of papers in the globe. True, for all he knew the globe might contain nothing more exciting than Balcourt's billetsdoux. Or it might contain papers vital to the defense of England. As if that weren't enough, he had entirely missed whatever had been going on in the courtyard. He had arrived just in time to see villainous-looking rascals trailing out into the night, and to hear Balcourt bidding Marston an uninformative farewell.

He probably should have tailed Marston home. Richard excised the *probably*. No doubt about it, the responsible thing to do, the Purple Gentian thing to do, was to follow Marston. Instead, the Purple Gentian had lurked in the bushes outside the Hotel de Balcourt, making sure that one Miss Amy Balcourt made it safely inside.

Richard grinned in recollection. Hell, it had been worth the missed intelligence just to watch Amy desperately trying to haul herself over that windowsill. She'd plant her elbows on the edge, screw up her face, wiggle in an exceedingly appealing way, and plop back down. Richard had admired her tenacity and her derriere.

One night's work—Richard sternly pulled his mind back to

the matter at hand. One night's work could be accounted lost with good grace. To lose another night's work verged on irresponsibility. Besides, Amy wouldn't be Amy if she didn't keep pestering him for his identity and a place in the League. Sooner or later, under the influence of her lips and arms and . . . anyway, sooner or later, he was bound to weaken on one or the other, and either would be disaster. Thus his resolution, as he trudged back home last night through the dark and smelly streets of Paris, that the Purple Gentian was to avoid Miss Amy Balcourt as though she were Delaroche himself.

Lord Richard Selwick, on the other hand, was quite free to call on Miss Balcourt.

After all, Richard reasoned with himself, as long as he confined his calls to nonspying hours, his relationship with Amy could be kept separate from his work.

He just had to charm Amy into liking him. It shouldn't be too hard. She might have kissed the Purple Gentian last night, but it was clearly Richard she was thinking about. Of course, it would be even better if it were Richard she was thinking about *and* kissing.

All he had to do was dispel her lingering anxieties about his character. Hmm. Richard paused next to a painting by David. That might be too difficult a feat without revealing his secret identity. Too much effort. No, he decided. Far better to seduce Amy out of her scruples.

Ah, now there was a plan worthy of the master strategist who had saved scads of French noblemen from the guillotine.

With that out of the way, Richard could once more concentrate on sallying forth and doing his bit to defend England against old Boney by drinking French brandy and winning at cards.

Richard dropped in on a record-breaking four salons and card parties between eight and eleven o'clock. At one, he eavesdropped on conversations under the cover of music; at another, he elicited information over cards; at yet another, he rifled through his host's desk while a poet declaimed in a room across the hall. It would have been five parties had he not spotted Pauline Leclerc as he entered the fifth salon. Grabbing his hat and gloves back from the astonished maid, he had barely escaped with his trousers intact.

Robbins dropped Richard off beneath the portico of Mme

Rochefort's town house, Richard's final destination, just after eleven. "Don't bother coming back for me," Richard told his coachman, as he swung out of the chaise. "I'll find my own way back."

"You're quite sure, my lord?" Robbins believed the population of Paris to be comprised entirely of footpads and assassins, all just waiting to leap out at his young master from dark alleyways.

"Quite sure. Get some rest."

"Aye, my lord."

As his carriage pulled away, Richard settled his hat more firmly on his head, gave his gloves one last tug, pasted on a social smile, and ascended the steps to the front door. He was let in by a maid, who took his hat and cloak and pointed him upstairs. Richard made his way up the marble staircase, skirting around a young dandy clinging to the bannister, who was already clearly the worse for drink. Richard feared for the next guest to pass below the staircase.

Reaching the landing, Richard considered his options. To his right, food had already been laid out in the supper-room, and a cadre of devoted gallants were making up plates for their beloveds of the moment.

Richard spotted his hostess in the crush, and nodded to her. Mme Rochefort waved her fan at him with more enthusiasm than decorum, a description that suited the majority of the guests rather well. Mme Rochefort's parties teemed with young adventurers, aging flirts, and hardened roués, all barely clinging to the fringes of society. Mme Rochefort herself fell into the second category; a former crony of Josephine's, she had been banished from the Tuilleries when Bonaparte had decided to become respectable.

Down the hall, the crowd in the card room was thinner than usual. Therese Tallien, another former friend of the First Consul's wife, was playing a rubber of whist with a brightly dressed dandy, a heavy-lidded young officer, and Desiree Hamelin, who was chiefly famed for having walked topless all the way from the Place Royale to the Luxembourg Palace in the harum-scarum days of the Directorate.

Richard wandered through the room, murmuring polite inconsequentialities to acquaintances, and declining the offer of a rubber of whist from Mme Tallien. Under fashionably languid lids, Richard's green eyes darted ahead of him across the room. Paul Barras, a former head of state (and, it was rumored, former lover of Josephine), sat over solitaire at a table near the door. He would be no use. Richard likewise dismissed a gaggle of giggling women in hideous striped turbans. Ah, but there, by the fireplace . . .

"Marston, old chap," Richard drawled. "Not having much luck at cards tonight, I see! Murat." Richard nodded to the Consul's brother-in-law, who was listing in his chair at an angle that declared that the snifter of brandy before him was by no means his first.

Marston kicked a chair at Richard. "Care to try your luck, Selwick?"

"Jolly good of you." Richard dropped lazily into the little gilded chair.

Marston rose and stretched, swaying only a bit in the process. "Think nothing of it. I'm off as soon as I win some of my blunt back from Murat here. Got an assignation with a hot piece of baggage."

Richard yanked his chair up to the table. "How much does she cost?"

Marston guffawed, baring large white teeth. "This one's free. Makes a nice change, eh?"

Richard politely bared his teeth in response, but since his interest in Marston's romantic affairs was about on a par with his desire to learn about the finer points of taxonomy, he quickly turned the topic of conversation to a more promising avenue.

"Any chance you're thinking of selling that curricle of yours?"

"What! Sell the Chariot of Love? It would send the ladies of Paris into mourning."

"And their cuckolded husbands would throw a fête."

Marston smiled smugly. "Tonight's lucky lady doesn't have a husband. Just a—"

"I ask," Richard interrupted, before Marston could embark again on his tedious tale of seduction and satiation, "because I have a friend who's looking for a carriage, and I know he admires yours."

"Who wouldn't?" Marston stretched out his legs. Richard wondered how they managed to support the weight of such a massive ego on a daily basis.

Concealing his distaste, Richard continued smoothly, "I've

advised Geoff that a closed carriage would be far more useful. What do you think?"

Marston snorted. "If you're an old lady! Women go mad for a nice little curricle. I can tell you about the time—"

"Curricles are very well for a spin about the park, but what about longer trips, or conveying packages? There's simply not enough privacy or room. Are you dealing, Murat?"

"I'll deal." Marston grabbed the deck of cards before his friend could respond, and began shuffling with the ease of a practiced gamester. "What's your game, Selwick? Commerce? Euchre? *Vingt-et-un*?"

"Whatever you were playing. So you'd recommend the curricle, would you? What about midnight assignations and that sort of thing?"

Marston flipped three cards Richard's way. "It's easy enough to hire a coach."

"Do you have any recommendations?"

"There's a little man in the rue St. Jacques," Marston said easily, kicking back and looking at his cards. "Has a plain carriage and doesn't ask too many questions, if you know what I mean."

"I'll remember that," replied Richard, with an amused smile. A little man on the rue St. Jacques . . . He would send Geoff down tomorrow to make inquiries. Richard mentally ticked off item one on his list. "How far does he let you take it?"

"I've been as far as Calais and back." Marston frowned and dealt himself another card.

"Did you have family visiting from England?" Richard inquired pleasantly.

"No, I—" Marston's mouth snapped abruptly shut.

Richard laughed the knowing laugh of the urbane man about town. "Say no more! Say no more!" he protested, holding out a hand. "The lady's reputation must be protected. I understand. Pass the decanter, would you?"

Visibly relaxing, Marston shoved the crystal decanter across the green baize tabletop. Richard raised it in a comradely gesture before pulling out the stopper and pouring some of the amber contents into a glass. Damn. Marston wasn't quite inebriated enough; if Richard probed further on that score, he would grow suspicious.

"To nameless ladies!" Richard pronounced, hoisting his brandy balloon aloft.

"I'll drink to that!" Marston downed the contents of his glass and reached across Richard for the decanter.

"Namelesh ladiesh," slurred Murat from his corner.

Now there was a man who was drunk enough to be of use.

"You've been at peace too long, Murat," Richard said cheerfully. "It's weakened your head for drink! Better work on that or they'll take away your commission."

"Him?" Marston jabbed a finger at his friend, who was listing like a frigate after a bad storm. "There's some perks to being the First Consul's brother-in-law, eh, Murat? Even if you do have to put up with Caroline!"

"Thash ri'," agreed Murat. "Have to put up wi' Caroline. More brandy?"

Richard helpfully leaned across the table and refilled Murat's glass. "Caroline giving you a hard time?"

"Thash a'ri'." Murat gestured expansively, sending half the contents of his glass sloshing down Mme Rochefort's rose silk moire walls. "Goin' away shoon."

Two glasses of brandy and several slurred sibilants later, Richard had managed to determine that Murat, if he was to be believed, had been promised a high position in the army for the invasion of England. Caroline, Murat said, had bullied her brother into it, which Richard could well believe. Caroline possessed the face of an angel and the ruthless ambition of, well, her brother Napoleon. Her brother Napoleon crossed with Lucrezia Borgia on a bad day. Richard felt mildly sorry for poor Murat.

His sympathy, however, dwindled as Murat continued to babble around the topic. It took nearly half an hour to ascertain that Murat didn't actually know when the expedition for England was to leave, just that it was to be soon. Soon being anywhere from two months to a year. Some help that. Napoleon was waiting for something. Caroline had yelled at Napoleon and he had protested that he couldn't do anything until the arrival of—

Richard hastily scraped his chair back as Murat was ill all over Mme Rochefort's prized Persian rug.

These were the moments, Richard reflected bitterly as Marston handed his friend a handkerchief and a servant came scurrying with rags and water, when he envied Miles his nice, quiet desk job at the War Office. His nice, quiet, *odorless* desk job at the War Office.

"Be ri' back," Murat announced, reeling off, hopefully to find a change of linen.

"Another glass of brandy and you'll be right as rain!" Marston shouted after him.

"Perhaps we might relocate to another table?" Richard suggested, his nose twitching.

"All right with me." Marston shrugged. "I'm leaving in ten minutes. The girl will be waiting for me at midnight. I might keep her waiting a few minutes—the suspense always makes 'em more eager—"

"How about this table?" Richard had no desire to hear any more of Marston's romantic advice. Before Marston could continue with his plans for the evening, Richard hastily complimented his jacket.

"I'll give you the name of my tailor," Marston offered generously.

Richard would rather face a firing squad than wear a peacock-blue frock coat with gold facings and cameo buttons, but the offer gave him just the opportunity he had desired.

"You're pretty chummy with Balcourt, aren't you? Couldn't you persuade him to patronize a different tailor? One who isn't color-blind? It's deuced hard on the eyes for the rest of us."

"Nature didn't give him much to work with." Marston snagged the brandy bottle and glasses from their old table, just as Murat wove his way back, minus his soiled cravat and waistcoat.

Richard feigned confusion. "I had thought you were friends."

Marston shrugged, evading the implied question. "Who would've thought the man would have such a toothsome sister?"

Richard fought back the urge to stop Marston's words with a fist. Richard had, admittedly, entertained much the same thought himself, but the gleam in Marston's eye brought out hitherto unsuspected proclivities towards violence.

"The cousin is reputed to be the beauty of the family," Richard threw Jane to the wolves without a qualm.

"Not my type. I like 'em little and cuddly, not cold and statuesque. Maybe you scholars lust after statues, but not me, no."

So, he was lusting after Amy, was he? Richard rather hoped that Marston was involved in shady business on behalf of Bonaparte, just so Richard would have official reason to thrash him.

Meanwhile, Marston had begun enumerating those attributes of Amy which he had noted the night before, none of which happened to be above her face. Richard considered accidentally hurling the leaded crystal decanter at Marston's head. Common sense intervened; he still had little idea as to Marston's true connection with Balcourt, and would be decidedly less likely to find out if he bludgeoned Marston senseless.

Holding up a hand, Richard protested, "Enough! You don't want to make the lady you're meeting tonight jealous."

"No danger of that!" Slapping his brandy balloon onto the table, Marston doubled over with laughter at a private joke. "Make her jealous! Ha! No danger of that at all!"

"Why not?"

Marston grinned wolfishly at Richard. "Because tonight's lucky lady *is* Amy Balcourt."

Chapter Twenty-one

R ichard saw red.
   He saw every shade of red imaginable, from crimson to scarlet, but mostly he saw himself driving his fist repeatedly into Marston's face. It took all of his considerable strength of will not to turn that vision into a reality.

Only Richard's hands, clenched into fists under the table, hinted at his inward struggle as he leaned back and drawled, "Really?"

"Some men have all the luck," hiccuped Murat, from somewhere just below the rim of the table.

"It ain't luck; it's my handsome face." Marston hauled his friend up by the collar and deposited him back on the seat of his chair. "Met the girl for five minutes last night, and already she can't keep her hands off me."

That wasn't the way Richard remembered it. Clearly, there was some mistake. Marston must have invented the assignation to impress his friends. Or he was meeting some other woman and had her confused with Amy. There had to be a simple explanation.

Through painfully tight lips, Richard got out, "What did she do? Accost you in your chambers after the party?"

"Nah." Marston flung a card on the discard pile. "She sent me an urgent message. Like that, do you? An *urgent message*?" Marston guffawed again. "She wants me badly."

"Nobody shends me meshages like tha' anymore," mourned Murat.

Marston dealt him a brotherly whack on the shoulder that nearly sent him flying over the arm of his chair. "That's because Caroline scares 'em all away!"

"Caroline," Murat groaned, and reached for the brandy decanter.

"An *urgent* message, you say?" queried Richard.

"That's women for you." Marston tossed back another snifter of brandy. "Says she must see me *urgently,* because she had something *terribly important* to tell me. Said I'd know what it was about after our conversation last night. Ha! As if any fool couldn't figure out what the girl wants, hey, chaps?"

"What about her brother?" Richard blurted out.

"What about him?"

"Won't he object to his sister arranging assignations with you?"

"Balcourt?" Marston threw back his head and laughed. Richard hoped the weight of it would cause him to overbalance, perhaps knocking himself out on a handy piece of furniture—there was the nice sharp edge of a card table right there—but Marston's luck was in and Richard's was out. Marston's head snapped back to center without Marston so much as wobbling. "Balcourt? He knows better than to come up stuffy about this."

That was taking French nonchalance too far, decided Richard. Not to mention that Balcourt was half English and thus should bloody well know better.

"But it's his *sister,*" Richard gritted out, pushing to his feet. "Rather a nasty trick to play on a friend, seducing his sister."

Marston shrugged. "Balcourt owes me. Good night, gentlemen."

"Do you need a ride?" Richard spoke rapidly as Marston began to move towards the door. "If you're willing to wait a moment, I'll send for my coach. I can drop you off on my way home."

And make good and sure you never make it to your assignation, Richard added grimly to himself. So many things might happen along the way. His English coachman, not knowing the streets of Paris well, might get lost, and drive about in circles for hours. At least long enough for Amy to think herself abandoned and leave in a fit of pique. Or the carriage might encounter a fatal pothole. Or Marston might pass out from drink, with a little help from his newfound friend. Or—

"Very decent of you, Selwick." Marston, who had paused for one glorious moment, set one foot in front of the other. And another. "But it's a short walk."

"Are you sure? Where are you meeting her?"

"The Luxembourg Gardens." Marston paused again. "Women and their romantic notions. I'd've preferred a bed."

Richard would have preferred to smash his fist right into Marston's smug mouth. Instead, he forced himself to bid Marston a pleasant good night. He contemplated giving him a little shove—just the slightest nudge—on the marble stair, but too many potential witnesses were milling about. Damn, how to dispose of Marston without drawing attention to himself? Attention the Purple Gentian could ill afford.

As he snatched back his gloves and hat from the maid at the foot of the stairs, Richard contemplated racing ahead of Marston, lying in wait, and knocking him down from behind. The streets of Paris abounded with footpads. That gold watch chain of Marston's shouted "grab me! grab me!" to any thief in a five-mile radius. Marston would be out cold, Amy would be safe, and no one would be any the wiser.

There was only, Richard realized, savagely crushing his hat in his hand, one slight problem. He had no idea which route Marston planned to take. Splendid. He'd lurk there in an alleyway by a street Marston might never walk past while Marston forced himself upon Amy in the Luxembourg Gardens.

What in the devil had Amy been thinking?

Bounding down the steps of the Rochefort town house, Richard saw Marston strolling towards the Seine, towards the bridge that separated them from the Luxembourg and Amy. Richard momentarily considered alerting Balcourt to his sister's peril, and just as quickly dismissed the idea. Even if he was to find Balcourt at home, even if Marston was wrong about Balcourt's indifference, he didn't like to think what might have befallen Amy by the time he wrenched Balcourt out of a chair and shoved him into his coach.

Besides, he didn't want to relinquish the pleasure of punching Marston.

There was only one thing to do. Damn, damn, damn. Richard rapidly changed course and headed for home. He stormed through the front hall of his house, capsizing a small table and knocking a picture askew. Charging into his study, he flopped to his knees and began flinging books from the bottom shelf of his bookcase.

What in the hell was Amy thinking, arranging assignations with strange men in the middle of the night? Had no one ever shouted any sense into her? Did she think she was invincible? When he found her, he'd shake her till she couldn't stand. And then he'd lock her into a room with a dozen locks—make that two dozen locks—so she couldn't send any more ridiculous notes to ridiculous men setting up ridiculous meetings at ridiculous hours of the night. Damn!

Seizing on a fold of black cloth, he yanked his cape out of its hiding place. No time to change his breeches; the cape would have to hide the tan cloth, and at least his boots were black up to the knee. The mask followed the cape, and Richard was up and running, mask dangling from his hand. Pushing past Geoff, responding to his, "Good God, man! What's wrong?" with a perfunctory, "Can't talk! Tell you later," Lord Richard Selwick bounded down the stairs of his town house.

Seconds later, the Purple Gentian sprinted in the direction of the Luxembourg Gardens and his damsel in distress. His resolution to avoid Amy Balcourt had lasted less than a day.

Amy shoved back her hood. Unfortunately, the removal of the draped fabric did little to improve her vision. "I knew I forgot something," she muttered. A lantern. She had the hooded cloak, the sturdy boots, the urgent information, but she had forgotten the lantern. And without a lantern, Amy had very little idea where she was. She did know she was in the Luxembourg Gardens. But beyond that, Amy was at a loss. One shrub looked very much like another in the darkness.

"Ah, there you are!" Marston's low voice carried down the long alley of trees as he emerged from around a bend. The large space distorted his voice, thickened it, made it sound unnervingly different than it had the night before. He was speaking English, Amy realized. Of course! Everyone's voice changed when they spoke another language. "I've been looking for you."

Marston's booted feet echoed on the flagstone path as he closed the distance between them, moonlight glinting off the gold embroidery on his coat. He wore the rich frock coat she had seen the night before at the Tuilleries, and his curly head was hatless. Amy fought down the sense of unease steadily rising like the fog around her. Why would he disguise himself in mask and cloak when she knew who he was? Surely, it showed good sense on his part not to parade about in costume.

"I'm sorry," Amy said, her own voice tinny to her ears. "I
ot a bit lost."

"You can make it up to me." Marston took her by the
houlders. "Like this."

Reminding herself again that he was the Gentian, and that
he'd embraced him last night, and enjoyed it very much, Amy
quished her stray qualms and went willingly into his arms. Let-
ng her eyes drift shut, she rested her cheek against his chest,
nd breathed a deep, contented sigh. . . . And her lashes popped
ack up.

He smelled wrong.

Amy rapidly pulled back, eyes wide with alarm. In that
rief moment she had been pressed to his jacket, she had
melled tobacco, brandy, and leather. No citrus cologne.

"Don't be such a tease," Marston growled, grabbing for
er.

Amy narrowly evaded his grasp. Oh goodness, he wasn't
he Purple Gentian. And he clearly thought that he . . . that
he . . .

"Come on! You know you want me!" Marston captured
ne of Amy's hands and reeled her in.

Damp lips descended on her own. Amy found her protests
eing displaced by a large tongue forging between her teeth.
Gagging at the intrusion, Amy shoved hard against Marston's
hest. The hard metal of Marston's watch fob scraped against
er palms, but Amy scarcely felt the pain as she strained
gainst him. Caught unawares, Marston stumbled back. Their
ps parted with a nasty sloshing sound.

Amy wiped her lips with the back of her hand. Marston's
yes narrowed dangerously.

"You seem to have the wrong idea! I mean . . . that is . . . I
lidn't invite you here to . . . to kiss you. I want to *talk* to you!
About . . . about Edouard's birthday!"

"About Edouard's birthday." Marston's voice dripped disbelief. Amy couldn't blame him; she scarcely believed her-
elf.

"Yes! I've been away so long that I scarcely know what he
ikes anymore, and I wanted to throw him a splendid birthday
celebration as a thank-you for bringing me out here," Amy
babbled, backing up towards the line of trees.

Stupid, stupid, stupid, she mentally berated herself. All
ight, you got yourself into this, Amy. Now fix it!

"I'm sorry if you thought . . . um," Amy stalled out. Biting her lip, she tried again. "I apologize for any confusion. You have every right to be angry. I didn't mean to bring you out here under false pretenses. Really! I am so very, very sorry."

Her apology seemed to have touched a chord in Marston.

Amy let out a sigh of relief. "Thank you for being so understanding."

Marston sidled towards her, and an arm snaked out, grabbing Amy around the waist. What she had said and what Marston had understood were two very different things. If she could just remove that crowbar of an arm of his from around her waist, maybe she could explain to him.

"There's no need to be shy," he crooned. "Come on now. You can tell me what you really want."

"You. Don't. Seem. To. Understand." Amy gasped out the words as she pushed against Marston.

His grip tightened around her and his mouth moved moistly against her ear. "Oh, I understand all right. You're just afraid to ask for it."

Marston's tongue flicked against her ear; he was holding her so tightly that her arms were pinned between them, the skin of her forearms scratching against the embroidery of his coat. Why wouldn't he let *go*? Amy wondered, the beginnings of panic spreading from her mind to her quivering hands. And Marston's mouth—it kept moving, following hers, trying to invade her lips.

Amy twisted her head to the side, struggling desperately to free her arms from Marston's embrace. She could hear the peaceful chirping of birds and the murmur of water in ironic counterpoint to the rasp of Marston's harsh breath in her ear.

"You don't understand," she panted again. "Surely we can discuss . . ." Marston's head followed hers. Amy's neck ached with the strain of pulling away. If only she could push him away long enough to make him listen to reason and understand that there had been a mistake! Wet lips trailed across Amy's cheek. Yanking an arm free, Amy shoved against Marston's face with all her strength.

Crunch!

She succeeded far better than she had imagined.

"You bitch!" Marston howled, releasing Amy. "You've broken my nose!"

Amy stared in horrified fascination at the dark liquid dripping through Marston's fingers. With his left hand, he yanked frantically at his cravat until the knot came undone, wadding the fabric up against his nose.

"I'm sorry," Amy gasped. "I didn't mean . . ."

Marston's pale eyes met hers over the crumpled cloth. His expression could only be described as murderous. With a low growl he flung aside the cloth and began advancing on Amy.

Apologies clearly weren't going to have much effect.

One yard, two feet. Marston was steadily closing the distance between them. "You're going to pay for this," he snarled.

Amy had the feeling he wasn't referring to monetary remuneration.

Amy set her arms the way she had seen her cousin Ned do when he was boxing with the stableboy. "If you don't stop right there, I swear I'm going to break something else! I will!"

"That will cost you," Marston warned.

His hands swallowed Amy's. Not altogether able to believe any of this could be happening, Amy felt her arms being forced around her back. In all of her twenty years, no one had ever treated her roughly or grabbed her in anger, and that this man, this friend of her brother's, should turn on her in violence was utterly inconceivable.

The pain in her shoulders brought her sharply back to reality. Amy pushed back with all her might, straining to keep his arms from closing around her, but years of lifting books in her uncle's library had done little to prepare her for a contest of strength; within moments, her arms were three-quarters of the way behind her. Her breath rasped anxiously in her throat. She supposed she should scream, but who would come at her call? Blood from Marston's nose dripped down onto Amy's cheek, and she gasped and wrenched her head away. The movement was all Marston needed to consolidate his victory. With a final burst of force, he twisted her arms behind her back, pinning them together with one large hand. Amy jerked against his grasp, arching away from him as far as she could, but he yanked her back against him. His fingers grasped her wrists as tightly as though they had been bound with a dozen sailor's knots.

No! Amy's mind shouted. Marston's arms around her

pinned her entire upper body immobile. With his free hand, he grabbed a handful of her hair, and yanked her head back. Amy's eyes teared with the unexpected pain.

"Now," he snarled, pulling savagely on her hair, "we can discuss what you can do to make this up to me."

"My brother will call you out for this!" spat Amy.

Marston chuckled unpleasantly, tugging her curls again, harder. "Your brother couldn't shoot a slug."

Amy's nostrils flared. "You value yourself highly, don't you?"

"Why, you little—arrrrrr!"

Amy's sturdy boot slammed down on Marston's little toe. The hard, square heel ground down into the leather with a marvelous crackling noise that was rapidly drowned out by a stentorian roar of pain. Twisting her wrists, Amy pulled free from Marston's loosened grasp. Blast! Marston's hands were already grabbing for her, pulling at her dress as she tried to run. She should have broken his fingers, not his toes. She heard the unpleasant sound of rending cloth, but Marston still held firm. Any moment now, Marston's other hand would shoot out and it would start all over again.

No! She wouldn't stand for it! Amy whirled and swung at Marston's face with her right fist. Her knuckles grazed the underside of Marston's chin and plunged into empty air.

Marston tumbled to the ground at her feet with a crash like the fall of Goliath.

Chapter Twenty-two

❦

Still struggling to catch her breath, Amy stared in confusion at Marston's fallen body. She really hadn't thought she had hit him that hard. And then she heard it. The sound of another person's breathing, issuing from the place where Marston had stood. Amy looked up abruptly, just as a shadowy figure bounded over Marston's body and stopped short in front of her.

"Did he hurt you?" it barked.

Amy blinked, glancing from the crumpled figure on the ground to the hooded phantom in front of her. "If you're not Marston, who are you?" she blurted out.

"You thought I was *Marston*? That's why you—never mind. We'll address that later." If a masked face in the dark could contrive to look stern, his did. "Did he hurt you?"

"No." Amy shook her head. Her heart still beat at triple the normal rate, but her thoughts scurried along even faster. How could she have ever thought Marston was the Gentian? Looking at the two of them together—admittedly, Marston was in a heap on the floor, which prejudiced the comparison somewhat—the distinctions were so obvious that Amy felt an absolute idiot for not having known, and run, the moment she saw Marston striding down that alley of trees. Where Marston was bulky, the Gentian had a graceful, slender strength. One broad-fingered hand lay on the ground near Amy's foot, brown hair sprouting around the knuckles. So very different from the long-fingered hands in black leather gloves clenched at the Purple Gentian's sides. Even Marston's teeth seemed larger and coarser than the Gentian's. Good heavens, could one have elegant teeth?

Amy pressed her palms to her face and rubbed them up and down, suppressing a gaggle of mad giggles.

"What in the hell were you thinking?" growled the Purple Gentian. "Well?" he bit out when Amy didn't respond immediately. "How in the hell could you think he and I were the same person?"

The Gentian glared fiercely at the body on the ground.

"You don't see the resemblance?" Amy shook with suppressed giggles. *Hiccup! Hiccup!* It was no use trying to contain it; her whole body quaked with laughter.

"Damn it, Amy, this is not funny!"

Amy doubled over, her arms wrapped around her stomach. "You look," she gasped, "s-s-so indignant!"

"You're bloody well right I'm indignant!" the Purple Gentian roared as he yanked Amy upwards until her streaming eyes peered directly into his. "Do you know what Marston was going to do with you? Do you? He was going to rape you, damn it!"

"I don't . . . I can't . . . Put me *down!*"

Eyes intent on hers, he opened his hands. Amy sat down heavily on the paced dirt of the pathway. Her legs didn't seem to want to lift her, and on the whole, Amy agreed with them.

"Is that what you said to Marston? Did he listen?"

At the sound of his name, the recumbent figure on the ground stirred and moaned. The Gentian crossed over to him in one quick stride and administered a brisk, brutal kick to Marston's jaw. Amy winced as Marston's head snapped back.

"Wasn't that a little . . . unnecessary?"

"Not at all. Do you want him waking up?" As Amy shuddered, the Gentian smiled nastily. "I thought not. You'd better hope that his brains are addled enough that he won't remember any of tonight's events. Let's make sure of that, shall we?"

The Purple Gentian's boot connected again with Marston's head, flipping Marston neatly over. The Gentian surveyed his handiwork. "Much better."

Amy scooted herself, crablike, away from Marston. Her arms throbbed where he had grabbed them and she could still taste his nasty slobbering mouth on hers. Amy wrapped her arms around her stomach and wondered what the Gentian would say if she was sick all over his shiny black boots.

"I think I'd like to go home now."

"I'm not done with you yet." The Purple Gentian crossed his arms over his chest and regarded Amy with asperity.

A bath. That was what she needed. She'd scrub out her mouth with tooth powder while the servants drew her a long, painfully hot bath.

"Please don't start screeching at me again."

"I am not screeching. Men do not screech. Damn it, stop looking at me like that!"

"Like what?"

"Like—" Richard bit off his words before they developed into a full-blown screech of the variety he had just denied indulging in. "Do you have no sense at all of the danger you were in?" Richard kept his voice cool and level. Ha! He'd defy her to label that a screech.

Amy frowned at him, stumbling slowly to her feet. "This would never have happened if you had told me who you were."

"Who told you to go looking for me?"

"I had something I had to tell you! And I had no idea if you were ever going to deign to contact me. After the way you ran off last night . . ."

"Now this is my fault? I run like a madman to rescue you—"

"And I already told you I didn't need rescuing!"

"So you were having a peaceful little chat with Marston when I approached? Was that it? And that's the least of it! You left the house alone, unchaperoned, unguarded, at midnight of all idiot times! You're lucky that Marston was the only one who attacked you! Footpads, pickpockets . . ."

Assaulted by images of Amy in danger—Amy being dragged into a dark alley, Amy being flung to the ground, Amy being hit over the head from behind, and, worst of all because it had been true, because he had seen it, because he couldn't seem to stop replaying it in his head with varying degrees of panic, Amy being overpowered in Marston's brutal embrace—Richard reacted without thinking. He reached out across the barrier of Marston's body and grabbed Amy by the shoulders and hauled her right over the fallen man. Too shocked to resist, Amy didn't struggle. She didn't even squeal. She did let out a small *whoosh* of breath as she smacked against Richard's chest, but that was clearly unintentional.

Richard didn't give her a chance to make any other sound.

His lips covered hers with an urgency that bordered on the savage. All the anger and tension Richard had been feeling since Marston had first uttered Amy's name poured into the kiss. His mouth molded against hers, pressing hard against it, as though the fabric of their separate lips could become one. Rather than shying back from the sheer force of his kiss, Amy threw her arms up around his shoulders, clasping him about the neck as she raised herself on tiptoe to match her mouth more perfectly to his. Richard groaned low in his throat and clamped her tighter to him, reveling in the way her body molded to his. Richard's breath came fast and his lungs ached as though he had been running for miles, but he didn't want to ever stop; he would keep running and running, with Amy's hands in his hair, and every muscle in his body alive where she was pressed against him; his thighs, his chest, his shoulders, all throbbing with the feel of Amy against him.

Amy clung to the Purple Gentian as his lips seared away the dreadful taint of Marston's unwanted kisses. Fire purifies, some dim part of her brain remembered. Amy blazed up, fired by the warmth radiating from the Gentian's arms, his lips enveloping her, the way his black cape enveloped her as it wrapped around her. She was the phoenix, reborn through fire, rising restored from the flames that consumed her. That explained the crackling in her ears and the flames behind her eyelids.

The Purple Gentian's lips left hers and his arms freed her waist. With an inarticulate gasp of distress, Amy lifted her face blindly towards his and locked her own arms more tightly about him. "Don't let go. Not yet . . ."

"Oh, Amy," the Purple Gentian groaned. Cupping her face in protective hands, the kid leather of his gloves soft against her skin, he pressed kisses on her forehead, her eyelids, her cheekbones, the tip of her nose, her lips. "God, Amy, you had me so worried. The thought of him touching you . . ."

"Didn't much appeal to me either," Amy riposted, leaning all of her weight against him. Just in case he had any ideas about pulling away again.

Amy rubbed her cheek against the Gentian's waistcoat—no hard metallic watch fob to bruise her, as there had been on Marston's clothes—and went limp with relief as she felt his arm steal back around her waist and his lips brush gently along the crown of her head.

"We should do something about Marston," Richard mumbled into Amy's hair, his voice scarcely louder than the muted rustle of the wind in the leaves.

"Couldn't we just leave him here?"

Regretfully, Richard straightened, gently putting Amy at arm's length. "It wouldn't be prudent."

"Should we return him to his house?"

"No. There's bound to be a valet or a servant about, and we don't want to cause too much comment."

Richard grimly circled the fallen form of Georges Marston, thinking what a bother the man had proven to be. If he had any recollection of tonight's activities, if he made the link between Richard and the masked man who had bopped him over the head, some of Richard's best intelligence sources would evaporate with all the speed of spilled water in the Egyptian sun. And, of course, there was the more immediate concern of what the devil one was to do with the lout. Why couldn't he have just collapsed from too much drink on the way over?

"Too much drink! That's it!" the Gentian announced with as much glee as though he had just cracked the code of the Rosetta Stone.

"You want a drink? Now?" Amy, puzzled by the workings of the masculine mind, stepped out of the way as the Gentian swooped down on Marston's recumbent body. "What on earth are you doing?" she demanded, as the Gentian began sniffing—sniffing!—at Marston's waistcoat.

The Purple Gentian rose easily to his feet and brushed off his hands. "Marston reeks of brandy. We can haul him over to the Latin Quarter and dump him behind a tavern. He'll fit right in with the other drunks passed out in the gutter."

"That should work." Amy's voice was unusually subdued as she joined the Purple Gentian in peering down at Marston's collapsed form. Stretched out on the dirt as he was, arms limp, hands limper, the bulk of the man still made Amy's flesh crawl. She took some comfort in the crooked angle of his nose, a sign that she had been able to protect herself, at least somewhat.

The Gentian had circled round to Marston's head, and was hauling the man's limp torso upright, long sleeves protecting his arms from the scratchy gold braid on Marston's jacket. Watching anxiously to make sure Marston's eyes didn't roll open, Amy took wary hold of Marston's boots.

They set off in silence down the path, between the row of silent trees, the Purple Gentian backing up with long strides that took two of Amy's shorter steps to match.

Amy gazed longingly at the tall, dark figure walking backwards in confident strides. If she asked, he would stop. And then she could bury her face in his chest and wrap her arms around his waist and let his strength support her. It was so terribly tempting. All she had to do was ask.

All she had to do was scuttle her pride.

Amy determinedly turned her thoughts to the quandary of filching the Swiss gold out from under the noses of Bonaparte's agents. And if she jumped nervously when a man with gold embroidery on his cloak swaggered past them into the gardens, well, the Purple Gentian made no comment. Amy glanced swiftly at the burden hanging between them, just to make sure Marston was still there, unconscious, limp, and harmless. Momentarily reassured, she returned to considering the benefits and drawbacks of gunpowder, though she still flinched every time the leaves around them rustled with the passage of a human body.

Much to Amy's relief, the gardens finally gave way to the busy streets of the Latin Quarter. Shouts and laughter spilled from brightly lit tavern windows, making Amy blink at the sudden glare; the sour reek of spilled spirits caused her to scrunch up her nose.

Through one window, a group of students was pounding out a bawdy ballad in Latin, punctuating their verses with swigs from a giant jug of Bordeaux. The group of sailors in the inn across the way was doing its best to outsing the students with an equally bawdy sea chanty. Just in front of them, a man reeled through a door into the street, nearly barreling into the Purple Gentian before collapsing in the gutter. In the open doorway, a massive woman in a soiled kerchief brushed her hands in the universal gesture of good riddance.

No one gave Richard and Amy a second look.

Amy could only conclude that hooded men and disheveled women bearing unconscious bodies weren't as unusual an occurrence as one would suppose.

Speaking softly under the cover of all of the merriment going on about them, the Purple Gentian leaned across Marston's unconscious body, and murmured to Amy, "Once we dispose of our cargo in a manner befitting him, I'll take you home."

"Cargo," Amy repeated. Keeping a firm grasp on Marston's feet, she hissed, "There's something I have to—"

"This looks like a promising alley, don't you think?" the Gentian interrupted, peering into a cul-de-sac between two noisy taverns. One man already occupied part of the gutter, arms flung wide, and one boot missing. "Let's drop him right over there, shall we? We'll even provide fitting company for him," the Gentian added with a chuckle.

Right. Now was probably not the best of times to relay Bonaparte's plans for invading England, Amy consoled herself. Certainly not over the body of a member of Bonaparte's military, unconscious though he certainly seemed to be. Could Marston merely be pretending to be unconscious, waiting for them to let go to wreak his revenge? Amy winced as she remembered the sound of the Gentian's boot connecting with Marston's chin and quickly discarded the possibility that Marston might be feigning oblivion. The man would have to have a head of steel not to be unconscious. Nonetheless, it probably wouldn't hurt to wait until they were in a less populated area before relaying her monumental information to the Gentian.

Amy hastily let go of Marston's feet as the Purple Gentian unceremoniously dumped Marston into a liquid that Amy hoped was spilled wine. Marston's body landed with a satisfying thump.

Brushing his hands together with the air of a man who considers a job well done, Richard took one last look at the crumpled figure in the gutter. Marston had begun snoring noisily, his mouth flopping open. His gaudy coat was smeared with dirt and mottled with blood. Between the state of his attire and his coarse expression, he looked like nothing more than a servant who had gone brawling in his master's clothes. All he needed to complete the scene was an empty bottle in his limp hand.

Richard glowered at the fallen body. "How could you think I was Marston?"

"Vanity, thy name is man?"

"Objecting to being compared to *that*"—the Gentian jerked a finger over his shoulder at Marston as he took Amy by the arm and steered her towards the river—"is not vanity. It's simple self-respect."

"The comparison made sense at the time," mused Amy. "No! No, I didn't mean it that way," she hastily amended as the Purple Gentian gave every sign of boiling over like an offended volcano. Taking care to emphasize that she found Marston in no way comparable to the Gentian, Amy explained the series of deductions that had led her to believe Marston must be he.

"After all, there he was in the courtyard, wearing a black cloak just like yours. What else was I to think?" she finished.

"It does make a certain amount of sense," the Gentian admitted grudgingly as they trudged down stone steps onto a pier to wait for one of the small boats that ferried passengers along the Seine for a fee. "Though why you couldn't tell the difference—"

"I had only met him once, and briefly, at that. And when I found the information . . ."

The Purple Gentian's eyes narrowed. "The information that was so vitally important that you had to set up an assignation in the middle of the night?"

Amy cast him a sidelong glance. "Do we really have to go into all that again?"

"Yes." The Gentian crossed his arms across his chest.

"You may change your mind when you hear what I have to tell you."

Even through his cloak and mask, the Purple Gentian radiated skepticism.

"All right, then. If you really don't want to hear about Bonaparte's plans for the invasion of England . . ."

Chapter Twenty-three

❦

"About *what*?" The Purple Gentian yanked Amy over to the side of the quay with such force that her cloak rippled out behind her like a pennant on a windy day.

"Bonaparte's plans! They were under his blotter on his desk."

Richard's memory momentarily clicked back to that afternoon, to Amy, flustered, running into him as she raced out of . . . Bonaparte's study. He'd been so delighted by the opportunity that her running into him had afforded him, so focused on flirting with her, that it had never occurred to him to wonder why she was scurrying through that particular anteroom.

"He plans to land a force of one hundred seventy thousand men with twenty-four hundred ships," Amy whispered urgently. "But Mme Bonaparte has emptied the treasury, so he can't do it until gold enough to finance the expedition arrives."

"So that's it!" That was what Murat had been about to say. Nothing could be done until the gold arrived. Richard could have kicked himself. After six years of close contact with the Bonapartes, six years of listening to Bonaparte rant about his wife's extravagance, you'd think he could have put two and two together. "Does he have the money?"

"That's the splendid thing!" Amy hugged the Gentian's arm in her glee. "He's arranged for a loan—as if he intends to pay it back—from Swiss bankers. It's due to come in by carriage to a Paris warehouse the night of the thirtieth. Don't you see, it's perfect! If we can just—"

"Intercept the gold before it reaches Bonaparte . . . ," the Purple Gentian continued for her, grinning broadly.

"We can stop the invasion of England and topple the government!"

"Shhhh!"

"Oh, sorry." Amy bit her lip. "I got a bit carried away. But can't you just see it? When that gold doesn't arrive . . ."

"But how do we keep it from arriving?" The Gentian paced in a little circle around the quay. Amy watched in appreciation, enjoying the way the cape swished about his booted legs as he walked, the way his jaw shifted as he thought through plans. Most of all, she basked in that thoughtless "we."

The Gentian whirled with a particularly satisfying swish. "How many men will be guarding it?"

"The letter didn't say," Amy admitted. "Fouché just wrote that it would be heavily guarded, whatever that means."

"Stealth, rather than force," muttered the Gentian, resuming his circles.

"What about a smaller version of the Trojan Horse?"

"A smaller what?"

Perching herself on a piling, Amy explained, "In Greek mythology, the Trojan Horse was a—"

The Gentian flapped his cape at her. "Stop! I know the story. You want to intercept the Swiss gold with a small wooden horse?"

"Not exactly." Amy swung her legs back and forth as she expounded, her heels hitting the wood block with a series of dull thuds. "But you could send a delivery of barrels or something to the warehouse—barrels of something they might want—and when they haul them inside, we can leap out and seize the gold."

Richard rather fancied the idea of springing out of a brandy barrel, rapier at the ready. "Not the vintage you were expecting, gentlemen?" he would drawl as he leaped out of the cask, brandishing the shining steel of his blade in their astonished faces. With a thrust to the left, and a stab to the right, he'd fight his way through the room, dueling personally with the man in charge, flipping his sword in an arc across the room. And then he'd deck the man guarding the gold with a quick uppercut, whirling to fight off the three men who'd jump on him from behind. He'd kick the first in the stomach, trip the second, and run through the third. And then he'd make some sort of witty remark. "Huzzah for the Purple Gentian!" his men would cheer.

If only it ever happened that way.

Ruefully, Richard shook his head, forcing himself to abandon his happy dreams of swashbuckling in favor of less glamorous realities.

"What if they don't stop to pick up the barrels? If they're Fouché's men, they'll be under strict orders. We could probably float by in a trunk with HUGE TREASURE IN HERE painted in foot-high letters across the top, and they wouldn't so much as glance at us."

"Drat." Amy absently kicked at the piling with her heel. "That also ruins plan B."

"Plan B?"

"Yes, I thought if the Trojan Horse idea didn't work, maybe Jane and I could pretend to be dancing girls looking for work, and—"

"Let's skip straight to plan C, shall we?"

"You don't like plan B?"

Like? What an incredibly inadequate word *like* was. To say that he liked the idea of Amy dressed up as a dancing girl would be like saying that Midas liked gold, or Epicurus liked food, or Miss Gwen liked poking her parasol at people. It didn't cover the half of it. By the same token, the word *dislike* didn't even begin to describe the revulsion that flooded through Richard at the thought of Amy exposing herself to a warehouse full of hardened French operatives. In comparison, it made the whole Marston incident look about as dangerous as a peaceful stroll through Hyde Park at five o'clock at the height of the season. Chaperoned.

"I loathe, revile, and detest plan B," Richard replied blandly. "Next?"

"Setting the warehouse on fire," Amy suggested promptly.

The Purple Gentian stopped his pacing and knelt beside Amy's makeshift pedestal. "Do you mean to try to burn down the building around the gold?"

Amy decided he really didn't have to know that burning down the building around the gold had begun as plan F on the walk over, been demoted to plan M, and finally discarded altogether as impracticable. "What we could do is start a small fire that will let off a lot of smoke—there must be some way to do that—and someone could start shouting *fire*. With any luck, the guards would panic, and leap out of the building. And even if they didn't, they would be so preoccupied with putting out the blaze that we could slip inside during the confusion and make off with the gold."

"The gold will be heavy," the Purple Gentian pointed out, but his tone wasn't dismissive. He sounded thoughtful.

"We set the fire, bash them over the head during the confusion, and *then* make off with the gold?"

"You might have something there. We'd have to find out how the men in the warehouse were to be dressed. My guess is they won't be in uniform. They'll more likely be disguised as workmen. If my chaps can slip in and blend with the guards . . ."

The Gentian hopped to his feet, nearly colliding with Amy's chin. "Wait! How do we know which warehouse it will be? We can't go up and down the streets setting fire to every warehouse we see."

Amy gave a little bounce on her perch. "And we don't have to! It's a lumber warehouse in the rue Claudius. A bit arrogant, don't you think?"

The Gentian's lips twisted wryly. "They picked the street for the name of the Roman emperor who conquered Britain? Clever. Very clever."

"But not clever enough for us!" Amy's outstretched hands and eager smile issued an irresistible invitation to the Purple Gentian to join in her exultation.

She laughed delightedly as he bypassed her outstretched hands, and, seizing her around the waist, whirled her in a triumphal circle. Amy felt the muscles of his shoulders move under her hands, the folds of his cloak swirl about her own legs, and tilted back her head with the dizzying joy of it all. It was better than a fair, better than a play, better than any daydream she had ever devised.

The Purple Gentian's arms tightened around her as he completed one last whirl. Amy's body brushed slowly along the length of his as he lowered her to the ground. Amy's wits seemed to have been shaken away while the Purple Gentian was spinning her in circles. After all, she should be thinking about defeating Bonaparte, not about the shocking intimacy of the Purple Gentian's cloak entangled with her skirts. Some witty comment was in order, Amy supposed, but the warmth of the Gentian's body against hers, the warmth of skin seeking skin through thin layers of fabric, made wit well nigh impossible.

With the uncomfortable feeling that somehow she was losing the thread of the conversation entirely, Amy dragged herself back to the matter at hand. "Where shall we meet to storm the warehouse?"

The Purple Gentian blinked once. Twice. "We?"

The pesky pronoun broke into Richard's enjoyable contemplation of Amy's lips. We. There was an ominous ring to that small word.

Amy nodded vehemently. "Of course! I can dress up as a workman. What do you think?"

Richard was spared from answering by the swish and bump of a boat pulling in against the quay. Richard silently promised to pay the boatman an extra large tip for extricating him from what would have undoubtedly been a highly uncomfortable discussion. True, he and Amy were bound to tackle the topic—if not each other—before the night was out, but it would be much better, Richard decided unilaterally, if they tackled it at Amy's door as he dropped her off. That way he could flee into the night when she disagreed with him. Yes, definitely better for all concerned. Shakespeare knew what he was about when he said that discretion was the better part of valor.

On no account would Richard allow the topic to be brought up while they were in the boat. He didn't care what ruses and distractions he had to employ; the waters of the Seine were cold and dirty—not to mention, wet—and he had no desire to sample them.

"You waiting for a ride?" the boatman called out, punctuating his words by spitting into the water.

"Yes," Richard replied, giving the boatman their destination, and hastily hustling Amy on board before she had a chance to demur. One of Amy's boots caught on the hem of her dress as Richard helped her over the rim of the boat. She pitched forward, making the boat rock back and forth, and the boatman curse in terms it was good Amy couldn't understand. Leaping lightly into the boat, Richard caught her before she had done more than stumble.

"Tourists," the boatman muttered, pushing off from the quay.

Richard steadied Amy and helped her down onto the bench. "All right, then?" he asked, settling himself down next to her, one arm around her shoulders—for warmth, of course.

"At least I didn't fall *off* the boat," joked Amy.

In her stumble, Amy had released her iron grip on her cloak. Richard's grin turned to a frown. "Your dress is torn," he said harshly, his arm tightening around her shoulders.

"Oh." Amy glanced down at the long tear stretching from the center of her bodice all the way to the ribbon marking the high waist of the dress. The fabric flapped open, revealing the filmy fabric of her chemise, and the curves below. Amy hastily pulled the edges back together, her face clouding. "That must have happened when I pulled away from Marston. I thought I heard—"

The hand casually resting on her right shoulder clamped into a viselike grip. "I should have hit him harder."

Something in the Purple Gentian's tone, an intense anger underlying the seeming calm, made Amy's eyes fly to his face. He *was* angry; it burned from every line in his face, from the stern cast of his lips to his narrowed eyes. But there was something more, something deeper, something that warmed Amy deep down under her ripped bodice and spread through her like strong spirits.

"I think you hit him more than hard enough," Amy reassured the Gentian, abandoning her hold on the edges of her bodice as she twisted on the bench to look him full in his face. "It's just a ripped dress. And I broke his nose, which I think is rather more than fair return for some torn fabric, don't you?"

The Purple Gentian failed to answer. For a moment, Amy was worried that he had been struck ill. His eyes were slightly glazed, and, goodness, crossed. Alarmed, Amy searched for the telltale signs of fever. His forehead didn't seem to be particularly flushed, but his breathing was certainly coming faster.

"Are you all right?"

The Gentian's head waggled in an indeterminate way that could have been either a shake or a nod.

You shouldn't, Richard was telling himself as his right hand hovered over the crevice in Amy's bodice. You really shouldn't. He knew he shouldn't have kissed her back there, in the gardens. Kissing her just made it harder for him to maintain his resolution not to see her—well, not to see her as the Purple Gentian, at any rate. He rather doubted that Lord Richard Selwick would be getting any kisses from Amy for, say, a week, or even two. Agony.

He shouldn't have kissed her in the Luxembourg Gardens, but he had. And if the kiss in her brother's study had been a mistake, this last one had been nothing short of a catastrophe; the kiss in the study had been enjoyable, but the kiss in the gardens had set him ablaze. If he gave in to the urge to touch her again, the result was bound to be something on the order of Pompeii: nothing short of mass destruction. There was no logical reason in the world for him to give in to the urge to slip his hand into the tear in Amy's bodice and every logical reason in the world for him not to.

Illogic had never looked quite so attractive.

In fact, illogic looked remarkably like a pair of well-rounded breasts, rosy areolae more revealed than concealed through the lace trim of a chemise.

"I'll just check for bruises," the Gentian said thickly as his finger dipped into the valley between her breasts.

"Oh, but I'm really not"—Amy gasped as the Gentian's hand slipped lower under her chemise, brushing against her nipple—"hurt," she finished weakly.

"Are you sure?" The Purple Gentian's palm flattened against her breast, the leather of his glove against her skin making her shiver in a way that had nothing to do with the cool night air rising off the Seine.

Amy reconsidered. "No," she said unevenly. "Not really." Maybe there were bruises there she hadn't felt before. Maybe that explained the sensations she felt as his hand grazed over her again as he hastily pulled it from her bodice.

Amy watched as the Gentian lifted his gloved hand to his lips and used his teeth to yank each finger free until the glove pulled loose and plummeted into Amy's lap.

Just a little touch, Richard promised himself, as his now bare fingers gently parted the torn fabric of Amy's bodice. He'd just allow himself the briefest of caresses—after all, there might be bruises there she should know about—and then he'd put Amy's dress back together and bundle her up in her cloak and behave just as properly as if Miss Gwen were sitting there on the other side of the boat chaperoning them.

As soon as Richard's fingertips touched the silky skin of Amy's breast, all resolutions were off. The specter of Miss Gwen splashed forgotten into the water, and all pretense of looking for bruises went the same way. He stroked a sensual semicircle around the top of her left breast, delving down into the shadowy area beneath her chemise. Surely the skin on the other side of her breast couldn't be nearly as soft. . . . But it could. And so could the pale skin all the way around her other breast. Richard traced a complete circuit around each, just to be sure, then trailed his fingers round again for good measure.

Reluctantly, Richard dragged his hand away from Amy's torn bodice, savoring the last brush of silky skin against his fingertips. "I don't think there are any bruises."

"Then why does it ache?" Amy asked, in such a quintessentially Amy tone of indignation that Richard just had to kiss her.

The kiss began as a spontaneous gesture of affection. It began as a quick smack on the lips. It didn't end that way. The minute Richard's lips touched Amy's, her mouth opened eagerly under his and her arms slid up around his neck. And somehow—Richard wasn't quite sure how it had happened, and, to be honest, wasn't wasting that much thought on the matter—rather than sitting next to each other on the bench, Amy had somehow slid sideways, and he was half atop her, one elbow propped against the wood of the bench, the other pushing that blasted cloak of hers out of the way.

"I think what you're feeling," Richard murmured, coming up briefly for air, "is"—*kiss*—"desire. Not"—*kiss*—"bruises." Having imparted that educational information, his mouth plunged back down on Amy's.

Amy gasped as the fabric of the Gentian's shirt brushed against her bare breasts, sending prickles of feeling along an area already teased to the point of agony. She wrapped her arms tighter around him. Pressing up against him, she kissed him as he had been kissing her, flirting with the tip of his tongue, nibbling the edge of his lips.

Richard made one last attempt to think logically.

"We're outside," he panted, tearing his mouth from Amy's.

Since organs other than Richard's brain were doing about three-quarters of his thinking for him, it wasn't the most wholehearted of protests. It had about as much effect as most of him had hoped it would. None.

Amy smiled dreamily up at him, lifting a hand to run it along his cheekbones down to his lips. "I know. Have you ever seen so many stars?"

Richard didn't bother to look up. He didn't need to. All the stars in the sky shone reflected in the blue depths of Amy's eyes.

"Shall I fetch you a necklace of them?" he asked tenderly.

Amy's hand stilled on the Gentian's cheek. She drew in a sharp breath. "A necklace of stars," she repeated, her voice unsteady.

Richard's desire-clogged brain registered alarm. Oh God, what had he said? He hauled himself up on both elbows, ignoring the splinters that plucked at his sleeves.

"Is something wrong?"

Beneath him, Amy's hair spread in a dark fan. It rippled around her pale face as she slowly shook her head.

"No . . ." Her glazed eyes snapped back into focus, glowing with joy. "*No.* Everything's *absolutely* right."

"Um, that's good," Richard ventured, but he was cut off somewhere around "goo" as Amy flung her arms around his neck and began showering his face with clumsy if exuberant kisses. She kissed his forehead, his cheekbone, the edge of his ear, the rim of his mask (that was clearly an accident), the corner of his lip, the curve of his chin (another accident), and the tip of his nose (which Richard thought might have been intentional, but couldn't be sure).

What *had* he said? Richard wished he remembered so that he could say it again, if this was going to be the reaction. But he was too busy enjoying the outcome—in this case, Amy trailing somewhat better-aimed kisses along his ear and his throat—to think too deeply about it. Richard groaned happily and plunged his hands into the lavender-scented mass of Amy's hair.

Brushing her hair back from her face, he leaned over to return the attentions, bracing his right elbow on the seat next to Amy. At least, he meant to brace his elbow next to Amy. Richard flailed for a moment as his body teetered on the edge of the bench, Amy's arms around his neck acting as a counterweight keeping him steady. Until, that was, Amy popped up to press a particularly exuberant kiss on his ear.

Ka-thunk!

They landed with a thud on the floor next to the bench, Amy sprawled on top of Richard. The boat careened back and forth as though they were on the high seas in a midwinter tempest, rather than on the Seine on a clear spring night.

Since Amy was perched on his rib cage, Richard was having somewhat more difficulty breathing than she was. But, given the view afforded by her gaping bodice, Richard had no inclination to complain.

Little trickles of water frothed up over the edge of the boat, and the boatman spat a curse. *"Amants!"* He made the word *lovers* sound like the rankest of insults.

"Amy, *amas, amants* . . ." Richard chuckled, holding a squirming Amy by the hips as she tried to wiggle off of him.

"Don't you mean, *amo, amas, amat*?" Amy giggled the conjugation of the Latin verb "to love."

"I like my version better," murmured Richard, nipping her ear.

Amy pushed at the Purple Gentian's chest with both hands, as she attempted to lever herself up. The boat rocked dangerously.

"I think you'd better stay here," he whispered, running a hand under her tumbled skirts to capture an ankle. "It's safer."

"For whom?" gasped Amy as the Purple Gentian's hand rose higher, sliding from her boot-top, following her silk stocking up along the curve of her calf and knee, pausing to toy with the ribbons of her garter. Amy jumped as his finger brushed along the bare skin of her thigh.

"For the boatman, of course." The Gentian grinned. "Less chance of us capsizing."

"Oh. I don't know if that's—" began Amy, only it came out as, "Iwa wo wo iwa," because the Purple Gentian made up for the shortcomings in his argument by twining his free hand in Amy's hair and making sure Amy couldn't argue back.

Long moments later, he grinned at a breathless Amy. "I thought you'd see it my way."

All Amy could see were stars, hundreds of stars, thousands of stars, dancing along the backs of her eyelids as he pulled her mouth back down to his, his lips moving on hers as velvet soft as the dark night. Their tongues twined together, warm and sweet. Amy swam in a dizzying wine-dark sea of sensation as the Purple Gentian's lips moved on hers and his knowing fingers teased the soft skin of her thigh. Was the boat swaying, or was she? Blindly, she slid her hands up under the Gentian's shirt, the ribbed muscles of his chest the only thing solid and sure in a wildly swaying universe. A dusting of hair tickled her fingertips.

Sensation after sensation assaulted Amy, the brush of hair across her palms and the moist thrust of the Gentian's tongue. The Gentian's fingers rubbed up against the fabric of her linen drawers, creating an odd tension that made Amy wiggle and arch towards him. The Gentian released her mouth and lifted his head to capture a ripe pink nipple in his lips. Amy drew back in surprise, but the Gentian refused to be dislodged, sucking and licking and tugging, until the fingers she had raised to his head to try to push him away were twined in the hair under his hood, pulling his mouth closer.

"Oh," she gasped. The Gentian didn't reply; his mouth was full.

An even louder "oh!" escaped her as the Gentian's fingers discovered the slit in her drawers and slid up into her liquid warmth, stroking, searching. . . . Amy cried out as a tremor of pleasure shot through her. Without withdrawing his intimate touch, the Gentian rolled them over so that she lay beneath him, blinking up at him with eyes dark with desire.

"I thought you'd like that," the Gentian murmured against her lips, before sliding his tongue into her ready mouth.

Moving her hips in restless circles against his fingers, Amy made wordlessly clear to him how much she liked it. She clutched at his shoulders as shivers ran through her that weren't shivers at all but little lightning jolts of intense pleasure. And then the storm itself broke, dispelling all the tension in her body as torrents of indescribable feeling thundered through her. It swept through her like a shower of shooting stars, touching every nerve in her body with celestial fire.

It was the most wonderful night of her life.

It was about to become the most awful night of his.

Chapter Twenty-four

R eason returned to Richard with the force of a blow.
    It took Richard, his hand on the buttons of his
breeches, a second to realize that it had indeed been a blow.
From the boatman's paddle. Accidentally, or otherwise, the
boatman had dealt Richard a stinging whack right on the back
of his head.

But the lump on his head was nothing to the bulge in his
breeches. Urgh. Now there was pain. Rather prominent parts
of his anatomy were screaming at him in intense irritation.
Below him lay Amy, her lips red and swollen, slightly parted,
her eyes misty with desire, damp, ready, willing. It would be so
easy—so natural—to ease up those tousled skirts. . . .

Richard hauled himself up onto the bench, and plunged
his hands over the side, letting the cold water wash the
arousing scent of Amy off of him. He would have stuck his
head over the edge, too, but he wasn't at all sure what might
be lurking in the water, and he wouldn't put it past that boatman to help the rest of him into the river with that con-
founded paddle. Although, Richard supposed, he really
ought to be thanking the boatman rather than cursing him.
If not for that fortuitous blow . . . Richard's face paled in a
way that had nothing to do with the icy temperature of the
water. Had he really been about to take Amy on the floor of
a dirty boat in the middle of the Seine? Oh God. What had
he been thinking?

He hadn't been thinking. That was the problem.

As cold water and equally chilly thoughts began to clear
the haze of lust from Richard's brain, he realized that the
murmuring noise he'd been half-hearing for some time wasn't
the swaying of the waves, but the monologue of the boatman,

who was muttering, "Go on. Act like I'm not here. Treat my boat like a brothel. Don't matter what I think, do it?"

The last time Richard had blushed had been in the summer of 1788, when, as a spotty twelve-year-old, he had been caught gaping down the bodice of the Duchess of Devonshire. Fifteen years' worth of embarrassed flush burned in his cheeks, mercifully hidden by hood and mask. Leaning over, he helped Amy up from the floor, trying not to look too closely at her pink cheeks and shining eyes.

"That was wonderful," sighed Amy happily.

For *wonderful* substitute *awful,* thought Richard grimly as Amy snuggled trustingly into his side. Idiot! Him, that was, not her. He could only thank whatever powers out there that were still keeping an eye on him for stopping matters before they reached the ultimate point.

"Do you want me to row back and forth—again?" the boatman asked sourly, flinging his rope expertly over a piling.

"No," Richard said shortly. He dropped a few coins in the man's calloused hand, so consumed with self-loathing that it took him a moment to realize that Amy was attempting to climb out of the boat on her own, teetering back and forth with one foot on the edge, and looking in imminent danger of toppling into the water at any moment.

Chalk up another point against him.

Richard handed Amy out of the boat and tried not to notice the way her fingers lingered on his arm or the glowing smile she cast up at him from under her too-large hood. Considering what had just transpired, she had every right to the possessive clasp, as well as to the smile that gave affection and assumed it in return. Hell, she had every right to an instant proposal, bended knee and all. Or at least the confession of his true identity.

But he couldn't give her any of those things. Not yet.

Tony's specter rose before Richard's eyes, blocking out Amy's smiling face. Not Tony as he had known him in life— that Tony, a dandy in an embroidered waistcoat, with a light foot for the dance and an appreciative eye for the female form, would have cheered on a bit of dalliance—but that other, awful Tony. The Tony lying bloody and abandoned on the dirt floor of a French hut because he, Richard, had been distracted from his duty by a woman.

Something else niggled at the back of Richard's mind,

something to do with the Swiss gold. Something he would have noticed before had his brain not been muddled with desire. How in the hell had Amy known about the Swiss gold? True, he had seen her come flying out of Bonaparte's study as though possessed of a dozen furies, but he had searched that same room not half an hour later and discovered no such information. If he had, he wouldn't have had to spend the evening trying to pry the same intelligence out of the First Consul's brandy-sodden brother-in-law. If Amy hadn't learned of the Swiss gold from searching Bonaparte's study, then where?

A chill that had nothing to do with the night air engulfed Richard. Based on Geoff's reports, and the evidence of his own eyes, Balcourt was up to something that involved the transport of mysterious packages. He spent that part of his day not occupied by his tailor lurking about the Tuilleries. It took no great leap of intelligence to jump from there to the conclusion that Balcourt was up to his neck in the affair of the Swiss gold. And Amy was his sister, mysteriously summoned back to France just as Napoleon commenced his plans for the invasion of England. What better way to entrap the Purple Gentian? Provide him some intelligence, discover his plans . . . and summon Delaroche. It would be a sure way to Bonaparte's favor for Balcourt and his sister.

Richard's eyes slid sideways towards Amy, down to the little hand resting so trustingly on his arm, and he swore silently.

Nobody could be that good an actress. Her reactions to her parents' deaths could have been feigned—but if so, she ought to be at Drury Lane, partnering Kean. Every one of Richard's instincts, well-honed over a decade of outwitting the French, screamed her innocence.

But he couldn't take that chance. How many of his men would be involved in the assault upon the coach bearing the Swiss gold? A half dozen at least. Geoff would insist on going along, Geoff, who was one of the two men Richard could unreservedly call friend.

He had to end it with her. And later, when it was all over, when the mission was safely accomplished, when the invasion of England was thwarted, he could make it up to her. There was no other choice.

Next to the Purple Gentian, his hand warm and strong

under her arm, Amy drifted through a world wreathed in magic. How could she have thought the streets of Paris dingy? The cobblestones glimmered in the moonlight, and the dark windows twinkled with stars. Beautiful, beautiful stars. Tilting her head back, Amy traced familiar patterns through the sky.

A necklace of stars. Amy hugged the phrase to her like a pile of love letters. When he had first uttered the words, she had been shocked speechless, more shocked than she had ever been in her life. That this man she had known for a mere two days—even if she had been daydreaming about him for most of her life—should be able to slip into her mind and retrieve one of her most precious memories . . . it was inconceivable. But then, somewhere between the stars and the tender expression on the Gentian's face as he looked down at her in that silly little boat, everything had made complete sense. This was her sign—practically a certificate of approval from her parents—that he was her true love. What other explanation could there be?

Far away, up in the darkness, Amy could have sworn one of the stars winked.

Amy's speculations were cut short as they turned along the side of the Hotel de Balcourt. The Gentian's head was turned away from her as he checked for an open window, his hood hiding all but the tip of his nose from Amy's view. Her hands still tingled with the feel of the short, crisp hair hidden under that hood. And the rest of her tingled with other memories entirely.

As they drew to a halt outside an unlatched first-floor window, Amy turned to face the Gentian, gazing up at the masked face revealed beneath his hood. "Thank you," she whispered. "Thank you for rescuing me, and thank you even more for everything else."

Rising on tiptoes, Amy swayed towards the Purple Gentian, lifting her face for a tender farewell kiss. She nearly toppled over as he took a jerky step back.

"I'm sorry," the Gentian said abruptly. "None of this should have happened."

He was back to being dark and inscrutable. In the shadow of the house, the Gentian's hooded face had all the expression of a faceless monk in a gothic novel. It was just the shadow of the house, cutting off light, which made the Gentian look so aloof, Amy reassured herself. This was, after all, the same man who had laughed with her, kissed her, and promised her a necklace of stars. Unlike the evening's earlier identity confusion, there could be no doubt that this was the same Purple Gentian of an hour or half an hour past, even if he was anonymously swathed in a dark cloak and hood. Amy had kept a hand on his arm at all times.

Until now.

Since that was clearly a situation that needed to be remedied, Amy took a step forward and rested a hand on the Purple Gentian's chest. "*Don't* be sorry," Amy said feelingly. "I'm sorry to have dragged you into a fight with Marston, but I can't regret anything else that happened. It was the most absolutely wonderful night of my life. *You're* the most absolutely wonderful—"

The Purple Gentian shook his hooded head. "Don't, Amy."

Under her fingers, the Gentian's chest was rigid, unmoving, as though he wasn't even breathing. Amy tilted her head back, back to the point of dizziness, to peer through the slits of his mask. "Are you worried that the praise will go to your head?" she teased. "And that it will puff up until you can't fit into your disguises anymore?"

The Purple Gentian redirected his gaze somewhere to the left of Amy's shoulder. Amy had to resist the impulse to turn around to see what could possibly be so engrossing.

"I'm serious, Amy," he said flatly.

"So am I," said Amy cheerfully. "I do think you're wonderful. How would you like me to prove it to you? I could follow you into Hades, like Orpheus after Eurydice. I could—"

"Amy, we can't see each other anymore."

The exuberant words Amy had been about to utter withered and died unspoken. She pulled back and stared at the Gentian. "What do you mean?"

Surely, there must be some other meaning to his words. Perhaps what he meant was that they couldn't go on meeting at night like this. She could agree with that. It would be much nicer to meet by daylight, to see his face when he spoke to her. Or maybe he meant his words literally; in the gloom, she really couldn't see him anymore either, Amy rationalized madly.

"I meant just what I said."

His words might have been uninformative, but the tone of

his voice, as stony as his motionless body, brooked no misinterpretation. Amy's spirits plummeted from the stars to the grimy cobblestones at her feet.

"You don't want to see me anymore?" Amy hated the little quaver she heard in her own voice.

The Purple Gentian nodded slowly.

It didn't make sense. It didn't make sense at all. It might as well have been a series of grunts, rather than words, for all the sense it made. Amy bit her lip on the anguished "why?" that was trying to burst out of her mouth and lowered her eyes to stare at the Gentian's scuffed boots. He liked her. She knew he liked her. Didn't he? After all, he had rescued her and kissed her and—oh goodness, there had been the necklace of stars. Surely, if he didn't love her, he wouldn't have done any of that. Would he?

Amy's hands curled into fists as she marshaled her panicked thoughts. There must be another reason.

"Are you worried about my reputation?" she blurted out. "Because as long as we meet discreetly there's really no cause to worry."

"That's not it." A wintry undertone of regret ran through the Purple Gentian's words, as chill and dead as a garden in December. Taking Amy's hand, which still rested forgotten against his heart, he gently returned it to her side.

Amy, who had been desperately searching for any signs of emotion, found herself wishing he would go back to his statue impersonation. Inscrutability was infinitely preferable to rue. And pity.

"I'm sorry, Amy," the Gentian was saying, with that same killing gentleness. "I wish it could be some other way."

The empty platitude scraped along Amy's heightened nerves, like a stone in her shoe that had to be flung out. "*What* other way?" she demanded. "You're talking in riddles! Why can't you see me again? I don't understand."

The Purple Gentian's jaw tightened, and he gazed out into the air over Amy's shoulder as though the answer might be lurking somewhere in those selfsame stars he had promised to her earlier.

Amy watched his averted face anxiously.

"It's the mission, you see," he said finally, awkwardly.

"Oh!" said Amy, then, "No, I don't see. My information was a help to the mission, wasn't it?" she probed.

"Yes."

"Then what? Are you worried about my being in danger? I promise, I'll be more cautious. I'll even—"

Lowering his hooded head to look at Amy, the Gentian pronounced with chilling finality, "I can't let infatuation get in the way of the mission."

"Infatuation," Amy repeated, her eyes begging him, willing him to take the word back. "Is that what you feel for me? Infatuation?"

A dreadful, frozen silence followed. The nightingales stopped chirping. The wind stopped blowing. The stars didn't dare twinkle. The moon looked as stiff and brittle as Amy felt.

And then the Purple Gentian shrugged.

"That's one way of describing it."

The moon crumbled into a thousand shards. Infatuation. Not even a poor cousin of love. All of her carefully hoarded memories rushed back at her in a new, unpleasant aspect. Instead of the Purple Gentian's kiss in the study, she saw his eagerness to leap out the window. Away from her. She was a liability. An impediment to the mission.

Had everything they had shared been no more than a distraction to him?

It could have been worse, she supposed. He could have left her with the illusion that he cared for her, kissed her goodbye, walked away, and never returned. At least he had been honest. At least he had shown her that much regard. She supposed she should be grateful for that. Her gratitude sat like ashes in her mouth.

"Thank you," Amy said tightly, "for not lying to me."

"It's not—I don't want you to think—Damn!" the Gentian cursed explosively.

Why wouldn't he just leave? The sight of him, looming there in his blasted black cloak, so dashing and handsome and—oh, anxiously boyish, stung like salt on a pricked finger.

"Good night." Amy nodded stiffly in what she hoped was the right direction. It was hard to tell with her eyes averted. But if she looked again, the tears might start, and that, above all things, was not to be borne. "Thank you for seeing me home. You can leave now," she added.

Only he didn't.

Just to be safe—since one really never knew with Amy—Richard took a quick peek under the desk. No, no Amy. Richard reminded himself that he should be experiencing relief, not disappointment.

Making his way to the globe, Richard took up where he had left off the night before. His fingers felt for that telltale crack along the equator, easing towards the tiny bump that must be . . . Ah! Richard smirked as the two halves sprang open. The catch.

Richard's smirk disappeared as his mouth dropped open in shock. What in the blazes? Plunging his hand into the rounded base, he ran it back and forth and around. He felt along the top of the globe to see if something might be glued to the inside. He stuck his head in so far that his nose bashed into the bottom. Clutching his wounded appendage, Richard staggered back and slammed the empty globe shut.

Someone else had gotten there first.

Chapter Twenty-five

꧁ ꧂

After the warm coziness of Mrs. Selwick-Alderly's flat, my own little gnome hole seemed even more desolate than usual.

The hall light had gone out again, leaving the blue-walled hallway in gloom, and the blue-carpeted stairs even gloomier. Juggling the caramel macchiato I'd picked up at the Starbucks next to the Bayswater Tube stop and the package under my arm, I picked my way downstairs, making a mental note to call the landlord about replacing the lightbulb before someone (that is, me) broke her neck on the stairs. I managed to insert key into lock on the third try, and blundered into my dark little entryway, fumbling for the light switch.

As furnished flats go, it wasn't too dreadful. There wasn't terribly much to it, just a narrow hallway with miniature kitchen appliances crammed against one wall, a tiny bathroom, and one rectangular room that tripled as living room, bedroom, and study. The conscientious owner had tried to brighten it up with cream-colored paint and flowered curtains and large landscapes of the Tuscan countryside. Unfortunately, the latter only emphasized the contrast between the Italian sunshine and the gray excuse for light that filtered through my scrap of window.

Dumping my coffee on the small, round table, and setting the plastic-wrapped package tenderly down on the bed, I toppled into a chair, and tackled my boots. The zipper on the left boot had gone stiff, probably in protest against the eternal rain. Another tug, and the zipper gave with that horrible tearing sound that anyone who has ever snagged a stocking knows all too well.

Ordinarily, I might have been mildly peeved about the

untimely demise of my last pair of stockings. But my mind wasn't on my wardrobe. Fueled by caffeine and caramel, it was replaying last night's scene in Mrs. Selwick-Alderly's kitchen in excruciating detail—the same way it had been doing since three this morning.

I'd tried to lose myself in Amy's letters, but the papers kept drifting down towards the coverlet as I would stare off into space, coming up with the five-hundredth witty parting line I ought to have fired after Colin Selwick. It is a truth universally acknowledged that one only comes up with clever, cutting remarks long after the other party is happily slumbering away. Somehow, I figured storming into Colin's bedroom, shaking him awake, and delivering my brilliant one-liner would only make me look more pathetic.

Besides, he might have gotten the wrong idea. To the male mind, female plus bedroom equals just one thing.

Colin hadn't been about when I dragged myself blearily out of the guest bedroom at seven that morning, and stumbled kitchenwards. Instead, I'd found Mrs. Selwick-Alderly at the pine table, drinking a cup of tea and reading the *Daily Telegraph*.

I'd veered between disappointment and relief. Disappointment, because there went any chance of delivering those painstakingly crafted retorts. And relief, because I know what I look like at seven in the morning.

Mrs. Selwick-Alderly had dropped her newspaper with flattering promptness, smilingly asking me how I'd slept, and pressed tea and toast upon me. I'd accepted the tea, declined the toast, and refrained from any mention of midnight encounters with her nephew. I wondered if she was going to bring up the presence of two chocolate-streaked mugs in the sink, but either she hadn't noticed, or didn't think it worth mentioning. Maybe Colin had midnight cocoa tête-à-têtes all the time.

Maybe I was being entirely ridiculous.

I gulped down my tea in record time.

"How are you finding our little archive?" Mrs. Selwick-Alderly asked, giving me a moment to recover from my burnt tongue.

"It's unbelievable," I said honestly. "I can't thank you enough for letting me use it. But . . ."

"Yes?"

"Colin—I mean, your nephew . . ." Damn. Mrs. Selwick-Alderly was well aware that Colin was her nephew without my telling her so. I started again. "Why doesn't he want me to have access to your papers?"

Mrs. Selwick-Alderly looked thoughtfully at the headline of the *Telegraph*. "Colin takes his position as guardian of the family heritage very seriously. What do you think of our Pink Carnation?"

"I haven't found him yet. I'm only about halfway through the papers you gave me. The handwriting took some getting used to."

"Amy's handwriting *is* awful, isn't it? Who do you think the Pink Carnation is?"

"Miles Dorrington seems like the best candidate." I watched Mrs. Selwick-Alderly closely, hoping for a reaction; something to confirm or contradict my hunch.

I didn't get one. Mrs. Selwick-Alderly went on calmly spreading marmalade on a piece of toast as she asked, "Why Miles?"

"The Pink Carnation's first recorded escapade isn't until late April of 1803. Miles is in constant contact with the Purple Gentian, so he knows everything that's going on in Paris; he has all the resources of the War Office behind him in London; *and*"—I brought forth my best piece of evidence so far—"he's in Paris in late April."

"How did you discover that, if you're only half finished?"

"I flipped ahead," I confessed. "I saw his signature on a letter that was dated Paris, April thirtieth. So I know he's at the right place at the right time."

"What about Georges Marston?"

"After his assault on Amy?" I exclaimed incredulously.

"Nobility of deed isn't always a sign of nobility of character," Mrs. Selwick-Alderly said quietly. "Great men have been known to be brutes in private life."

I made a face, resisting a five-year-old's impulse to stamp my foot in protest. "Not the Pink Carnation," I said firmly, trying to ignore the little trickle of unease that slithered down my spine like the snake along the tree of knowledge.

That would explain Colin's reticence . . . the Pink Carnation, a would-be rapist. I banished the thought as an impossibility. Marston couldn't be the Pink Carnation. If he were, we'd have heard something about him prior to April 1803;

Marston had been in Paris for months, ever since his defection from the English army. Miles. It had to be Miles.

". . . with you," Mrs. Selwick-Alderly said.

"Pardon?"

Mrs. Selwick-Alderly repeated herself. I gaped in incomprehension.

"You can't mean it." That had just been an offer to take the manuscript home with me, hadn't it? I tended to be a bit out of it in the morning, but not entirely delusional. I must have misheard.

"You must finish the story," she said, folding her paper and putting it aside. "And then we can discuss whether the Pink Carnation lives up to all your expectations."

"But what if I lost them?" I protested. "I might drop them on the Tube, or they might get damaged by the rain, or . . ."

"That sort of thinking," Mrs. Selwick-Alderly said with great satisfaction, "is exactly why I have no hesitation about entrusting them to your care."

After that, how could I argue? Especially when I wanted to finish reading those papers more than I wanted anything in my life. Retrieving the papers from her guest room, she had first placed them in their special, acid-free box, wrapped the box in a clean linen sheet from the airing cupboard, and folded the entire bundle into no fewer than seven thick plastic bags before placing the bulky package into a Fortnum's carrier bag. They were on short-term loan—I was to return the pile the following day, presumably before Colin discovered they were missing.

The safety of the papers was one thing, but Colin Selwick's obsession with secrecy was quite another. I was still smarting over his high-handed directive of the night before. Nothing goes beyond this flat, indeed!

I could understand not wanting his family's name dragged through the muck of the tabloids—but what sort of scandal was big enough to catch the public's attention two hundred years later? Maybe his great-great-great-grandfather, the Purple Gentian, *had* sold out to the French, and had been unmasked by the Pink Carnation, and that's why Colin Selwick wanted to keep it all under wraps, I hypothesized. Even so, I couldn't imagine that generating more than scholarly interest, or, at most, a couple of paragraphs towards the middle of the *Mirror* on a particularly slow news day. It wasn't exactly stop-the-presses sort of stuff.

Besides, as far as I could tell from the documentation I'd been reading, the Purple Gentian was fanatically devoted to his cause. The worst I'd been able to discover about him was that he had played nasty games with the heart of Miss Amy Balcourt. Poor Amy. Reading that entry of her diary in the wee hours of dawn—just before my eyelids finally gave in to gravity and my body to sleep—I'd wanted to slug Lord Richard for her. And he had sounded so charming. But, then, they all did. Even Grant had been charming in the beginning.

Now, what was he still doing in my head? Out, out damned ex!

Scowling, I gulped down the remains of my coffee, and went to toss the empty paper cup in the trash. I dumped it into the bin with unnecessary force.

It wasn't as though I was pining for Grant, I groused to myself as I stomped back over to the bed. Things had begun to go sour long before the advent of Alicia the art historian. For those last few months, we'd stayed together as much out of convenience as anything else, just because it would be too much trouble to find someone else to fill up those empty Friday nights.

I plopped down onto the flowered coverlet, and reached for the plastic-wrapped package. Unfortunately, I knew exactly what I was suffering from. LIPID (Last Idiot Person I Dated) syndrome: a largely undiagnosed but pervasive disease that afflicts single women.

My roommates and I had come up with the term in college, to explain the baffling phenomenon of nostalgia for one's most recent ex. No matter how absolutely awful that person had been at the time, after a few weeks, the relationship would take on a rosy tint, and wistful little phrases would begin to creep into conversation, like, "I know he cheated on me with three people at the same time, but he was such a fabulous dancer," or "All right, so he was a raging alcoholic, but when he was sober he did such sweet things! Remember those flowers he bought for me that one time?" Inexplicable, but inevitable. A few weeks of singledom render even the most inexcusable ex charming in retrospect.

Hence, LIPID syndrome. As everyone knows, lipids are fats, and fats are bad for you, and therefore ex-boyfriends must be avoided at all costs.

This is what comes of having a bio major as a roommate for four years.

The one sure way to fight off LIPID syndrome was to distract oneself. True, the only foolproof cure is a new relationship, thus knocking the LIPID back down the dating chain into harmless obscurity, but there are other, temporary diversions. Reading a novel, watching a movie, or delving into the private lives of historical characters.

With an anticipatory grin, I eased the bundle in my lap out of its first layer of wrappings, a green Harrods bag, and began slowly unwinding the next layer, a turquoise bag from the Fortnum & Mason Food Hall. I had just gotten down to layer three—another Harrods bag, relic of last year's January sales—when my raincoat began bleating out a Mozart sonata.

Setting aside my bundle, I leaped for the vibrating pocket of my raincoat, yanking out my mobile just as it got to the third measure.

It was still only eight in the morning. Who would call at such an uncivilized hour? Mrs. Selwick-Alderly demanding the papers back? A furious Colin Selwick, accusing me of grand manuscript theft and threatening to sic Scotland Yard on me?

PAMMY, proclaimed the screen in capital letters.

I should have known.

Pammy and I had attended the same all-girls school in Manhattan until tenth grade, when Pammy's parents split, and her English mother took off for London, Pammy in tow. But we'd kept in touch, first by scrawled schoolgirl letters on overly cutesy stationery, and later via marathon e-mail sessions. I loved her. I did. But Pammy was . . . Pammy. Over the top. Unique. About as sensitive as a construction crew. *Not* the person to tell about the Selwick saga.

For a moment I considered pushing the little red end-call button. But Pammy is a force of nature not to be denied. She'd only keep calling back till I gave in. I hit receive.

"Hi, Pammy."

"What are you wearing tonight?" she demanded without preamble.

Oh, God, tonight. I'd completely forgotten. Damn. I knew I should never have picked up the phone.

Pammy, as she airily informed people at cocktail parties, did PR, which, as far as I could tell, involved throwing very expensive parties on other people's tabs. Tonight's extravaganza celebrated the launch of the Covent Garden store of a hot new designer, hot and new meaning that the clothes were all either tattered in mysterious places, or made from exotic materials like genuine imported Tibetan yak skin (dry clean only). Pammy, who tended to know about these things, swore he was the next Marc Jacobs. It would be, like all of Pammy's parties, hot and crowded and filled with impossibly glamorous people with hip bones so sharp they could qualify as concealed weapons.

"Pammy, no; I can't," I moaned.

"Don't even *think* of backing out," she ordered. "If you don't show tonight, I will personally march over to Bayswater and drag you out."

She would, too. This was, after all, the same girl who had marched Andy Hochstetter over to me at a Goddard Gaities dance in sixth grade, and threatened to strangle him with his own tie if he wouldn't dance.

"I'm really tired . . . ," I hedged.

Pammy snorted. "So take a nap! It's not like you have to go anywhere."

Pammy had never grasped the concept that grad school actually required work.

"I have a ton of manuscripts to read. . . ."

"These people have been dead for five hundred years, Ellie. What does an extra day matter?"

Pammy had also never grasped the concept of time periods. I had given up trying to explain to Pammy that 1803 was only two hundred years ago, and, no, the Pink Carnation didn't wear armor like the people in *A Knight's Tale*.

"It's not like it's going to make any difference to them if— what the fuck do you think you're doing?"

Since that last was followed by a screech of tires, it clearly wasn't intended for me.

"Are you okay?" I shouted above the din of cursing motorists.

"Idiot drivers," muttered Pammy, who'd nearly mown down three pedestrians driving me home from her flat two nights before. Her tone switched to wheedle mode. "Come on, Ellie, if you don't go, you're just going to sit alone in your flat feeling sorry for yourself. Wouldn't you rather be out, doing something? It will be fun."

"Fun," I echoed flatly. Stick-thin models parading around in clothes that looked like something out of a surrealist painter's disturbed dreams while the self-proclaimed glamorous screeched at each other over lukewarm glasses of champagne. Hmm, champagne. Pammy did generally order excellent alcohol.

Pammy scented weakness. "Good! It's just a few blocks off the Covent Garden Tube stop . . ." Without pausing for breath she rattled off the address. "Did you get that?"

"No."

"Ellie!"

I fetched pen and paper. One could sooner argue with a hurricane. "Repeat," I directed.

By the time she was done, I'd covered two sides of a piece of notepaper. Knowing my propensity for getting lost, Pammy gave me what she calls Ellie directions: complicated lists of every single landmark in a ten-block radius of where I was supposed to be going. "If you see a Starbucks, you've gone too far," she finished. "And I'll have my mobile on. I probably won't be able to hear it," she added pragmatically, "but call if you get lost, and I'll try to come out and find you."

"No Starbucks . . . ," I repeated, scribbling away. "Will anyone I know be there?"

Pammy rattled off a list of names, some of which I recognized from her previous parties, including her current crush, an investment banking type notable only for his surprisingly bright ties.

"And I've invited a few St. Paul's people," she finished, referring to the London private school she'd transferred to after leaving Chapin, "but I don't think you've met any of them. Now," she said briskly, having gotten the preliminaries out of the way, "what are you going to wear?"

"I hadn't thought about it," I admitted; Pammy's parties were always impossible to dress for.

Phone pressed to my ear, I wandered over to the wardrobe, and regarded my limited London wardrobe. The sight that greeted me was uninspiring. Tweed, tweed, everywhere, as far as the eye could see. All right, so I'd taken the whole dressing-like-an-academic thing a little too much to heart.

"I can loan you something," Pammy offered a little too promptly. "There's the cutest little outfit I bought just the other day. . . ."

"What about my little black dress?" I countered, pushing past rows of herringbone and plaid.

"Ugh," Pammy said eloquently. "It makes you look like a Chapin mother."

Now that wasn't fair. True, it was a classic little black sheath dress, but it was made of a soft, clinging fabric that draped in a way utterly inappropriate for a parent-teacher meeting. I'd bought it miraculously on sale at Bergdorf's the previous winter, and it had become my cocktail fallback dress. Definitely not a Pammy sort of outfit, though.

As for what was a Pammy sort of outfit . . . "Listen, I'm going down into the Tube now, so we might be cut off. But how about this. All you need are two scarves. Just tie one around your chest as a top, and the other—"

Mercifully, the Tube yanked Pammy out of range before she could finish the thought. Even Scheherazade was allotted a few more layers than that.

Slamming the wardrobe doors shut, I retreated to the bed. I'd deal with the outfit issue later. With any luck, Pammy wouldn't change her mind and decide to show up at eight o'clock with an outfit that she just knew would look fabulous on me. The last time she had attempted to dress me for a party, it had involved a red leather bustier. Enough said.

Plumping up my pillows, I fell gratefully back onto the bed, and regarded the plastic bundle from a prone position. Nap? Or manuscript? My body was definitely urging nap . . . but I found myself reaching for the manuscript anyway.

Just one or two pages of Amy's diary, I promised my tired body. Just enough to find out what happened when she went to view Lord Richard's antiquities.

Chapter Twenty-six

Dawn had barely broken over the spires of Notre Dame. In the twisted streets of the city, fires remained unlit and responsible citizens slumbered soundly in their beds. But in the Ministry of Police, Gaston Delaroche was already at his desk.

Outside his office, four people stood waiting. One wore the clothes, and bore the reek, of an onion seller. He juggled three onions as he waited. Another was dressed for travel in spurs, cape, and hat. He feigned interest in the pattern of tiles on the floor, ducking the occasional flying onion. The third was female, a burly woman in brown wool with her hair piled atop her head, examining her nails in the flicker of the torches on the wall. The final member of the quartet was the sort of street urchin one might encounter on any street on any day in any major city, a skinny thing held together by dirt and rags. He stood picking at the specks on his arms.

The silent denizens of the hallway possessed two things in common. The first was a certain blandness of expression. Despite their varied costumes, anyone walking down the hall would be hard-pressed, upon being asked, to remark upon the particulars of any one of them.

The second common element was Delaroche.

Each waited for admission to the inner sanctum, as they had waited each morning since he had summoned them. As they would continue to wait each morning until he gave them leave to go.

They were his . . . ah, but spy was such a nasty word. They were his intelligence gatherers, his eyes, his ears, his pursuers of the elusive and the dangerous. Each had come to him through paths so shadowed that not even his extensive files bore the record of their existence. Each owed him a bond of obligation as deep as life or death.

By courtesy, the lady, however dubious her claim to that title, was summoned first, by a red-eyed sentry who opened the door at Delaroche's command, and closed it again behind. It amused her to vary her accent as she spoke: one moment the purring tones of a polished courtesan, the next the shrill shriek of a fishmonger's wife. In this patchwork way, she reported that Augustus Whittlesby had spent the past day prostrate at the feet of a minor statue of Pan, and the past evening pursuing his muse in the arms of one of the girls of Mme Pinpin's house of pleasure.

"Not enough. Not enough," muttered Delaroche, and waved her away.

The onion seller entered next. He informed the assistant to the Minister of Police that Sir Percy Blakeney had passed the previous day reading in his library, playing picquet with his wife, and entertaining his brother and sister-in-law. No unknowns had entered the house nor had Sir Percy gone out.

Third came the traveler, spurs clicking with authority against the tiled floor. His voice, when he spoke, failed to match his stride. Hesitant and apologetic, he confessed to losing Georges Marston at Mme Rochefort's party, and only finding him again lying senseless in a cul de sac in the Latin Quarter.

"Fool!" Delaroche hissed, slamming his palm upon his desk. "Careless fool!"

The traveler slunk out of the office, spurs grating against stone as he dragged his feet. The others drew back from him as if from one with the plague. One never knew how the taint of displeasure might spread.

Last entered the street urchin, slipping through the door with the beggar's ragged grace. In the harsh light of the candles on Delaroche's desk—both illumination and weapon— the urchin's begrimed face hovered uncertainly between youth and age.

In a light voice that could have been a boy's treble or a man's tenor, he reported that Lord Richard Selwick seemingly had done nothing but engage in amorous endeavors. Two nights previous, Selwick had undertaken an assignation with a young woman in the Balcourt household.

"And last night?" Delaroche's eyes narrowed.

Last night, explained the urchin, Selwick had engaged in a brawl with Georges Marston over some wench in the Luxembourg Gardens—the urchin's smudged face cheered somewhat at the mention of bloodshed—but once Marston had been knocked cold, not much of a fight at all, Selwick had gone off with the girl, engaging in activities better conducted behind closed shutters.

"So Marston was felled by Selwick." Two suspects disqualified by a chit of a girl! Marston's crumpled body in the park had seemed so promising, but to hear that his state was brought on by nothing more significant than a fracas over a female . . . Delaroche's nostrils flared with ire. That left him, once again, with Sir Percy and Whittlesby. Delaroche's mind sped feverishly back over the testimony of his agents. There must be something there. Some clue.

The urchin's lips twisted in the flickering candlelight into a fey smile. "Lord Richard Selwick," he added softly, "was hooded and masked."

Delaroche had been on the verge of dismissing his last and youngest agent; the boy's words stayed his hand.

"Masked."

"Lord Richard returned to his lodgings prior to both assignations. He emerged wearing a black cape, a black hood, and a black mask. A cape, hood, and mask such as are worn by the Purple Gentian."

"It's not enough," Delaroche muttered to himself. "Anyone might wear a black cloak. Even the mask might be explained. We need more. We need . . ." Delaroche fixed his ferocious gaze on his agent. "Two women, you say? One each night?"

"Yes." The agent had learned that it was best to answer simply.

"Ah." Delaroche leaned back in his chair with a nasty smile, a smile akin to that bestowed by the spider upon the fly. "Therein lies the answer to our riddle."

"Sir?"

"But isn't it obvious?" Delaroche barked with humorless laughter. "Come! Even you must see the fatal flaw in his alibi! Selwick is . . . English!"

"English." Understanding began to dawn in the agent's eyes.

Delaroche rubbed his palms together in an orgy of self-congratulation. "If Selwick were French, the tale would be believable. We could dismiss him now. But he is English! And everyone knows that the English are a cold, passionless people, incapable of grand stirrings of the blood. For an Englishman to have seduced two women in as many nights is inconceivable."

Rising from his chair, slowly, deliberately, Delaroche strolled to the window. "You," he said in a voice so pleasant that the boy-man, who had faced the point of a knife more than once without a wince, trembled with fear. "You are to watch Lord Richard Selwick day and night. Keep a detail of soldiers within call. Do not let him leave your sight."

"Yes, sir."

"Didn't you hear me?" Delaroche turned abruptly on one heel. "I said watch him! Go, damn you!"

Without another word, the boy fled the room.

Delaroche's nose quivered like a dog scenting blood. The Purple Gentian was growing careless. One could tell by the foolish mistake he had made of trying to disguise his meetings with agents as affairs of the heart.

Lord Richard Selwick had powerful friends in the government, friends no less formidable than the stepchildren of the First Consul. It was said that the First Consul himself was unaccountably fond of the man. But how fond would the First Consul remain of his director of Egyptian antiquities once his less-scholarly activities came to light?

Delaroche's lips curved into the shape of a scimitar. "One more mistake, Selwick. All it will take is one more mistake."

Chapter Twenty-seven

"Good morning, slugabed!" Jane's voice came from somewhere close at hand. Amy rolled over, the covers still bunched up around her shoulders, as Jane continued, with the unconscious condemnation of the naturally early riser, "It's past eleven already. You've lost half the day."

"No great loss," muttered Amy. Despite the comfort of the familiar dialogue, a sense of malaise weighed heavily over her. Her eyes felt scratchy under their lids and the back of her throat ached as though with the onset of the grippe. Memories of the night before began to return slowly, in patches. Marston on the ground. All the stars shining at her. The Purple Gentian telling her . . . oh. Amy squeezed her eyes even more tightly shut. As if shutting her eyes could block out the memory of the Gentian saying, "We can't see each other anymore."

"I brought you chocolate," Jane's familiar voice wheedled. "And I have something to tell you."

Amy slowly pushed the covers back from her chin, and blinked blearily at Jane. In her Grecian-style gown, her hair in a knot at the back of her head, a pile of papers in one hand, and a fluted chocolate pot in the other, Jane looked a bit like a minor classical deity. Amy envied her cousin's serenity.

"I thought that would roust you out," Jane said with some satisfaction. But her tone changed as she took in Amy's reddened eyes. "Are you all right?" she asked anxiously.

The sight of her cousin exuding love, concern, and hot chocolate—since Jane, focused entirely on Amy, hadn't noticed the way the chocolate pot in her hand was tilting, or the trickle of chocolate freckling the pale blue counterpane—made tears prick in Amy's eyes.

Pulling her pillow over her head, Amy grumbled, "Not if you wake me at this hour of the morning."

"I'm not sure this even counts as morning anymore." Jane put down her papers, tugged the pillow away, and handed a reasonably dry-eyed Amy a porcelain cup of lukewarm chocolate.

"What happened last night?" Jane asked, settling herself down on the bed in the hollow next to Amy's hip. Her skirts blended with the sheets, white on white. "I stopped by after I heard your door click closed, but you were lying so still I couldn't bear to disturb you. Did you speak to your Purple Gentian?"

"I think we may have to restore the monarchy without the Purple Gentian," Amy said, her eyes on her cup of chocolate. She looked up at Jane with a false, strained smile. "That will give us much more freedom of movement, don't you think?"

Jane watched the contortions of Amy's lips with alarm. "What's wrong, Amy?"

"Nothing's wrong. The Purple Gentian and I just realized we had different . . ." Different depths of emotion? Different ideas of the value of a kiss? Amy pressed her lips together tightly. "Objectives," she finished brightly. "He wants to stop the invasion of England, and I want to restore the crown. That's all."

"The two aren't necessarily incompatible."

The Purple Gentian seemed to think so. He found her a distracting infatuation, incompatible with stopping the invasion of England. Incompatible with him.

The rich chocolate tasted like acid in Amy's mouth.

"Who needs the Purple Gentian?" declared Amy, hauling herself up on her elbows. "Just because he's"—*handsome, charming, witty, tender,* her traitor mind supplied—"had more experience doesn't mean he's indispensable. We'll do just as well on our own."

An ache of emptiness overtook Amy on that last word. Maybe she could pretend she had never found him, never believed she loved him, had lost nothing but daydreams.

"Something happened last night with the Purple Gentian. Was he uncouth?" Jane asked darkly. "Did he hurt you?"

"No! Nothing like that. He just—"

"Just what?" prompted Jane, a deadly hint of steel in her gray eyes.

"It's complicated."

Jane refilled Amy's cup of chocolate and handed it back to her. "It can't be that complicated."

So Amy explained. She told her about the meeting in the study, the fracas in the gardens—Amy rapidly hurried through that bit, as Jane's face darkened in a way that foretold lectures to come—and the dreadful walk home. The events on the boat, aside from a chaste kiss or two, Amy omitted. And she left out any mention of stars, especially in the form of a necklace.

Jane listened thoughtfully. "I'm not sure this means what you think it means."

Amy plucked listlessly at an embroidered lily on the edge of her eiderdown. "I'll never see him again, and that's all there is to it."

"Amy, you can't just—"

"Romance would get in the way of my mission, anyway. It already has."

"Birds of a feather," muttered Jane. "That sounds a great deal like—"

"When you woke me up, you said you had something to tell me?" Amy cut in.

Jane retrieved her tidy stack of papers. "It will keep till later. We're to go to the Tuilleries at four, and I have some little odds and ends I want to tie up before then."

Amy buried her head again in her pillow. "I'd forgotten. Lord Richard's antiquities."

Her spirits were still low hours later as Miss Gwen shepherded them into the Tuilleries to keep their appointment with Lord Richard. Amy derived less than the usual enjoyment from watching Miss Gwen make loud demands in English and poke the baffled guards with her parasol. An entourage of three footmen, all clutching their sides in pain, eventually escorted them to Lord Richard's office.

The room was smaller than Amy had anticipated. Or maybe it merely seemed small due to the clutter of objects that filled the room. Long tables ran down both sides and the center of the room, their surfaces covered by vases, pottery, fragments of jewelry. Crates, lined up one after another, formed a solid block beneath the tables and rose in tottery piles at the corners of the room. At the very end of the room sat Lord Richard, nearly hidden behind a stack of immense, leather-bound ledgers. He was, Amy saw as they moved farther into the room, squinting at a shard of pottery, the quill in his other hand poised over a page already half filled with tidy script.

And he wasn't fully clothed.

Amy didn't mean to stare, but Lord Richard's jacket was slung over the back of his chair, his waistcoat hung open, and the linen of his shirt was so very fine. The healthy sheen of skin showed through the white fabric. Amy watched, fascinated, as the sleeve bunched and pulled against the sleek muscles of his arm as he reached over to dip his quill in the inkwell. Her eyes traveled up the length of his arm, to the loosened knot of his cravat, the pulse moving in the hollow of his bare throat.

"Hrrrrmph!" Miss Gwen cleared her throat forcefully enough to create a hurricane three counties away.

"I do beg your pardon." Lord Richard grabbed for his jacket. "I hadn't expected you for another quarter hour yet. Welcome." He ushered them into the room, turning his devastating smile in special welcome upon Amy.

"When were you in Egypt?" asked Miss Gwen in her peremptory way, saving Amy from having to say anything at all.

"I went over in ninety-eight with Bonaparte's expedition and returned later that year," Lord Richard said, not meeting Amy's eye.

Blast! Trust Miss Gwen to bring up an awkward topic, when the point of the visit was to charm Amy into liking him as himself. A few more mentions of the Egyptian expedition, and she'd be scowling at him again as though he had single-handedly guillotined half the French aristocracy. But could he really blame Miss Gwen for bringing up Egypt when he'd invited them to view Egyptian antiquities? Hmm. Richard considered that conundrum. Unfortunately, he didn't have any nice, safe Roman or Greek antiquities lying about, and he couldn't very well ask them to leave for a few hours so that he could procure some.

"You were in Egypt when Nelson destroyed the French fleet?"

"Yes."

Miss Gwen's steely eyes were rather too probing for Richard's peace of mind. He hastily picked up a necklace from one of the long tables lining the sides of the room. "This is a necklace made of faience, which is—"

"Where were you?"

The necklace dangled in the air in front of Amy, shades of dusty red and blue, as Lord Richard turned to cock a confused eyebrow at Miss Gwen. "Where was I when?"

"Never mind." Miss Gwen waved an imperious hand. "It doesn't signify."

Jane stepped in to rescue him. "What's this, my lord?" she asked, indicating a piece of stone, engraved with what looked to be little squiggles and pictures, which stood propped against the wall.

"We think that might be a funeral stela," explained Lord Richard, running a finger fondly along the carvings. "See the pictures on top? That's the pharaoh in the middle, giving offerings to a god—that's the chap with horns, on his right. His queen, with the tall hat, stands on his left."

"Who was she?" asked Amy, moving to stand next to him, drawn in despite herself.

"We don't know," Lord Richard admitted, grinning boyishly down at her. "Would you like to hazard a guess? Perhaps a princess from a faraway land, brought overseas from her home."

"Shipwrecked on the coast of Egypt," suggested Amy, "like the heroine of a Shakespeare play. Forced to disguise herself as a boy, until her innate nobility shines through her humble robes. She catches the eye of the pharaoh. . . ."

"And they live happily ever after," finished Lord Richard.

"I wonder what really happened to her," Amy said, eyes scanning the unreadable symbols in front of her. It reminded her of the first time she had looked at the Greek letters on the page of one of Papa's books, how it seemed impossible that the strangely configured strokes of ink could resolve themselves into the love of Ariadne and the treachery of Theseus. Amazing how many stories dwelled on men repudiating the women who loved them. Theseus and Ariadne, Jason and Medea, Aeneas and Dido. Too bad she hadn't learned her lesson well enough from her storybooks.

"You don't think she lived happily ever after?" Lord Richard asked softly, his fingers brushing past Amy's as she traced the contours of a small bird.

"That's an ending for books, not for people."

"What are books about, if not people?"

Richard yielded to the temptation to lean just a little bit closer to Amy. The lavender scent of her hair filled his nostrils. His gaze roamed over the dark curls of her hair, the gentle curve of her cheek, the kissable little dent at the base of her throat.

Amy backed away from the force of Lord Richard's gaze. "Why don't you ask Miss Gwen," she suggested. "She can tell you all about the characters in her horrid novel, I'm sure."

Lord Richard didn't so much as glance at Miss Gwen. His green gaze narrowed even more intently on Amy. What was it about his voice, his presence, his talk of happy endings that was making her so nervous? Amy felt a slight flush rising in her cheeks at the sight of Lord Richard's tapering fingers stroking the stone tablet, caressing the contours of the carvings. She focused her eyes on Lord Richard's face. She could see the little crinkles at the corners of his eyes, the gold tips of his lashes, the slight dusting of pale hairs across the bridge of his nose.

"Uppington," announced Miss Gwen out of nowhere. Lord Richard started and banged his head against the stela. Amy let out the breath she'd been holding in a giggle.

"The Selwick Marquesses of Uppington of Uppington Hall. In Kent, unless I mistake myself," Miss Gwen continued.

Rubbing the bump on his head—Richard wondered if he'd find hieroglyphs embedded on his skull from the force of that blow—he smiled ruefully at Miss Gwen. "You know your *Debrett's* well."

Miss Gwen sniffed. "Young man, I live in the countryside, not the wilds of America. We are not entirely cut off from the civilized world."

"My apologies."

"When I made my debut, I knew my peerage better than any girl in London. I could identify the crest on a carriage from five streets away. The Uppington estates are adjoined by those of the Blakeneys, are they not?"

"Does that mean you know the Scarlet Pimpernel?" Amy asked breathlessly.

Lord Richard's face stilled into a mask as imperturbable as that of the carving of the pharaoh on the stela. Amy blinked. She must have imagined the expression. Lord Richard was smiling, all affability, at Miss Gwen as he replied, "Yes, I spent much of my youth raiding the Blakeney kitchens. Would you like to see a mummy?" he added. "It might prove a useful device in your novel."

Richard took Miss Gwen's bony arm, and steered her down the center of the room, away from Amy.

Amy hurried after them. "What is the Scarlet Pimpernel like?"

"Percy is a splendid chap," Richard said warmly. "He never even scolded me for picking all of the plums out of his plum pudding."

Amy smiled. Richard smiled back. They smiled together. It was quite definitely a *moment*.

It was, alas, only a momentary moment. Miss Gwen spoiled it by banging her parasol against the flagstones of the floor. Richard supposed he should be grateful that it had been the floor, rather than his toe.

"We have trespassed on your hospitality long enough." Miss Gwen shook off Richard's arm, and grabbed Amy's. "I have learned all I desired . . . about Egyptian antiquities. Come along, Jane, Amy. Don't dawdle. I'm sure Lord Richard has much to do."

"I'll see you to your coach," Richard offered as Miss Gwen chivied her charges forward with the tip of her parasol.

This Miss Gwen graciously permitted. Richard regaled Amy with tales of his childhood exploits and Percy's benevolence all the way through the palace. Amy, enthralled, didn't seem to notice that all of his stories stopped at least a year before Sir Percy became the Scarlet Pimpernel. She countered with her own tales of training to be a member of the Pimpernel's band, all of the midnight escapes from the nursery, and costumes filched from the scullery or her uncle's wardrobe.

"Don't forget the time you tried to train the sheep to stampede at the sound of a whistle," chimed in Jane.

Lord Richard arched a quizzical eyebrow at Amy.

"I thought they might be useful in an attack," Amy protested, lips twitching with suppressed laughter. "After all, we didn't have any cavalry at hand, so I had to make do with what we had."

"Tell me," he said, lowering his voice in a tone of mock confidentiality, "did you actually try to *ride* the sheep?"

Amy flushed, looking, one might say, somewhat sheepish.

"Waving a wooden sword and shouting battle cries," confirmed Jane.

"I was only eight," Amy defended herself.

"Yes, but you were twelve when you set your hair on fire."

"Let me guess," Lord Richard ventured, grinning at Amy. "You were experimenting with gunpowder to blow up the Bastille."

"Actually," Amy corrected him loftily, "I was applying ashes to my hair to see if they would make me look convincingly aged and gray-haired. The only problem was that I didn't stamp out all of the embers quite thoroughly enough. Uncle Bertrand wouldn't let me have any gunpowder," she added wistfully as they stepped outside.

Lord Richard flung back his head and guffawed. The courtyard of the Tuilleries rang with his laughter as he escorted the three ladies to Edouard's carriage. He made his bows to Miss Gwen and Jane, handing them into the carriage. Finally, Amy stood alone before the open door.

His voice lowered to an intimate murmur that made the skin on Amy's arms prickle, and ought to have caused her chaperone to drag her away at once. "Stay away from gunpowder," he cautioned, bowing over Amy's hand. With a quick, mischievous glance into the carriage to make sure Miss Gwen was occupied in conversation with Jane, Lord Richard flipped Amy's hand over, and pressed a lingering kiss on the sensitive skin of her palm.

Amy's shocked gaze flew from her palm to Lord Richard's laughing eyes. She stared at him, her confusion palpable on her face. In the fraught moment before she turned to climb up into the carriage, he ran his thumb in an intimate caress over her palm. And then he winked.

He told *her* to stay away from gunpowder?

Chapter Twenty-eight

Amy stumbled into the carriage in an extreme state of confusion.

Confusion seemed to be her normal state, nowadays. Amy tried to remember what it felt like to feel sure of herself and her plans and her opinions and the people around her, and failed miserably. First, there had been the Purple Gentian, who had baffled her by seeming to care for her, then repudiating her. And now Lord Richard! Lord Richard who, whenever she thought she had him pegged—as a charming antiquarian, as an evil abettor of the French, as the lover of Pauline Leclerc—did something to confuse her. How could he speak so warmly of Sir Percy, and yet himself have aided the French? How could he bedevil her one moment and charm her the next?

Maybe, thought Amy, her hands pressed tightly together in her lap, she was just too easily charmed. It said something rather unpleasant about the shallowness of her own character that she could fancy herself in love with the Purple Gentian one day and be fascinated by Lord Richard the next. Oh, but she had been so sure of her feelings for the Gentian! And of his for her. His promise of a necklace of stars had seemed to be a sort of divine seal of approval, marking him out as her official, one and only true love.

The phrase fluttered in circles around her head. Something about it nagged at her memory. A necklace of stars . . . a necklace of stars. But she had never told the Purple Gentian about her father's promise; she had never even told him about her parents' death. Only one person in France knew about her childhood memory. One person who had grown up next door to Percy Blakeney, who had been in Egypt when Bonaparte's fleet was destroyed. One person who had been sporting tight tan trousers the previous afternoon. One person who always wore citrus-scented cologne.

"That cad!" Amy breathed.

Jane broke off midsentence in her conversation with Miss Gwen and touched Amy's hand. "Are you feeling quite all right?"

Oblivious to Jane, to Miss Gwen, to discretion, Amy jerked her hand away and slammed it back down against the seat. "That utter sniveling, lying *cad*!"

"Um, Amy? Would you like to tell me what's wrong?" Jane was hovering from a safe distance, lest Amy strike out again. Amy could have told her she was safe—the only person Amy wanted to hit, again and again and again, was several yards back in the Tuilleries—but at the moment, Amy wasn't capable of uttering anything quite that coherent.

"Cad . . . disgusting . . . urgh!" she muttered.

Amy's arms flailed wildly. Jane scooted a little farther back on the seat and looked anxiously at Miss Gwen. "Should we . . . ?"

Miss Gwen, however, was smiling quite unconcernedly, if slightly maliciously, at Amy. "You certainly took your time figuring it out."

"You knew?" Amy's eyebrows flew up till they nearly reached her hairline. "All this time, you knew? And you didn't *tell* me?"

Jane looked brightly from Amy's agitated face to Miss Gwen's smug one. "Oh, are you talking about Lord Richard being the Purple Gentian?"

"Arrrrrrrrrrrrrgh!" Amy flung herself face-first into the seat cushions.

"If it makes you feel better, I only figured it out this morning," said Jane apologetically, wrenching a corner of her skirt out from under Amy's head.

"Wonderful," sputtered Amy, lifting a flushed face from the bench, "just wonderful. *Everyone* knew except me."

"The First Consul doesn't know yet," volunteered Jane. "Nor does the Ministry of Safety."

"Yes, but they haven't been kissing him!" cried Amy heedlessly.

"I take that to mean that you have?" Miss Gwen's beady eyes fixed on Amy like a vulture sighting prey.

"Um . . ."

"I will refrain from comment on your reckless disregard for your reputation," Miss Gwen's voice scraped across Amy's raw nerves like talons clawing flesh. "Your morals I leave to your conscience. Since what is done cannot be undone, it remains only to take what little good one can from this unfortunate episode."

"You mean that now I've learned my lesson and know never to kiss anyone ever again?"

Miss Gwen impaled Amy on a look of utter contempt. "Lesson, indeed! Kindly contrive not to be more absurd than the good Lord made you. No. I require a full description of the kiss or kisses for incorporation into my novel."

The world and everyone in it had gone mad. That was the only explanation that Amy could come up with. Lord Richard Selwick, Bonaparte's antiquarian, was the Purple Gentian. Miss Gwen, rather than scolding her for improper behavior, wanted to use it in her novel. What next?

Bewilderment momentarily distracted her from Lord Richard's deception. But only for a moment. "How could he be so *cruel*?" she whispered, her eyes clouded.

"Why don't you go to him and tell him you know who he is?" suggested Jane.

Amy shook her head so vehemently that her loose curls whipped across the end of Jane's nose. "You don't understand, Jane. I want to make him *suffer*."

Miss Gwen emitted a cracking noise that might have been a laugh. "Ah. Young love."

Amy scowled at her. "What in heaven's name are you talking about?"

"You shouldn't take heaven's name in vain, missy. You might want to go there someday." Miss Gwen smirked. Amy simmered. When Miss Gwen felt Amy had simmered for a suitable length of time, she spoke. "It's quite simple. You wouldn't hate him so much unless you loved him. Hmm. I like that. Maybe I'll use it in my book."

"At least *someone* benefits from this farce," bit out Amy.

"Don't take that tone with me, young lady. I'm on your side in this. You needn't goggle your eyes at me. The young man played with your affections in a most inappropriate way and deserves whatever punishment you choose to mete out." Miss Gwen considered for a moment before adding, "Excluding physical mutilation. One must acknowledge the bounds of decency."

Amy gave a laugh that sounded suspiciously like a sob.

"How do you intend to wreak your revenge?" Miss Gwen asked briskly.

Amy plunged with relief into her favorite distraction. Planning. Planning almost anything was a dependable remedy for weepiness. Planning ways to wreak devastation, vengeance, and mayhem upon the guilty golden head of Lord Richard Selwick was even better. Amy rubbed her eyes clear and set to work.

The ideal revenge would be to serve back to him the bitter brew of his own devising. Perhaps she could appear at his chambers in disguise, heavily veiled in black, and convince him that she was a secret agent sent by the War Office. Or, even better, she could be a French agent defecting to the English. He wouldn't see her face, and she would speak in a heavy accent—a Provençal dialect, perhaps, southern and exotic, with echoes of the troubadours and courts of love—so he wouldn't recognize her voice. And once he was terribly, painfully, in love with her, she could repudiate him on a dark midnight, and leave him standing broken beside his own house. An eye for an eye, a tooth for a tooth, and a deception for a deception. Justice in its purest form.

The plan was perfect.

And entirely impracticable. There was nothing to guarantee that she could make him love her. Besides, one yank of her veils, and the whole plan would be undone. Amy sank back into thought.

What mattered most to him? What would it pain him most to see taken away?

"I'll beat him to the Swiss gold. I'll show the Purple Gentian that he isn't the only one who can thwart Bonaparte."

Miss Gwen leveled an appraising gaze at Amy. "I thought there might be some mettle in you."

Both Jane and Amy stared openmouthed at Miss Gwen.

"Was that a compliment?" whispered Amy to Jane.

"It sounded like one," Jane agreed, eyes wide.

"Don't allow it to go to your head," Miss Gwen interrupted dryly. "I spoke solely of potential. You may yet prove the contrary."

"Thank you," said Amy.

"I like this plan much better than tormenting Lord Richard," contributed Jane, leaning forward on the seat.

"Oh, I still intend to do that, too," responded Amy stubbornly. "Miss Gwen's right. He broke the do-unto-others rule, and now he's going to get his just deserts. It's too bad *I* can't pretend to be two people, just to show him what it feels like."

"Let's not go into that again," Jane put in hastily. "How shall we intercept the gold?"

"We already had a plan." Amy's lips twisted in a rueful grimace as she relayed the plan she and the Purple Gentian had contrived together the night before. Miss Gwen listened intently. "If that is the plan the Purple Gentian intends to employ, we must find another one."

"We don't have enough people for it," pointed out Jane, ever practical. "The Purple Gentian has a league; we just have us. Not that we aren't formidable," she added hastily, with a glance at Miss Gwen.

"Why shouldn't we be a league?" demanded Miss Gwen.

"That's it! Amy—" Jane's mouth was a round O of amusement. Speechless with mirth, she rocked back against the seat, one hand pressed to her chest, the other held out to her cousin.

"Out with it!" snapped Miss Gwen.

"The Pink Carnation!" gasped Jane.

Miss Gwen looked at her as though she was considering transporting her immediately to Bedlam.

"You must remember, Amy! Before the Purple Gentian appeared, when we were going to be our own league, and call it—"

"The Pink Carnation," Amy finished, the beginnings of a smile glimmering across her unhappy face. "We liked it better than the Invincible Orchid," she finished, her voice cracking slightly.

"Shall we?" asked Jane breathlessly, a faint pink flush rising in her pale cheeks. "Shall we become the Pink Carnation?"

"Oh, Jane!" Amy launched herself across the seat to hug her cousin. "I would like nothing better! We'll make Bonaparte quail at the very sight of a Carnation!"

"*I* prefer the Invincible Orchid," announced Miss Gwen.

Neither of her charges listened. They were too busy planning the career of the Pink Carnation.

Chapter Twenty-nine

I only got lost three times on the way to Pammy's party. That I didn't go farther astray was entirely due to the excellence of Pammy's directions, which were of a see-Jane-run level of simplicity. I'm not exactly a brilliant navigator at the best of times; in my current daze, it was only a wonder I hadn't accidentally wound up in Scotland. By the time I'd retraced my steps all the way back to Covent Garden from High Holborn (don't ask how I wound up over there), I was all but ready to hop right back on the Tube and head home. Only a marked disinclination to be alone with my own thoughts drove me to dig out Pammy's directions from the pocket of my raincoat and try again.

I needed a glass of champagne. Badly.

Spotting me at the door, Pammy waved a tiny pink purse over her head like a lasso and shouted, "Ellie!" Bowling models out of her way, she rushed over, pushing past the bouncer to join me on my little patch of cold sidewalk. We exchanged the sort of effusive greetings usually reserved for released captives rather than friends who just had dinner on Tuesday.

Even through my preoccupied fog, I couldn't help gaping at Pammy's latest outfit. She was wearing bright pink snakeskin pants. Species *Christianus Lacroixus*, that elusive denizen of the fashion jungle. She had paired the flaming fuchsia snakeskin with a bright Pucci top in swirling blue, pink, and orange that clashed dreadfully with the pants, and even more so with the faux red streaks in her short blond hair. It should have looked dreadful. Instead, she looked like she'd just stepped off the cover of *Cosmo*.

I'd settled on one of my favorite dresses, a little beige suede sheath from BCBG. From the front, it looked perfectly demure, but the back was bare from the waist up, with the exception of one asymmetrical scrap of cloth that tied across the middle of my back, and served more to emphasize the gap than cover it. It was my "I need an ego boost" dress. The creamy color made my hair look more russet than red, and the dramatic back made me feel glamorous, in an old Hollywood sort of way.

Pammy observed my ensemble with a critical eye.

"Oh well, at least you're not wearing your pearls."

Pressing a neon green glow stick into my hand (she had a pink one, presumably to go with the pants), she yanked me past the red ropes and into a room already so crowded that people were perching on the edge of the DJ's booth just to get out of the way. At the far end of the room, a temporary catwalk had been set up. Two women with fashionably bored expressions were posing with shoulders back and hips out, ignoring the inebriated party guest who was trying to claw her way up onto the platform. Since there was clearly no coat check, or, if there ever had been it had long since been overrun by the partygoing hordes, I wriggled out of my raincoat and slung it over my arm.

"Oooh, bubbly!" Pammy exclaimed, as a waiter shimmied by several yards away. "Yoo-hoo!" she caroled. "Over here!"

A glass was shoved into my hand; Pammy introduced me to someone; we shouted pleasantries over the throbbing music and moved on.

I jostled along through the crowd in Pammy's wake, nodding absently in response to her whispered asides ("That jerk Roderick! Can you believe he . . ."), but I only caught about a third of it. I couldn't blame it on the music, or the crowds, or the strobe light that seemed personally out to blind me; my mind was elsewhere entirely, back in 1803.

My dashing hero, my paragon of manhood, my lover of moonlit daydreams, was a woman.

The Pink Carnation was a woman.

I'd read the passage in Amy's diary where she described the inception of the Pink Carnation right before I left for Pammy's party. I'd been dressed already, perched on the edge of my bed, bag and coat ready next to me, reading just one more page before I really had to go. I'd been longing to find out whether Lord Richard would break down and tell Amy his identity, crossing my fingers and hoping for Amy's sake that he would.

Maybe that's why the revelation caught me quite so off guard. I hadn't been looking for it. It had never occurred to me that the Pink Carnation could be anyone other than a man—most likely Miles Dorrington, but maybe Geoffrey Pinchingdale-Snipe, or even Augustus Whittlesby. I had given up expecting to hear anything about it in Amy's diary, which was crammed full of her personal concerns. If—when—I came upon the Pink Carnation, I'd expected it to be in one of Miles's letters to Richard: "Hullo, old chap. The War Office is sending me along to take your place. Aside from a silly flower name, should be jolly good fun," or something along those lines. Never, in a million years, would I have imagined . . . this.

I had sat there numbly, manuscript pages fanning out in my beige suede lap, thinking back over all the clues I'd missed. Amy's accounts of her childhood exploits, her determination to dethrone Napoleon, her anxiety to join a league. I should have known. I should have expected.

But who would ever have imagined that the Pink Carnation could be a woman?

I grasped at straws. It wasn't entirely certain that the Pink Carnation was Amy. She'd only just come up with the idea, after all. Maybe she came up with the idea, and then mentioned it to . . . whom? Geoff? Not likely. Geoff was Richard's friend, not Amy's. Whittlesby? Amy thought he was a blithering idiot. And why would Amy ever, ever hand her league over to someone else?

There was no logical way around it. The Pink Carnation was a woman.

I had sat on the Tube in a trance. Another passenger, an elderly woman with a woolly hat and bad teeth, had asked me if I was ill. I'd shaken my head, and thanked her politely, the words scarcely registering over the turmoil in my head.

How could I have missed it? As a scholar, how could I have been so careless? That stung, that my preconceptions had so blinded me to the truth of what I was reading. What kind of a historian was I, blundering along blindfolded by my own imagination?

All right, that hurt, but it wasn't what hurt the most. What hurt the most was the loss of the daydream. I wonder if that was how Amy felt, when she realized her Purple Gentian, her daydream prince, was Lord Richard Selwick, and suddenly everything she had thought to be true needed reevaluating.

My image—my imaginings, as I now, painfully, knew them to be—of the Pink Carnation had been so real, so solid. In my head, he'd been something of a cross between Zorro and Anthony Andrews as the Scarlet Pimpernel. A rakish grin, a cocky tilt of the head, a steady sword arm. I could close my eyes and conjure him up, even now. But none of that had ever existed. Poof! All gone! And in my wonderful Zorro/Anthony Andrews hybrid's place there stood a bouncy little twenty-year-old English girl in a sprigged muslin dress.

And Colin Selwick had known. My face grew hot as I remembered my spirited defense of the Pink Carnation's manhood. How he must have been laughing at me!

"At least we agree on that much," he had said, about the Pink Carnation's not being a transvestite. That dry note of mockery in his voice—at the time, I'd thought he'd been ironically amused by the idea of our agreeing on anything, but now I knew I'd been the butt of that joke. Of course, the Pink Carnation wasn't a transvestite. Amy wore dresses and named herself after a pink flower because she was female. Not a cross-dressing male with a carnation fixation, or even a Regency dandy with a penchant for pink. And Colin Selwick had known all along.

Nodding and smiling at yet another of Pammy's numerous acquaintances, I downed my glass of champagne, and reached for another.

"Pardon?"

One of Pammy's friends was actually trying to make conversation with me. On my third glass of champagne—or was it my fourth?—it took me a moment to focus. I looked up to see a tallish man with dark, wavy hair like Colin Firth's. Not at all bad looking in a dark, smoldering Rufus Sewell sort of way.

"Arrr rrrrr rrrr rrrr," he repeated.

"Oh, absolutely!" I said airily. "Couldn't agree more!"

Curly-haired Chap gave me an odd look and turned away.

"Um, Eloise?" Pammy hissed in my ear. "He asked what your name was."

"Well, I thought it was a very valid question!" I hissed back.

That's the lovely thing about champagne. After a few glasses, one loses all ability to feel like an idiot.

"Oh! Look who's there!" Pammy was still looking in the direction of Curly-haired Chap, but her attention had shifted to someone just beyond him. Curly-haired Chap was pointedly ignoring both of us. Since Pammy had exclaimed the same thing several times in the past hour, I didn't pay much attention. "I never thought she'd show. Serena! Yoo-hoo! Serena!"

Curly-haired Chap edged back a bit, and through the gap I saw Chic Girl. Also known as Serena. And behind her was Colin Selwick.

Something cold and wet dripped down onto my sandaled toes. Ooops. I hastily righted my champagne glass before I poured any more libations to my feet.

"Yoo-hoo!" Even over the din, Pammy managed to make herself heard. "Over here!"

With a tentative smile, Serena gave a little wave back, said something to Colin, and began to wend her way through the intervening bodies towards Pammy.

"You know her?" I hissed as Serena navigated her away around Curly-haired Chap, Colin in tow.

"She's one of the St. Paul's crowd," Pammy whispered back. "A little shy, but a sweetie. Darling!" She launched herself at Serena, kissing her on both cheeks. "And this is my very old friend Eloise. Eloise, I'd like you to meet Serena and her—"

"We've already met," I cut in, with a wave of my champagne glass. "Hello, Serena." I smiled sweetly at Serena, who did seem rather a sweetie, even if she was wearing another pair of to-die-for boots, this time soft black leather, paired with a very un-Chapin-mother little black dress.

"You." I pointed the champagne glass at Colin.

I had a feeling I was going to hear about this from Pammy later, but champagne is the better part of valor, and I needed, desperately needed, to talk about the Pink Carnation. The female Pink Carnation.

"I need to speak to you."

Colin raised an eyebrow. "What about?"

"Yes, what about?" echoed Pammy shamelessly.

I glowered at Pammy. "Not here. Come with me. Back in a moment," I assured Serena, and towed her boyfriend off across the room. There was a pocket of relative privacy at one corner of the catwalk. The models had long since abandoned their platform, and two drunken guests were gyrating to the music, one of them wearing a green sequinned dress that made her look like a walking Christmas tree.

Colin submitted to being towed, but freed himself as soon

as we'd reached the corner. "Bond, James Bond?" he quipped quizzically.

"She's a woman!"

Colin regarded the Christmas-tree woman with a puzzled frown. "I wouldn't be so sure about that."

I hit him with my glow stick, which had long since ceased to glow. "Not her! Oh, for goodness' sake, don't be dense! You know very well who I mean! The Pink Carnation. Is. A. Woman."

That got his attention. "Shhhh."

I made an exasperated face. "Do you really think anyone here would care? They'd probably think I was talking about a new rock group."

His face relaxed into amusement. "True."

"Why didn't you tell me?" I demanded.

"You didn't ask."

"That is the most puerile excuse for an answer I've ever heard."

Colin plunked his empty champagne glass down on the edge of the catwalk. "Well, what was I supposed to say?"

"You let me go on about the Pink Carnation, all the while knowing . . ." I bit down on my lip, hard.

Colin stared at me, uncomprehending. "All the while knowing what?"

"That the Pink Carnation was female!"

"You're quite upset about this, aren't you?"

"Urgh!" Ten points to Let's State the Bleeding Obvious Man.

Looking completely baffled, Colin snagged two more glasses of champagne from a passing tray, and pressed one into my hand, closing my fingers around the stem. "Here. Drink. You look like you need it."

Despite the fact that it came from Colin Selwick, that was excellent advice. I drank.

"I know you didn't want me there, but it still wasn't nice to make fun of me," I blurted out.

"When did I make fun of you?" he asked, with a good imitation of surprise.

I eyed him suspiciously. "Last night."

Colin contemplated this. Understanding dawned in his hazel eyes. "You mean the nightdress? You must admit, you *did* look like Jane Eyre."

I could only deal with one grievance at a time. "Forget about that."

"How can I?" Colin's lips were twitching. "It's not often a Brontë heroine—"

"Stop it!" I gave a little bounce of irritation. "I wasn't referring to that! I wasn't talking about your making fun of me for looking like a demented gothic heroine—"

"Not necessarily a *demented* gothic heroine," Colin broke in, grinning.

"Oh, be quiet!" I howled, undoubtedly changing his mind about the whole demented thing. "I'm talking about the Pink Carnation being manly, and it wasn't nice of you!"

"Come again?" said Colin.

I gripped the stem of my champagne glass, took a steadying breath, and started over. "I am referring," I said with deliberate gravity, "to your allowing me to go on about the Pink Carnation being manly, when you knew, all along, that the Pink Carnation was Amy."

"You think the Pink Carnation is—" Colin stopped abruptly. "Never mind. Let's go back to the beginning, shall we? First of all, I have no recollection of your saying anything about the Pink Carnation being manly."

Hadn't I? I racked my champagne-slogged brain. He'd said something about that researcher thinking the Pink Carnation was a transvestite, and I'd said . . . what *had* I said? I couldn't remember. Damn.

"Oh," I said in a small voice. Maybe champagne didn't completely dull one's ability to feel like an idiot.

"Second," he began, "I never—" but I was spared the second blow to my ego. Someone tugged at Colin's elbow, causing him to break off midsentence. We both looked over sharply. It was Serena.

"Colin?" she said in a piteous little croak, "I don't feel very well."

Colin's expression immediately switched to affectionate concern. He put a protective arm around her shoulders. "Do you want me to take you home?"

I stood back, feeling like the proverbial third wheel. Colin's attention was focused completely on Serena, his blond head bent attentively towards her dark one. I watched the way his brows drew together in concern, the way his bent body shielded her from the jostling crowds, and felt an emptiness in the pit of my stomach that had nothing to do with skipping dinner.

I knew exactly what it was, and I was too champagne soaked to lie to myself about it.

I was jealous.

It wasn't that I wanted Colin Selwick, I assured myself. Good heavens, no! I wanted what he stood for. I wanted someone who would drop a conversation when I appeared, who would worry if I said I felt sick, who would automatically shield me from being jostled without even stopping to think about it. It had been a very long time since anyone had taken care of me like that.

You learn how to work around it. You make sure you never drink so much that you can't get home on your own. You mark out friends you can rely on. You program emergency numbers into your cell phone, bring Band-Aids in your bag, and always carry extra money for late-night cabs. But it's not the same. I envied Serena that.

At the moment, she wasn't looking particularly enviable. She sagged against Colin, both arms wrapped around her stomach.

"Look, why don't I go find a cab?" Colin suggested desperately. "I'll just go—"

Serena shook her head. "I don't—" she began, and then pressed her lips tightly together. Her face had gone from pale to an alarming greenish color. "I think I'm going to—" She clamped her knuckles over her mouth and swallowed hard.

"Oh, hell. Um . . ." Colin cast a look of complete panic around the room. "There must be a loo somewhere."

"I'll take her." I stepped in, slipping an arm through Serena's. "I think I saw one just over that way."

"Thank you," Colin said with palpable relief. "I'll just be out here."

Taking Serena by the arm, I steered her towards the ladies' room, rudely pushing through chattering groups of people. I got Serena to the bathroom just in the nick of time. There was a line, of course, but we pushed past, Serena's greenish complexion and hunched posture doing more to explain than I could.

There was a huffy "Well!" from one woman in the queue, but I noticed she moved her Manolo Blahniks quickly out of the potential line of fire.

As I had for drunken roommates back in college, I knelt

behind Serena with one arm around her shoulders, the other holding her long, dark hair back from her face, while I murmured silly, soothing things, like, "That's right, get it all out," and "Don't worry, it's all okay, you'll feel better in a minute, just get it all out."

There was an awful lot to get out.

Between bouts, she looked up at me with tearstained eyes. "I'm so embarrassed," she murmured. "I can't imagine why ... I only had one glass ... I don't usually ..." And she lurched back over the porcelain goddess.

"There, there." I recaptured some escaping strands of dark hair. "Don't worry. Maybe it was something you ate. Trust me, no one will think the worse of you. At least you made it to the toilet," I said encouragingly. "I once threw up all over an ex-boyfriend's shoes."

A giggle emerged from the depths of the toilet bowl.

I gathered up a handful of toilet paper as she settled back on her haunches, and handed it to her in lieu of tissues. "Unfortunately, he was a rather nice ex-boyfriend, so I can't even claim it was done in revenge." I kept my tone deliberately light as I funneled her tissues. "And they were new shoes, too."

"Wha-what did he say?" Serena ventured, blowing her nose.

"He was very nice about my throwing up on him," I recalled. "What he found harder to forgive was my pointing at his shoes and bursting into uncontrollable laughter. Ah, well. Feeling better?"

Serena nodded tentatively.

I hauled myself to my feet with the help of the toilet paper dispenser, and held out a hand to her. "Why don't we go rinse your mouth out then, and I should have some mints in my bag. . . ." Fumbling in my little Coach bag, I pushed open the door of the stall with one shoulder, ignoring the glares of the women waiting outside. It's an endless mystery to me the way lipsticks, hairbrushes, and mints can all find places to hide in a bag two inches tall by four inches long.

Feeling a light touch on my arm, I looked up inquiringly.

"Thank you," Serena said softly. Her mascara had run, and her nose was red, but her eyes were clearer and some color had returned to her cheeks. "You really have been lovely."

I shook my head, resuming my mint search. "It's really not a big deal. We've all been here. Well, not here, in particular, but you know what I mean. Mint?" I shook two tiny little Certs into my hand and held them out to Serena.

"Thank you." She leaned over the sink, splashing cold water on her face. I handed her a paper towel. "About yesterday," she said hesitantly, taking the paper towel and dabbing at her damp face, "I've been wanting to apologize."

"You had nothing to apologize for," I said firmly. Except for owning nicer boots than mine, but I decided to keep that bit to myself.

"Colin was impossibly rude."

That I could agree with. Emphatically. I wondered if he'd told her of our midnight chat in the kitchen. I smiled noncommittally and handed her my mini mascara.

"He really isn't usually like that," she continued anxiously, her large, hazel eyes following mine in the mirror. I'd seen eyes of that same color before recently, but couldn't peg where. "He felt awful about it afterwards."

I admired her loyalty, but had little interest in hearing an apologia for Colin Selwick.

"I think we're being glared at," I put in quickly. "If you're feeling better, we should probably free up the mirror space."

Gathering up my toiletries, I hustled Serena out of the bathroom. Colin and Pammy were waiting for us by the door. I handed Serena over to Colin, who helped her into her coat, and asked the bouncer to whistle for a cab. As Serena said her good-byes to Pammy, Colin turned slightly so that he and I were blocked off from the other two.

"It was very kind of you to take care of Serena," he said quietly.

"Just polishing my halo," I proclaimed with a cavalier wave that nearly sent me toppling over. Two hours of sleep plus four—or was it five?—glasses of champagne were taking their toll.

Colin grabbed my elbow. "Steady there. Are you sure you don't need someone to take care of *you*?"

It had definitely been five glasses of champagne. Smiling, Colin looked just like he did in the photograph on Mrs. Selwick-Alderly's mantel—only without the horse. I pressed my eyes briefly shut to make the world stop spinning and shook my head.

"Nope. I'm absolutely all right. Not a bit"—I had to fling a hand out for balance as he let go—"unsteady."

"Right," Colin agreed with unconcealed amusement.

I made a concerted effort to stand up straighter.

The laugh lines at the corners of Colin's mouth deepened. Taking a step back, Colin slung an arm around Serena's shoulder. "Ready, Serena?" She nodded, snuggling trustingly against his shoulder. "We could drop you off home if you like," he suggested to me.

My champagne buzz was wearing off, leaving me feeling tired, and mildly ill.

"No, thanks," I said brightly, snatching up a glass of champagne I had absolutely no intention of drinking and holding it aloft. "I'm sticking around with Pammy. The night is young! Right, Pams?"

Pammy gave me a you-are-a-great-big-weirdo look. "Sure, Ellie."

"In that case"—Colin steered Serena towards the door— "good night."

He was probably relieved to have to deal with only one wobbly female, and afraid I was going to change my mind.

"Good night, Eloise," murmured Serena, peering around his arm. "Thank you, again."

I watched them disappear behind the red ropes, the unwanted glass of champagne hanging heavily in my hand.

Pammy stared at Colin's back as he helped Serena into the cab. "I don't remember Serena's brother being quite that hot."

I pivoted to face her. "Who?" I demanded.

"Serena's brother," Pammy repeated. "You know, tall, blond guy, English-sounding name—Cedric, or Cecil, or . . ."

"Colin."

"Yeah, that's it. He's gotten much better looking."

"Her brother."

"No, the Pope. *Of course* I meant her brother. Poor Serena," Pammy rattled on, "she had a bad breakup last month, so her brother's been keeping an eye on her. She told me about it while you were off whispering with him. What were you guys talking about over there, anyway, Ellie? Ellie? Yoo-hoo! Earth to Ellie! Are you okay? You look a little out of it."

My eyes remained trained on the doorway, where Colin— and his sister—had exited a moment before.

"Out of it does not even begin to describe it," I said grimly.

Chapter Thirty

❧❧❧

The Purple Gentian, blissfully unaware of the creation of a rival flower, bounded joyously up the steps of his town house, flinging open the front door without waiting for Stiles to get there first. All the way home, he had savored the memory of Amy's face as he had kissed her hand good-bye. He had lingered happily over the confused pleasure in her eyes as he whistled through the Tuilleries garden, and he had grinned over her slightly parted lips as he evaded the slops a brawny maid was tossing from an upper window. Operation Charm Amy was going splendidly, he gloated to himself as he strode into his front hall and tossed his hat onto the front hall table.

There was only one slight problem.

The front hall table wasn't there. Or if it was, he couldn't see it. His foyer was entirely filled with piles of bandboxes and his . . .

"Mother?"

Richard blinked once, then twice. His mother was still there.

"Oh, hello, darling." His mother waved a hand at him in greeting before returning to harassing his butler. "Now let's get this straight. Those two hatboxes go in the front bedroom, and the large trunk goes in—"

Stiles emitted one of his theatrical groans. Richard envied him that.

"Um, Mother?"

"Yes, dear?" His mother thrust another hatbox on the pile Stiles was already holding. "Oh do stop whining! You have the build of a man half your age."

"He is half his age," Richard said dryly. "Mother, what are you doing here?"

He'd meant the question to come out calmly, but his voice reverted to somewhere preadolescent on the last word.

"Oh, how silly of me!" Stiles took advantage of Lady Uppington's momentary distraction to scuttle behind the pile of luggage. The marchioness beamed at her son. "We came to help you, of course!"

Richard's head reeled, and he sat down rather abruptly on a huge trunk, into which, by the size of it, his mother had packed a full silver service, two wardrobes, and perhaps a footman or two. Or at least her shoe collection.

Richard tackled the most pressing question first. "What do you mean by we?"

"They were here a moment ago." His mother peered at the mountain of baggage as though expecting half of *Debrett's Peerage* to pop out. "I suppose Geoff must have taken them into the drawing room. Your father is here, of course. It's been so long since he and I have been to Paris together." The marchioness smiled mistily. "You came along after our last trip to Paris, dear."

"Mother!" Richard yelped.

What deity had he offended? Maybe there was something to all of those rumors about curses on those who profaned the tombs of the pharaohs.

Taking pity on her son, who had gone red straight up to the tips of his ears, Lady Uppington informed him, "Henrietta's here too. A little continental polish will be just the thing to set her off for her next season."

Lady Uppington might have said more, but her words were abruptly truncated by the cacophony of several loud thumps, an ear-curdling shriek of rage (which Richard was able to identify as part of Stiles's King Lear impersonation), and a hearty masculine yelp.

Richard frowned. "That does not sound like Henrietta."

"Well, no. We also brought along—"

"Hullo, Richard!" Miles bounded around the pile of boxes, pushing a floppy lock of blond hair out of his eyes. "Why does your butler hate me?"

"Don't flatter yourself. He hates everyone." Richard turned to look at his mother. "Is there anyone else you brought who you'd like to warn me about? Great-aunt Hyacinth? The underfootman from Uppington House?"

"Always happy to see you, too, old chap." Miles whacked

Richard on the shoulder. "Stop grousing and come along. Geoff's got tea and crumpets for all of us in the drawing room."

Richard scowled at the back of Miles's head as he followed him into the drawing room.

Henrietta stood on tiptoe to press a quick kiss to Richard's cheek. "I'm sorry, Richard," she whispered. "I know I should have tried to stop them."

"Thanks, Hen." Richard squeezed his sister's shoulders.

"But, well, I rather wanted to see Paris, so . . ." Henrietta shrugged apologetically.

"Thanks," Richard repeated dourly. "Thanks a lot."

Hen covered her mouth with her hand and retreated to her chair. "Sorry."

"Is that picture crooked?" Lady Uppington bounced into the room behind Richard and moved the simpering Watteau shepherdess above the settee a fraction to the left. "Really, Richard, I don't understand how you young men manage to live in such a state of chaos. Dirty cravats under the settee, empty brandy glasses on the table, and is that a piece of cheese under Henrietta's chair?"

With a swish of petticoats, Henrietta expeditiously relocated to the settee.

Lady Uppington shook her head and straightened another picture. "I'll talk to the maids after we've had our tea."

"I'm assuming you haven't come all this way to supervise my housekeeping."

"That would be silly, wouldn't it?" replied Lady Uppington tartly. "Oh, do sit down, Richard. You're making me dizzy prowling about in circles like that. It's like watching one of the lions in the Tower."

Richard felt a great deal of sympathy for the Tower menagerie as he flung himself into a chair, which, of course, promptly skidded back a good six inches. His mother watched him indulgently. *Empathy* for the animals in the Tower might be more like it. Richard loved his mother; he would be the last to deny that. She was a very paragon of a mother, and he was awfully glad he had been born to her and not some other woman and so on and so on and so on. But at the age of twenty-seven, you would think one deserved a certain amount of privacy, wouldn't you? He was sure he had to be the only agent operating in France—or England or Russia or the farthest wilds of the Americas—whose mother showed up at random on his doorstep. It just wasn't right.

"As soon as you left, I started thinking . . . ," began Lady Uppington.

"They do that, you know," Richard's father observed from the safety of his chair.

Lady Uppington swatted him, a gesture more symbolic than practical, as the marquess was seated a good three feet out of range. "As I was saying," she continued, with a pointed look at her spouse, "after some thought, your father and I decided that your mission would go much faster if we came over and helped you."

Richard swung around to glare at his father. Making little pointing gestures at his wife, Lord Uppington affected an expression of innocence. Richard wasn't fooled. His father had been angling to be involved in his missions for years. Hell, he was worse than his mother. Richard looked hard at Lord Uppington. Being a peer of the realm, a man of dignity and substance, master of four estates and hundreds of dependents, Lord Uppington did not blush or squirm. He did, however, discover a sudden deep interest in the folds of his cravat.

"Help me." Richard repeated. "Mother—"

Just when he thought nothing worse could happen, just as he was about to tackle the catastrophe at hand, another disaster erupted.

Miles leaped up from his chair next to Geoff and hooted, "Richard's in love!"

All activity in the room drew to an abrupt close. Geoff's teacup halted guiltily in between the table and his mouth. Henrietta dropped her biscuit. His mother stopped straightening the pictures on the walls. His father looked up from his cravat.

"In love!" Lady Uppington opened her mouth in a delighted O. "Oh, Richard!"

"Miles, blast you! I am not in—urgh!" Richard emitted a strangled noise.

His mother tugged at his arm. "Darling, how wonderful! Who is she?"

Richard shrugged away. "But I just said—argh!"

Miles nodded sagely, a great, big, infuriating grin spreading across his face. "Yes. Clearly a victim of Cupid's amorous dar—oof! You know, throwing that cushion at me just proves my point. What do you say, Henrietta?"

"Henrietta," Richard pronounced chillingly, "is not going to say anything at all. Not if she doesn't want to be bodily lifted onto the next packet for Dover."

Henrietta's mouth snapped shut.

Miles, too large to lift, was less easily silenced.

"I, for one, want to meet this paragon," Miles announced. He struck a lovesick pose and strummed a chord on an invisible lute. "Does she have a balcony under which we might stand and call for her? Oh Amy, Amy, wherefore art thou—"

"Not long for this earth," Richard uttered through clenched teeth.

Miles retrieved his hand from its languishing position on his brow. "Is that any way to speak of your beloved?" he clucked reprovingly.

"I was speaking of you."

"Why, Richard, I never knew you cared."

"Do be quiet, Miles." Henrietta "accidentally" stepped on Miles's foot in passing with a force that ensured that the only noises emerging from his mouth were inarticulate ones indicating pain. "We'll never get anything sensible out of Richard if you don't stop provoking him."

His large hands closing around Henrietta's waist, Miles lifted her off his foot and set her down firmly on the settee. "But what's the fun of sensible?"

"Miles does have a point," mused Lady Uppington.

Five heads twisted sharply her way. Or, rather, six heads, if one counted Stiles, who was listening outside the half-open door.

"My dear," remarked the marquess mildly, "I have known you longer than anyone else in this room, and I must say that you have always struck me as a supremely sensible woman. I would rather object to your altering your character at this late date."

"Thank you, darling." Lady Uppington blew a kiss to her husband. "I'm rather fond of your character, too. But I was referring to Miles's suggestion that we meet this Amy. If we were to call on her after dinner . . ."

"It will be too late to call," Richard put in dampeningly.

"Don't be ridiculous!" his mother replied blithely. "We're in France. They don't keep proper hours here."

Richard turned in silent appeal to Lord Uppington.

"Don't look at me," his father said, stretching out his legs. "I've learned when not to get in the way of your mother."

"Thank you, darling." Lady Uppington beamed. "That's one of the things I love about you."

"I'll accompany you, Lady Uppington," Miles offered angelically.

"Nobody asked you," snapped Richard.

"Is that any way to treat your oldest friend?"

"Don't you mean my *former* oldest friend?"

"Don't yell at me; yell at Geoff. He's the one who told me about Amy."

"If Miles gets to go, I get to go, too!" put in Henrietta, looking mutinous. "After all, *he's* not even family. If Amy's going to be my sister, I ought to get first crack at meeting her."

"Before you reserve the chapel," Richard drawled, in his most obnoxious London man-about-town voice, "there are a few things that ought to be made clear."

"Darling, you aren't afraid we'll embarrass you, are you? I promise, we'll be on our best behavior, even your father." The marchioness wrinkled her nose playfully at the marquess.

"Mother, would you stop flirting with Father for a moment and listen?"

"I never stop flirting with your father," said Lady Uppington complacently. "That's why we have such a happy marriage. And I hope that all of you find spouses with whom you can happily flirt for the rest of your lives." She and Lord Uppington exchanged a look that Richard could only label *gooey*.

"It's a wonder that we've turned out as normal as we have, isn't it?" whispered Henrietta, coming up behind Richard's chair.

"I still haven't forgiven you yet," Richard cautioned her.

"Oh, but you will," Henrietta said blithely, leaning over to kiss his cheek. "I'm your favorite sister, remember? Besides," she added, casting a glance around the room, "you know you'll need my help keeping them in line tonight."

"That assumes we're going somewhere."

Henrietta gave Richard a pitying look that said, louder than words, You can delude yourself if you like.

Henrietta knew too damn much for a nineteen-year-old.

Chapter Thirty-one

"Where is she? Where is the little witch?" An extremely irate Georges Marston burst lopsidedly through the door of the dining room where the Balcourts were partaking of supper. His angry blue eyes lit on Amy. "You!" he bellowed, limping down the length of the table.

"Sir!" Miss Gwen's voice stopped Marston dead in his tracks. "What is the meaning of this intrusion?"

"Her." Marston pointed at Amy, all but frothing at the mouth. "Her!"

"She," Miss Gwen corrected primly.

"Yes, *her!*" Marston's lip curled in a manner that made Amy wish to find some pressing reason to adjourn to another room. Preferably with the door locked behind her. Her arms ached with the memory of Marston's painful grip. She wouldn't let him touch her again. She'd break her wineglass over his head and ward him off with the fragments. She'd break his other toe—no, that would require an unpleasant proximity.

Miss Gwen sighed. "No, Mr. Marston. Not her, she. Did your father's family teach you no English grammar? Or has life in the army whittled away at your verbal skills until you are capable of nothing save the occasional incorrect monosyllable? Following the implied verb 'to be,' the noun must always be in the nominative, rather than the accusative."

"Accusative," repeated Marston, with a nasty look in his eye that Amy feared had little to do with grammar. "I'll show you accusative! I accuse her!" One beefy finger pointed straight at Amy.

Amy shot up in her place. "And I accuse you of behavior unbecoming to a gentleman, and I demand you leave my house at once!"

"I think I'll leave," murmured Edouard, heaving his bulk out of his chair.

"Sit!" Miss Gwen commanded. Edouard sat. So, unexpectedly, did Georges Marston.

"I've always been very good at dealing with dogs," commented Miss Gwen.

Georges Marston promptly stood back up.

Miss Gwen lifted an eyebrow. "Some need more training than others."

Marston ignored her, and started again towards Amy. "What do you mean, your house? It's *his* house, and he'll do as I say, or suffer the consequences, right, Balcourt?"

"Um . . ." Edouard, having been forbidden to leave the table, seemed to be attempting to cram himself under it.

"Why don't you take a seat, Mr. Marston, and I'm sure we can get this all sorted out," suggested Jane.

Intent on his prey, Marston paid Jane no more mind than the candlesticks at the table, or the silent footmen by the sideboard. If Marston were to attack her, Amy wondered, would any of those white-wigged men come to her defense?

"I'm so glad you stopped by, Mr. Marston," Jane put in, her voice pitched to carry. What on earth was Jane talking about? Amy certainly didn't share the sentiment. "I've been wanting to ask you about the tea and the India muslin."

Marston stopped dead two chairs away from Amy, his eyes and tongue bulging like those of a dog whose owner had yanked too abruptly on the leash.

"Tea," he croaked, not turning.

"And India muslin," Jane reminded him softly. Amy could have sworn she saw a glint of amusement in her cousin's eye, but Jane's demeanor was as self-contained as ever and her voice devoid of any hint of mockery. "Tell me," she asked, in a tone that contained only innocent inquiry, "do the authorities know of your import business?"

Kaleidoscope images shifted in Amy's head into a complete whole. The strange packages in the ballroom that Amy had hoped might contain supplies for the Purple Gentian, but hadn't. The dirt-blackened doors and windows of the west wing. Now that Jane had put the pieces together, it was as patently obvious as Marston's guilty fury. Edouard had never had anything to do with the Purple Gentian. Nor had Marston.

Her brother and Marston were smugglers.

Marston's eyes darted from side to side, landing on Edouard. Turning an alarming shade of green, Edouard shook his head violently.

"But . . . the wounded man?" Amy heard herself say.

"A customs official named Pierre Laroc," replied Jane, her gaze never wavering from Marston. "How much did you pay him to forget that little incident, Mr. Marston?"

"I don't know what you're talking about," Marston growled, stomping across the room to loom over Jane.

"Really? And I suppose my cousin doesn't know anything either," she added gently, glancing at Edouard, who was still shaking, not only his head, but the rest of his portly body as well. His cravat quivered with agitation. Jane sighed. "I suppose there is nothing for it but to ask the authorities to settle my curiosity over the tea and muslin in the ballroom. The *British* tea and muslin."

Marston's broken nose turned bright red with rage. "You wouldn't dare!"

"You, Mr. Marston, are not in a position to make terms."

"You can't prove anything." Small flecks of saliva spattered the air as Marston blustered. "The ballroom's empty. You don't have any proof."

"I fear, Mr. Marston, that you are mistaken on that score. You see"—Jane smiled, a gentle curve of the lips that held the entire room silent—"I do have proof. I have your records and your correspondence. I found them secreted in a hollow globe in my cousin's study. Your own pen tells against you."

Marston's large hands flexed dangerously. Jane didn't so much as flinch.

"Touch Miss Balcourt again," Jane warned, her voice as steely as her spine, "in anger, in lust, or even in greeting, and those papers go directly to the authorities."

The tense silence was broken by the dry sound of Miss Gwen clapping. And then the room dissolved into madness. With a roar, Marston flung himself at Edouard. Edouard pleaded and shrieked and babbled. Marston's hands closed around his throat, turning his protests to gurgles. China crashed into fragments against the parquet floor. Amy ran and hugged Jane. The footmen wisely sneaked out the door while no one was looking. Miss Gwen whacked the back of Marston's head with her soupspoon, calling him an insolent son of a rabid dog.

. And the butler cleared his throat.

"Ahem!" He had to try several times before the room stilled, raising his voice to a level that would have rendered a man of lesser vocal capacities mute for a month. Miss Gwen paused with her spoon raised above Marston's head. Marston stopped with his fingers digging into Edouard's vocal cords. And Edouard stayed just as he was, his tongue hanging slightly out, pop-eyed with terror.

The butler proffered a card on a silver tray to Edouard. Miss Gwen snatched it on his behalf.

"Lord and Lady Uppington would like to pay their respects," the butler intoned, his gaze fixed somewhere above the bizarre tableau created by his master, Marston, and Miss Gwen.

"Put them in the green salon," instructed Miss Gwen, since Edouard seemed incapable of speech. To be fair to Edouard, Marston's hands were still locked about his throat, so his incapacity might have been due to dearth of air rather than lack of wit. "And you!" She dealt Marston another smart whack with her now-rather-dented silver soupspoon. "Stop throttling Mr. Balcourt and take your leave at once! Shoo!"

Marston shooed. With an eloquent sneer at Jane and Amy, who stood with their arms about each other's waists for support, he sauntered out the door after the butler.

"One can only hope he will not encounter the Uppingtons," declared Miss Gwen, dropping her soupspoon into her bowl with a clatter.

Uppington. The name sounded familiar, but Amy was too busy making sure Marston's retreating back kept retreating to give it any thought. "When did you find out about the smuggling?" she whispered to Jane.

"Last night," Jane whispered back. "I was going to tell you this morning, but . . . Why are we whispering?"

"I don't know." Amy shrugged helplessly. "It just seemed the thing to do."

"Come along, girls." Miss Gwen propelled them out of the dining room. "We don't want to keep our guests waiting."

"I'm surprised you're taking this so calmly," Jane hissed to Amy as they approached the threshold of the green salon.

"Well, I was a little worried, but you dealt with him splendidly."

Jane looked at her confusedly. "Oh, do you mean Marston?

I was talking about"—the footman, walking before them with a candelabrum, flung open the doors of the green salon— "Lord Richard," Jane finished weakly.

Amy's mouth opened but no sound emerged.

Lord Richard Selwick leaned nonchalantly against the mummy case, his arms crossed over his chest. At Amy's entrance, he uncrossed his arms and smiled with a depth of welcome that made Amy's stomach do more flip-flops than an entire troupe of acrobats at a village fair.

Those lips, curved into a devastating smile, were the ones that had so passionately claimed hers last night. That hand, so idly playing with his quizzing glass, was the one that had cupped her face and stroked her hair and caressed her . . . um, well. Amy's cheeks flared with color.

Uppington. Amy would have whacked her head with the heel of her hand if too many people hadn't been looking on. That's what she got for reading Latin and Greek when she should have been memorizing *Debrett's Peerage*. As Miss Gwen had so helpfully pointed out that afternoon, the Selwick family bore the Uppington title.

A petite woman in a green-and-blue gown was poking interestedly into a funeral urn, while the somewhat taller brunette beside her protested, "But Mama, do you really want to know what's in there?"

As Amy and Jane approached, Jane keeping a hand on Amy's arm for moral support, both looked up. Dropping the lid of the urn, the woman in green swept forward with a warm smile distressingly like Richard's. "I do hope we're not intruding! I was all agog to meet our dear Richard's traveling companions. You must be Miss Balcourt?"

The brunette waved enthusiastically over her mother's head. "Since we're introducing ourselves, I'm Henrietta! You know, Henrietta? Hen? The little sister? Didn't Richard tell you about me?"

Next to Henrietta, a broad-shouldered man in a crumpled cravat rolled his eyes. "Surely he must have mentioned me, the best friend?" he simpered, in obvious imitation of Henrietta's enthusiastic greeting. "You know, the best friend? Miles?"

Amy saw murder written in the brunette's hazel eyes.

"You can be so juvenile sometimes, Miles!"

"The next packet to Dover, Henrietta," Richard warned in awful tones.

Henrietta's mouth snapped shut. She even refrained from responding in kind when Miles stuck out his tongue at her.

"They were just fed," Lady Uppington explained apologetically.

Rap! Rap! Rap!

"Young man!" snapped Miss Gwen, leaning on the parasol she had just pounded against the floor. "Kindly replace that object in your mouth!"

Miles's tongue disappeared behind his lips with the speed of an army retreating into a castle and yanking down the portcullis.

"How splendid!" Lady Uppington bustled forward, laying a friendly hand on Miss Gwen's bony arm. "You *must* tell me how you do it. And who you are," she added as an afterthought.

Miss Gwen, with an angle to her chin that amply portrayed her disapproval of the impropriety of the proceedings, even if the cause of the mayhem was a marchioness, made herself known to Lady Uppington, and presented Jane and Edouard, the latter still a bit purple about the throat and bulging in the eyes.

Lady Uppington ignored the disapproval emanating from Miss Gwen and beamed directly at Amy. "I still haven't introduced myself, have I? I am Lady Uppington, and this"—a wave of an emerald-laden hand at the silver-haired man looking on with amusement a few feet away—"is Uppington, and that's—oh, well, you know, Henrietta." Henrietta dimpled. "And the ill-behaved young man with the unkempt hair—"

Miles's hand went anxiously to his head. Henrietta smirked.

"—is the Honorable Miles Dorrington. Let's see, you all know Richard already. Have I forgotten anybody?"

The brunette, otherwise known as "you know, Henrietta," twined her arm through Lady Uppington's. "You left out Geoff again."

"Geoff, darling!" Lady Uppington let out a cry of distress and held out a hand to a quiet young man standing near Richard. "I didn't mean to neglect you."

"He's used to it by now," Henrietta explained in an aside to Amy.

"*That*"—Lady Uppington leveled a quelling glance at her daughter—"was unkind. Geoff is just so much better behaved than the rest of you that it's easy to forget he's there."

"Was that a compliment?" Miles inquired of Geoff.

"Do you see what I mean?" sighed Lady Uppington to Amy.

Amy, utterly bewildered by the entire Uppington invasion, did the only thing she could do. She smiled. She was rather thankful for Lady Uppington's cheerful volubility. It saved her from having to speak to Lord Richard. By dint of keeping her eyes fixed on Lady Uppington and Henrietta, she could almost pretend he wasn't there. Almost. The more she told herself not to look, the more her eyes strayed towards him.

How should she behave towards him? Amy wondered as the Uppingtons and their entourage continued to bicker among themselves. She couldn't scream or throw things; that would certainly alert Lord Richard to her newfound knowledge of his double life. Tormenting him had seemed like such a splendid idea in the carriage, but Lord Richard's presence turned simple things complicated. Revenge, for example. Such a nice, simple idea. But whenever Lord Richard smiled at her over his mother's head, Amy wanted to smile back.

Maybe that wasn't such a dreadful idea, Amy rationalized. After all, she did need to lull him into a false sense of security before she meted out her revenge. She would flirt with him, repudiate him, and then best him at espionage. It was all part of the plan.

After much altercation, Lady Uppington finally got around to introducing Geoffrey, Second Viscount Pinchingdale, Eighth Baron Snipe.

"So many titles, so little Geoff," sighed Miles, stretching to emphasize his two-inch advantage over the viscount.

"So much brawn, so little brain," countered Henrietta good-naturedly.

"Who beat whom at draughts last week?"

"Who underhandedly caused a diversion by bumping into the board?"

Miles assumed an angelic expression. "I don't know what you could possibly be referring to. I would never do anything so low as to knock over the board and rearrange the pieces."

"Richard never cheats at draughts," Lady Uppington whispered to Amy.

"No, only at croquet," Miles put in sarcastically. "Or did that ball just move two wickets all by itself?"

"You," drawled Lord Richard, strolling forward to join the

little group around Lady Uppington, "are merely sore because I sent your ball flying into the blackberry brambles."

"Thorns all over my favorite breeches," mourned Miles.

"Oh, that's what became of those!" exclaimed Henrietta.

"Did you think Miles had suddenly discovered good taste?" Richard grinned.

"I don't know why I put up with this family," Miles muttered to Amy and Jane.

"It's because we feed you," Henrietta explained.

"Thanks, Hen." Miles ruffled her hair. "I would never have figured that out on my own."

"He's like one of those stray dogs that follows you home," Henrietta continued, warming to her theme, "and once you've given him a meal, keeps scratching on the kitchen door, and looking up at you with big mournful eyes."

"All *right,* Hen," said Miles.

"Madness only runs in part of my family," Richard said softly to Amy. "My brother Charles is quite sane, I assure you. And Miles isn't related at all."

"Third cousin twice removed!" protested Miles.

"By marriage," corrected Richard, his eyes not leaving Amy's. "I trust you had a pleasant afternoon?"

Amy had spent the remainder of the afternoon on her stomach on her bed, contemplating the relative merits of boiling him in oil as opposed to hanging him by his feet and hitting him with a spiked stick.

"Yes. Quite." Amy belatedly remembered that she was supposed to be flirting with him, and added, "I *especially* enjoyed the antiquities."

"Ah, so you like antiquities!" Lady Uppington broke in, with a significant look at Richard. "How splendid! Do tell me more. . . ."

Within ten minutes, Lady Uppington had deftly extracted the information that Amy had been born in France, raised in Shropshire, and didn't much care for turnips. Richard listened, mute with horror, as Lady Uppington ferreted out Amy's literary preferences, and political leanings. She seemed on the verge of inquiring about her shoe size, when Henrietta fortunately intervened.

"Has Mother told you yet about the time Richard tried to tear up the floor of the gazebo with a pickax?"

Richard ceased feeling thankful. Over Henrietta's head, he

saw Miles bearing purposefully down on them. The room began to feel uncomfortably close.

"Miss Balcourt"—he broke into his mother's wildly exaggerated account of the time he had accidentally skewered a gardener while fencing with the topiary—"the statues in the courtyard appear to be exceptionally fine. Would you do me the honor of showing them to me?"

Amy's skin tingled with excitement at the invitation. Every sensible instinct in her body told her to decline. But there were certainly more than enough people about to chaperone them, Amy persuaded her sensible side. This was a perfect opportunity to put her plans for revenge into practice—what could be more romantic than a moonlit garden?—and she'd be a fool not to leap at it.

"Yes, I'd like that," Amy responded with scarcely a moment's hesitation.

". . . blood spurting everywhere! Wait, what did you say, dear?"

"I asked Miss Balcourt if she would take a turn in the courtyard with me. She said yes. And I would like to make clear that I barely scratched his hand."

"The courtyard! What a good idea! I mean, you shall have to be chaperoned, of course. Henrietta, darling, why don't you go with them."

"How can I *be* a chaperone when I *have* a chaperone?" protested Henrietta.

Tapping her foot in impatience, Lady Uppington whispered something in Henrietta's ear. "Oh, right!" Henrietta waggled her eyebrows meaningfully at her mother.

"Shall we?" asked Richard dryly, extending an arm to Amy.

Brother and sister exchanged a long look as they exited through the French doors onto the balcony. Henrietta yawned ostentatiously and collapsed onto a stone bench. "It has been an awfully long day! I'll just sit down here and watch the stars, if you don't mind terribly."

"Thank you," Richard mouthed at her.

Tucking Amy's arm more firmly through his, Richard led her down the three shallow steps into the moonlit garden.

Chapter Thirty-two

∞⚜∞

Amy cast about for something to say as they wandered towards the fountain in the center of the courtyard.

Lord Richard's booted feet kept pace with hers on the walkway. Amy forced herself to look up from her contemplation of four sets of toes (two in ribbon-bedecked slippers, two in shiny black boots) and face her nemesis. Something about the angle of his head as he glanced down at her was so like the Purple Gentian that it made Amy's heart contract. Idiot, Amy told herself, forcing a fixed smile onto her lips in the face of his quizzical gaze. Of course he looked like the Purple Gentian. The blasted man *was* the Purple Gentian. Amy hoped the crunching of gravel underfoot sufficiently masked the gritting of her teeth.

"Did you really duel with hedges?" asked Amy. She was strong, Amy reminded herself. She was stonyhearted.

"Only because my father told me that they were dragons," Lord Richard responded, with a grin that could melt stone. Amy rapidly adjusted her recital to ironhearted instead. Lord Richard waved his left hand in the direction of the shadowy clumps of shrubbery. "I assure you, your brother's garden is safe from me."

"A little hacking with a sword looks like it might do some of these plants good," Amy commented, stooping to touch a leaf on an overgrown rosebush. "Ouch!"

"Prickly things, aren't they?" Lord Richard took the hand Amy was flapping about and turned it over to examine the pricked pad of her finger. His fingers burned against her wrist and palm.

"They have to protect themselves somehow." Amy wrenched her hand away.

"You sound like you empathize."

"My aunt Abigail is a great cultivator of roses." Amy evaded the implied question and Lord Richard's amused gaze, turning from the rosebush to wander along a small graveled path. She was doing quite well, she congratulated herself. She was keeping the conversation light, and his touch hadn't affected her at all. Or at least not that much. Oh, heavens, she hoped he hadn't felt the way her pulse was racing in her wrist.

"Perhaps I should speak to her about the removal of some thorns."

Forget touch. The hideous man didn't even need to touch her to send shivers down her spine.

"Shouldn't we look at some statues?" Amy suggested breathlessly. "After all, that is what you told your mother."

"Oh, that. I am sorry about inflicting my family on you like this."

Just because he sounded like a chastened schoolboy didn't mean she should feel sympathy for him, Amy told herself. It didn't change the way he had played with her affections. Bluebeard had probably had a mother, too.

"I think they're lovely," Amy said stoutly, and meant it.

"Most of the time," Richard replied wryly, glancing back to the balcony where Henrietta was sitting with her head ostentatiously tilted up towards the night sky, "I would agree with you."

"You are lucky to have them."

Lord Richard glanced down at her with too much comprehension in his green eyes. "I am sorry about your parents. Truly sorry."

Amy shrugged uncomfortably. "We don't need to revisit all of that."

"But I think we do." Richard stopped as they rounded an overgrown bush and reached for Amy's hand. "We started off badly on the boat and I want to fix it."

"There's no need." Amy hastily shifted her hand out of reach. Not quite sure what to do with it, or with her other, equally vulnerable hand, she clasped them behind her back. Unfortunately, that had the effect of propelling her bosom into more than usual prominence. Lord Richard's gaze plummeted like a hawk descending on its prey.

Resisting the urge to tug at her bodice, Amy let her hands

fall back to her sides. "You've been more than kind. Having us to see your antiquities, for example," she continued a little too brightly. "That was terribly, um, kind of you. So now that's all settled."

Clearly, it wasn't. Lord Richard moved closer. "What can I do to convince you I'm not an evil regicide?"

The bush prickled through the thin fabric of Amy's frock. When, she wondered indignantly, had she lost control of the conversation? She was supposed to flirt with him, he was supposed to fawn besottedly, and she was supposed to crush his hopes under her dainty slippered heel. Not *this*! His tangy cologne filled her nostrils, blotting out the scents of the garden, assaulting her with memory, weakening her with desire.

"I'm convinced," Amy blurted out to his cravat. He was so close that the ends of the starched fabric practically tickled the end of her nose. One more step and his knees would brush against hers. "Really!"

The cravat receded. "Good."

Amy let herself look up. It wasn't one of her wiser decisions.

"I wouldn't want you to think ill of me," he said softly, so softly his words stroked Amy with the evening breeze. His hand moved to brush a lock of hair off her cheek. Slowly. Gently. His green eyes sought hers in a lingering caress as his head tilted towards hers.

"No!"

Amy yanked her head back so violently that her hair tangled in the branches of a bush. Her blue eyes were wide with panic. "No! I—I can't. I just can't."

Lord Richard took a step back, hands in his pockets. "Why not?" he asked neutrally. "Do you still dislike me that much?"

Dislike. Oh goodness. What an inadequate term. She wanted to take him by the shoulders and shake him until his teeth rattled and then kiss him till they were both gasping, and he asked her if she *disliked* him? Amy hadn't the slightest notion what exactly she felt towards him—the English language didn't contain words enough to encapsulate the blizzard of emotions storming through her—but it certainly wasn't dislike.

How could it be possible to desire and despise someone quite so much all at the same time? Was there a word for that in any language?

"No," she croaked. "I don't dislike you."

Lord Richard's face relaxed almost imperceptibly. "Then why . . . ?"

She could tell him the truth, Amy thought madly. She could call him to account for his actions and give him the chance to explain himself. She drank in the features of his face: the straight slope of his nose, the watchful green eyes, the clean angles of cheekbones and jaw. The Purple Gentian, unmasked.

The bracing memory of his deceit stiffened Amy's resolve to make him suffer as much as possible.

Casting her eyes to the side, she declared, with all the conviction she could force into it, "I love another."

Of all the responses Richard had expected—and Amy had stood there thinking for so bloody long that he'd had time to come up with an entire encyclopedia's worth of them—that one hadn't been on the list.

"Who is he?"

"Please don't ask me that."

Richard's mind—and stomach—churned. Who could it be? Whoever it was, it would give Richard great satisfaction to drive a fist into his jaw. It couldn't be Marston, not unless Amy had a hidden streak of perversion. Who in the hell else did she even know in France? Did she have a beloved back in England? Was that the answer? And what was she doing kissing the Purple Gentian when—oh. Oh no. The terrible truth hit Richard like a whack from a falling column.

He was jealous of his own bloody self.

When, he thought furiously, in all the annals of the world, had there ever been a situation so ludicrous? At least King Arthur and Menelaus and all those other chaps had been cuckolded by genuine rivals. It was positively embarrassing to be thwarted in love by one's own bleeding self. What sort of idiot got in the way of his own courtship?

Lord Richard Selwick, the Purple Gentian, that was who. *Urgh.*

Like Amy, Richard found the English language entirely inadequate for the situation.

"Tell me more about your perfect love," he clipped.

"I never said he was perfect."

"He's not?" Richard was offended. What was wrong with the Purple Gentian? He was a paragon of a man, a hero, a— oh, wait, he was supposed to be his rival.

Amy's eyes slanted up at him from beneath dark lashes. "You heard Miss Gwen. There's no such thing as a perfect man."

"What's wrong with him?" Richard quickly cataloged possibilities. Was it his breath? That blasted cloak?

"He didn't trust me as he should," Amy replied promptly, glowering at Richard.

Hell. It would have been much easier to deal with getting a new cloak.

This was ridiculous! He didn't know whether to defend himself—the Purple Gentian bit of himself, that was—or to be jealous of his Purple Gentian self on behalf of his himself self. Devil take it, even his thoughts were in a deuced tangle. There was one way to end all the tangles and confusion.

Richard's mouth opened but no sound came out. He'd thought he would feel better when he told Deirdre, hadn't he? And look what had come of that. Who would the casualty be this time? Geoff? Miles?

Richard's mouth shut into a very tight line.

Amy was watching him closely. "Were you about to say something?"

Richard shrugged. "Merely that your secret love, whoever he may be, is a very lucky man. Shall we return to the others?"

The walk back across the garden was considerably quicker than the stroll out; Amy had to scurry to keep up with Richard's brisk strides. Maybe it had to do with being out of breath, but victory didn't leave nearly as sweet a taste in Amy's mouth as she had anticipated. Could one really use the term victory, when Lord Richard hadn't so much as glanced at her since they had started back down the path?

If he had ever really cared, he would never have given up that easily. Clearly, thought Amy savagely, she hadn't even been an infatuation. She had been nothing more than a *dalliance*.

Henrietta looked up eagerly as Richard and Amy hove into view. "Did you have a nice . . . ," she began brightly, but the phrase trailed off as she caught sight of her brother's stony face.

"I'll leave you here to get acquainted." Richard all but shook Amy's fingers off his arm, executed a bow in her general direction, and plunged through the French doors into the drawing room.

"Richard! Pssst!" His mother's arm shot out and dragged him behind a faux mummy case. "Over here!"

"Ouch." Richard rubbed his wrist and glowered down at his mother. When in matchmaking mode, somehow his diminutive parent's strength was as the strength of ten. Ten pugilists, that was.

"Sorry, darling," the marchioness absentmindedly patted her son's wrist, but her solicitude was short-lived. "What happened? You were outside with her for ages!"

Richard gave evasion a try. "Is Miles flirting with Hen?"

Lady Uppington rolled her eyes. "If Miles is flirting with Hen, I'm sure Hen is happily flirting back. Besides, they're perfectly well chaperoned by that nice Miss Meadows. Do stop trying to change the subject, Richard. I don't know why you children always think you can distract me like that."

"When have we ever tried to distract you, Mother? You're far too sharp for us."

Lady Uppington narrowed her eyes. "Let's see. . . . There was the time you and Charles . . . Oh no. I'm not falling for *that* old dodge. Come now, darling, won't you talk about it to your"—Lady Uppington patted the side of the mummy case—"*mummy*?"

Richard groaned. "That was beyond awful, Mother."

"Some children have no gratitude. What happened, darling?"

"Amy thinks she's in love with the Purple Gentian."

"But you *are*—"

"I know!"

It was at that highly edifying moment that Miles chose to pop behind the mummy case. The marchioness looked miffed.

"Why so gloomy? Is it . . . the mummy?"

Richard glowered at his best friend. "Don't you start."

"I promise to behave as long as you provide refuge from the hen party—and I do mean, a *Hen* party—on the balcony. They've all got their heads together, and when I wandered over, Hen flapped her hand at me and told me I was superfluous. I'm not sure which was more provoking, the sentiment or her vocabulary."

Miles heaved a disgruntled sigh. Lady Uppington beamed with maternal pride. Richard noticed none of this; his head was craning around the edge of the mummy case, peering at the little grouping beyond the French doors. It was, terrifyingly, just as Miles had described: Jane's fair head, Henrietta's glossy chestnut, and Amy's bouncy curls all bent close together. A steady sibilant sound drifted through the air. Richard didn't want to know what they were talking about. Which meant, of course, that he rather desperately wanted to know whether they were talking about him.

Richard strained to listen, his fingers grasping the side of the mummy case. "No!" Henrietta exclaimed, bouncing on her bench. "You can't be serious!" The heads swooped back together. *Hiss, hiss, hiss . . .*

Had Richard known what was being said on the balcony, he would have been even more alarmed.

"What do you *mean* he didn't tell you who he was? That's appalling!"

Within ten minutes, by means of ambiguous half-statements and strategically raised eyebrows, Amy had managed to ascertain that Henrietta knew of Richard's dual identity. Once that was out of the way, the conversation became much more direct.

"How could he let you think he was two people?" Henrietta glowered in the direction of her brother. "That's . . ." Having already used *appalling*, she cast about for another term. "Unconscionable!" she finished triumphantly.

"I feel an idiot for not having realized. If I hadn't been so convinced that he was utterly under Bonaparte's thumb . . ."

"It is a wonderful disguise, isn't it?" Henrietta belatedly remembered that they were excoriating Richard, not praising him. "But he *still* should have told you."

"What hurts the most is that he didn't trust me enough to tell me," Amy confided. "Just now, when I told him I loved another, he could have made amends by simply saying . . ."

" 'By the way, that other happens to be me. Sorry. Forgot to tell you before'?" Henrietta supplied.

Amy grinned despite herself. "Something like that."

"Oh no. That would have been far too easy. He's an absolute dear, and a wonderful brother, but he *is* a boy." Henrietta shook her head in irritation. "He has delusions of authority. They all do. He thinks he always knows what's best for everyone and how to organize their lives."

"That's *exactly* the problem!" Amy waved her hands about excitedly. "He needs to be shown that he can't always organize everything for everyone."

Henrietta looked gratified. "Oh, absolutely!"

"Something must be done."

"I couldn't agree more." Henrietta nodded emphatically. "They need to be taken down a peg or two occasionally. For the good of womankind."

"Amy, are you going to?" Jane put in.

"Do you have a plan already? Oh, please tell!" Henrietta swished her long hair out of her face, and leaned forward imploringly. "I won't utter a word."

"We do have a plan," Amy uttered thrillingly.

Henrietta listened, enthralled. "Smashing!" she exclaimed, when Amy and Jane had finished filling in the details. "The Pink Carnation! I love it! Especially the name." She giggled. "How may I help?"

"Shhh!" Jane hissed abruptly. "He's coming!"

All three girls instantly sat up straight and folded their hands in their laps.

Richard glowered suspiciously at his sister as he stepped out onto the balcony. Henrietta smiled at him with an innocence that informed him instantly that his worst fears were correct.

Richard kissed his sister on the cheek, and bowed over Jane's hand.

He didn't bow over Amy's hand. He didn't nod. He simply looked at her. Only there was nothing at all simple about the way he was looking at her.

His eyes burned into hers with a mixture of longing and pain that held Amy transfixed. Returning the stare, pain for pain, longing for longing, Amy fought the urge to grab his hand. Even had she not had her pride to consider, a hand would have been redundant. Their eyes locked them closer than any handclasp, closer than speech.

Richard broke the gaze first.

With a toneless "Good night, Miss Balcourt," he turned on his heel and left the balcony. His unyielding back strode out the French doors, through the salon, and disappeared from sight.

Richard's sister slid her arm through Amy's and squeezed. "Courage," Henrietta cheered her. "Remember the good of womankind."

"Right," Amy muttered, eyes still on the door through which Richard had exited a moment before. "The good of womankind."

She could be heard muttering the phrase through her teeth at intervals for the rest of the evening.

Chapter Thirty-three

❦

In a dark house in a dark street in the predawn blackness of the Ile de la Cité, a single candle burned. The grudging light of the candle illuminated a chamber as meager as the single flame itself. A narrow bed, unwelcoming and unslept in, stood against one wall, flanked by a barren nightstand. A pair of ancient leather slippers lay at uneven angles on the scarred wooden floor. In a straight-backed chair by the room's sole window sat Gaston Delaroche.

At half past two the signal came, the sound of an owl hooting in the alleyway behind the window. The Assistant Minister of Police raised the sash of the window, and a slight, dark figure joined the shadows under the crooked overhang of the second story of the old house. If words were whispered, the sound was submerged under the million nighttime noises of the crowded street. The abrupt snuffle and hiss of snoring men, the creak of rope beds, and the rustle of feather ticks created a monotonous hum. From the upper reaches of Delaroche's boardinghouse came the sharply muffled cry of a small child, and a man's irritated grumble. The sash of Delaroche's window slid silently closed. The shadows were once again merely shadows.

The warped table tottered as Delaroche seated himself again in the rickety chair. The candle flame flickered, threatening to go out. Delaroche appeared not to notice.

Twice. Lord Richard Selwick had been seen twice in the company of Mlle Amy Balcourt. They had been seen first in the courtyard of the Tuilleries. Later, Selwick had been spied entering the gates of Balcourt's town house with a larger party, consisting, Delaroche's spy informed him, of the Englishman's family.

What drove a man to see a woman twice in one day?

Delaroche rapidly dismissed the possibility that the Balcourt girl might be an agent. Her brother was well known as a hanger-on at the First Consul's court. That in itself was no guarantee of the girl's innocence. Family ties, ha! Blood might be thicker than water on the floor of the interrogation chamber, but Delaroche had long since concluded that the truism had few other applications. Family ties were an impediment. A prop for the weak, an encumbrance for the strong.

But Delaroche would have heard long since had a new spy been in operation in Paris. There would have been ripples and reverberations across the dark pools of his subterranean world, whispers and rumors. There had been none. The Balcourt chit was innocent—of spying, at least.

Which brought Delaroche back to his initial question: Why would the Purple Gentian waste precious hours on a chit of a girl?

It was at the Balcourt town house that Lord Richard had first been spotted in amorous embrace with an unnamed female two nights previously. Delaroche himself had observed them in flirtation at one of Mme Bonaparte's salons. A slow, contemptuous smile broke across the face of the Assistant Minister of Police.

Every man had a weakness, even the oh-so-intrepid Purple Gentian.

"One mistake, Selweeck," Delaroche crowed softly in the darkness. "All it takes is one fatal mistake."

To snare the man, one need only lay hold of the girl.

Delaroche snuffed the candle.

Chapter Thirty-four

Unbeknownst to either the Ministry of Police or the Purple Gentian, in a large town house on the other side of the city, the League of the Pink Carnation was planning its first escapade.

Considerable thought was expended as to how the illustrious career of the Pink Carnation ought to begin. Miss Gwen, under whose high-necked bodice lurked the sort of bloodthirsty spirit that accounted watching gladiators being gored by lions rather good fun, would be satisfied with nothing less than running through a Frenchman (Miss Gwen graciously left the choice of Frenchman up to committee), and hanging him by his feet from the blade of the guillotine.

Jane, after a startled look at Miss Gwen, suggested filching some files from Delaroche's office, a plan which was instantly voted down by both of the others; Amy dismissed it as insufficiently daring, Miss Gwen as boringly bloodless. Amy's plan A, that they sneak into the Temple prison in cunning disguises and liberate some deserving prisoners, met with equal scorn. As did plan B, plan C, and even plan D, which involved dressing up in the clothes of the previous decade, dusting themselves all over with flour, and flitting about Bonaparte's bedside as the ghosts of murdered aristocrats. "Like Richard III being haunted by his victims!" explained Amy with relish. Miss Gwen, scenting potential fodder for her horrid novel, was intrigued, but in the end ruled that scaling the windows of the Tuilleries dressed in three-foot-wide panniers and covered in flour would be both difficult and messy.

Jane's alarmed face relaxed.

"We don't have to do anything too spectacular," she pointed out hastily, before Amy could outline plan E. "After all, this is merely a calling card. Something to make the Minister of Police aware that he has a new adversary."

"A *better* adversary," amended Miss Gwen with a sniff.

"Since our real mission is the retrieval of the Swiss gold," Jane continued, "shouldn't we keep this one simple?"

"Oh! I have an idea!" Amy sat bolt upright on the settee, blue eyes gleaming with mischief. "Why don't we sneak into his bedchamber and leave a note and a pink carnation on his pillow?"

Miss Gwen's thin lips, which had begun to move automatically into their sneer position, relaxed into speculation instead.

"I like it!" seconded Jane, sounding rather insultingly surprised.

"We could write it in rhyme," giggled Amy. "How about, 'Seek me where and when you will/ The Pink Carnation will best you still'?"

"It doesn't scan," said Miss Gwen dampeningly.

"Well, I only just made it up off the top of my head."

Miss Gwen's narrowed eyes implied that she thought little of the top of Amy's head.

"Maybe we should stick to prose," Jane suggested tactfully. "Something—"

"I know, *simple.*" Amy cast Jane a fond look. "In that case, why not just leave him a note telling him that he can thank the Pink Carnation for the disappearance of the Swiss gold? We could leave it right before taking the gold."

The idea passed the Committee of the Pink Carnation by unanimous vote. It all seemed an excellent idea at the time, with even Miss Gwen deigning a rare nod of approval. Jane, the Carnation with the neatest handwriting, drew up the note to Delaroche. Miss Gwen procured their costumes, a task accomplished with one quick raid on the grooms' quarters. Discovering the best time to enter Delaroche's lodgings was left to Amy, who struck up a conversation with Delaroche's groom as she waited for the Balcourt carriage to be brought around after an evening party at the Tuilleries. If he was nonplussed at being addressed by a lady, the groom failed to show it. He proved surprisingly helpful in apprising her of his master's schedule, repeating several times that Delaroche had an engagement outside of Paris on the evening of the thirtieth. Amy ought to have been pleased that it had been so easy. But by the time two days had passed, Amy found herself wishing she had been assigned something a little more, well, active. Something that would keep her mind off Lord Richard.

This latter task wasn't in the least helped by the fact that Lady Uppington had enthusiastically adopted both Jane and Amy, and persisted, with significant sidelong glances at Amy, in relating many adorable tales of Richard's youth. Amy tried not to listen too eagerly, but how could she help herself? She could just see a miniature Richard jauntily leveling a sword at a yew bush, and from there it was only a short step to picturing the very devastatingly adult Richard facing off against Marston, and from there . . . From there, Amy tended to blush a very deep red at memories that had no business coming to mind in the presence of Richard's mother and sister.

If she was being honest with herself, it wasn't just in the presence of Richard's family members that memories plagued her. They leaped into her head when she was plotting with Miss Gwen, flitted in front of her when she was brushing her hair at her mirror, and positively taunted her as she lay unsleeping in bed. It was utterly infuriating to be sitting at the breakfast table, staring at the remains of a brioche, and to hear the whisper of the Purple Gentian's voice in her ear and feel the brush of his hand across her cheek. And Amy's heart leaped painfully into her throat every time she saw a black cloak swishing down the street.

Why couldn't he leave her alone? Oh, but there was the rub—Lord Richard, and his alter ego, the Purple Gentian, *were* leaving her alone. When she and Jane called on Lady Uppington and Henrietta for tea, he kept scrupulously to his study. He stayed towards the other side of the salon at Mme Bonaparte's receptions. (Amy surrounded herself with very tall officers to physically block off the temptation of glancing in his direction to see if he might possibly be glancing at her.) When she loitered in the corridors of the Tuilleries on her way back from her weekly English lesson with Hortense, he whisked so rapidly around a corner that all she saw was the glint of a familiar golden head. Nor had there been any midnight visitations from the cloaked and masked form of the Purple Gentian.

But that was all right, wasn't it? She only had to see him once more, one meeting to crow over her triumph, and then he'd flee back to England in embarrassment, and she would be done with him forever. No more Lord Richard Selwick. No more Purple Gentian.

Amy scowled at yet another mutilated brioche.

On the day the Swiss gold was due to arrive, Amy paced back and forth in front of her window, watching as the streaks of sunset wended their painfully slow way across the sky— why wouldn't the sun just *set* already? Amy began dressing a good hour before the time they had appointed to leave, drawing out the process as long as she possibly could.

Binding her breasts proved much more difficult than Amy had imagined. How did all of those Shakespeare heroines who disguised themselves as boys manage it? Amy scowled at the long strip of white linen that had untied itself—again. After another three tries, and several cries of pain, the binding found its way onto the fire. After all, the shirt was loose, and billowy, and maybe if she hunched over a bit, no one would notice.

Wriggling her nose in distaste, she shrugged into the grimy trousers—their color was indeterminate, and might have been anything from black to brown originally—and pulled the coarse beige linen shirt over her head. It smelled regrettably of stableboy.

Fully garbed, down to a pair of muddy brown boots, Amy found herself once again without anything to do—and with an offensive stench. Next time, she resolved grimly, they would go disguised as something more glamorous. Something less smelly. Maybe they should have pretended to be ladies of the night going to meet a client.

Jane rapped on the door as Amy glowered at an infuriating streak of orange in the darkening sky.

"Ready?" she asked.

"An hour ago."

Jane's lips quirked as she looked pointedly at the grimy men's clothes and the streaks of soot adorning Amy's face. "I guessed as much. I just spoke to Miss Gwen and she says she'll meet us back here at eleven so we can all leave for the warehouse together."

"She's not going to go with us to leave the note?" Amy scraped back her hair with one hand, and felt around on her dressing table for a ribbon with the other.

"No." Jane took the ribbon from her and began tightly winding the mass of dark curls so they would fit under a knit cap. "She's saving herself for the real mission. When I went in, she was skewering pillows with her parasol."

"Some chaperone," muttered Amy.

"Fortunately for us," Jane countered wryly, knotting the ribbon. "I'm going to get dressed—are you sure you're all right?"

"Just fidgety." Amy demonstrated the proof of her words by resuming her pacing, scattering flecks of dried mud across the carpet. "But I'll be *perfectly* happy tomorrow once Lord Richard is gnashing his teeth in frustration because we bested him."

"Aren't we supposed to be besting Bonaparte?" Jane inquired delicately.

"Two birds with one stone," proclaimed Amy with a toss of her head.

Jane shook her head and headed for the door. "I'll be ready to leave in five minutes," she reassured her cousin.

Amy glanced at the clock. Nearly half past seven. By eight o'clock . . .

At half past seven, in a small house across the city, Geoff poked his head around the door of Richard's study.

"Would you like some tea?"

"You can come in, you know," Richard said crossly, pushing back his chair from the desk. "I'm not going to bite."

"Do you promise?" Geoff pushed the door the rest of the way open. Richard kicked a chair in his direction. Since the floor of the study was covered by a Persian rug, the chair didn't go awfully far, but Geoff took the point and the chair. "I thought you were going to skewer Miles with your butter knife tonight at dinner."

"Well . . . Miles." Richard shrugged as though that explained it. "Brandy?"

"Thank you." Geoff accepted a snifter. "Why don't you just talk to her?"

Richard stiffened, the brandy decanter poised over Geoff's glass. "To whom?"

Geoff gave him a look. "The Queen of Sheba, who else?" Richard focused on pouring the amber liquid. "Amy, of course."

"Oh." Richard corked the brandy decanter and sat back in his chair. "Darts?" he suggested hopefully.

Geoff, however, was not to be deterred. "You are going to do something about her after tonight's mission, aren't you? I don't really care what, but you've been increasingly unpleasant to live with."

"Thanks."

"Think nothing of it. Well?"

"I hadn't really thought about it," Richard grumbled, not meeting Geoff's eye. That was the problem with friends who had known you since you were just out of the nursery. It was far too easy for them to detect lies—and they had no shame about pointing them out. All right, so Richard had thought about it. Incessantly. He had rehearsed about twenty variants of a speech along the lines of, "Only the need to save England prevented me from revealing to you . . ." No, he had scrapped that one as too pompous. "By the way, thought you might like to know, I'm the Purple Gentian. Will you marry me?" seemed a bit too offhand. And they just got worse from there.

"I was thinking about doing a bit of reconnoitering before tonight's mission," Richard announced loudly. True, Geoff was only two feet away, but raising his voice helped to drown out all of that silent skepticism radiating from his friend.

Richard hauled himself out of his chair. He hadn't really considered reconnoitering before, but now that he'd declared the intent to do so, it did seem rather a good idea. It would give him something to do, keep his mind off Amy, and get him in the right mood for tonight. "I might drop by Delaroche's lodgings and see if there's anything about the gold in his secret files there."

"The ones he keeps under his pillow?" Geoff asked, diverted. "How such an accomplished agent chooses the most idiotic hiding places . . ."

"Shocking, isn't it?" Richard agreed heartily, seizing the change of subject and making a rapid dash towards the door before Geoff could remember his initial purpose. "The desk drawer in his office and under his pillow. It takes all the challenge out of it. Well, I'm going to go change. I'll meet you back here by ten or so."

"Anything else you need me to do?" Geoff asked.

"Just dissuade my mother if she has any ideas of coming along tonight. Other than that, I can't think of anything that could go wrong," Richard said breezily, and exited to undertake the calming, and familiar, task of burgling Delaroche's lodgings. He glanced at the clock: just past seven thirty. He could easily be there within the next half an hour and back by ten.

By eight o'clock, Delaroche's empty lodgings had become an unexpectedly lively place.

Perched with one leg on the lintel of Delaroche's window-sill, Richard froze at the sound of a door being eased open. Trying to ignore the discomfort in his leg muscles (after all, it wasn't the most convenient of poses), Richard watched as the wood swung open in a slow semicircle and a dark-clad frame slid into the small room.

Delaroche? No. The figure, even if somewhat hard to make out in the dark room, was clearly too small to be Delaroche, weedy little man though the Frenchman was. Besides, why would Delaroche be slinking around his own bedroom? The man was odd, and probably mildly mad, but Richard still couldn't see him prowling around his own darkened room for fun. He preferred to prowl around other people's darkened rooms for amusement, a pastime Richard had to admit he rather sympathized with.

The small figure stole towards the bed, hips swaying. Hips doing what? Something about the way the prowler was moving nagged at Richard's memory. Heedless of caution, Richard leaned sharply forward. Intent on tiptoeing, the intruder didn't notice. The very *female* intruder. The ... good God, it was Amy. No wonder that backside looked familiar. He'd certainly spent enough time staring at it over the last few weeks.

The intruder was *Amy*.

Devil take it, what was Amy doing in Delaroche's bedchamber?

Amy swerved at the sound of the window sash being raised behind her—and tripped over a leather bed slipper that Delaroche had inconsiderately left lying on the floor beside his bed. She hit the dusty ground with an *ooof* that obscured the sound of the first footfall, picking herself up off the floor just in time to see a second booted leg join the first. Her gaze traveled up from the scuffed black boots ... to the hem of a black cape swinging in dark folds against the boot calves. Oh no.

Amy's hands went cold.

In fact, her entire body must have turned to ice, because

she stayed frozen in her half crouch, one hand still touching the dusty floorboards. Her horrified eyes strayed upwards, over a pair of tightly fitted black breeches, black gloved hands loosely resting on the windowsill. . . .

It wasn't *fair*. What was he doing here, now, when she was so close to taking her well-deserved revenge? Why couldn't he have put in an appearance at tea yesterday, or Mme Bonaparte's salon the day before? Why plague her *now*? Amy's whole body began to shake as she took in the lean line of his throat, the familiar angles of his face under the shadowy circle of his hood. She would *not* fling herself into his arms. It had been a very bad habit, and, besides, he clearly didn't want her in them anyway. All that was over, over, over. But why did he still have the power to reduce her to an emotional blob of jelly? It was worse than unfair; it was wrong.

"What are you doing here?" she demanded, brushing her dusty hands against her knees. With his back to the window, blocking what little moonlight there was, it was all she could do to make out his face, let alone any expression.

"I might ask the same of you," retorted the Gentian, stepping away from the window in a swirl of black fabric.

Amy automatically took a step back towards the bed, as if putting a few more inches of distance between them would dull the impact of his presence. It didn't. She still felt his nearness along every inch of skin, raising goose bumps under the coarse linen of her shirt, prickling along the roots of her hair. Amy's fingers tingled. Hoping it would drive the tingles away, she balled her hands into fists. The tingles spread into her palms.

The Gentian shook his hooded head. In a voice warm with amusement, he said, "You don't give up easily, do you?"

Amy's chest constricted with the injustice of it. So it wasn't enough to repudiate her? He had to laugh at her, too.

"Not on the things that matter," she bit out.

"I take it you weren't just out for an evening stroll?"

Amy felt the card containing the Pink Carnation's note to Delaroche stiff in her pocket. Whatever happened, it was imperative, absolutely imperative, he not discover the existence of the Pink Carnation. Amy clung to that one thought in a mind rapidly turning to mush as Richard took yet another casual step closer. The backs of Amy's knees banged against Delaroche's mattress. Thank goodness it was a deep pocket!

"If you're looking for Delaroche's secret files"—the Purple Gentian leaned towards Amy—"I'll give you a little hint. He keeps them under his pillow."

"Right," Amy stammered, leaning back so far her head was nearly level with her shoulders. "Thank you."

"Don't you want to look at them?"

Whomp! It happened in seconds; the Purple Gentian reached over Amy to the pillow. Amy tried to lean back further, lost her balance, and toppled backwards onto the bed. It was a disaster. Not only was she sprawled flat on her back, with her bottom half off the bed, and her trouser-clad legs flung apart, the Purple Gentian's hand was trapped under her head.

Amy's wide eyes flew to Richard's face. He was still smiling, but it wasn't a teasing grin; the curve of his lips was . . . predatory. Through the slits of his mask, Amy could see his green eyes narrow on her lips. Amy's breathing quickened, her lips parting in alarm—it had to be alarm—as the edges of his cape brushed her arms and the familiar scent of his cologne filled her with yearning memories. His hand turned to cup her head, tangling in her hair, massaging her scalp.

"This is not happening," bleated Amy.

"All right," murmured the Purple Gentian softly, his face so close she could feel the gentle puff of his breath across her lips. He smelled of brandy and cloves and something else indescribably his. "This is not happening."

Chapter Thirty-five

❧

But it *was* happening, and Amy didn't want it to stop. His lips reached hers, and reality disappeared in a floating mist of taste and touch and scent; his tongue burrowed deep into her mouth, and, unthinking, Amy lifted her arms to clasp tightly about his neck. They kissed with the savagery of long separation; lips slanting together, tongues twining, bodies pressing together. Richard's hand slid under Amy's back, molding her to him, while his thigh pressed between her legs.

Amy gave a little cry and arched up against him, kissing him back hungrily. Why couldn't she have just this one last time? she thought hazily. Just one last memory to store up to savor on all those long, empty nights ahead. . . . Knowing that this would be the last time, the very last time she'd feel his lips, his caress, his strong body against hers—that this wasn't supposed to be happening but it *was*—magnified every sensation. The crisp brush of his hair against her sensitive fingertips, the flick of his tongue around the curves of her lips, the warm pressure of his hand along her spine. Just this one time . . . she promised herself. Since she would never have the chance again . . . Amy greedily tugged the Gentian's shirt from his waistband, sliding her palms along the smooth skin of his back. She traced the contours of his muscles, memorizing their shape and texture.

The Gentian's lips left Amy's to trail along her cheek, down the curve of her chin. Amy gave a little cry of protest, and pressed harder against his back, trying to urge his mouth back up to hers, but Richard just grinned wickedly, and trailed his tongue along the curve of her neck, and . . .

Richard's nose twitched. He sniffed Amy's neck. He frowned. He sniffed again. "What," he asked dazedly, "is that smell?"

Amy's own nose had long since become accustomed to the eau de unwashed groom that permeated her borrowed clothes. Besides, she didn't want to speak. If they spoke, she might have to think.

"Don't breathe," she advised huskily, yanking his head back down towards hers.

The Purple Gentian showed no signs of disagreeing. His mouth reclaimed hers with alacrity. His hands slipped into the loose waistband of Amy's trousers, molding her against the bulge of his arousal.

Amy's legs instinctively closed around his waist, and she moaned in a voice that was half-protest, half-plea, "Richard . . ."

Suddenly, the Purple Gentian's hands grasped her shoulders in an iron grip, yanking her into a sitting position. "What did you say?" he bit out.

"I said . . . oh." Amy gulped. Her head swam from being yanked upright, but even through her vertigo Richard's green eyes on hers were as implacable as the jade eyes of an ancient statue. "I don't suppose you'd believe me if I said I only just guessed?"

Richard gave her a little shake. "How long have you known?"

Amy considered prevaricating, but something about the way Richard's fingers bored into her shoulders and his gaze into hers warned her that that would be a very bad idea. "Since the day after the Seine."

"That night in the garden? You knew?"

Amy could barely nod.

"Damn you, Amy!" He let go of her so abruptly that she almost tumbled back onto the mattress, grabbing at the end of the night table to steady herself. "All the while I was eating my heart out—with jealousy of my own bloody self, no less!— you knew?"

"I wanted—" Amy's throat was so dry that it took an effort to force out the words. She licked her swollen lips. "I wanted you to know how it felt. To be played with like that. I'm sorry." She only half heard her own words. Jealousy? He was jealous?

"You're sorry. *Now* you're sorry." With the amount of sarcasm dripping from his words, Amy was surprised she didn't dissolve into nothingness on the spot.

Amy caught herself on the precipice of an apology and sprang up from the bed. "I don't know why I should be. *You* repudiated *me*, if you remember correctly."

"Only because I had to." Richard frowned under his mask, not liking the way the conversation was turning.

Amy took a step forward, hands on her hips. Richard would have enjoyed the sight—they were, after all, a very nice pair of hips—if the expression on her face hadn't been quite so ominous.

"And then you flirted with me the next day!"

"It made sense at the time."

"For all I knew, you were just playing with me out of some . . . some malicious whim!"

"You were never a whim."

"It certainly doesn't feel that way. For all I knew you might have been the sort of cad who enjoys driving women mad just for the sheer joy of it. You told me I was an *infatuation*."

"I had good reasons."

"All right, then. What are they? Or do you need time to invent some?"

Richard bit down the automatic urge to snap that it was none of her affair. Because it was her affair, and had been ever since he had kissed her in her brother's study. Looking down at Amy's flushed face, Richard felt oddly sheepish. It was an unpleasant feeling, a feeling entirely unsuited to an intrepid secret agent, and Richard did his best to squelch it. He *had* had good reasons, he reminded himself. Deirdre. The mission. Saving England, and all that. Surely saving England counted as a good reason. If he could only convince Amy of that then . . . well, then maybe he would stop feeling like such a complete heel.

"There was someone. Someone I fancied myself in love with. A long time ago."

Amy swallowed the impulse to demand sarcastically if this nameless someone had been more than a mere infatuation. She wondered if he'd kissed her on moonlit nights on the Seine. If he'd taken her to see his antiquities. If she'd been prettier and wittier than Amy. If she'd been blond.

"Who was she?"

Richard shrugged. "The daughter of neighboring gentry." He paused, trying to think how to go on. For all that the images of Deirdre's betrayal and Tony's death were emblazoned into his brain in precise detail, he'd never actually had to put any of it into words before. Those who knew, knew. Geoff, Miles, Sir Percy, his parents . . . None of them had ever taxed him with an explanation. They just knew. And they never discussed it.

"I fancied myself in love with her," he repeated, as if by focusing on the foolishness of the lovelorn swain he had been, he could put off the other part, the darker part. "It was nearly six years ago."

"Are you still in love with her?" Amy croaked.

Richard's head snapped down towards Amy. "In love with her? Zounds, no! It was . . ."

"An infatuation?"

The sarcasm was wasted on Richard. "An infatuation," he agreed. "She was young, pretty, and nearby. I was impressionable."

Amy sniffed scornfully.

"I had a rival. A middle-aged widower. I'd been running missions for Percy for just over a year. I thought that if I told her . . . Hell, I was bursting to tell her. To tell anyone. I was young, and stupid, and I wanted to boast. Even if Baron Jerard hadn't been involved, I would have told Deirdre about the League sooner or later."

Deirdre. The name somehow made the woman more real to Amy. Deirdre. It was a nasty name, Amy decided viciously, despite the fact that she'd heretofore always rather liked it, and when she was ten had given the name to her third-favorite doll.

"Her maid was a French operative."

Amy's eyes flew up to his face in surprise.

With the grim air of a man running a gauntlet, Richard plunged on. "I made the mistake of telling Deirdre, in some detail, of a mission we had planned for the following month. Her maid alerted the Ministry of Police. They preceded us to our meeting place."

"Were you hurt?"

"I?" Richard laughed bitterly. "Not a scratch. They arrived at the cabin just before T— one of our best men showed up with a French count he had rescued from the Bastille. By the time Geoff and I arrived, the count was recaptured. Tony was dead. I was unhurt. It didn't take long to trace the link to Deirdre."

"I'm so sorry."

"So was I." Richard shook his head. "But that didn't make any difference to Tony."

Remembered grief incised deep lines on either side of Richard's lips, and chiseled away at Amy's anger. It had seemed so straightforward just moments before. He had wronged her. He had played her for a fool. He was in the wrong, and no excuse, no excuse at all (short of memory loss, or an evil twin) was going to set that right. When he mentioned Deirdre, Amy had bristled with righteous indignation. It would have been so easy to scoff at a betrayed love, to fling shrill derision at him like poison-tipped arrows.

Even knowing the rest of it, part of Amy still wanted to fly at him like a harpy, and screech, "That was *it*? You played games with *my* heart because another woman—a woman who was not me—betrayed your trust years ago? You made my life agony for *that*?"

But she couldn't.

Not when his remorse hung between them like a living thing. Or did she mean like a dead thing? Tony.

"But I'm not Deirdre," she blurted out.

"I couldn't tell you, Amy," Richard said quietly. "There were too many lives at stake."

Amy stared at him dumbly. You didn't have to dally with me, she thought. You could have just left me alone. Or you could have trusted me. I wouldn't have told. She desperately rehearsed all the grievances that had fueled her since that afternoon she had realized his double identity. But all of them scattered in the face of those horrible, weighty words, *too many lives at stake*.

Amy shook her head and took a step back. "I can't . . . ," she began, but choked on her own confusion.

How could she say she couldn't accept that, when she knew he was right, that he had done the honorable thing? Her hurt feelings were insignificant when weighed in the balance against a man's life. She knew that. A line from one of her favorite poems flitted through her head: "I could not love thee dear so much, loved I not honor more." It had always seemed such a noble sentiment. But here the sentiment stood embodied before her, and Amy wanted to scream and rail. How had everything turned upside down? Five minutes ago, he was a rogue, and a deceiver, and she a maiden wronged.

Now, Amy's head ached with the uneasy sense of being wrong rather than wronged.

But he hurt me, her heart argued back.

Why couldn't he have been the despicable cad he seemed, so she could just hate him? None of these horrible, messy, confused emotions.

"I'm going home," she said thickly.

Richard immediately stepped forward. "I'll see you back."

"No." Amy shook her head as she flung her legs recklessly over the side of the window. She wanted to walk and walk and go on walking as though, if she moved quickly enough, she might outpace the confused thoughts that pursued and pricked her.

"No," she repeated, "I'll be all ri—aaaaah!"

Amy's words turned into an agitated cry as a pair of hands closed around her midriff and jerked her down from the window.

"Let *go*!" Amy drove an elbow into her captor's arm, earning a muffled *oof*. In retaliation, the arm around her stomach tightened. Amy gasped for breath, ineffectually trying to kick backwards, as she was hauled inexorably into the alleyway behind Delaroche's lodgings.

Richard flung himself out of the window after her in a swirl of black cape—and froze, as a phalanx of military men materialized out of the darkness. The brass on their uniforms might have been somewhat dull in the dark, but it didn't take much moonlight to see that their muskets were primed and ready.

A short, bandy-legged man strutted through the semicircle of musket points. "The Purple Gentian, I presume?" Delaroche sneered.

Chapter Thirty-six

"Unhand her," Richard snapped.

He knew he had made a tactical error when Delaroche's smile widened. "Such a touching tête-à-tête," the little man crooned. "And so very . . . convenient."

Fifteen men. Richard rapidly assessed the situation. Fifteen burly infantrymen crowded into the little alleyway behind Delaroche's lodgings. Of those fifteen, fully three were occupied in subduing Amy. A shako hat rolled through the dust as Amy rammed into one of her captors, sending him reeling. Another darted back and forth, trying to avoid Amy's flailing feet as he wound a rope around her wrists. A third still held her around the waist, but his nose oozed blood onto his white cross straps from a well-placed butt of Amy's head.

Which only left twelve infantrymen pointing muskets at Richard.

"Move," cautioned Delaroche, "and my men will shoot the charming Miss Balcourt."

Twelve muskets hastily shifted target.

"You're warring on women now, Delaroche?" Richard didn't have to feign the disgust in his voice. "Needed to find someone smaller than you to beat up on, did you?"

"Insults will not alter your predicament, my friend." Delaroche smirked. "You fell into my trap, just as I knew you would."

"Trap?" Amy gasped.

"Trap," Delaroche repeated smugly. "Every man has a weakness, Monsieur Purple Gentian. For some, it is drink. For others, it is cards. For—"

"Is the treatise on human nature really quite necessary?" Richard interjected, glancing sidelong at Amy. The rope had finally made its way around her arms.

"For you," Delaroche continued, as though Richard had never spoken, "it is a woman. That woman."

"She has nothing to do with this, Delaroche."

"Oh no, Monsieur Purple Gentian? She led you to me. Just as I knew she would."

"No!" Amy squirmed in her captor's grasp. "I wouldn't—" Her words ended abruptly as a heavy hand clamped down over her mouth. A masculine yelp followed as the guard snatched his bitten palm away from her mouth.

Horrified comprehension swept through Amy. That groom of Delaroche's, that smirking, spotty boy, who had been so forthcoming in telling her exactly when his master would be out of his chambers. Amy doubled over, feeling sick for reasons that had nothing to do with the bulky arm clamped around her ribs.

Richard forced his body to relax, forced himself to wave a languid hand in Amy's direction. "Quite a fuss over a bit of fluff."

"A bit of fluff?"

Richard studiedly avoided Amy's eyes, hoping to hell that she would realize what he was trying to do. "A light-skirt," he clarified, in his best man-about-town air of bored sophistication, "a mere spot of dalliance. Don't you French know something about that sort of thing? Or did you lose your talent for amours along with your monarchy?"

"A mere spot of dalliance," Delaroche repeated, turning the unfamiliar English words scornfully on his tongue. "Or so you claim. We have ways of testing the truth of your words. Pierre?"

A heavy hand crashed against Amy's face, snapping her head back. Amy gasped in surprise and pain.

"Antoine?"

Metal gleamed at Amy's throat. A knife.

"He is under orders to use it," Delaroche said softly. "A bit of fluff, you say?"

A strangled yelp emerged from Amy's throat as the knife pressed against her skin, raising a thin red welt.

"What do you want?" Richard asked grimly.

"That, Monsieur Gentian, ought to be obvious."

"Not to all of us," Richard snapped.

"Your confession and surrender."

"Don't!" Amy cried out. "Don't do it! You've made a mistake, Monsieur Delaroche! He doesn't care for me. Really! It's not worth—urgh! Keep your bloody hand off my mouth! Owwwww . . ."

"On one condition!" Richard's voice rang out over Amy's cries. The soldiers holding her froze. "You leave the girl alone. Otherwise there's no deal. No confession. No surrender. I want your solemn word, Delaroche, that the girl will be left here. *Unharmed.*"

Delaroche nodded. "Unharmed." The knife fell away from Amy's throat, and the hands yanking her bound arms behind her back slackened.

The little Frenchman's eyes gleamed with triumph. "Your mask, Gentian."

Richard's hands went to the lacings of his black mask.

"No!" Amy protested, as his gloved fingers plucked at the knot. "You mustn't!"

Amy pulled against the arms holding her, frantic to get to Richard before he could reveal his identity once and for all to Delaroche. She couldn't let him do it! She couldn't let him lose everything, all that he had worked and fought for and perhaps his life into the bargain, all because of her. If he did . . . Amy's stomach lurched as the knot gave and the strings loosened. If he did, she would be worse than Deirdre.

The mask tumbled to the ground.

An inarticulate murmur of distress rose from Amy's throat, inordinately loud in the hushed silence that had swept the alleyway. All eyes were riveted on Richard's pale face in the moonlight, on the straight line of his nose, the cool glimmer of his green eyes, the gilded gleam of his hair as he pushed back the hood of his cape, all the features that marked him damningly and irrevocably as Lord Richard Selwick, enemy of the French Republic.

"You can still run!" Amy cried desperately. "You don't have to do this, Richard!"

One by one, his black gloves joined his mask on the ground. His long, slim fingers, now bare, went to the frogs holding his cloak closed. Sweeping off the garment, Richard sketched an ironic bow.

"Here I am, Delaroche. Unmasked, unveiled, and at your service. Now release the girl."

With a snap of Delaroche's fingers, Amy tumbled, still bound, to the dirt. Using her shackled wrists as leverage, she scooted painfully towards Richard. Desperately, she tried to come up with a plan. If she could create a distraction . . . a fire, maybe? Only she had nothing with which to create fire, even if her hands had been free. Jane! Why wasn't Jane doing anything! Amy knew she was back there in the shadows, hiding and waiting, biding her time as only Jane could bide, but why oh why couldn't she just do something? Fling a match, cry murder, stumble in pretending to be a drunken manservant, anything!

Under Amy's horrified gaze, Delaroche wound a rope around Richard's outstretched wrists. Fifteen musket-bearing soldiers closed ranks around them, their high-crowned hats blocking Richard from Amy's sight.

"You won't get away with this!" she railed at the row of blue-clad backs, propelling herself unevenly forward across the ground. "The Pink Carnation will rescue him and see you hanged!"

Preoccupied with Richard, no one paid the slightest bit of attention, except one infantryman, towards the edge of the group, who turned back and jerked a finger at Amy. "What about the girl, sir?"

Without removing his eyes from his long-awaited prize, a bound (if not yet humbled) Purple Gentian, Delaroche shrugged.

"Leave her to the dogs."

As the booted feet receded into the distance, Amy could hear Delaroche utter, "We have much to talk about, you and I, Monsieur Selweeck. And you *will* talk."

Richard never looked back.

Amy stared after the retreating party of soldiers, her indignant cries frozen on her lips, the enormity of the situation only gradually beginning to dawn. She half expected to hear the sounds of a fray, to see a black-garbed figure break away from the group and dart for the shadows. But he didn't.

"Amy!" Jane bent anxiously over her. "Lean forward so I can untie you."

"They have Richard," Amy whispered incredulously.

"I know." Jane tugged at the tail of the rough-hewn piece of rope. "I saw."

"Why didn't you do anything?" Amy twisted towards Jane, chafing her sore wrists as Jane pulled the rope free.

"Amy, there were *fifteen* of them." Jane thriftily coiled the rope and looped it around her arm. "I considered going for help but it seemed more prudent to wait and see what happened before charging off."

Prudent. The word tasted sour on Amy's tongue. "Well, now you know." Amy stumbled to her feet. "So let's go after them!"

Jane grabbed her by the wrist, making Amy wince as her hand closed around skin chafed by the rope. "Not alone," Jane protested. "We'll be no use to him alone. They'll simply capture us and use us against him."

"As they already did." Amy's face twisted. "But we can't leave him there! We can't! Jane, the *Ministry of Police* has him! Do you know what they do to people? Oh, God . . . there's no time to be lost!"

"Stop that!" Jane shook Amy sharply. "What good do you think you'll do him running off after him alone?"

Amy stared at Jane with wide, horrified eyes. "What would you have me do? Sit and wait for him to be executed? Jane, I can't! I'd rather be caught and tortured!"

"We will save him." Jane took a deep breath, her own face pale and miserable in the moonlight. "We will. You wanted to be the Pink Carnation, Amy? Now's your chance. You need to *think* like the Pink Carnation. Not like . . . like the heroine of a silly horrid novel running pell-mell into disaster! Show some *sense*! We need reinforcements and we need a plan," Jane finished decisively.

Amy drew a shuddering breath, knowing Jane to be right, and hating it. "His family. We can go to Lord Richard's town house. There must be some members of his league there who can help us."

Amy didn't waste any more breath; she set off at a run. They both knew the reputation of the Ministry of Police for cruelty. Abuse, torture, even mention of the dark arts. Tales of English agents captured and never seen again. Or, worse— could it be worse?—released as vestiges of their former selves, their minds as broken as their bodies, babbling like village idiots as they limped along on crumpled limbs.

They ran down twisted streets, past drunken carousers, through puddles of filth. Jane slipped in a patch of mud, and Amy yanked her upright and hauled her forward.

Hideous thoughts chased Amy. Oh, heavens, Richard had been right; her involvement had been fatal for him. If he had never met her, he would still be free, not in the hands of a fanatical maniac intent on torturing him for both professional and personal reasons. If she hadn't been so credulous . . . why hadn't she realized that Delaroche's groom was parting with information far too freely? Even a child could have realized it was a trap! But, no, she, Amy, in all her hubris, had just assumed that their instant success was due to her innate knack for espionage, not because she was an unresisting pawn in the hands of the French Ministry of Police. If that weren't bad enough, she had kept Richard there arguing—what had possessed her to stand there bickering with him in the chambers of the Assistant Minister of Police? Good heavens, she couldn't have done him more disservice had she been in Delaroche's pay!

Being the Pink Carnation had seemed such a grand idea, thumbing her nose at Richard and at Revolutionary France all at once. Why had she never thought of the consequences? She *was* worse than Deirdre. At least the loathsome Deirdre had merely been thoughtless. She, Amy, had known the risks Richard ran as the Purple Gentian, and set out deliberately to thwart him. She ought to have foreseen the dangers. She ought to have *known*.

While her lungs twisted, and her leg muscles ached, Amy played her painful game of If. If she hadn't let wounded pride rule her . . . If, if, if. If she had only told him in the garden that she knew who he was, and that she loved him anyway.

If she could only have him back, she would beg him to forgive her. She would never ever quibble with him over trivialities again. She would revel in the luxury of just gazing at his face. And it wouldn't even matter if he loved her back, just so long as he was safe and well.

Amy clutched a tattered image of Richard, his green eyes glinting with mischief, his mobile lips twisted with amusement. Richard with his clever turns of phrase and moments of disarming boyishness. Richard taking her hand and teasing her about thorns.

They had only been to Lord Richard's house once before, for tea with Lady Uppington, and even Jane's excellent sense of direction wasn't enough to keep them from becoming hopelessly muddled in the tangled streets of Paris. A dangerously long amount of time elapsed before the two scrambled up the steps to Lord Richard's front door. Amy pounded anxiously with the big metal knocker, knocking over and over until the door jerked open. Amy tumbled over the threshold.

The silver-haired butler sniffed as though he smelled something nasty (which, as Amy's clothes had formerly belonged to an undergroom, he probably did), and nudged her recumbent form with one polished toe. "Tradesmen to the back," he said disdainfully.

The heavy wooden door began to close.

"Who is it, Stiles?" Lady Uppington's voice carried through the hallway, and in the crack of the door left open, Amy could just see her standing at the top of the stairs, like a guardian angel in robe and ribboned nightcap.

"It's Amy Balcourt and Jane Wooliston," called out Amy, struggling to her feet.

"We're sorry to call at such a late hour," Jane added politely.

"Do move away, Stiles, and let them in!" Lady Uppington declared, hurrying down the stairs. "What . . . ?" The marchioness enjoyed a rare moment of speechlessness as she surveyed Amy's and Jane's outlandish attire.

"It's Richard," Amy said urgently, grabbing her hand. "They've taken him. The Ministry of Police."

In the light of her candle, Lady Uppington's face went gray. She put the candle down abruptly on the newel of the stairs, and said, "Well, we shall just have to rescue him then, shan't we?"

"Mother?" Henrietta tumbled down the stairs in a flurry of white linen flounces. "Is something the matter? Oh, hello, Amy. What are you doing here?"

Meanwhile, Miles and Geoff had filtered into the foyer from a door down the hall, and the form of Lord Uppington could be seen at the top of the stairs. Lady Uppington set her jaw in a way that reminded Amy painfully of Richard and looked around the expectant faces. "Richard has been taken by the Ministry of Police. Uppington—"

The marquess didn't have to wait for his wife to finish the sentence. "I'll go to Whitworth at the embassy straightaway."

"Thank you." The marquess and marchioness exchanged a look that made Amy's throat go tight.

"What happened?" Henrietta scurried across the hall to Amy. "Did the mission go awry? And what was Richard doing there?"

"Mission? What mission?" As the marquess accepted his hat and coat from Stiles and hastily departed, Lady Uppington turned her attention back to Amy. And to Henrietta. Her anxious green eyes snapped with maternal alarm as she took in her daughter's diaphanous attire.

"Henrietta Anne Selwick, put on a dressing gown at once!"

Her words had somewhat the reverse of the desired effect, since both Miles and Geoff instantly snapped to attention. Miles's jaw plummeted, and his lips moved in what might have become a whistle had the female in question not been his best friend's sister. As it was, he couldn't quite restrain an incredulous, "Zounds, Hen!" Geoff had the grace to look embarrassed.

Henrietta ignored them both. "But I might miss something," she protested.

"You clearly already know about this so-called mission," Lady Uppington said ominously.

"But—"

"Go!"

Henrietta went.

Lady Uppington looked around the anxious group in the hall and seemed to come somewhat more to herself. "There's no point to us all standing about like this," she declared. "Let's all go sit down in the drawing room. Geoff, dear, have Stiles bring us some tea—we're going to need something to fortify us for the evening's activities. Amy, would you like to explain what happened?"

Thus marshaled like a small but well-disciplined army, they all followed Lady Uppington into the drawing room, while Amy explained the plan to beat Richard to the gold. She didn't explain the motivation behind it, but Lady Uppington's shrewd eyes wrinkled around the corners with something that would, at any other time, have been amusement.

"It was an excellent plan," Lady Uppington said, adding nostalgically, "I would have done the same myself." Seating herself in a large brocaded chair at the front of the room, she said briskly, "That's all neither here nor there. The important thing is getting Richard out. Geoff?"

"Yes, Lady Uppington?"

"Where will they have taken him?"

Geoff didn't hesitate before answering. "Delaroche has an

extra-special interrogation chamber he uses for important prisoners. He'll put Richard in a cell for a few hours, let him stew, and then transfer him to the interrogation chamber. None of the rooms on that level of the ministry have windows, so there's no breaking in that way."

"Could we infiltrate the guards?" asked Amy anxiously. "Knock them over the head, take their uniforms, that sort of thing?"

Geoff shook his head. "I wouldn't recommend it. There are too many of them."

Henrietta barreled through the door, hastily dressed in a dark, high-necked gown with all the buttons in the wrong holes. "Have I missed anything?"

"We're trying to rescue your brother," Lady Uppington replied.

"Oh, what about bashing the guards over their heads—"

"You're a bit late on that one," Miles cut her off. He looked her up and down, then, as if relieved to see the old, fully clothed Henrietta back, relaxed in his chair and added, "Miss Balcourt has already tried that one."

"Do you have a better idea?" Henrietta demanded, seating herself next to Amy.

"Now," interposed Lady Uppington tightly, "is not the time to bicker. Ah, the tea is here. Henrietta, why don't you pour?"

"I do have an idea, actually," Miles said, with a lofty look at Henrietta, who was scowling over the tea things. "Geoff and I could go to the ministry and pretend to turn ourselves in. Then we can turn on the guards and—"

"Bash them over their heads?" finished Henrietta, handing him a cup of tea.

"Precisely. You learn, my child."

"It sounds too uncertain," Jane broke in thoughtfully. Even wearing offensively dirty men's clothing and a penciled-on mustache, she still somehow contrived to look neat and composed. "It's too likely that they would secure you, leaving us with three people to rescue instead of one. I believe we need to move away from the whole subject of bashing, and think of something a bit more subtle."

"Infiltration!" blurted out Amy. The polite trappings of the tea party grated on her nerves, and she squirmed in her gilded chair. "Who could we disguise ourselves as?"

"Geoff does a smashing Fouché impression," volunteered Miles.

Five indignant pairs of eyes glowered at him. "I was serious!" Miles protested. "He does! And who better to have free access to the Ministry of Police than the Minister of Police? Think about it!"

Jane shook her head regretfully. "Unfortunately, Lord Pinchingdale-Snipe doesn't look at all like M Fouché."

"A large hat?"

"Miss Wooliston is right," countered Geoff, gulping down his third cup of tea in as many minutes. "Even a big hat can't disguise our differences in height, and the sentries there see him often enough to have a pretty good idea of what he looks like."

Amy stood abruptly. "Let's just think of something, for heaven's sake! Haven't you rescued people before?"

Geoff perked up for a moment, then shook his head. "Only from the Bastille. We've never tried to get anyone out of Delaroche's lair."

On that deflating note, Lord Uppington entered. It was plain to see from the droop of his shoulders that his own task had been equally fruitless.

"Whitworth was no help," he said wearily. "He had some sort of row with Bonaparte the other night—over Malta, he said. He was all but packing his own bags when I called. There's nothing he can do for Richard."

"So we are on our own," said Lady Uppington. "As we expected."

The marquess took her hand and squeezed it. "As we expected, my dear." He cast a keen look at Geoff. "I suppose this Delaroche chap won't be susceptible to bribery."

"Not a chance of it, sir."

"I feared as much. There's nothing worse than an incorruptible madman."

Jane's lashes lifted over clear gray eyes. "There might be another solution, sir. Amy, do you remember the soot on our teeth?" she asked in the infuriatingly enigmatic way she had whenever she had a truly inspired idea.

Amy nodded hesitantly, trying to figure out what Jane could mean by it. "Yes, of course. When we used to . . . Oh! Servants! That's it!"

"Could you enlighten the rest of us?" asked Miles.

"Do you want to use servants to storm the ministry and rescue Richard?" Henrietta looked up interestedly from her cup of tea. "That would be splendid."

"No." Amy shook her head so rapidly she knocked off her cap. "We could *be* servants. Surely someone must clean the Ministry? And who would ever look at a charwoman with a bucket? Jane, you're brilliant!"

"An excellent idea!" seconded Lady Uppington. "You're quite right. Nobody ever looks closely at staff. Geoff, dear, you can forge us some sort of pass, can't you?"

"I do have a copy of Delaroche's seal," Geoff admitted, "but, surely, you can't be thinking of going yourself?"

The room broke into an alarming hullabaloo as Lord Uppington, Geoff, and Miles tried to remonstrate with Lady Uppington and Amy—as Amy quickly made quite clear that the only way to prevent her going was to lock her in a tower without doors or windows, of which there were few in the vicinity. Miles kept insisting that as Richard's best friend, he really ought to go; the marquess thumped for his paternal privileges; and Geoff's usually quiet voice rose to unusual levels as he reminded them all that only he actually knew where Richard was being kept.

"You would all make appalling women." Lady Uppington cut forcibly through the babble. "And if Amy and I are caught—yes, I do admit the possibility!—they are far more likely to deal leniently with us than with you."

"Besides," pointed out Jane coolly, "someone still needs to intercept the Swiss gold."

"Oh hell," Miles groaned. "The Swiss gold."

"The Pink Carnation will steal the gold just as we planned," Jane said firmly. "With the Purple Gentian incarcerated, there's all the more need for the Pink Carnation. But if Amy is rescuing Lord Richard, we need a replacement for her."

Miles nodded, hair flopping up and down over his brow. "Count me in."

"And me!" chimed in Henrietta.

"You," said Lady Uppington tersely, "are staying home. One child in the hands of the French is more than enough for any mother to have to bear. It's settled, then," she said, before Henrietta could launch into full-scale protest. "Amy and I will rescue Richard; Geoff, I believe you should come along with us as guide; Miles, Jane, and Uppington will intercept the Swiss gold. Shall we?"

The entire party surged to their feet, shoving teacups back on the tray, and quibbling over details. Amy declared her intent to get clothes from the servants' quarters; Jane directed a footman to take a note to Miss Gwen to alert her to join them at Lord Richard's house; and Henrietta's voice rose in agitated protest.

"But, Mama . . ."

"No buts, Henrietta!"

Henrietta pressed her lips together in extreme irritation. "I'm not going to waste time by teasing to come along. But you've all forgotten something. How are we going to get Richard out of Paris?"

Miles dropped his teacup. The point was so simple, and so essential, that Amy couldn't believe that none of them had thought of it. From the looks of stupefaction on the faces of Richard's family and friends, none of them had considered it either. Perhaps, thought Amy rapidly, they could secrete Richard in the Hotel de Balcourt till the hullabaloo quieted down and the French agents had some other poor hero to persecute.

Jane suddenly smiled. "Oh, I think we have an answer to that. There is a certain gentleman of our acquaintance who possesses both a carriage and a boat, which I believe he will be more than happy to place at our disposal."

"Marston!" exclaimed Amy.

"The very one," agreed Jane. "If someone would be so kind as to remind him of some papers of his I hold, I have no doubt he'll be agreeable."

"Give me his direction, and I'll see to him." Lord Uppington strode across the room to Jane.

Jane nodded her thanks. "It might be wise to take the precaution of replacing Marston's coachman and sending some of our own men ahead to Calais to secure the boat. I wouldn't trust Mr. Marston's word."

Miles, for once all seriousness, yanked the bellpull. "Richard's coachman can take care of the carriage, and Stiles and five of the footmen can ride ahead for the boat. I'll speak to them directly."

"Can we go now?" prompted Amy anxiously, halfway out the door.

Following her, Lady Uppington stuck her head around the door of the drawing room one last time.

"Have the carriage brought to the Hotel de Balcourt," instructed Lady Uppington. "If these French have any sense, they'll be watching this house. I don't think they have much in the way of sense, but we can't rely on that. We'll meet you there by one. If we're not there . . ."

Amy hurried ahead of Lady Uppington towards the servants' quarters, blocking out her last words. That the plan might go awry was not to be thought of. Any more than she could bear to think of what Delaroche might be doing to Richard at this very moment.

Chapter Thirty-seven

B ooted feet slapped to a stop outside the door of Richard's cell.

Levering himself on his bound wrists, he wriggled to a standing position from the floor where the guards had thrown him with unnecessary force several hours before. He had informed them that the use of that much force was a waste of their energies, but they had just grunted in response to his kindly professional advice. They had also proved churlish in not giving him opportunity for the escape ploy in which they bent over to untie him, and he bashed them over the head with his bound wrists, then stole their clothes. A pity, that. It had worked so well in 1801. Maybe the word had spread. At any rate, they had avoided that prospect by simply declining to untie him. So Richard had spent the past several hours reclining, still bound, on the straw-scattered floor, his mind turning anxiously elsewhere. Not to Delaroche and the tortures the disturbed little man was arranging for him, but to Amy, lying bound and helpless on the cobblestones outside Delaroche's lodging.

A key squeaked in the lock. The door shuddered. "Open it, you fools!" a voice thundered.

"Um, it's stuck, sir," someone quavered.

A very loud curse from the other side of the door, and then the door shuddered again and popped open. Two sentries tumbled to the floor. Behind them stood . . . Delaroche. He really ought to be a comical figure, Richard thought. Small and skinny, dressed all in black like a cut-rate Oliver Cromwell, strutting forward in boots that could use a polish. Richard hopped forward on his hobbled legs and executed what he hoped was a mocking bow.

"So," Delaroche snarled, "we meet at last."

"Actually," Richard responded blandly, "I believe we were first introduced at Mme Bonaparte's salon, if I remember correctly."

"Your powerful friends cannot help you here. You are in *my* domain now." Delaroche laughed. Evilly.

"You should really get that rattle in your throat looked at," suggested Richard, peering earnestly at Delaroche. "It must be from all this loafing about in drafty dungeons. Terrible for your health, you know."

"It is *your* health you should fear for." The evil laughter was beginning to grate on Richard's nerves. Not to mention that his neck hurt from trying to keep an eye on Delaroche as the man paced in circles around him, his boots crunching on the straw and debris scattered about the floor.

Delaroche strode on bandy legs to the door, clapped his hands together, and bellowed, "Prepare the interrogation chamber!"

"The regular interrogation chamber, sir?" one guard ventured, keeping well on the other side of the stone doorframe.

"Oh no." Delaroche unleashed another of his humorless laughs. "Take him to the extra-special interrogation chamber!"

It didn't raise Richard's spirits that the guard himself blanched at the suggestion.

Down several flights of stairs, nestled in a catacomb of underground cells, Delaroche flung open the door of his extra-special interrogation chamber with housewifely pride.

"Behold!" Delaroche crowed as the guards gave Richard a little push towards the center of the room, fleeing back towards the corridor.

Skidding a bit on the straw that covered the floor, Richard beheld. He and Geoff had heard rumors about the extra-special interrogation chamber—it was the sort of thing that was whispered from agent to agent—and had even speculated on breaking into it, as part of their what-can-we-do-to-annoy-the-Ministry-of-Police campaign. But they had never gotten around to it. And Richard had always, in the back of his mind, assumed that the whole extra-special interrogation chamber was most likely a rumor fabricated to terrify the enemies of the Republic. Sure, maybe Delaroche had a little room somewhere where he quizzed his hapless victims; maybe he even owned a pair of thumbscrews; but a whole torture chamber?

The whole idea was just too medieval, too melodramatic, too . . . Delaroche.

Damn. He should have known better.

"Friends of yours?" he inquired, waving a hand at the skulls standing on pikes around the walls.

"No," Delaroche bit out. "But they'll soon be friends of *yours*."

Richard didn't much care for the sound of that. He was also running out of dazzling repartee in the face of what looked like an increasingly bleak situation. Delaroche was more of a madman than even he had realized. While the skulls might be a bit dusty, the extensive collection of torture tools arrayed about the room gleamed sharp and clean. Delaroche must have scoured the dungeons of castles across the breadth of Europe to acquire his toys, which looked like they included not only the full collection of the Marquis de Sade, but a representative sampling of the best the Inquisition had to offer. In his quick sweep of the room—it wouldn't do to take his eyes off Delaroche for too long—Richard noted no fewer than two iron maidens, thumbscrews in ten different sizes, and a deluxe rack. Delaroche greeted each implement of torture personally—as far as Richard could make out, he hadn't named them (though Richard wouldn't have put it past him to do that), but he stopped by each one to touch spikes and grind levers with macabre tenderness.

Across the room, Delaroche carefully eased a double-headed ax onto a specially designed stand that showed off both blades to their best advantage. "Where shall we begin?" Delaroche mused, crossing his arms across his chest as he strutted toward Richard. Richard had rather hoped he wouldn't get to that stage for a while yet. Didn't he have more instruments of torture to caress first? "Something appropriate, something tasteful. Torture is an art, you know," Delaroche chided. "A skill that must be practiced with care and finesse. What is it that you use in your English prisons? The rack? Your fists?"

"Actually," Richard drawled, "we use a little thing called due process."

Delaroche looked momentarily intrigued, then shrugged. "Whatever that is, it is the work of amateurs to use the same instrument for all crimes! Here, we very carefully match the punishment to the crime."

"How very refined."

"Your compliments will not help you, Selweeck. I could give you a painful poison in that tea you English love so well, nothing that will kill you—no, no!—but something that will make you writhe with pain and beg to confess. Or I could cut off an appendage for every enemy of the state you stole from Mme Guillotine. . . ."

"Why not start with my head?" Richard suggested.

While Delaroche vacillated among his toys, Richard once again twisted his wrists to test the slack in his bonds. There wasn't any. It could have been worse, though. At least they had bound his wrists in front of him, instead of behind. If Delaroche would come close enough, he had the chance of mustering enough force to strike him a blow on the head, something the Assistant Minister of Police was clearly not expecting. Ideally, he'd follow that up with a kick, but his feet were tied tightly enough that in the attempt he would more likely bowl himself over than his adversary.

"Ah! I have it!" Richard had stopped listening about four suggestions ago, but the glee in Delaroche's voice yanked his attention away from his escape plans. "Since you are so fond of the company of the fairer sex," Delaroche sneered, "we shall start with an introduction to the lady in the corner."

He gestured towards the iron maiden, and Richard's eyes involuntarily followed. It was, most certainly, the most deluxe iron maiden imaginable. Like the mummy cases Richard had seen in Egypt, the casing had been painted to resemble a woman. Knowledge of what lay inside suggested a rapacious slant to that red mouth, and a hungry glint to the painted eyes.

Delaroche grasped the handle cleverly concealed among the lady's red-and-gold skirts; inch by ominous inch, the gaudy façade of the iron maiden jerked open, revealing its spiky intestines.

For the first time in a long and successful career, it occurred to Richard that he might actually be facing death, a very painful death, and that there was little more he could do to outwit it.

Death was, of course, a possibility he had considered in the past. Percy had counseled them all very seriously about it when they joined the League of the Scarlet Pimpernel. Mortality hadn't seemed all that pressing at the time, but then, after Tony's death, Richard had been convinced that his own turn was bound to come at any moment, his life forfeit for Tony's. Given the suicidal recklessness with which he had rushed into missions for months thereafter, death had seemed a probability, if not an inevitability. But he had survived. Fate was funny like that.

All those times he'd contemplated his potential demise—in the moments before he'd crawled through a Temple prison window, or plunged into a group of armed French agents—he had consoled himself with the thought that he'd left a legacy of which he could be proud. He had done something heroic with his life. How many men could say the same?

Blast it all, why wasn't that enough anymore? Glory, he reminded himself. Think of Ajax, of Achilles. Glory, glory, glory.

But all he could think about was Amy.

When he tried to picture Henry V, plunging into the breach at Honfleur, instead he saw Amy, popping out from underneath a desk. Instead of Achilles roaring beneath the walls of Troy, there was Amy, swinging a punch at Georges Marston. Amy, Amy, everywhere—and usually somewhere she wasn't supposed to be, Richard thought, with what might have turned into a grin, if Delaroche hadn't tested one of the spikes of the iron maiden, and sprung away, holding a handkerchief to his bleeding finger.

Devil take it, he didn't want to die. Not that he'd ever really *wanted* to die, even after Tony, but now . . . how in the blazes was he supposed to tell Amy he loved her if he was dead?

Delaroche dropped the bloody handkerchief and bore down upon Richard.

"Selweeck," he panted triumphantly, "meet your doom!"

Richard hoped to hell that Miles and Geoff had come up with a rescue plan.

"I didn't think there would be so many of them," whispered Amy.

The uneven stones of the wall rasped against Amy's back as she cautiously tilted her head around the corner of the corridor for a second glance. Drat. They were still there. Three sentries in dark blue coats, muskets at their sides, ranged in front of a large wooden door banded with iron. There were five other doors on the corridor, four of them mere grilles, revealing the cells within. When she craned her neck, Amy could see a hint of movement in one, and something that might have been a bony arm in another. The fifth portal was a smaller version of the guarded door, a heavy oaken affair hinged and studded with iron, with a tiny shuttered window at the height of a man's head. Amy's gaze darted back to the largest portal. The window was closed, the thick wood of the door and the massive stone walls muffling any sounds from within. But Amy had no doubts that they were finally within view of Delaroche's extra-special interrogation chamber. And Richard.

And three armed sentries.

And she had thought that just getting into the building had been nerve-racking. There had been that heart-stopping moment when the guard at the front entrance of the Ministry of Police had demanded their passes. He had peered at the seal Geoff had purloined from Delaroche with a care that could denote either suspicion or poor eyesight. Amy and Lady Uppington had avoided looking at one another, lest they betray their fear in a guilty glance. But after an agonizing hour of scrutiny (which in reality had been thirty seconds at the most), the guard had shoved the papers back at Amy, with a grunted "All in order."

He had, nonetheless, demanded to see the contents of their pails. "The minister thinks there might be trouble tonight," he growled by way of explanation, as the water sloshed in Amy's bucket, and the rag that had been draped over the side slid down into the liquid with a slow plop. Amy had endeavored to look nonchalant, but the unaccustomed bulk of her dagger's sheath burned against her calf. She tried to stand as a charwoman would stand, perhaps with a bit of a slump from the weight of the bucket.

Glancing over at Lady Uppington, Amy couldn't help but be impressed by Jane's handiwork and the older woman's acting abilities. There wasn't a hint of the English marchioness left in the woman beside her. Lady Uppington's silvering blond tresses had been liberally combed through with ashes, to turn them a rough, dirty gray, and then covered with an equally sooty kerchief, that looked as though it had served as both a cleaning rag and someone's handkerchief before being pressed into duty as a head covering. Her tattered brown dress hung shapelessly from her form as she slouched forward, unspeakably aged, clutching two voluminous shawls around her shoulders to warm her old bones and make up for the ripped and patched state of her sleeves. Even her face looked different. Jane had accentuated her crow's-feet with a careful web of lines drawn in charcoal, but it was more than that. Something about the slack hang of the mouth, the tired droop of the eyelids.

Past the first obstacle, Lady Uppington and Amy had scrubbed their way down the midnight hallways of the Ministry of Police. Torches along the walls cast flickering reflections in the water in their pails as they lurched through the halls in search of the staircase that would lead them down to the dungeons and Richard. They stayed in the pools of light, rather than the shadows. "Less suspicious that way," Miles had advised. "Why would a washerwoman hide unless she wasn't really a washerwoman?"

The flagstones of the ministry provided echoing warning of anyone's approach—unless that person had, like Amy and Lady Uppington, removed their shoes. But the only people to pass them had been soldiers, whose booted and spurred feet gave the alarm in ample time for Lady Uppington and Amy to fall to their knees and pretend deep absorption in grime removal.

All their earlier trials paled when compared to the prospect of having to fight their way past three sentries with what Amy had to confess to herself was a fairly meager arsenal. In her daydreams of espionage, she had always been armed with an epée and a pistol (never mind that she had never been taught how to use either), and an escort composed of well-muscled members of the League of the Purple Gentian, who presumably knew how to employ both sword and firearms. Never had she imagined that she would find herself in the dungeons of the most closely guarded building in Paris, accompanied by an aging English noblewoman, with an armory consisting of one dagger strapped to her calf, one elderly dueling pistol (courtesy of Lord Uppington, who had last fired it in 1772), and a bottle of drugged brandy. Jane had insisted on the brandy, over Miles's protests that opiates had little place in hand-to-hand combat. Amy supposed they could always use the bottle as a club.

A dagger, a pistol, and a bottle against three large men armed with muskets.

"Do you think he'll have more men inside with him?" Amy whispered to Lady Uppington, leaning over to make sure her dagger was still safely in its sheath.

"We'll face that when we get there. Or rather"—Lady Uppington patted the dueling pistol tucked beneath her voluminous shawl—"*they* will face *us*. Ready, my dear?"

Amy loosened the ribbons securing her bodice and edged her neckline down to the verge of immodesty. Four weapons, she thought with a surge of optimism. After all, even Revolutionary guards couldn't be entirely proof against the male propensity to make utter cakes of themselves when faced with a shapely female form. Jane had garbed her with just that prospect in mind, ransacking the wardrobes of Richard's maids until she had found a low-cut blouse that laced up the front, and a wide woolen skirt that stopped an inch short of Amy's ankles and accentuated the sway of her hips.

"Ready," Amy whispered.

Dropping to hands and knees, the two women rounded the corner, swirling their dirty cloths over the flagstones. *Slosh, swish. Slosh, swish.* Two yards closer to the guarded door ... another swipe of the dirty cloth and another yard disappeared under a slick film of water. Amy wondered if the three guards, visible to her only as three pairs of boot-tops and three pairs of black gaiters, would realize that their charwomen were scrubbing very lackadaisically and neglecting whole swaths of floor. Although, from the state of the flagstones, it didn't appear that anyone had scrubbed down in the dungeons for a very long time. Ugh, was that clotted blood? Amy scuttled around a particularly nasty brownish stain, yanking her woolen skirts out of the way.

"You!" One set of boots detached itself from the row and tromped up to Amy.

Amy's head flew up, past black gaiters and dark blue breeches, at which point her neck refused to bend back any further. Settling back on her knees, she tilted her head up to a broad face sporting three days' worth of fair stubble. The guard who had stepped forward was the largest of the three, and clearly their leader, a hulking Goliath of a man, with jowls sagging around a beefy face, and a shock of pale hair of an indeterminate shade. He wouldn't be easily subdued, thought Amy grimly. Behind him, poised on either side of the massive door, the two others looked on. If the first guard was Goliath, then the second guard, considerably shorter than his companions, had to be David; Amy's gaze caught him halfway through a yawn. As for the third, he was lean and dark; a thin mustache, not unlike the one Amy had drawn on Jane's face earlier in the evening, shadowed his lips. There was a dangerous stillness about him, as though he was holding himself taut, waiting to spring. Like a slingshot, decided Amy. He would be one to watch carefully.

"You!" the big soldier—Goliath—barked again.

"Yes, sir?"

"What do you think you're doing down here?"

Amy glanced down at her bucket, then over at Lady Uppington, who continued to ply her dirty cloth in slow circles, around and around the same flagstone. "Cleaning, sir?" she replied.

"I can see that." The guard rasped his hand through the stubble on his chin. "Did no one tell you you're not to clean down here?"

He sounded irritable, but not suspicious. Amy breathed a silent sigh of relief and feigned confusion. "No, sir," she said eagerly, making a show of stumbling to her feet and brushing off her patched skirts. "We was just told to scrub. Did you hear that, Ma?"

"Yes, yes," Lady Uppington croaked in cracked tones, the one word she could be trusted to say without alerting a listener to her English accent.

The guard nodded. "I can see as how it's an honest mistake. Big place like this . . ."

Amy nodded enthusiastically; the guard didn't seem to notice as she edged a few inches closer to the door with the movement. "You don't know what a relief it is not to have to do this floor, too. Why, we thought we wouldn't see our beds before dawn, and me ma, well, she has another job days, at a big, fancy house in the Faubourg Saint-Germain." Amy drawled the last name with the contempt appropriate to any good revolutionary.

"Long night," the guard agreed with a nod.

"Yes, yes," Lady Uppington cawed again in her crone's cackle.

To Amy's surprise, the guard actually smiled. "Agreeable woman, your ma."

Lady Uppington smiled broadly in acknowledgment, revealing a mouthful of blackened teeth. Amy had always known that trick with the soot and gum would come in handy someday. "Yes, yes."

Amy might have been tempted to laugh, had she not caught the hint of a sound from behind the door. Any potential amusement at Lady Uppington's performance drained away from Amy instantly. Richard was behind that door, being questioned and possibly—no, probably—tortured. Enough chitchat.

Amy flung back her shoulders and leaned forward so that her loosened bodice gaped. So did the short guard. His jaw fell appreciatively open, and his musket sagged several inches. Following up on her advantage, Amy twined a dark curl around one finger. "Long night for you all, too, ain't it?"

"Oh, it's not all that bad," David babbled, staggering forward a few steps from the door to get a better view of Amy's charms. One down, she thought. Lady Uppington was nudging her bucket slowly along the flagstones, closer and closer to the door.

Amy took a little step back, drawing David out farther from the door, and focused the force of her smile on Goliath. "Must get pretty boring just standing here all night," she said with a show of sympathy. "Don't know how I'd stay on my feet that long. But then, I'm not a big, strong man like you."

Something like a snort emerged from the shawl-covered form of Lady Uppington, but Goliath's chest puffed out. "Doesn't take much strength," he said gruffly.

"Just staying power," put in the little one, waggling his eyebrows suggestively.

Amy wasn't quite sure what he meant, but from the accompanying leer, it was obviously meant to be prurient, so she grinned back at him as though she understood and waggled her eyebrows back for good measure, with an extra dip designed to show a maximum amount of cleavage.

The only one who didn't show any sign of succumbing to Amy's charm or her bosom was Slingshot, who stood just as firmly at his post as he had five minutes before, his hands just as firmly on the stock of his musket. And he was eyeing Amy's antics with a decidedly inimical eye. Drat! Either he was fanatically devoted to duty, or smarter than the others, and had smelled a rat. Neither option suited Amy.

A rat. Amy's face almost broke into a genuine grin as an

idea hit. That was how she would disarm Slingshot! Goliath was still modestly disclaiming any extra standing abilities. Amy gave an agitated squeal—not loud enough to disturb the inhabitants of the room, but just shrill enough to get the attention of all three guards.

"Raaaaaaaat!" she cried, yanking her skirt up around her ankles and hopping from one foot to the other. "Ooooh! Ooooh! There's a raaaaat! Save me!"

She flung herself straight at Slingshot. Taken by surprise, the guard staggered sideways—away from the door. Amy grabbed his arm, and yanked him back towards the center of the corridor, squealing and hopping all the while.

"There!" she panted, pointing a quavering finger at an imaginary spot down the hall. "I saw it right there! All dark and furry with them little sharp teeth! Ooooooh!" She flung both arms around Slingshot, immobilizing him in the middle of the hallway. Through the crook of his arm, she could see Lady Uppington, poised right outside the heavy oak door. But she wasn't opening it. Amy made little flapping motions with her hands. Lady Uppington shook her head. Drat! What was she waiting for?

Amy frowned. Lady Uppington mimed glugging noises—and hurriedly bent again to the floor as David glanced her way. Right. The brandy.

Goliath patted Amy heavily on the shoulder. "There, there, miss. It's gone now."

Amy whirled away from Slingshot, making sure to keep one arm linked through his, and gazed up at Goliath with big anxious eyes. "Are you sure? *That* big it were." She sketched with one hand. "I could just *feel* it brushing against my leg."

Amy yanked up her skirts and stared down at the limbs in question. Three pairs of masculine eyes followed.

"I'll keep the big, bad rat off your legs," the little one offered with a leer.

"I think . . ." Amy sagged artistically against Slingshot. He might have been staring at her ankle with the rest, but she still had a feeling that he'd bolt for his post the minute she released him. "I think I need a drop of brandy." She pulled the bottle out of the large pocket in her voluminous skirt, uncorked it, and, turning her head to the side, made a show of drinking deeply.

"Greedy me!" She giggled, ostentatiously wiping droplets off her chin. "Would any of you gentlemen like a drop?"

"We're not supposed to . . . ," began Goliath, with a longing glance at the flask.

Amy thrust the bottle at him and batted her eyelashes. "Oh, go on! I won't tell!"

"Yes, go on," urged David. "But leave some for me!"

Goliath took a long swig and passed the bottle to David, who glugged greedily, and offered it to Slingshot. The dark man shook his head. "We're on duty," he cautioned with a glower.

"What harm can it—"

Thud!

David broke off midsentence as the dungeon door swung open, banging into the wall. The ragged form of Lady Uppington darted through. Slingshot made a belated grab for Amy as she hastily yanked her arm from his, sprinting after Lady Uppington. The other two guards stood frozen with surprise, as, through the open door, the ragged old charwoman drew forth an elegant gold-chased dueling pistol from the folds of her grimy shawl.

Lady Uppington leveled her husband's pistol at Delaroche with the skill of an assured duelist.

"Drop those thumbscrews and step away from my son."

Chapter Thirty-eight

❧∾⌘∾❧

"Mother?" Richard gasped. Good God, Delaroche hadn't even started torturing him, and already he was hallucinating. But that certainly looked like his mother, and right behind her was ... Amy?

Richard blinked. It was undeniably Amy—and a good deal of Amy was on view thanks to the unlaced state of her blouse.

"Don't even think of moving," Lady Uppington snapped at Delaroche as Amy sprinted past her and made straight for Richard. Behind her three guards, one fat, one short, one tall and thin, crammed through the entrance and stumbled to a stop just short of Lady Uppington and her pistol.

"Did he hurt you?" Amy grabbed at Richard's bound hands, and began plucking at the complicated series of knots. "I don't see any blood."

Amy concentrated on picking the fibers free from Richard's wrists, trying not to look at the iron maiden that gaped open in the corner of the room. The straw underfoot pricked at Amy's bare feet and the stench, a dank stench of rooms long unaired, with a fetid hint of something even more distressing, of blood and fear, made Amy's stomach clench. She dug her nails into the rope.

Over Amy's bent head, Richard saw his mother carefully circle so that she could keep the guards within her sights as well as Delaroche.

"Drop those muskets! Drop them, I said!" Lady Uppington harrumphed in annoyance. Three dull thuds followed.

Lady Uppington glowered over the sights of her pistol. "If any of you so much as consider moving, I shall shoot Monsieur Delaroche. Do you understand?"

Much shifting from foot to foot and mumbling ensued from the guards.

"No talking!" admonished Lady Uppington with a wave of her silver-handled pistol that made Delaroche flinch. "Oh, don't be such a coward, you nasty little man. I assure you, I'm a crack shot. I won't hit you unless I *intend* to hit you."

As far as Richard knew, his mother had never been near a pistol in her life. But who really knew what women got up to in their spare time? It was a terrifying thought. But it wasn't quite as terrifying as the sight of Amy reaching under her skirts and sweeping up with a dagger in her hand.

"The rope is all bunched together," she explained in response to his horrified glance. "I can't untie it."

"How in the blazes did you get in here?" Richard asked dazedly, trying to keep his eyes off the blade sawing back and forth between some very vital veins. A fiber snapped and he felt the rope slacken a fraction.

"I'll explain later." Amy cast a quick, anxious look at the three exceedingly restless guards. Richard flinched as the knife nearly went into his palm.

How long until the sleeping draft took effect? Jane had emptied well over ten doses of the white powder into the small bottle of brandy, enough, she had promised Amy, to put an elephant to sleep for a week. Goliath might look a bit like an elephant, but neither he nor David showed any sign of succumbing to lengthy slumber, and Amy had her doubts as to how much longer Lady Uppington could hold them back. Could Jane have been mistaken about the dosage? David yawned, but, then, he had been yawning before, and it was well past midnight. True, both the big man's and the little man's movements seemed slower, but that might be a result of Lady Uppington's pistol, not the drug.

"Ouch!" Richard yelped.

"Sorry, sorry," Amy muttered, turning her attention back to his hands. Another fiber snapped, and another. With a determined twist of his wrists, Richard broke free of the rope.

Amy dropped to her knees and began frantically sawing on the ropes binding Richard's legs. She didn't like the way that Slingshot was eyeing Lady Uppington, or the way Delaroche was edging closer to a lethal-looking double-headed ax mounted on a crimson velvet stand.

"I'll take over." Richard leaned over, wafting Amy away

from his legs. Between his mother holding a gun on Delaroche and Amy untying him, he was beginning to feel uncomfortably peripheral to his own rescue. Miles would never let him hear the end of it. Hell, he'd never be able to show his face in male company again. He might as well resign his memberships in his clubs and join a sewing circle. His mother, blast it, was getting far too much enjoyment out of poking Delaroche in the ribs with her pistol.

"Stop!" Lady Uppington snapped as the little guard staggered a few paces sideways. A few steps closer to the pile of muskets. The little guard stopped, swaying on his feet.

"Sleepy," yawned the little guard, sagging against the wall.

Richard wrenched at the knots binding his legs, pulling a tail of rope loose with a satisfied grunt. Nearly free.

Thump!

Straw and dust scattered in all directions as the large guard fell heavily to his knees and toppled over facedown on the floor. His smaller colleague gave another large yawn and tumbled on top of him, snoring. Delaroche wrenched his head around in shock. So, too, did a startled and delighted Lady Uppington. Her pistol wavered forgotten in her hand for a mere moment as she beamed at the small pile of sleeping men.

That moment was all Slingshot needed. Moving with all the coiled energy Amy had feared, he knocked the pistol out of Lady Uppington's hand and grabbed her from behind, wrenching her back with such force that her feet rose off the ground. The pistol skittered across the straw-strewn dungeon floor.

Dropping the dagger with a clatter, Amy dove for the pistol—as did Delaroche. Hampered by her broad skirts, Amy pounced on the pistol just as Delroche's bony hand swept it up off the flagstones. Her hand clutched empty air and a handful of stray straws. Her left arm banged painfully against the flagstones as she plummeted heavily forward. Winded, Amy gasped for air, but her breath caught in her throat as the long barrel of a silver-and-gold dueling pistol filled her vision.

Amy scrabbled at the dirty floor, hastily scooting backwards as Delaroche followed, a self-satisfied smile on his angular face.

Kicking her legs free of the enveloping folds of her skirt, she lurched to her feet. Delaroche followed her movements with the pistol. Behind Delaroche, Amy could hear the sounds of Lady Uppington's scrimmage with Slingshot, but she didn't dare take her eyes off the gleaming pistol barrel pointing directly at her heart. To her left, she could hear Richard's labored breathing and the desperate scrape of the dagger against the ropes that still bound his legs.

"You, Mlle Balcourt"—Delaroche stepped deliberately forward, forcing Amy to slink backwards, her eyes fastened on the pistol—"have outlived your usefulness. You have become . . . how do you say in your barbaric tongue? Ah, yes. A nuisance. But not, I think"—Delaroche herded Amy inexorably backwards—"for much longer."

Amy skittered to a stop as a disquieting smile disfigured Delaroche's thin face. Wrenching her head around, she froze as her horrified gaze encountered the bristling embrace of the iron maiden, two feet behind her. Amy made an inadvertent mewing noise of distress. That . . . he couldn't . . .

"You fiend!" she gasped.

"As you wish," he replied with a smirk. "Now, if you would be so kind?" Delaroche waved the pistol in a macabre parody of politeness.

Amy cast a quick, panicky gaze around her. To her right, the open lid of the iron maiden blocked a sideways leap. To her left . . . Amy's breath rushed out of her lungs in a grateful sob as Richard bounded to her side. With one fluid movement, he yanked her out of the path of the iron maiden and positioned himself between Amy and Delaroche. A ragged tail of rope still trailed from his left leg.

"You've had your fun for the night, Delaroche," he said grimly, brandishing Amy's dagger. "Now it's time for you to fight like a man."

Delaroche snarled.

"Richard," Amy whispered, "he still has a pistol."

"Mother!" Richard's eyes didn't leave Delaroche. "Is that blasted thing loaded?"

"I don't—urgh!" Slingshot tried to clap his hand over Lady Uppington's mouth, but she administered a sharp elbow to the rib. "—know, darling!"

"Brilliant," muttered Richard, circling Delaroche to put the maximum distance between himself and the iron maiden. Trust his mother to bluff her way into the dungeons of the Ministry of Police with a possibly unloaded pistol.

"There is one way to find out," Delaroche chortled. He aimed the pistol at Richard's heart. "Farewell, Selweeeck."

Amy struck at Delaroche's arm as his finger closed over the trigger, knocking his aim sideways. The pistol discharged, knocking a fragment of stone off the wall. Make that a loaded pistol, Richard concluded as he came up from his defensive roll. The force of the recoil sent Delaroche reeling several steps backwards. Amy sneezed uncontrollably as acrid black smoke trailed from the pistol.

Delaroche stared in alarm at the smoking firearm. With a sudden movement, he dropped the useless pistol and darted for the double-sided ax.

"Richard!" Amy screamed. She tugged at a broadsword mounted on the wall between two grinning skulls. The weight of the weapon sent her stumbling backwards. Richard raced to her side, grabbing the sword from her just as Delaroche wrenched the ax free of its mount. "Here, take this," he ordered, pressing her dagger back into her hand. "Free Mother."

Delaroche swung at Richard, the double blade arcing in a deadly circle through the torchlight. Richard jumped back, leaving the edge of the ax to strike sparks against the stone of the wall. Richard tried to heft his sword one-handed, as he would an epée; his wrist nearly snapped under the strain. Hastily readjusting both hands on the hilt of the weapon and raising it with an effort, Richard cursed softly. Angelo's fencing academy had never prepared him for this. Devil take it, this was the sort of sword one of his ancestors might have wielded at Agincourt. It had been made for burly barbarians wearing armor and riding massive warhorses—not a civilized nineteenth-century gentleman accustomed to dealing with the niceties of epées. Hell! Richard swung again, a clumsy stroke that missed Delaroche by half a foot.

Clang! The ax clashed against the broadsword, taking a chip out of the blade. Reverberations trembled up Richard's arms.

Who would have thought that Delaroche would have so much strength in him?

Richard retreated, trying to remember everything he had read in his inquisitive boyhood about medieval warfare. It wasn't much. Just something about having to strike from above rather than stab with a broadsword, and he wasn't even sure that was right.

Delaroche's ax whistled by him again; Richard jumped back as the blade passed within an inch of his abdomen. Delaroche staggered with the force of the swing.

Getting the feel of his weapon, Richard swung again at Delaroche, hoping to catch him off balance. He missed, but the weapon moved more smoothly this time, and his adversary stumbled backwards, the ax dragging visibly. Richard's lips curved into a predatory grin.

Amy's ears rang with the wild clatter of their weapons as she ran to the aid of Lady Uppington, still struggling with her captor on the other side of the room. Lady Uppington's kerchief had been torn off and her sooty hair straggled wildly around her face. The skin around one eye was already beginning to purple and swell, but Lady Uppington fought on undaunted, kicking at her assailant's calves with her bare feet as he tried to pin down her flailing arms. Blood trickled down Slingshot's face from a series of nasty scratches that raked from eye to jaw.

"Unhand me, you vile, vile man!" she panted. "Didn't your mother"—*kick*—"teach you any manners?"

"Don't you be saying anything about my mother!" With a growl, Slingshot's hands shifted from Lady Uppington's arms to her throat. Lady Uppington made little choking noises as he began to squeeze.

"Nooooo!" Amy launched herself at the guard. Her dagger tore through his sleeve, opening a long, bleeding rent along his upper arm. Roaring with pain, he dropped Lady Uppington, who stumbled, gasping, backwards. Enraged, he turned on Amy. Amy was dumbly regarding the blood darkening the keen metal of her dagger. Oh goodness. She had stabbed a man. And might have to do so again, if the expression on the guard's face was any guide. Amy hastily yanked her bloodied dagger back into ready position.

Lady Uppington rushed for the fallen muskets, grabbing one off the pile.

"I'll do it again!" Amy threatened shrilly as the guard advanced on her, his face mottled with rage and blood.

But there was no need. Behind the guard, Lady Uppington laboriously raised the musket. The heavy wooden stock crashed down on his head. Slingshot dropped, unconscious, to the ground.

"Ha!" Lady Uppington exclaimed raggedly. "And about time, too."

Littered with bodies, the interrogation chamber was beginning to resemble the last scene of *Hamlet*. In the center of the room, Richard and Delaroche continued to bludgeon each other with weapons that had been old when Shakespeare was young. It wasn't like any duel Amy had ever imagined; there was no graceful interplay of blades, no quicksilver parries, no lightning footwork. Instead, the combatants lurched awkwardly backwards and forwards, propelled by the sheer weight of their weapons. Both were breathing heavily; both clutched hilts slick with perspiration. Richard limped slightly where Delaroche's ax had nicked him just above the knee. Delaroche favored his left arm, where Richard had whapped him with the full force of the flat of his blade.

"We should stop them," Amy breathed as a reckless swing of the ax passed uncomfortably close to Richard's left arm.

Lady Uppington's color was as high and her eyes as bright as her son's. "Don't, my dear. You'll only be in the way."

Delaroche lunged; Richard whacked the blade away. "Tsk, tsk, tsk," he scolded, breathing heavily. "That wasn't very polite."

"I don't need lessons in etiquette from you, Selweeck!" snarled Delaroche raggedly.

"Given what I've seen of your entertainment of guests, I wouldn't be so sure."

Delaroche growled with rage and swung wildly—too wildly. "For our first lesson"—Richard's blade thrust under his guard—"we'll discuss the rules of surrender." With a hearty heave, Richard levered his sword against the handle of the ax, sending Delaroche's weapon spiraling out of his hands.

Delaroche skidded back. "Your surrender, Selweeck! Not mine!"

Richard advanced. "Your surrender, Delaroche. Or next time my blade strikes home."

"Arrogant . . . ," sputtered Delaroche. "English . . ." He whirled, and ran for the door to the dungeon. Richard dropped his broadsword and sprinted in pursuit.

"Guards!" hollered Delaroche.

But only a strangled "Gua—" emerged from his mouth as he tripped over a fallen musket and plummeted heavily to the floor. Richard skidded to a stop just in time to save himself from tumbling over Delaroche's prone form. Seizing the advantage, Amy grabbed the closest object to hand—Lady Uppington's discarded bucket—and emptied the contents over Delaroche's head just as he opened his mouth to bellow again. A whoosh of dirty water turned his cry to an indignant splutter. A sodden rag flopped from one ear.

"Quick!" Lady Uppington grabbed the rag and shoved it into Delaroche's mouth, just in case he harbored any more thoughts of calling for reinforcements. Amy quickly bound his legs, while Richard secured his flailing arms. With his trussed limbs, his popping eyes and the ball of fabric in his mouth, Delaroche made a particularly unappetizing suckling pig.

Lady Uppington stood back and glowered at their adversary. "I say we throw him into the iron maiden."

Whack! Delaroche's head sagged forward as Richard dealt him an economical blow with a musket barrel. Richard grabbed his mother with one hand and Amy with the other. "I say we leave—now!"

Amy and Lady Uppington were only too happy to comply.

Chapter Thirty-nine

❧

An air of suppressed excitement emanated from the small group in the Balcourt courtyard. Even the horses harnessed to the plain black carriage that stood in the center of the cobblestones seemed to feel the tension, moving restlessly back and forth, swishing their brown manes. As three disheveled figures stole through the gates, the group let out a ragged cheer.

"You made it! Huzzah! I knew you could do it!" Henrietta flung herself at her mother and brother.

"What took you so long?" demanded Miles, pounding his best friend on the back.

Amy hung back behind Lady Uppington, watching as Richard was overwhelmed with joyful welcome. Henrietta clung to Richard's arm, chattering and exclaiming, Geoff kept shaking his head and muttering, "Thank God," Miles bounded by Richard's side like a faithful hunting dog, and Lord Uppington took Richard's hand with a solemnity that was enough to make anyone tearful. Even Miss Gwen unbent enough to announce that she was pleased to see him return unharmed, which, for Miss Gwen, represented a great excess of emotion.

The courtyard resounded with good cheer. Except for Amy, who wanted nothing more than to sit down heavily on the cobblestones. It had, after all, been a long and anxious night, after all the excitement of planning the raid on the Swiss gold, and the fight with Richard, and the anxiety of his rescue . . . not to mention running across half of Paris in the dead of night. Anybody's legs would feel wobbly after all that exertion.

Amy tried to join in the jubilant spirit. After all, they had rescued Richard. Huzzah! Even in Amy's head, the *huzzah* lacked conviction. She might have rescued Richard—with a great deal of help from Lady Uppington and her antiquated pistol—but there was the pesky matter of why Richard had needed rescuing in the first place. How he must despise her! He hadn't said anything on the way back—Lady Uppington had spoken enough for all three of them—but, then, he didn't have to, did he? She knew what he must be thinking. She had vindicated his mistrust ten thousand times over; she had done what even vile Deirdre had failed to do: She had ended his career as the Purple Gentian.

It was all over. Not only Delaroche, but fifteen—fifteen!—of his men had seen Richard unmasked, by his own hand, as the Purple Gentian. It would be all over Paris by morning, and in the London illustrated papers by noon the next day. Richard could never return to Paris again. He might not be dead, but the Purple Gentian was. Delaroche would be proud, Amy thought bitterly.

She wanted to crawl into the house, bury her head under a pillow, and hide.

"Amy!" Henrietta darted over and dragged Amy into the circle. "You're such a heroine! What was the torture chamber like?"

"Torture chambers are so trite," sniffed Miss Gwen.

Henrietta ignored her. "Was it truly ghastly?"

Amy scarcely registered the exchange because Richard's eyes were on her, casting her another unreadable sidelong look. The entire way back to the Hotel de Balcourt, he hadn't directed one solitary word her way. Just those *looks*.

Amy nodded absently. "Ghastly," she echoed. She wished he would just explode already and have done with it. Tell her he hated her. Tell her she'd ruined his life. Tell her . . .

"Oooh, splendid! You must tell me all about it later. But now"—Henrietta twirled in a circle in an impromptu victory dance—"guess what we have in the carriage!"

"We?" Miles waggled his sandy eyebrows at Henrietta. "Just who went on this mission?"

Under cover of their bickering, Richard edged towards Amy, wishing that they were anywhere but in the middle of the circus he termed his family. All the way home from the Ministry of Police, he had searched for opportunities to speak to her. But his mother had hurried them so rapidly through the streets of Paris that speech had been impossible.

Geoff said something to him, but Richard ignored him, keeping one eye on Amy, who was half hidden behind his mother. Richard had already tried to make his way over to Amy no fewer than three times. The first time, Miles had cornered him, demanding to know the details of the escape. Not to be outdone, Henrietta begged a full description of the torture chamber. And his father, in his own quiet way, had proved very insistent about recounting the saga of the Swiss gold in epic detail. Lord Uppington, after seven years of following his son's exploits from his favorite armchair in the library at Uppington House, was over the boughs at having finally been out on a mission. Richard listened with half an ear to the mechanics of constructing a barricade to stop the progress of the carriage bearing the gold. He downright ignored his father's account of calming the horses while Miles fought it out with the coachmen. By the time Lord Uppington got around to the bit where Miss Gwen disarmed one guard and rammed another in the stomach with her trusty parasol, Richard gave up all pretense of paying attention and left his father in the middle of a sentence.

He wanted to ask Amy why she looked so woebegone. He wanted to make sure she knew he'd never meant that about her being a bit of fluff. Or a light-skirt, or a mere dalliance. He wanted . . . Oh hell, he just wanted Amy. Cavemen had had the right idea, Richard thought disgustedly. Just knock the girl on the head and bear her home to your cave. None of this having to express emotions that made a man feel like his still-beating heart was being torn from his ribs and mounted on a spike for all to jeer at.

Right. He dug his hands into his pockets and rocked back onto his heels. He'd just tell her he loved her and get it over with already.

"I'm so sorry," Amy blurted out wretchedly, cutting Richard off before he could begin. "I know I've ruined everything, and I wish there were some way I could make it up to you."

"Ruined everything?"

"The Purple Gentian." Amy shifted on her dirty bare feet. "Your mission. Everything."

"Not quite everything," broke in Miss Gwen smugly. "We have the gold, and we'll soon have Lord Richard safely out of Paris."

"We have a boat waiting for you," Miles called, loping

around Miss Gwen. Any hopes Richard might have had for a private chat with Amy rapidly evaporated.

"The boat formerly belonging to Georges Marston," Geoff put in smugly, joining the group.

"Don't worry," Miles added. "We sent Stiles along to clear it out for you."

"We'll pack up your things and follow in a few days," Lady Uppington contributed. "We have it all taken care of, darling. You needn't worry about a thing."

"You seem to have it all planned," Richard said levelly.

Don't go, Amy wanted to beg. But she couldn't. Delaroche knew Richard's identity; to stay in Paris was to flirt with the gallows, if not something far worse. Miss Gwen was right. He had to go, and quickly.

Amy's entire body ached with the strain of holding back tears. She tried to console herself with the prospect of carrying on the Pink Carnation—which was, after all, what she had come to Paris to do. But, somehow, the prospect of espionage had lost its luster for her. How could there be a Paris for her without Richard? His presence would haunt her in the corners of Mme Bonaparte's yellow salon and the corridors of the Tuilleries. And then there was the Seine . . . the boat . . . the carriage . . . even her brother's house. There wasn't a place in the city that hadn't been imprinted with the memory of Richard.

Even the sparkling stars in the night sky above her belonged to Richard.

"May I come with you?"

Henrietta's mouth snapped shut midsentence; Miss Gwen ceased poking Miles with her parasol; the entire courtyard went still, everyone's attention riveted on Amy. It was like being in Sleeping Beauty's castle, surrounded by frozen figures caught in an enchantment.

"I want to come with you," Amy repeated, her voice unnaturally loud in the lull. "That is," she added, as Richard made no response, no movement, "if you'll have me?"

"Will I have you?" Richard repeated incredulously. "Will *I* have *you*?"

Uncomfortably aware of the seven pairs of eyes upon her, Amy flushed a deep red. "Well, yes," she muttered. "That was the question."

"Will I have you!" Richard whooped. Swooping, he jerked

Amy off her feet, and whirled her in a dizzying circle. "Oh, no, no! You have it all wrong. The question," he pronounced, lowering her very, very slowly to her feet, "is, will *you* have *me*? After all, I'm the one who made a muddle of everything by not telling you the truth. . . ."

"But I made you reveal your secret identity," Amy said breathlessly.

Richard grinned down at her. "I should have revealed it to *you* days ago."

Could a person explode from sheer joy? If so, Amy knew her time was limited. Her heart was pounding so hard it was about to burst right out of her chest; the sides of her face were about to split from the smile that was spreading across them; and her head was so light it was about to float right off the rest of her body. "You don't hate me for exposing you to Delaroche?"

"Not if you don't hate me for calling you a light-skirt."

"It was the bit of fluff that hurt," Amy countered giddily, reveling in the press of Richard's hands on the small of her back and the way his green eyes crinkled at the corners as he smiled down at her.

"Give me a half century or so, and I'll make it up to you."

"I think he's trying to propose to you," interjected Henrietta delightedly.

"Don't you have someplace else you need to be?" Richard scowled.

"You're going about this all wrong," interrupted Henrietta again. "You're supposed to get down on one knee and—argh!" She subsided with a muffled yelp as Lady Uppington clamped a hand over her daughter's mouth.

"Don't interrupt them or you'll spoil it," Lady Uppington hissed in a stage whisper.

"Can't you all just go *away*?" Richard roared.

Amy would have seconded the sentiment had she not been in love with the whole world (even Bonaparte and his Ministry of Police) at that very moment.

"This is all very charming," announced Miss Gwen, "but I believe *you* are the one who needs to go away, my lord, before someone from the Ministry of Police alerts the guards at the gates of the city."

Richard glowered at Miss Gwen before turning back to Amy. Taking her hand, he said softly (the entire assembled crowd strained forward as one) and rapidly, "Amy, I love you. I want to marry you. I'll get down on as many knees as you require of me—as soon as this lot *goes away*." His voice dropped again. "Will you come with me?"

"To the wide world's end," replied Amy. "Or to Calais— whichever is closer."

Richard grinned. "Definitely Calais, then. Does this mean you love me?" he asked in a voice pitched for Amy's ears only.

"Yes, yes, *yes!*"

"Ah, my excellent powers of seduction persuaded you . . ."

"Ha!" yelped Miles from the background.

"Oh, do be quiet!" scolded Henrietta, who was quite curious to hear more about seduction techniques, even if they were her brother's.

Amy bit her lip. "Do you really think we should be talking about seduction in front of your family?"

She looked so adorable in her embarrassment that Richard didn't much care whether his family was breathing over their shoulders or stranded in the farthest Antipodes. He just knew he had to kiss her. Right that very moment.

"It's all right," he murmured, leaning in. "We are going to be married."

"Oh, in *that* case . . ."

"Shhh!" Through a fog, Richard heard Henrietta hush Miles on the threshold of a snide comment. "I think he's going to kiss her!"

Richard's face froze a hair's breadth from Amy's. His jaw clenched. Amy, meanwhile, had gone bright red again, and banged her forehead against Richard's chest, on the time-honored theory that if she couldn't see anyone, they couldn't see her.

"Right," Richard said through compressed lips. "That's enough. Let's go."

"Wait, we want to see your technique!" Miles jeered. "Ow!" Miss Gwen had applied her parasol to Miles's arm with immediate effect. "Owww . . ."

"You can't just take Amy and go!" Lady Uppington protested, looking uncharacteristically perturbed. "I know I've been a rather permissive mother"—Henrietta made a noise that quickly turned into a cough—"but I really cannot countenance your going off alone with a young lady of good family.

And overnight, no less! No, Richard, you'll just have to wait until we bring Amy back with us, and then we can arrange everything properly. We'll have the wedding breakfast at Uppington House, Amy dear, unless you think your aunt and uncle will object? Hmm, I wonder if the dear archbishop . . ."

Amy put her arm firmly through Richard's. "What if someone were to chaperone us?" She looked appealingly at her cousin. "Jane?"

Jane's brow furrowed. She clasped her hands together at her waist. "Amy, I'm not going back."

"What do you mean?" asked Amy.

Little circles of pink burned in Jane's pale cheeks. "I know it was always your dream, Amy, but, if you don't mind terribly, I'd like to stay on as the Pink Carnation."

"Oh. Of course I don't mind. Just, are you sure that's what you want, Jane?"

"More than anything," Jane said simply.

"What is the Pink Carnation?" whispered Richard to Amy.

"I'll explain later," Amy whispered back.

"And I"—Miss Gwen thumped her parasol for attention—"am staying with her, so don't look to me for a chaperone, missy."

"Not bloody likely," muttered Richard.

"I'd be your chaperone," volunteered Henrietta, "only Mama would never let me."

"Besides," Miles pointed out, ignoring the increasingly ominous expression on his best friend's face, "the more people go along, the more difficult it will be to smuggle you all out. Kiss your betrothed good-bye, old chap, and have a pleasant journey home."

"Enough!" Amy stamped her foot, and the sturdy boot she was wearing made a satisfying reverberation on the cobbles. Whoever had given permission for her future, hers and Richard's, to be decided by committee? It was time to take action. Grabbing Richard's hands, she announced, "Richard, I give you my full permission to compromise me."

"Why aren't we all that lucky?" sighed Miles into the shocked silence.

"Amy, you don't mean that," interjected Lady Uppington.

"I certainly hope you do," breathed Richard into Amy's ear.

"Oh, I do," Amy whispered back wickedly, loving the way his hands started trembling in hers.

"Your reputation . . . ," continued Lady Uppington.

"If anyone hears that I was alone with Richard, can't we just bruit it about that we were already secretly married in France? Nobody except all of us here will ever know the difference." Amy sent an appealing glance around the group in the courtyard. Henrietta looked like she was on the verge of applauding. Miss Gwen eyed her coldly. "Please. I don't want to be separated again."

"I second that," put in Richard, squeezing Amy's shoulders possessively.

Support came from an entirely unexpected source. From the edge of the group came a rich chuckle. "Who are we to stand in the way of young love, Honoria?" the marquess said good-humoredly. "After all, if you remember . . ."

The marchioness turned bright pink.

The marquess patted his wife's hand, smiling broadly. "I thought so, my dear."

Richard looked in horror from one parent to the other. "I don't want to know. I just don't want to know," he muttered.

"You shall use your consequence to protect Miss Balcourt's reputation, and no one will dare to say anything against her."

Amy liked Lord Uppington more by the moment. She beamed at the marquess, and nearly dropped Richard's hand with shock when Richard's dignified father dipped an eyelid at her in a small but undeniable wink. "Welcome to the family, my dear. Now don't you think you ought to be going?"

Chapter Forty

"You do know that I didn't consider you an infatuation, a light-skirt, or a bit of fluff?" Richard said for at least the tenth time since they had left Paris.

Amy snuggled into the curve of his arm, feeling more perfectly happy than she had since ... well, than ever. On the desperate ride from Paris to Calais, she and Richard had been hidden, rather uncomfortably, in large wine barrels. But Amy hadn't felt any of the pins and needles in her legs or cramps in her arms, because every so often Richard would whisper through the bunghole in his barrel to the bunghole in her barrel to reassure her of his deep and sincere sentiments for her. Amy finally understood what Hamlet meant when he said he could be banded in a nutshell and count himself king of infinite space; it perfectly described how she felt about Richard. She might be squinched into a shape resembling a giant walnut, but every time Richard said something like, "I couldn't sleep all last week for thinking of you," her spirit soared to heights beyond the infinite.

Of course, she was rather glad to be out of that barrel, infinite space and all. Trying to kiss Richard through the barrels' bungholes had resulted in a splinter in her lip.

Amy took advantage of being uncasked to press a kiss to the hand that was stroking her hair. "You can keep trying to convince me of it for, oh, the next sixty or so years."

Richard considered. It sounded to him like a very good bargain, especially once he factored in the different ways he could persuade Amy of the extent and durability of his affections. Most of them involved removing a great deal of clothing.

"That sounds fair," Richard assented.

They were standing on the deck of Marston's boat, watching the widening strip of water that separated them from

Calais, France, and the infuriated minions of the Ministry of Police. Marston's crew, at the sight of a few gold pieces, had happily defected to the nearby taverns and been replaced by Richard's staff. Richard only hoped that at least one or two of his men knew something about sailing, or it might be a very wet swim home. On the other hand, Richard reflected, Amy would look rather nice wet. He considered the subject more deeply, and decided the same pleasing effect could be obtained with rather less risk to their lives in the privacy of their own room with the help of a bathtub and some nice fluffy towels. And maybe some oils . . .

Richard groaned.

"Are you all right?" Amy asked drowsily, her sleepless night in a barrel beginning to catch up with her. She turned languidly in Richard's embrace to glance up at his face, which had the unfortunate corollary of bringing her breasts into contact with his side.

Richard gritted his teeth. After all, it would only be a week or so until they were married. So close! He was so close! He could wait that long, couldn't he?

Certain parts of his anatomy strongly disagreed.

"Mother'll probably insist on getting the Archbishop of Canterbury," he muttered. "And how long does it take to prepare a wedding breakfast for five hundred people?"

"Five hundred people? Hmmm?" Amy yawned.

Richard seized Amy by the shoulders. Her eyelashes flew up. "Ships' captains can perform wedding ceremonies, can't they? It's legal, isn't it?"

"Did I miss something?" Amy scrubbed her eyes with her fists. "I'm sorry. I must have been dozing off. Five hundred ships' captains . . . ?"

"Let's get married!"

"Wasn't that the plan already?"

"No, I mean right now. Here. We can have the captain marry us. Whoever the captain is."

"But why?" Amy began bemusedly. Richard tipped her back over the rail of the ship for a long, searing kiss. Fortunately, Marston's boat was in far better repair than the packet they had taken over, or they would have both been thrashing about in the waters of the Channel.

Amy's face looked considerably less sleepy as comprehension dawned. "What a splendid idea."

"Excellent!" Richard grabbed Amy's hand and tugged her away from the rail. "Who's acting captain?" he hollered across the deck.

"I am!"

It was Stiles, striding across the deck, only . . . Richard blinked. He couldn't tell whether his hair was still dyed gray, because it was covered by a bandanna of blinding red. One silver hoop swung from Richard's butler's ear. A white shirt billowed over breeches that had to have been deliberately frayed along the hems. And to top it all off, a stuffed parrot perched upon Stiles's shoulder.

"Awk!" screeched the parrot.

Make that a live parrot, Richard revised.

"Arrr, I be the captain," Stiles growled.

"Amy, you do remember my butler, Stiles, don't you?"

"There'll be no time for butlering on the high seas, me laddie," Stiles grumbled darkly. "I'll be busy fightin' off the sea serpents and battlin' the raging waves, waves that can bury a ship and none the wiser."

"Ah, but can you perform a wedding service?"

With a great many *arrs* and expressions of nautical incomprehensibility, Stiles averred that he could, and went off in search of a *Book of Common Prayer*. As Marston's crew hadn't been much given to spontaneous religious ceremonies, the search proved fruitless. So Stiles improvised.

It wasn't like any wedding Amy had ever imagined. The midmorning sun shone down on them like a benediction. The air smelled of fish and brine; music was provided by the waves lapping against the keel; the wedding guests, Richard's footmen, staggered from side to side with the rocking of the boat. Amy's veil was a scrap of sailcloth, and the parson was an actor turned butler turned pirate, whose interpretation of the wedding service would have made the Archbishop of Canterbury take to his bed. Amy loved every moment. After all, if they were standing in the apse of Westminster Abbey, she rather doubted Richard would be allowed to stand with his arm around her waist and his head resting on hers. Nor would Richard have been permitted to kiss the bride for a full five minutes, which, the bride decided, would have been a sad loss.

"I do! Awk! I do!" croaked the parrot, who seemed to feel he had deserved a more central role in the ceremony.

Amy's eyelids fluttered open as the long kiss ended. "I'm not sure this is entirely legal, but I don't really care."

Richard grinned, and swept his new, if perhaps not entirely legal, wife up in his arms, and kissed the tip of her upturned nose. "I adore you, Amy. I really do."

Amy blew a kiss back up at him. "Despite my dubious morals, letting you compromise me like this?"

Richard squeezed her a little tighter as he carried her down the narrow stairs to Marston's cabin. "I promise you," he said with an exaggerated leer, "I really don't consider that a drawback." Turning to the side, he shouldered open the door of Marston's cabin.

Amy took in a brief glimpse of sunlight slanting across scarred wooden boards, a heavy table and chair, and a substantial bed. It was just like Marston to deck his bed out with red velvet draperies.

"Your threshold, my lady," Richard announced, carrying Amy over it.

Amy rubbed her head against his shoulder and started laughing. "Isn't it just like us?" she gasped between giggles. "We can't do anything properly! We don't even have a wedding night; we have a wedding *afternoon*." The statement sent her into further paroxysms.

Richard maneuvered Amy through the door, kicking it shut behind them. "Look at it this way," he suggested, lowering her gently onto Marston's gaudy red silk coverlet, "we get a wedding afternoon *and* a wedding night."

"Lucky us," agreed Amy breathlessly as Richard's lips brushed across hers in an achingly tender kiss.

"It's so glorious to be able to kiss you and know it's you," said Amy several long kisses later, twining her arms tighter around Richard's neck.

"Do you miss the Purple Gentian at all?" asked Richard, twirling one of her dark strands of hair around his finger.

Amy considered for a moment, leaning her head back on the pillow in a way that bared the white arch of her neck. Unable to resist, Richard ran a finger down the line of her throat, following it with his lips.

"Oooh. You know, it's not at all easy to think when you do that. No. No, I don't miss the Purple Gentian. He was a lovely romantic dream, but I much prefer—oof!" The force of Richard's arms around her rendered finishing the thought impossible.

"Right answer."

"*True* answer. Besides," Amy added breathlessly, grinning up at him, "the mask chafed."

If he had ever taken the time to envision his wedding night—or, in this case, wedding afternoon—shouting with laughter wouldn't have been on the agenda. But that's just what he was doing. It was as if all the joy welling up within him needed an outlet. There were also other things demanding an outlet, but Richard wanted to keep those in check as long as possible, since Amy deserved the best wedding afternoon anyone had ever had.

He smoothed her hair away from her face. "I love you."

"Say it again," Amy begged, her blue eyes sparkling. "I can't ever hear you say it enough."

"I love you." Richard kissed the tip of Amy's nose and she giggled.

"I love you." Amy's giggle turned into a gasp as his lips touched the sensitive hollow above her collarbone.

"I love you." His lips descended into the deep cavity of her bodice. "All of you," he amended, sitting back on his heels, his gaze raking down Amy's body from the loose neck of her blouse to the way the coarse wool of her skirt molded against her legs. "And I would love you"—he yanked on the laces of her bodice—"even better without all these clothes in the way."

"Wait," Amy said huskily, stilling his hand on the laces of her bodice. "Don't I get to see you?"

Although reluctant to leave off unlacing Amy, whose bodice had already dipped to show a tantalizing amount of nicely curved flesh, Richard didn't need too much encouragement to comply. Amy lifted herself up on one elbow to watch as he dragged his shirt up over his head. How could she have ever thought he looked like an illustration of Horatius? Apollo the Sun God was closer to the mark. Richard glowed. Sunlight reflected off the wiry gold hairs dusting his chest, and turned him into an object of worship. And he was hers. Utterly, entirely hers. Amy thrilled to the thought.

Never one to allow new toys to sit and gather dust, Amy reached out and tentatively touched her palms to the smooth skin of Richard's stomach, loving the way his muscles tensed under her fingers. She slid her hands upward, fascinated by the heat that radiated from his skin, the unfamiliar brush of hair against her fingers.

Richard's hands clamped down on Amy's wrists, placing her hands firmly on the gaudy silk coverlet. "Your turn," he announced unevenly.

"But you're still wearing—" Amy's words were abruptly cut off as Richard whisked her shirt and chemise over her head in one hearty tug.

"Much better," he decreed, flinging them aside. "Much, much better. You do not know how much I've been looking forward to this," he muttered, as he gently cupped a breast in each hand.

"I thought"—Amy paused with a gasp as Richard brushed his palm against the puckered nub of her nipple—"that you would never touch me like this again."

Looking genuinely horrified, Richard's hands closed possessively over her breasts. "Perish the thought! I intend to touch you like this again . . ."—his mouth gently brushed one nipple—"and again"—he visited the other—"and again." His mouth fastened on the first nipple and Amy lost all interest in conversation. She whimpered as he withdrew his mouth, flicking her hardened nipple teasingly with the tip of his tongue. She arched up against him, pulling at his hair.

"Someone is getting impatient," he murmured, running his hand down along Amy's torso to the lacings of her skirt.

"Patience," Amy said fiercely, twining her fingers in his golden hair and yanking his mouth towards hers, "is not one of my virtues."

She couldn't say what exactly she was impatient for, but the feel of Richard's leanly muscled body against hers, the wiry hair on his chest brushing against her aching breasts, made her strain against him in inexplicable agitation. Running her hands along his shoulders, she felt his muscles bunch as he eased her skirt down her hips. He freed his mouth from hers and slid down to follow the path of her skirt, kissing each inch of skin as it was bared, the indentation of her waist, her thighs, her calves, the very tips of her toes.

Richard tossed her skirt and drawers into a far corner of the room—the farther away the better, as far as he was concerned—straightened, and stared. He had imagined, of course. What redblooded man wouldn't? But the daydreams didn't even come close to the reality of Amy, her skin milky pale against the red silk coverlet. Richard just stared, openmouthed, at the perfection of her, of her perfectly proportioned arms and legs, the gentle swell of her stomach, the curves of her hip bones.

"You're so little," he marveled. "So little and so perfect."

Amy leaned up towards him, twining her arms around his neck. "So are you," she announced as his hands locked around her waist and began to ride up her rib cage towards her breasts.

"Ow!" He pulled away in mock offense.

Amy blushed. "Not little. Perfect, I mean. At least, I think I mean—"

She looked so charmingly befuddled that Richard decided there was only one humane thing to do. He stopped her mouth with a long, passionate kiss.

Arms, legs, and lips intertwined, they slid sideways towards the pillow. Richard's hands roamed the length of Amy's body, igniting urgent prickles of sensation wherever they touched. He ran his tongue along the rim of her ear, and Amy squirmed, murmuring incoherently. She squeezed him tighter, clutching the warm skin of his shoulder blades, pressing up against him so close that she could feel the groan that welled up in his chest. She touched her own tongue delicately to his ear and was rewarded by a shudder that ran through his entire body. She heard the sharp hiss of his indrawn breath, and then . . .

Amy frowned in confusion. "Why are you counting in Greek?" she asked.

"So I don't"—Richard's hand slid up the inside of her thigh, toying with the dark tangle of curls at the base of her legs—"explode."

"Oh," said Amy, who didn't quite understand, but didn't at all care, because one of Richard's nimble fingers had slipped past her curls into the moist core of her, and, oh goodness, was it *possible* for anyone to feel like that? He was touching her the way he had touched her that night on the Seine, only this time, with Richard's naked body pressed against her, his unmasked face taut with passion above hers, it felt ten times better and Amy wasn't sure she would live through the experience. She cried out as he slipped a finger into her slick sheath.

"Oh, bloody hell," groaned Richard. Pulling away, he tugged at the buttons of his breeches. One popped off and ricocheted off the wall. Amy half-giggled, half-sobbed, her hands joining his in peeling off the tight buckskin. "Damn!" cursed Richard as the trousers bunched around his ankles.

Frantically kicking them off, he rolled back towards Amy, grabbing her up in his arms and kissing her with a passion unabated by stubborn articles of clothing.

"Where were we?" he wheezed.

Taking his hand, Amy showed him. Richard's blood went from overheated to boiling in the space of a second. He would have started counting in Greek again but he didn't think it would do any good. Feeling her begin to squirm again beneath him, he slowly eased his hand away and replaced it with the tip of his shaft, biting down hard on his lip in the effort not to plunge straight in.

Amy quivered as the unfamiliar fullness eased between her legs, her body straining upwards, desperately wanting more. "Please . . . ," she breathed.

"This . . . might . . . hurt." Richard's words emerged in a series of pants.

Amy's nails dug into the hard muscles of his upper arms, the pressure of his arousal against her sensitive nub driving her half wild with unfulfilled desire. "Oh, Richard . . ."

It was more than flesh and blood could bear. With the sound of his own name whistling in his ear, Richard plunged, checking only slightly as he felt the barrier of her virginity giving way. Amy stiffened beneath him. "Should I stop?" Richard asked, steeling himself to withdraw.

Amy bit down on her lip and shook her head. "Don't." She lifted her face to his. "Don't stop, *please.*"

Richard wasn't sure he could have if he wanted to, but he tried to move more slowly as Amy's body adjusted to his, his tongue sliding through her lips in unconscious imitation of the movement of their bodies. Slowly, clumsily, she began to rock her hips in small circles against his, whimpering as her passion built to a crescendo. She locked her legs around his back, drawing him deeper inside, pushing, straining, begging for more.

Richard abandoned all attempts at restraint. With a primal cry he drove deeply into her. Kissing him frantically, nails clawing into his back, Amy bucked against him. She cried out her pleasure as a thousand diamond sparkles exploded across the back of her eyes and bathed her body in effervescent splendor. A moment later, as she quivered beneath him, Richard gave a hoarse cry and collapsed against her.

Still incapable of speech, Richard rolled Amy over so that she was lying half on top of him.

Amy reveled in the feel of Richard's warm, wonderfully male body under hers. Her leg snuggled comfortably between his thighs, and her breasts squished against his side. She flung an arm across his chest, and rubbed her cheek in the perfect hollow between his shoulder and neck, a space clearly formed with Amy's head in mind.

"Mmm," she murmured, rubbing her fingers idly through the damp hair on his chest. "So happy."

"Mmm," Richard agreed, blowing away a strand of dark hair that had decided to invade his nose. "I don't know how I'm going to keep my hands off you when we get back to London."

"Do you have to?" Amy lifted her head, looking gratifyingly distressed by the notion.

"Until we're officially married."

"How long can that possibly take?"

"Weeks! Months!" howled Richard. "All of those ... *things* that go into a wedding," he added with disgust.

"Drat," said Amy. "Maybe we should just stay on the boat."

"Not a bad idea."

"Do you think it might storm?" The words plucked at Amy's memory and she smiled to herself as she remembered the last time she had uttered something similar, on another little boat making its way across the Channel.

Richard's eyes fastened on hers. "I know one particularly rough crossing that took four full days."

Amy lifted herself up on one elbow and gazed down into Richard's face. "Do you have a distinct sense of *déjà vu*?" she asked conversationally.

"Hmm. There are," Richard mused with mock seriousness, "some crucial differences."

"And those might be?"

"Last time"—Richard's hands slid up Amy's ribs to her breasts—"you were fully clothed."

"That's only one difference."

"But a crucial one, don't you agree?"

"I've thought of one," Amy said, when she could speak again.

Richard considered. "I'd still have to pick your not being fully clothed."

Amy shook her head. "Think."

"I give up."

"*This* time, I love you."

Chapter Forty-one

Onslow Square looked much prettier in the sunlight.

    Or it would have, had I not been in the grip of a massive hangover which turned the sunlight glinting off iron railings and car windows into a direct affront. I huddled into the entryway of Mrs. Selwick-Alderly's building and contemplated the buzzer. Part of me was inclined to pop two more Tylenol, call Mrs. Selwick-Alderly with dire tales of bubonic plague, and flee home to my darkened flat.

    Of course, that meant getting back on the Tube. The Tube is not the place for a queasy stomach.

    If it had just been a matter of an unsettled stomach, I might have braved the Tube. But I was weighted in place by the bundle in my arms. In a capacious Waterstone's bag, I carried the bulging, plastic-wrapped package of manuscripts. I had promised Mrs. Selwick-Alderly that I would return it today, so return it today I must.

    Last night . . . what had I been thinking? I resisted the urge to bang my head against the intercom. I had made an absolute ass of myself in front of Colin Selwick. Oh God. I hadn't fallen over, had I? Or sung anything? I desperately searched my mental archives, wincing as I flipped through last night's collection of embarrassing memories. No falling and no singing. I could always call Pammy tonight and make sure. I didn't think there were any big black spots in my memory, but that's the problem with black spots, isn't it? You can't know they're not there because you can't remember them in the first place. Urgh.

    What I did remember was bad enough. Why in the hell did I have to hit him with that glow stick? And the glow stick was minor compared with grabbing him and yanking him across the room. Not that any of it mattered, I reminded myself for the fiftieth time. If anyone ought to be ashamed, it was Colin Selwick. What was the idea of letting me think his sister was his girlfriend? To be fair to him, I was the one who had leaped to the conclusion that she was his girlfriend. But he might have disabused me of the notion. The only reason I could come up with to explain why he hadn't done so was that he was afraid I would fling myself at him if I thought him girlfriendless. Not exactly flattering. Do I look that desperate?

I really hoped Colin Selwick had gone back to Selwick Hall. Or out to a movie. Or anywhere. I didn't care where, just so long as it wasn't 43 Onslow Square.

Okay. Enough dithering. I would return the manuscript, have a cup of tea with Mrs. Selwick-Alderly, and go home. Nothing to make a big deal about. I pressed the buzzer.

"Yes?"

"It's me, Elo—"

"Come right up, Eloise," Mrs. Selwick-Alderly called down, only in the way of buzzers, it came out, "Grrr grrr grrr, rrrr." The metallic crunching noises reverberated through my skull.

Hauling my aching head up to the first landing, I was trying to arrange my face into a suitably amiable expression when I caught sight of the open door. And its occupant.

So much for the attempt to smile.

"Feeling a bit rough?" inquired Colin Selwick from his spot against the doorframe.

"Whatever gave you that idea?" I muttered. It wasn't fair. He'd been out last night, too, tossing down the champagne, and there wasn't so much as a dark shadow under his eyes. All right, so I'd had a four-glass head start on him, but still. He had no right to look quite that bright and alert and well rested.

Since I couldn't express any of that, I vented some of my disgruntled emotions by shoving the plastic-wrapped pile at him. "Here. I've brought your aunt's manuscripts back."

From the look on his face as he accepted the package, it didn't look like his aunt had ever gotten around to informing him about the manuscript loan. The only word to describe him was nonplussed. Fortunately, Mrs. Selwick-Alderly appeared before Colin could regain his powers of speech.

"Eloise! Welcome!"

"I've brought the manuscripts," I repeated, for lack of anything better to say. Colin, fortunately, seemed to have passed from alarm to resignation without passing rage; or, if he was angry, he was holding his tongue as he passed the manuscripts silently to his aunt. "They're all there," I added, for Colin's benefit.

"I'm sure they are." Mrs. Selwick-Alderly ushered me into the parlor, Colin following silently behind. Damn, I had been hoping he would go away. How could I ever speak freely to Mrs. Selwick-Alderly with Colin lurking there? I couldn't look at him without wincing.

The parlor looked much the same as it had the day before yesterday, right down to the tea tray, only this morning the fire was unlit. And there were three cups on the tray instead of two. Damn, damn, damn. I sank onto the same side of the sofa I had occupied on my last visit, Mrs. Selwick-Alderly to my left. Colin flung himself into the overstuffed chair next to my side of the sofa.

"How's your sister doing?" I asked pointedly.

Colin didn't miss a beat. "Much better," he said promptly. "She thinks it was a dodgy prawn sandwich she ate for lunch yesterday."

"What's all this?" Mrs. Selwick-Alderly looked up from the tea tray in some concern. "Is Serena ill?"

Colin explained, while I accepted a cup of tea from Mrs. Selwick-Alderly and browsed among the biscuits, searching for something plain. "You've won an admirer for life, Eloise," he finished, stretching his long legs out comfortably in front of him. "She was singing your praises in the cab home."

This was not what I had expected. I cast a suspicious sideways glance in his direction.

"That was very kind of you, dear," Mrs. Selwick-Alderly said approvingly. "Biscuit, Colin?"

Colin took three.

Since he clearly wasn't going anywhere, I decided to just go on as though he weren't there. Putting my teacup down on the coffee table, I leaned towards Mrs. Selwick-Alderly, effectively cutting Colin out of the conversation.

"What did happen after Richard and Amy returned to England?"

Mrs. Selwick-Alderly tilted her head to one side in thought. "They were married, of course. Both Jane and Miss Gwen returned briefly from France for the occasion—Edouard as well. The Bishop of London performed the ceremony at Uppington House, and the Prince of Wales himself attended the wedding breakfast."

"Good old Prinny," commented Colin. "Probably hoping to revive the droit de seigneur."

I ignored him. Mrs. Selwick-Alderly had more effective tactics. "Colin, dear," she asked, "would you fetch down the miniatures?"

Colin loped across the room to fetch. Carefully, he freed the two small portrait miniatures that hung above the trunk from their tiny hooks and brought them over to Mrs. Selwick-Alderly.

"These were painted shortly after their wedding," Mrs. Selwick-Alderly informed me as Colin dragged his chair closer. Planting an arm against the side of the sofa, he leaned over my shoulder to look at the miniatures. I scooted closer to Mrs. Selwick-Alderly. "This"—she passed me the first painting, a man in a high collar and intricately tied cravat—"is Richard."

I had expected him to look like Colin. He didn't.

Lord Richard's face was narrower, his cheekbones higher, and his nose longer. The coloring was similar, but even there Lord Richard's hair was a shade lighter, and his eyes were, even in the tiny portrait, a distinct green. I suppose it shouldn't be surprising after two hundred years for a family resemblance to have died out. It was Amy's comments about blond hair and a supercilious expression that had led me astray. I considered the latter. Hmm, maybe the family resemblance hadn't entirely died out after all.

"And this"—Mrs. Selwick-Alderly handed me the second miniature, as I settled Lord Richard carefully in my lap—"is Amy."

Amy's dark hair was pulled into ringlets at either side of her face, like Lizzie's in the BBC's *Pride and Prejudice,* and she wore a plain, high-waisted, white muslin gown. In her hand, extended as though towards the occupant of the other miniature, she held a small flower, shaped like a bluebell, but of a deeper hue. Purple, in fact. Despite my lack of horticultural knowledge, I had a feeling I knew which species of flower Amy was holding. Cute. Very cute.

Amy herself was more cute than pretty, with her bouncing curls and her rosebud lips scrunched into a barely repressed grin. She looked like the sort of girl who would lead a midnight kitchen raid at a slumber party. Or burgle Napoleon's study.

I settled Amy next to Richard in my lap. They looked quite pleased to be reunited; Amy's eyes glinted mischievously over her oval frame at Richard, and Richard's expression looked less supercilious, and more "I'll see *you* later."

I wondered if Amy had found life in England intolerably dull after her adventures in France. Did she, in the end, resent having to turn over the title of Pink Carnation to Jane? I hated to think of her becoming old and bitter, and resenting Richard for depriving her of the adventures she might have had.

"Were they . . . happy?" I asked.

"Did they live happily ever after, do you mean?" Mrs. Selwick-Alderly clarified.

A sound suspiciously like a snort emerged from the chair to my right.

"As much as any two persons of strong temperament could," Mrs. Selwick-Alderly continued. "There is still a stain on the upholstery of one of the dining room chairs from a decanter of claret that Amy emptied over Richard's head one night."

"He complained that she hadn't used a better vintage," Colin put in through a mouthful of chocolate-covered biscuit.

"He should have thought of that before he provoked her," I suggested.

"Maybe that was why he did it," riposted Colin. "Get the bad wine out of the way."

Something in that struck me as logically flawed, but I was too headachy to isolate it. "He could have just drunk it."

"Like last night?" Colin murmured, with a smile that invited me to share in his amusement.

I pointedly turned my attention to my tea.

Resting both elbows on the armrest of his chair, Colin tilted towards me and asked, "Now that you've found what you're looking for, will you be returning to the States?"

"Certainly not!" He could be a little less obvious about wanting to be rid of me, I thought indignantly. "I have hundreds of questions that still need to be answered—Jane Wooliston, for example. Did she remain the Pink Carnation?"

I fixed Colin with a sharp look; I hadn't forgotten his aborted "You think the Pink Carnation is Amy?" He could have just told me that it was Jane who eventually became the Pink Carnation instead of letting me find out for myself this morning as I slogged through the last of the manuscripts. But, no, that would have been too helpful.

I wasn't taking any chances this time. "Is Jane the one who stops the Irish rebellion and helps Wellington in Portugal, or is it someone else using the same name?"

"Oh, it's Jane all right," Colin acknowledged affably.

"What else did you want to know, my dear?" asked Mrs. Selwick-Alderly.

There had been an intriguing tidbit in the last letter I had read, a letter from Amy to Jane (Jane was back in Paris by then) dated just after Amy's wedding. Rather than letting their spying skills go to waste, Amy proposed opening a school for secret agents, based at Lord Richard's estate in Sussex. But it had only been mentioned in passing, and might, like so many of Amy's plans, never have come to fruition. Still, it didn't hurt to inquire. . . .

"The spy school," I asked eagerly, "did it actually happen?"

"Look," Colin broke in, sitting up straight, "this is all very interesting, but—"

"The best description of the spy school was written by Henrietta," contributed Mrs. Selwick-Alderly placidly.

"Lord Richard's little sister?"

"The very same. Richard was furious with her, and insisted she leave it at Selwick Hall. They were doing their best to keep word of the spy school from getting around, you see."

"Is it here?" After all, there were all those other papers in the trunk. The manuscripts that I had been given were a mere fraction of the folios and manuscript boxes I had glimpsed inside the trunk two days ago. They could just be nineteenth-century laundry lists, but . . .

"All of the papers relating to the spy school"—Mrs. Selwick-Alderly tilted her head towards Colin—"are still at Selwick Hall."

"They're in very poor condition," Colin countered.

"I'll follow proper library procedure," I promised. "I'll wear gloves and use weights and keep them away from sunlight."

If he wanted, I would wear a full-body hazard suit, disinfect my eyelashes, and dance counterclockwise around a bonfire under the full moon. Anything to be allowed access to those manuscripts. I could deal with talking him into letting me publish the information later.

"Our archives"—Colin dropped his teaspoon onto his saucer with a definitive clatter—"have never been open to the public."

I wrinkled my nose at him. "Haven't we had this conversation before?"

Colin's lips reluctantly quirked into a faint echo of a smile. "I believe it was a letter, actually. At any rate," he added in a far more human tone, "you'll find Selwick Hall an inconvenient trip from London. We're miles from the nearest station, and cabs aren't easy to come by."

"You'll just have to stay the night, then," said Mrs. Selwick-Alderly as though it were a foregone conclusion.

Colin gave his aunt a hard look.

Mrs. Selwick-Alderly gazed innocently back.

I very carefully lowered my teacup into my saucer. "I wouldn't want to impose."

"In that case—"

"But if it wouldn't be too much of a bother," I rushed on, "I'd be very grateful for the opportunity to see those papers. You wouldn't have to entertain me. You can just point me to the archives and you won't even know I'm there."

"Hmm," expressed what Colin thought about that.

I couldn't blame him. As someone who likes her own space, I wouldn't much like to be saddled with a weekend houseguest either.

"I'll even do my own dishes. Yours, too," I threw in as an additional incentive.

"That won't be necessary," Colin replied dryly. "I'll be there this weekend," he continued, "but you must already have plans. Why don't we meet for drinks sometime next week, and I can summarize—"

Trying to fob me off with drinks, was he? I put an end to that.

"No plans at all," I countered cheerfully. Pammy would understand why I was ditching our Saturday shopping spree— at least, she would if I mentioned Serena's surprisingly hot brother rather than nineteenth-century manuscript material. "Thank you so much for the invitation."

It hadn't really been an invitation. He knew it. I knew it. Undoubtedly, Mrs. Selwick-Alderly and the portrait miniatures in my lap knew it, too. But once the words were out of my mouth, there was little he could do to deny them without seeming rude. Thank heavens for social conventions.

Colin tried another tack. "I was planning to drive down this afternoon, but I imagine you'll need—"

"I can be packed in an hour."

"Right." Colin's lips tightened as he levered himself out of his chair. "I'll just go and make the arrangements, then, shall I? Can you be ready to leave at four?"

The answer he was clearly hoping for was "no."

"Absolutely," I chirped.

I recited my address for him. Twice. Just so he couldn't claim he had been waiting outside the wrong building, or something like that.

"Right," he repeated. "I'll be outside at four."

"Till then!" I called after his retreating back. Amazing the way the prospect of a treasure trove of historical documents can cure a hangover. My head still hurt, but I no longer cared.

In the hallway, a door slammed.

That did not bode well for our weekend.

Rising, Mrs. Selwick-Alderly began to gather up the tea things. I leaped up to help her, but she waved me away.

"You"—she wagged a teaspoon at me—"should be packing."

Over my protests, she herded me towards the door.

"I look forward to hearing the results of your researches when you return," she said firmly.

I murmured the appropriate responses, and started towards the stairs.

"And Eloise?" I paused on the top step to look back. "Don't mind Colin."

"I won't," I assured her breezily, waved, and continued on my way.

Manuscripts, manuscripts, manuscripts, I sang to myself. But despite my cavalier words to Mrs. Selwick-Alderly, I couldn't help but wonder. A two-hour drive to Sussex—could we make polite conversation for that long? And then two nights under the same roof, two days in the same house.

It was going to be an interesting weekend.

Historical Note

At the end of any historical novel, I'm always plagued with wondering which bits really happened. Richard and Amy's exploits, along with the whole host of flower-named spies, are, alas, purely fictional. Napoleon's plans for an invasion of England were not. As early as 1797, he had his eye on the neighboring coastline. "Our government must destroy the British monarchy . . . That done, Europe is at our feet," Napoleon schemed. Even during the short-lived Peace of Amiens (the truce that enabled Amy to join her brother in France), Napoleon continued to amass flat-bottomed boats to convey his troops to England. In April 1803, on the eve of the collapse of the peace, Napoleon sold Louisiana to the United States to raise money for the invasion—a more reliable method of fund-raising than bullying Swiss bankers.

As for the Bonapartes and their hangers-on, while caricatured a bit (something of which Amy's beloved news sheets would no doubt approve), they have been drawn largely from life; Napoleon's court boasts a rich collection of contemporary memoirs and a mind-boggling assortment of modern biographies. Josephine's extravagances, Napoleon's abrupt entrances to his wife's salons, Pauline's incessant affairs—all were commonplaces of Napoleonic Paris. Georges Marston's drinking buddy, Joachim Murat, suffered a tumultuous marriage to Napoleon's sister Caroline; Josephine's daughter Hortense took English lessons at the Tuilleries until her tutor was dismissed on suspicion of being an English spy; and Beau Brummel really was that interested in fashion.

In the interest of the story, some rather large liberties were taken with the historical record. Napoleon inconsiderately sacked Joseph Fouché and abolished the Ministry of Police in

1802. Both were reinstated in 1804—a year too late for the purposes of this novel. But no novel about espionage in Napoleonic Paris could possibly be complete without Fouché, the man who created Napoleon's spy network and cast terror into the hearts of a whole generation of Frenchmen and English spies. In addition to rehiring Fouché a year too early, I also made him the gift of an impressive new Ministry of Police on the Ile de la Cité. No existing building possessed an extra-special interrogation chamber ghastly enough for Gaston Delaroche.

I also rearranged England's secret service a bit. During the Napoleonic Wars, espionage was coordinated through a sub-department of the Home Office called the Alien Office—not the War Office. Given the strong fictional tradition of ascribing dashing spies to the War Office, I just couldn't bring myself to have Richard and Miles reporting to the Alien Office. I could picture the wrinkled brows, the raised eyebrows, and the confused "Shouldn't he be going to the War Office? Where do aliens come into it? I didn't know this was *that* kind of book!" As a compromise solution, while I call it the War Office, any actual personnel, buildings, or practices described in conjunction with Richard's and Miles's work really belong to the Alien Office. For the little-known story of the Alien Office and much more, I am deeply in debt to Elizabeth Sparrow's wonderful book, *Secret Service: British Agents in France 1792–1815,* which is, essentially, Eloise's dissertation. Eloise, however, is not jealous, since she a) has that fabulous scoop about the Pink Carnation, and b) is fictional.

The
Secret History
of the
Pink Carnation

Lauren Willig

A CONVERSATION WITH LAUREN WILLIG

Q. Where did you get the idea for The Secret History of the Pink Carnation?

A. Baroness Orczy used to say that the Scarlet Pimpernel strolled up to her one day at a Tube stop. My introduction to the Purple Gentian was far less dramatic. After years of exposure to the Scarlet Pimpernel and his swashbuckling brethren, it occurred to me that the Pimpernel and Zorro and all those other masked men really had it way too easy. Their plans were seldom foiled; they always landed on their feet when swinging through windows; and, for the most part, their heroines stayed out of the way, cheering from the sidelines. Clearly, this state of affairs couldn't be allowed to continue. I set about plotting mayhem, and quickly decided that an enemy would be an insufficient obstacle to fling into my suave spy's path. Enemies were too simple, too easy. I would bedevil my hero, not with an enemy, but with an unwanted ally. A strong-minded heroine set on unmasking him—so she can help him. It was every spy's worst nightmare. Once that crucial question was resolved, the plot rapidly fell into place. Napoleon's interest in antiquities and the archaeological aspect of the Egyptian expedition provided a cover for my hero, and the guillotine a motive for my heroine. After that, however, the characters pushed me aside and took over. Richard flatly refused to swing into rooms on a rope, and the smuggling subplot, which was originally accorded a much larger role, all but disappeared. As for Jane . . . let's just say that Jane was originally supposed to be meek and mild.

Q. Why did you pick this particular time period?

A. When I was ten, one of the inevitable Napoleon and Josephine miniseries aired on television. Enthralled, I badgered my father, a former historian, for books on the topic. He replied with a pile of heavy tomes. They might be dusty on the outside, but on the inside, they teemed with color and intrigue. I laughed over Josephine's pug dog biting Napoleon on their wedding night and cried over the unhappy marriage of Josephine's daughter to Napoleon's brother. I even named all of the guppies from my fifth-grade science project after Napoleon's numerous relations. Although the guppies long ago departed for that great fishbowl in the sky, my interest in the Napoleonic Wars has remained, from the English side as well as the French. With Waterloo so firmly fixed in our imaginations, sometimes it's hard to remember that the threat of French domination seemed a very real thing to contemporaries, as gallant little England held out alone against the growing forces of France (England's Continental allies showed a distressing habit of surrendering every time Napoleon defeated them in battle). It was a time of flux and turmoil as England reacted to the shocking news and ideas pouring across the Channel, fearing rebellion within as well as invasion without. Uncertainty and upheaval may not make for comfortable living, but they provide great fodder for both historians and novelists.

Q. You're in graduate school and law school, and yet still find time to write novels. How do you juggle?

A. It helps that I have very poor television reception. Aside from the lack of distractions, it all comes down to what I think of as the Theory of Productive Procrastination. It's a sad fact of human nature—or, at least, my nature—that one never wants to do what one is actually supposed to do. The minute I undertake a task, I would instantly rather be doing something else. Laundry, for example, or cleaning out the bottom of the closet. Writing *The Secret History of the Pink Carnation* gave me something to do while avoiding working on my dissertation. Of course, the dissertation still needed to get done, so I had to add on law school. In comparison with doing my torts homework, the dashing Royalists who form the subject of my dissertation suddenly took on a renewed allure. And to get myself to do my law school homework . . . well, there's always the new book to procrastinate from now, even if it does mean that my closet is still messy and likely to remain so. I find the same rule applies within the *Pink Carnation* books; whenever the historical characters begin to weary me, there's always Eloise to play with, and vice versa.

Apart from the procrastinatory imperative, juggling multiple careers has proved unexpectedly productive in other ways. I wrote the *Pink Carnation* over summers, on either side of my third year of graduate school. That nine-month hiatus in between, while frustrating at the time, gave the plot and characters time to simmer on the back burner and mature in ways I had never anticipated. Recently, I took a break from the third book in the *Pink Carnation* series to work at a law firm for several months. The interactions and intrigues of the office provided all sorts of insights into human nature and ideas for future plot twists. One of the glorious aspects about writing is that nothing is a wasted experience; one never knows when a scrap of dialogue, a historical fact, a bit of legal jargon might suddenly come in handy, popping to the surface from the subterranean reaches of one's brain. While the writer as introvert in a garret is a well-established trope, venturing out into the workaday world keeps dialogue and characters grounded in some semblance of reality.

Q. Like Eloise, you have spent the past six years working on a graduate degree in English history. Did your historical training aid in researching The Secret History of the Pink Carnation?

A. Yes and no. I had done a field on Modern Britain (which is defined as anything post 1714), which left me with a bookcase full of monographs on Georgian England, and I was a past master at wandering through the stacks of Widener Library with my head at a forty-five-degree angle, just in case there might be something on the shelves the library catalog had missed. I knew how to work the microfilm reader, and where to look for the more obscure historical journals. At first, it all seemed to be going well. I even had all sorts of choice historical tidbits gleaned from contemporary memoirs (Napoleon's relatives always make for colorful reading)—and then I hit a snag. Amy was about to fling herself into a chair, and I had no idea what the chair looked like. I turned to my bookshelves, but none of the scholarly works that weighed down my shelves contained anything remotely useful. Fifty-odd books on Georgian England, and not one description of a chair. All of this is a rather long way of saying that training as a historian goes only so far in writing a historical novel. Bit by bit, I learned to look farther afield for those pesky period details one couldn't find in the traditional histories, developing a collection of books on antiques, architecture, costume, and even cookbooks. Historical maps suddenly became items of desire. I haunted the period rooms in the Metropolitan Museum, squinted at little plaques in folk museums in England, and discovered a wealth of resources on the Internet, especially writers groups devoted to the time period.

Q. Why a book within a book?

A. Too much caffeine? Aside from the effects of overcaffeination, the Eloise chapters arose out of a combination of factors. During my year in England, I'd gotten hooked on chick lit, and was eager to try my hand at it. As a writer, I enjoyed the challenge of working with different voices and styles within the same book. The Delaroche chapters, deliberately penned in a style that I think of as "High Melodrama 101," arose out of that same impulse. Writing in the first person provided a whole new set of challenges to work through. How do you adequately describe a character from within her own head? Since everything is filtered through that character's viewpoint, how do you allow her to cherish her misconceptions while putting the reader in the know?

As a historian, I had another hobbyhorse to ride. One of the greatest challenges for both the historian and the historical novelist is rendering the past accessible to a modern audience. In juxtaposing the historical and modern chapters, I hoped to play up the commonalities that persist across the centuries, despite changes in costume and custom. Over my years dipping in and out of archives, I've repeatedly been struck by how little human nature changes. By far my favorite example of this comes from a set of fourteenth-century letters, in which a teenage boy writes home from boarding school because his favorite tunic needs washing and he's short of funds (which sounded eerily like my brother's calls home from boarding school), and a grown daughter fumes to her brother that if she has to spend one more day in the same kitchen with her mother, one of them isn't going to make it out alive (we've all been there). I've also seen the son of a sixteenth-century queen write to his mother that his grandfather is a big meanie because he won't let him go riding, he's grown two inches, and when is she going to come home so that he can show her his brilliant new toy sword? *Plus ça change, plus c'est la meme chose.*

Q. You and Eloise are both Harvard grad students who spent a year abroad in England. How much of the book is autobiographical?

A. The answer to that is probably best summed up by a college roommate, who, upon reading the book, exclaimed indignantly, "But Eloise isn't anything like you!" We do share a predilection for three-inch heels and toffee nut lattes, but, other than that, Eloise's adventures are entirely her own. My own researches take place two hundred years earlier than Eloise's, in the seventeenth century rather than in the nineteenth, and I did not, much to my chagrin, stumble on a cache of undiscovered family papers. Instead, I developed an intense attachment to my favorite desk in the manuscript room on the third floor of the British Library, and spent several weeks learning how to work the watercooler in the lunchroom of the Public Records Office. In my own defense, it was a very confusing watercooler.

Nonetheless, while Eloise and I are far from the same person, we occupy very similar worlds. Making Eloise a graduate student in the Harvard history department was a sop to all those years of English teachers who sternly admonished me to write what you know. I hated that advice. I didn't want to write what I knew; I wanted to write about dashing men in knee breeches dangling improbably from ropes, conducting daring midnight escapes. But, despite all my fuming and fidgeting, I have to admit the wisdom of their advice. Placing Eloise in the same academic program and lending her my basement flat in Bayswater made her much easier to write about. I could picture her route to the British Library every morning, the kebab shop where she buys her fish and chips, even the clothes hanging in her closet. Even the party where Eloise attacks Colin with a Glo-Stick has a basis in a similarly bizarre bash I attended while overseas. There's a certain nostalgic pleasure to revisiting my old haunts through Eloise's eyes.

Q. The Secret History of the Pink Carnation borrows elements from a number of different genres. While the debt to Baroness Orczy is clear, which other authors influenced you in your work?

A. Cursed with literary schizophrenia, I grew up reading mysteries, romances, suspense, fantasy, spy novels, nineteenth-century fiction, and those wonderful multigenerational historical epics that proliferated through bookstore shelves back in the eighties. My father had a taste for historical fiction, and my mother for Japanese and Russian literature of the more lugubrious sort, so we had very eclectic bookshelves. I read anything, anywhere, at any time (although reading while roller-skating was not one of my better ideas). I've been staggering between genres ever since.

If I had to narrow it down to a crucial few, I would say that my imagination was molded by a combination of Alexandre Dumas, Margaret Mitchell, and Judith McNaught. I dashed down narrow alleyways with d'Artagnan, ran blockades with Rhett Butler, and exchanged quips with supercilious heroes in Regency ballrooms. But my stylistic sensibilities were shaped in the school of L. M. Montgomery, Nancy Mitford, and Elizabeth Peters, who, despite writing in completely different genres, all have a knack for an ironic turn of phrase and a winning way of highlighting life's absurdities. When Judith Merkle Riley's *A Vision of Light* came out, followed by Diana Gabaldon's *Outlander*, it was the best possible combination of both tendencies: vivid historical scenes presented with a wry twist.

Q. What was the most difficult or frustrating part of the writing process?

A. It's hard to pick just one. I'd have to go with those days when I sit down at the computer, and no one's there. My characters are all out to lunch. Even the villain can't be rousted out of his bed to do anything dastardly. I sit and scowl at the screen, drink ludicrous amounts of tea, check e-mail every three minutes, and generally work myself into a snit. The English language becomes an unfamiliar wilderness and words, with all the recalcitrance of a herd of stubborn sheep, refuse to allow themselves to be arranged into any semblance of coherence. And then, on the flip side, there are those days when the characters are jumping up and down in my head, shouting, "Pay attention to me!" and fluid lines of perfect prose are unrolling through my head—but I can't act on any of it, because there's something else I have to do, like grade student papers, or it's four in the morning and I've already turned my computer off. Having learned from past experience that such moments are fleeting, I try to always keep paper and pen somewhere in the vicinity so I can catch at least a fraction of those fragments of narrative and dialogue before they scuttle away again. Of course, those instances—both sets of them—are more than outweighed by those glorious moments when the characters frolic across the page, doing all sorts of wonderful things I never expected them to do.

Q. Will Eloise and Colin's story continue into the next book?

A. Although Eloise and Colin's story continues, the next book, *The Masque of the Black Tulip*, belongs to Henrietta Selwick and Miles Dorrington, the Purple Gentian's little sister and best friend. When Eloise follows Colin back to Selwick Hall to plunder the family archives, she discovers that there's a new French spy on the loose: the Black Tulip. (My apologies to Alexandre Dumas for stealing the name!) The Black Tulip is under orders to find and eliminate the Pink Carnation—which means, naturally, that someone will have to find and eliminate the Black Tulip. And who better to do so than Miles? Of course, Henrietta, the girl whose earliest words were "me, too!" insists on pursuing her own investigations. As I was writing *The Secret History of the Pink Carnation*, it became gloriously clear that Henrietta and Miles were perfectly suited—and equally clear that they were sure to fight it every step of the way. I'm happy to say they have proved me right on both counts.

Q. When will Jane get her own book?

A. I'm not sure how much I should give away . . . but the short answer to that is, not for a while yet. One of the constraints of working in the early nineteenth century is that heroines tend to marry young, much younger than suits our modern sensibilities. If they don't, the author is forced to engage in alarming contortions to explain why the heroine has been left on the shelf for so long—forced to take care of the family estates, without the money to afford a

Season, kidnapped by bandits and locked in a box till after she turned twenty-one, and so on. An interesting trend recently has been to have older, widowed heroines, where the age problem is dealt with by the expedient of an earlier marriage and a conveniently deceased husband. With Jane, however, this problem is moot. Jane has a wonderful reason for not marrying young: she's too busy saving civilization from the depredations of Napoleon's armies. I will say, however, that Jane does get her romance eventually, and I know exactly who it is—but that's between me and Jane.

QUESTIONS
FOR DISCUSSION

1. Meg Cabot called *The Secret History of the Pink Carnation* "a genre-bending read." The book contains elements of chick lit, mystery, comedy, adventure stories, and historical romance. Discuss how the story uses and subverts these various traditions. How would you classify the book, and why?

2. In the transition between 2003 and 1803, we become intimately acquainted with two very different sorts of heroines. How does Amy's character contrast with Eloise's?

3. Discuss the effect of the book in a book. Are there parallels between the modern and historical stories? Is Eloise a frame or a foil?

4. Amy's "necklace of stars" attains great significance in her interactions with Richard. What does the necklace of stars symbolize? What does it mean to Amy?

5. When Amy discovers a wounded man in the ballroom, she immediately assumes he must be a member of the League of the Purple Gentian. Who did you think the wounded man might be?

6. Due to experiences in his past, Richard decides early in the novel not to share his secret identity with Amy and holds to that resolution, despite their growing intimacy. Do you find Richard's reasons compelling? Is he driven by

loyalty to his League, or fear of having made another romantic misjudgment? If you were Amy, would you find his actions forgivable?

7. What do Richard's interactions with his family tell us about him as a character?

8. The Purple Gentian takes his place as part of a long tradition of fictional spies. Discuss the ways in which Richard embodies or deviates from the trope of the dashing hero. Do his deviations from the archetype undermine his role or make him a more convincing hero? Do you take Richard's role as a spy seriously, or is he more of a parody?

9. Amy and Jane serve as foils for each other throughout the novel, yet Jane's decision at the end of the novel calls into question the depth of the differences between them. In what ways are Amy and Jane secretly alike? Is Jane really the sensible cousin?

10. To what extent are both the modern and historical characters' actions driven by a fascination with the past? Are they more affected by the historical past, or their own personal pasts?

11. Growing up in Shropshire, Amy considers herself a stranger, both in England, and in her uncle's family. Once in France, Amy pretends not to speak the language, and finds very little in common with her brother. By the end of the book, would you say that Amy considers herself English or French? How would she define her relationship with her family? What does this say about the nature of belonging?

12. Although the historical story revolves around Richard and Amy, much of their tale, including their final declaration of their feelings, takes place in the midst of a group of their friends and relations. Do you feel that the presence of secondary characters adds to or detracts from Amy and Richard's love story? Does the ensemble cast steal the show?

Read on for an excerpt of

*THE MISCHIEF
OF THE MISTLETOE*

a brand-new book in Lauren Willig's
bestselling Pink Carnation series.

Available from New American Library
in November 2011.

"I am for teaching," announced Miss Arabella Dempsey.

Her grand pronouncement fell decidedly flat. It was hard to make grand pronouncements while struggling uphill on a steep road against a stiff wind, and even harder when the wind chose that moment to thrust your bonnet ribbons between your teeth. Arabella tasted wet satin and old dye.

"For what?" asked Miss Jane Austen, swiping at her own bonnet ribbons as the wind blew them into her face.

So much for grand pronouncements. "I intend to apply for a position at Miss Climpson's Select Seminary for Young Ladies. There's a position open for a junior instructress." There. It was out. Short, simple, to the point.

Jane screwed up her face against the wind. At least, Arabella hoped it was against the wind. "Are you quite sure?"

Sure? Arabella had never been less sure of anything in her life. "Absolutely."

Jane hitched her pile of books up under one arm and shoved her ribbons back into place. "If you rest for a moment, perhaps the impulse will pass," she suggested.

"It's not an impulse. It's a considered opinion."

"Not considered enough. Have you ever been inside a young ladies' academy?"

Arabella made a face at the top of Jane's bonneted head. It was very hard having an argument with someone when all you could see was the crown of her hat. Jane might be several years her senior, but she was also several inches shorter. The combination of the two put Arabella at a distinct disadvantage.

Six years older, Jane had always been as much an older sibling as a playmate, telling stories and bandaging bruised knees. Arabella's father had been at one time a pupil of Mr. Austen's at Oxford, when Mr. Austen had been a young proctor at St. John's. Back in the golden days of childhood, Arabella's father's parish had lain not far from Steventon, and both books and children had been exchanged back and forth between the two households.

This happy state of affairs had continued until Arabella was twelve. She remembered her head just fitting on Jane's shoulder as she had cried on it that dreadful winter, as her mother lay still and cold among the gray sheets on the gray bed, everything hued in ice and shadow. She remembered the clasp of Jane's hand as Aunt Osborne's carriage had come to carry her away to London.

"And what of your aunt Osborne?" Jane added. "I thought you were only visiting in Bath. Aren't you to go back to her after Christmas?"

"Mmmph." Arabella was so busy avoiding Jane's eyes that she stumbled. Flushing, she gabbled, "Loose cobble. You would think they would keep the streets in better repair."

"How singular," said Jane. "The cobbles are perfectly stationary on this side of the street. Why this sudden desire to improve young minds?"

That was the problem with old friends. They saw far too much. Arabella developed a deep interest in the cobbles beneath her feet, picking her steps with unnecessary care. "Is it so unlikely I should want to do something more than be Aunt Osborne's companion?"

"You have a very comfortable home with her," Jane pointed out. "One aging lady is less bother than fifty young girls."

"One aging lady and one new uncle," Arabella shot back, and wished she hadn't.

Jane looked at her, far too keenly for comfort. But all she said was, "It is final, then?"

"As final as the marriage vow," said Arabella, with an attempt to keep her voice light. "My aunt and Captain Musgrave were married last week."

"But isn't he...."

"Half her age? Yes." There was no point in beating around the bush. It had been all over the scandal sheets. "But what are such petty things as numbers to the majesty of the human heart?"

Jane's laughter made little puffs in the cold air. "A direct quotation?"

"As near as I can recall." Arabella hadn't been in a position to memorize specific phrases; she had been too numb with shock.

Captain Musgrave had made a pretty little speech out of it, all about love defying time, all the while holding Aunt Osborne's jeweled hand in an actor's practiced grip, while she fluttered and dimpled up at him, her own expression more eloquent than any number of speeches. In the half-dark dining room, the candle flames created little pools of light in the polished surface of the dining table, oscillating off Aunt Osborne's rings and the diamond pendant in her turban, but nothing shone so bright as her face. In the uncertain light, with her face lifted towards Captain Musgrave, tightening the loose skin beneath her chin, one could almost imagine her the beauty she once had been. Almost.

Even candlelight wasn't quite that kind.

One of her aunt's friends had dropped a wineglass in shock at the announcement. Arabella could still hear the high, tinkling sound of shattering crystal in the sudden silence, echoing endlessly in her ears like the angry hum of a wasp. Arabella had made her way through the wreckage of shattered crystal, spilled claret staining her slippers, and wished them happy. At least, she assumed she had wished them happy. Memory blurred.

He had never made her any promises. At least, none that were explicit. It had all been done by implication and innuendo, a hand on her elbow here, a touch to her shoulder there, a meeting of eyes across a room. It was all very neatly done. There had been nothing concrete.

Except for that kiss.

"It would make an excellent premise for a novel," said Jane. "A young girl, thrown back on her family after years in grander circumstances. . . ."

"Forced to deal with carping sisters and an invalid father?" The wind was beginning to make Arabella's head ache. She could feel the throb beginning just behind her temples. It hurt to think about what a fool she had been, even now, with two months' distance. "If you must do it, at least change my name. Call her . . . oh, I don't know. Elizabeth or Emma."

"Emma," said Jane decidedly. "I've already used Elizabeth."

Arabella smiled with forced brightness. "Did I tell you that

I finished a draft of my novel? I call it *Sketches from the Life of a Young Lady in London.* It's not so much a novel, really. More a series of observations. Sketches, in fact."

Jane ignored her attempts to change the subject. "Your father said you were only home until the holidays."

"I was. I am." Arabella struggled against the wind that seemed determined to wrap her skirt around her legs as she labored uphill. What madman had designed the streets of Bath on a nearly perpendicular grade? Someone with a grudge against young ladies without the means to afford a carriage. "Aunt Osborne expects me back for Christmas. I am to spend the twelve days of Christmas with her at Girdings House at the express command of the Dowager Duchess of Dovedale."

The invitation had been issued before Captain Musgrave had entered onto the scene. An invitation from the Dowager Duchess of Dovedale was something not to be denied. The Dowager Duchess of Dovedale possessed a particularly pointy cane and she knew just how to use it.

Arabella's aunt attributed the invitation to her own social consequence, but Arabella knew better. The house party at Girdings was being thrown quite explicitly as a means of marrying off the dowager's shy granddaughter, Charlotte. The dowager needed to even the numbers with young ladies who could be trusted to draw absolutely no attention to themselves. After years as her aunt's companion, Arabella was a master at the art of self-effacement.

She had been, to Aunt Osborne, the equivalent of a piece of furniture, and to her aunt's friends something even less.

The first person to have looked at her and seen her had been Captain Musgrave.

So much for that. What he had seen was her supposed inheritance. His eyes had been for Aunt Osborne's gold, not for her.

"And after Twelfth Night?" Jane asked.

She wasn't going back to that house. Not with them. Not ever. "What newlyweds want a poor relation cluttering up the house?"

Jane looked at her keenly. "Has your aunt Osborne said as much?"

"No. She wouldn't. But I feel it." It would have been so much simpler if that had been all she felt. "It seemed like a good time to come home."

Except that home wasn't there anymore.

When she thought of home, it had always been of the ivy-hung parsonage of her youth, her father sitting in his study, writing long analyses of Augustan poetry and—very occasionally—his sermons, while her rosy-cheeked sisters tumbled among the butterflies in the flower-filled garden.

To see them now, in a set of rented rooms redolent of failure and boiled mutton, had jarred her. Her father's cheeks were sunken, his frame gaunt. Margaret had gone from being a self-important eight-year-old to an embittered twenty. Olivia had no interest in anything outside the covers of her books; not novels, but dusty commentaries on Latin authors dredged from their father's shelves. Lavinia, a roly-poly three-year-old when Arabella left, was all arms and legs at fifteen, outgoing and awkward. They had grown up without her. There was no place for her in their lives.

No place for her in London, no place for her in Bath. No place for her with her aunt, with her father, her sisters. Arabella fought against a dragging sensation of despair. The wind whistled in her ears, doing its best to push her back down the hill up which she had so laboriously climbed.

Absurd to recall that just three months ago she had believed herself on the verge of being married, living every day in constant expectation of a proposal. It was a proposal that had come, but to Aunt Osborne, not to her.

A lucky escape, she told herself stoutly, struggling her way up the hill. He had proved himself a fortune-hunter and a cad. Wasn't she better off without such a husband as that? And she wasn't entirely without resources, whatever the Musgraves of the world might believe. She had her own wits to see her through. Being a schoolmistress might not be what she had expected, and it certainly wasn't the same as having a home of one's own, but it would give her somewhere to go, something to do, a means of living without relying on the charity of her aunt. Or her new uncle.

Uncle Hayworth. It made her feel more than a little sick.

"She must not have been able to do without you," said Jane.

Arabella wrenched her attention back to her friend. "Who?"

"Your aunt." When Arabella continued to look at her blankly, Jane said, "You hadn't heard?"

"Heard what?"

Jane shook her head. "I must have been mistaken. I heard your aunt was in Bath. A party came up from London. There's to be an assembly and a frost fair."

"No. I—" Arabella bit her lip. "You probably weren't mistaken. I'm sure she is in town."

Captain Musgrave had expressed a desire to go to Bath. He had never been, he said. He had made serious noises about Roman ruins and less serious ones about restorative waters, making droll fun of the invalids in their Bath chairs sipping sulfurous tonics.

Jane looked at her with concerned eyes. "Wouldn't she have called?"

"Aunt Osborne call at Westgate Buildings? The imagination rebels." No matter that Arabella had lived under her roof for the larger part of her life; Aunt Osborne only recognized certain addresses. Pasting on a bright smile, Arabella resolutely changed the subject. "But Miss Climpson's is within easy distance of Westgate Buildings. I'll be near enough to visit on my half days."

"If you have half days," murmured Jane.

Arabella chose to ignore her. "Perhaps Margaret will like me better if she doesn't have to share a bed with me." She had meant it as a joke, but it came out flat. "I don't want to be a burden on them."

It was as close as she could come to mentioning the family finances, even to an old family friend.

Jane made a face. "But to teach . . ."

"How can you speak against teaching, with your own father a teacher?"

"He teaches from home, not a school," Jane pointed out sagely. "It's an entirely different proposition."

"I certainly can't teach from my home," said Arabella tartly. "There's scarcely room for us all as it is. Our lodgings are bursting at the seams. If we took in pupils, we would have to stow them in the kitchen dresser, or under the stove like kindling."

Jane regarded her with frank amusement. "Under the stove? You don't have much to do with kitchens in London, do you?"

"You sound like Margaret now."

"That," said Jane, "was unkind."

Arabella brushed that aside. "If I ask nicely, perhaps Miss

Climpson will agree to take Lavinia and Olivia on as day students."

It was a bit late for Olivia, already sixteen, but would be a distinct advantage for Lavinia. Arabella, at least, had had the advantage of a good governess, courtesy of Aunt Osborne, and she knew her sisters felt the lack.

"It will not be what you are accustomed to," Jane warned.

"I wasn't accustomed to what I was accustomed to," said Arabella. It was true. She had never felt really at home in society. She was too awkward, too shy, too tall.

"It is a pretty building, at least," she said as they made their way along the Sydney Gardens. Miss Climpson's Select Seminary for Young Ladies was situated on Sydney Place, not far from the Austens' residence.

"On the outside," said Jane. "You won't be seeing much of the façade once you're expected to spend your days within. You can change your mind, you know. Come stay with us for a few weeks instead. My mother and Cassandra would be delighted to have you."

Arabella paused in front of the door of Miss Climpson's seminary. It was painted a pristine white with an arched top. It certainly looked welcoming enough and not at all like the prison her friend painted it. She could be happy here, she told herself.

It was the sensible, responsible decision. She would be making some use of herself, freeing her family from the burden of keeping her.

It wasn't just running away.

Arabella squared her shoulders. "Please give your mother and Cassandra my fondest regards," she said, "and tell them I will see them at supper."

"You are resolved, then?"

Resolved wasn't quite the word Arabella would have chosen.

"At least in a school," she said, as much to convince herself as her companion, "I should feel that I was doing something, something for the good of both of my family and the young ladies in my charge. All those shining young faces, eager to learn . . ."

Jane cast her a sidelong glance. "It is painfully apparent that you never attended a young ladies' academy."